CITY GIRLS FOREVER

Also by Patricia Scanlan

Apartment 3B
Finishing Touches
Foreign Affairs
Promises, Promises
Mirror Mirror
Francesca's Party
Two for Joy
Double Wedding
Divided Loyalties
Coming Home for Christmas
With All My Love
A Time for Friends
Orange Blossom Days
The Liberation of Brigid Dunne
(also published as A Family Reunion)

Trilogies

City Girl
City Woman
City Lives

Forgive and Forget
Happy Every After
Love and Marriage

Open Door

Second Chance
Ripples
Secrets
Voices (ed)
Legends (ed)

Short Story Collection

A Gift For You

Non-fiction

Winter Blessings
Bringing Death to Life

Patricia Scanlan

CITY GIRLS FOREVER

SIMON & SCHUSTER

London · New York · Amsterdam/Antwerp · Sydney · Toronto · New Delhi

First published in Great Britain by Simon & Schuster UK Ltd, 2025

Copyright © Patricia Scanlan, 2025

The right of Patricia Scanlan to be identified as author of this work has been asserted in accordance with the Copyright, Designs and Patents Act, 1988.

1 3 5 7 9 10 8 6 4 2

Simon & Schuster UK Ltd
1st Floor
222 Gray's Inn Road
London WC1X 8HB

Simon & Schuster Australia, Sydney
Simon & Schuster India, New Delhi

The authorised representative in the EEA is Simon & Schuster Netherlands BV, Herculesplein 96, 3584 AA Utrecht, Netherlands. info@simonandschuster.nl

www.simonandschuster.co.uk
www.simonandschuster.com.au
www.simonandschuster.co.in

A CIP catalogue record for this book is available from the British Library

Hardback ISBN: 978-1-3985-3834-4
Trade Paperback ISBN: 978-1-3985-3835-1
eBook ISBN: 978-1-3985-3836-8
Audio ISBN: 978-1-3985-3837-5

This book is a work of fiction. Names, characters, places and incidents are either a product of the author's imagination or are used fictitiously. Any resemblance to actual people living or dead, events or locales is entirely coincidental.

Typeset in Bembo by M Rules
Printed and Bound in the UK using 100% Renewable Electricity at CPI Group (UK) Ltd

MIX
Paper | Supporting responsible forestry
FSC® C171272
www.fsc.org

I dedicate this book to you, dear reader. And to *all* my wonderful and loyal readers who have been with me since I first introduced Devlin, Caroline and Maggie in *City Girl*.

Your continuing support and loyalty – and especially the kindness of my Facebook followers – has been a great gift and source of encouragement to me throughout my writing career.

Warmest wishes and many blessings to you. I hope you enjoy reading about our City Gals in their prime. XXX

'Rare as is true love, true friendship is rarer.'
Jean de la Fontaine

PART ONE

CHAPTER ONE

Devlin/Caroline/Maggie

'Would you look at *"Me! Me! Me!"*. She looks like Spock's granny! Those eyebrows! McDonald's arches have nothing on hers. She must be seventy if she's a day,' Maggie whispered to Devlin and Caroline.

'Maggie!' hissed Devlin. 'Stop it! We're at a *funeral.*' The trio of friends were at the funeral of a highly regarded photographer, Jason King, who'd shot the photos for Devlin's 'City Girl Gym & Spa' brochure more than thirty-five years ago and taken their photos many times, at various social events they'd attended over the past three decades. The church was packed. Dublin's glitterati had come to pay tribute. Many of them original members of City Girl, prompting Maggie's irreverent comments. A sea of well-known faces gazed solemnly at the priest as he mournfully read, 'Length of days is not what makes age honourable, nor number of years the true measure of life; understanding, this is man's grey hairs, untarnished life, this is ripe old age.'

'Not very appropriate,' murmured Maggie sotto voce, 'considering that Jason was as bald as a coot. Would you look at the hair extensions on The Merry Widow. She'd give Rapunzel a run for her money!'

Devlin snorted, and hastily pretended to cough. Caroline's shoulders shook with silent laughter and she buried her face in her hands.

'I'm *never* sitting beside you at a funeral again,' Devlin informed Maggie as the priest led the coffin down the aisle past them, followed by the grieving family.

'Why?' Maggie asked, the picture of innocence.

'*Rapunzel!*' retorted Devlin, unable to keep her face straight as the choir swelled into the final verse of 'Going Home'.

'Must be the writer in me.' Maggie grinned as they joined the queue to write their names in the book of condolences.

'Have we time for a cuppa anywhere?' Devlin asked when they emerged into the sunlight, blinking after the cool dimness of the church.

'I've an hour to spare, where's handy?' Caroline eyed Maggie. 'You free?'

'You bet I am. I didn't come all this way from Wicklow not to have a catch-up with my gals.' Maggie linked Caroline's arm as they made their way through the throngs of mourners towards their cars.

'How about the Bots?' Caroline suggested. 'We can park there. It's only five minutes away.'

'Perfect!' Devlin agreed.

'Give ya a race!' Maggie laughed.

Fifteen minutes later they sat outside in a small courtyard, in the Botanic Gardens, with pots of tea and coffee in front of them and a selection of wraps and buns. The midday sun was warm in a cerulean sky and birdsong filled the air.

'So peaceful here. The scent of the orange blossom makes me think I'm abroad.' Devlin inhaled deeply.

'I wish we *were* abroad! Just the three of us.' Maggie bit into a tuna wrap.

'We need to get away for a few days. We haven't been away in such a long time,' Caroline agreed. 'Feckin Covid.'

'Oooh that would be blissful,' Devlin enthused. 'Let's think about it. Are you up for it, Maggie?'

'Sure am.'

'Caroline, how are you doing time-wise at work?'

'I'm fairly booked up with appointments for the next couple of months but, if you give me an idea of when, I can scale them down and pencil in some holidays. How about you?'

'Well, apart from trying to get City Girl back on track after the last couple of years I'm not too bad. We were so lucky we didn't go under. Shame we had to close Belfast, but Galway's doing fine, thank goodness, and Dublin's flying it. *And* I have to come up with some plans to celebrate City Girl's thirty-fifth anniversary—'

'*What!*' exclaimed Maggie, shocked. 'Thirty-fifth anniversary? How can that be? It only seems like yesterday!'

'I know.' Devlin shook her head. 'It's like a dream. Imagine: there weren't even mobile phones when it opened.'

'Oh the excitement of it. Remember? Dublin's poshest gym and beauty spa. Everyone wanted to have membership. Half the people at the funeral today were members then,' Maggie observed. '"*Me! Me! Me!*" was one of the first. She asked me what I did, one day after a stint on the treadmills. I told her I was a nurse and she had the cheek to ask, "How can you afford membership?" As I recall she was dressed in a tiger-print leotard and the kind of pink tights Jane Fonda used to wear when she was "going for the burn". She looked more like a cross between Tigger and Piglet, if the truth be told.' Devlin and Caroline guffawed.

'I feel old!' Maggie groaned.

'Well, you *are* a few years older than us,' Devlin teased.

'What are you going to do to celebrate the anniversary?' Caroline asked.

'I don't know. Seeing "*Me! Me! Me!*" and Rapunzel and a few of the other original Grandees at the funeral gave me a bit of a shock. When I look in the mirror *I* get a bit of a shock too, to be honest,' Devlin admitted.

'You're singing to the choir, sista!' Maggie nodded. 'At least we're still ticking the fifties box. I suppose that's some small comfort.'

'Speak for yourself.' Devlin scowled. 'It was bad enough ticking the forties. I'm married to a man who's ticking a different box! Luke's in his *sixties*!'

'Let's not depress ourselves, Dev,' Caroline remonstrated. 'You could be *moi*: childless and manless, at my age—'

'Lucky you,' Maggie interjected sourly. 'Much as I love my children, I could do with a break from their snowflakey problems. Where did I go wrong? I ask myself. We just had to get on with things. Now they're all going to therapy and swallowing anti-depressants like they're Smarties.'

'Different pressures, societal changes. It's hard for them.' Caroline patted her arm.

'I know. I just have no patience anymore. It's the friggin' menopause, I suppose.'

'Let's not even go *there*,' Devlin groaned, biting into a cupcake. 'I flew off the handle with Luke because he decided to cut the grass last Saturday morning when I was trying to have a lie-in. I *screeched* at him! Like a fishwife!'

'Oh dear,' murmured Maggie, laughing. 'You love your lie-ins.'

'My patience threshold is zilch lately,' Devlin admitted.

'Mine too.' Caroline sighed. 'I have a client who really isn't interested in moving forward no matter how hard I encourage her to – she has issues with her older sister, but she's definitely partly to blame – you have no idea how close . . . how *close*,' she joined her two fingers together, 'I came to telling her to get over herself yesterday. That's *baaad*!'

'Look what we've turned into: the City Aul Wans!' Devlin grinned.

'When you mention having a party I'm just thinking maybe you could do an event for charity, like one all those social butterflies go to: they're all loaded. Make it the society bash of the year, lots of publicity, must-have tickets, prizes of free spa days, gym membership, facials, massages,' Caroline suggested, having attended many such soirees when she was married to Richard, all those years ago.

'A big City Girl bash!' Maggie exclaimed. 'Woohoo! There'll be a lot of face-lifts for that. And I'll be having the first one. Once a City Girl, always a City Girl. That's us.'

'We could put on the invite, "City Girls Forever!"' Devlin exclaimed, eyes alight. 'Ladies, *this* is going to be fun.'

CHAPTER TWO

Devlin

Devlin turned off the car's engine and had a quick scroll through her messages. One from Madalina, her PA, made her stomach give a sickening lurch.

> Lady wants to know if u could call her to speak about a retired gynae consultant u both worked for. She needs some advice. U can call her on the No I've copied u in on, or I can tell her ur busy.

Devlin exhaled. A consultant gynae. Colin Cantrell-King.

Who was this woman? Why did she need advice about Colin Cantrell King? That misogynistic, cold-hearted, controlling bastard. The man who had fathered her precious daughter, Lynn. The sorry excuse of a man who had wanted to abort his own child. A wave of unexpected grief engulfed Devlin.

A sharp toot of a car horn startled her and through tear-smeared eyes she saw a hard-faced blonde wave gaily at her.

'Bloody hell!' she muttered. Lianna Griffin, owner of a chain of nail salons, was the last person she wanted to see. Lianna would expect Devlin to wait until she had parked her massive SUV to walk into City Girl with her. Being seen with the owner of Dublin's iconic Health Spa and Gym would be good for Lianna's business. She'd want a selfie, to post on her numerous social media pages.

I can't stay here, Devlin thought in panic, wiping her eyes and starting the ignition. She drove out of her parking space and emerged onto the side street that led to St Stephen's Green. Merging into the traffic, she touched the car's screen and rang Madalina.

'Hi Devlin,' her PA's crisp, accented tone filled the car.

'Mad, I'm not coming back this afternoon: can you let Liz know? I was supposed to meet her at three-thirty.' Liz, who was once her PA, now managed City Girl. 'I'll get back to you in a while about the stuff you've sent me.'

'No probs, Dev. Drive carefully,' Madalina responded. In the background Devlin could hear the office landline ringing. 'Have to take this, bye.'

Devlin managed a small smile. Madalina was a godsend. She'd come to Ireland from Romania, years ago, and had got a job as a beauty therapist in the City Girl spa. Before long, she was the deputy spa manager. Now she was Devlin's PA. She ran a tight ship. Focussed, efficient: she was the most organised person Devlin knew and had no time for her boss's moans about menopausal 'brain fog'.

'Pish. If you say it, it vill happen. Stop that talk! Take my grandmother's remedy.' Madalina's grandmother had 'remedies' for everything. Devlin had a store of such goodies in her bathroom cabinet.

The traffic was heavy and she had to concentrate on her driving, her sat nav telling her Pearse Street and across the Liffey at Butt Bridge was her fastest route. She didn't want to go home, to Howth, right now but she wanted a place to sit and think for a while. The Bull Wall was one of her favourite haunts. She could get a coffee at the Happy House and allow the memories that she kept such a tight lid on to surface.

Twenty-five minutes later she walked along the sand-blown path with a cup of steaming coffee in her hand, the breeze from the Irish Sea lifting tendrils of hair off her face. The salty tang was reviving and she sat on one of the seats and stared unseeingly across to Dublin Port, the iconic red and white chimneys piercing the cobalt sky. Little wisps of angel-wing clouds drifting gaily along did not soothe her heavy heart, as they normally would. She sipped her coffee, as memories swirled around her.

Colin: her boss, her very attractive boss, with whom she'd thought she was madly in love! The innocence of her. The stupid naivety of her twenty-year-old self. When he'd taken her virginity in the examining room of his posh D4 consulting rooms, a sordid episode that had taken less than five minutes, she'd been stunned. She had thought their first lovemaking would have been tender and loving and romantic. Not a pain-filled, undignified . . . assault really. She acknowledged what she'd call it now, Devlin thought miserably, remembering how shocked, disappointed and let down she'd felt at the time. And then discovering she was pregnant and his cold fury when she'd told him. He'd arranged for an abortion and she'd travelled to London but, unable to go through with it, she'd come back home and faced the wrath of not only Colin but her mother, Lydia, as well. Only for the stoic support of her father, Gerry, the loyal friendship of Maggie and Caroline and her adored aunt, Frances, Devlin would have gone under.

The joy her precious daughter had given her, despite the hardship of being a single mother living in Ballymun, had kept Devlin going, until that life-altering, catastrophic day when a juggernaut had slammed into the car that Devlin, her toddler, and aunt had been travelling in to Wexford. Her two-year-old daughter and aunt had died, and she'd sustained serious injuries.

Despite the heat of the late spring sun, Devlin shivered and her hand shook, causing her to spill her coffee as a wave of sadness swept over her and tears streamed down her face. Even after all these years the depth of the sorrow could still surprise her. She had lived a very full life since that horrific time – marrying her beloved Luke, having their son Finn, building the City Girl brand, seeing it savaged in the economic crash of the mid-nineties, then revived, and smacked down again in the Covid pandemic – but always, in the secret compartment of her heart, that was Lynn's and her aunt's, the mourning of their loss lived on.

She rooted in her bag for a tissue and wiped her eyes. Make-up, mascara and eyeshadow stained the tissue and she grimaced knowing that she probably looked a sight. She kept her head down as a couple with a Labrador walked past and then glanced up at the towering statue of Our Lady, which stood at the end of the narrow finger of land that pointed into the sea. 'I put my child in your care when she died, take my grief away,' Devlin whispered, before standing up and walking back to her car.

Luke was on his bi-monthly visit to his London office. She was glad. He would have taken one look at her and known something was up and she didn't want to trouble him with her sadness, preferring to keep it to herself. Finn was a chef in a seafood restaurant in Barcelona, so the house would be empty and that suited Devlin fine. She glanced at her watch. It was after four. She'd go home, catch up on her emails, try and ride out the tsunami of grief that had unexpectedly come roaring back to swamp her.

Would she get in touch with the caller whose message had triggered her heartache? Devlin didn't know.

CHAPTER THREE

DEVLIN

Five days after Devlin had received Madalina's message about the woman who wanted to make contact with her about CCK, as Devlin called him, she finally bit the bullet. Hard as she had tried to dismiss it from her thoughts, she couldn't.

'What's bothering you, Dev?' Luke had asked bluntly, at breakfast earlier.

'Nothing,' she said lightly. 'Just a bit preoccupied with work.'

Her husband leaned across the table and stared into her eyes and, even after all their years together, Devlin never failed to appreciate how a look from those intense hazel eyes, ringed by a sweep of black lashes she would have given anything for, could sometimes take her breath away.

'Stop looking at me like that,' she said, flustered.

'Something's up and it's not about work,' Luke said calmly, gently touching her cheek with a long forefinger. 'Is there anything I can do to help?' His tenderness undid her, and tears brimmed in her eyes. 'What's wrong, can't you tell me? Is it anything I've done or not done?'

'Ah, no Luke, it's not you.' She gulped.

'Come on, let's go sit on the sofa and tell me what's troubling you.' He got up from the table and took her hand and they walked over to the big squishy sofa that faced wall-to-ceiling patio doors looking out over Howth as far as Wicklow. The view of a sun-sparkled sea glittering and shimmering like thousands of silver sequins never failed to delight Devlin. Her home was her greatest sanctuary, but even home could not drown out the memories that had come back to haunt her.

She sat beside Luke and snuggled in against him, feeling the steady beat of his heart as she rested her cheek against his chest. Her husband's arms tightened around her.

'... it was just so unexpected and out of the blue, it brought everything back,' she said shakily after telling him of the message she'd received. 'I thought my grief was very manageable, but it feels so raw. I can't believe it.' She shook her head and again the tears came and she cried. Luke held her, silently, until she composed herself.

'I don't think *anyone* ever gets over the death of their child,' he said quietly. 'It's a grief different to all others. You live with it but, like now with you, memories come back and you have to endure it until your equilibrium returns, and it *will*.'

'I wonder what that woman wants?' Devlin wiped the tears from her face.

'Perhaps you should make the phone call and see. At least you'll know then, and it won't be agitating you,' Luke suggested.

'I suppose so. I'll do it today, after I've had the Zoom meeting with the Belfast people.' Devlin sighed. City Girl's Belfast operation had been the worst hit by the pandemic despite the stringent, precautionary measures they'd taken when the business had reopened. With the landlord insisting on an unreasonable rent increase, it hadn't been viable to keep the business going and Devlin had made the decision to close before incurring any more loses that would endanger the brand elsewhere. There were a few details to sort before everything was finalised.

'OK, take your Zoom and then just get that call to that woman over and done with, and take it from there.' Luke smiled at her, and she smiled back. Her husband's pragmatic approach to problems always calmed her.

Two hours later, Devlin sat in her car in the car park on Howth Summit, sipping a takeaway coffee and staring unseeingly out over the magnificent views of Dublin Bay across to the Sugar Loaf. She hadn't wanted to make the call at home, hadn't wanted to bring the energy of her past into her sanctuary.

She scrolled to Madalina's message and clicked on the number. Her heart began to pound, her palms dampening, as the phone dialled the number and it rang.

'Hello?' a soft-accented voice answered.

'Nenita Santos?' Devlin managed to keep her voice steady.

'Yes!'

'I'm Devlin Delaney. I believe you wanted to get in touch with me,' Devlin said briskly.

'Oh! Oh my goodness, I didn't think you would get back to me.' The other woman was edgy.

'May I ask what you want to connect with me about?' Devlin asked, just wanting to have the call over and done with.

'Ms Delaney. I'm so sorry I can't talk right now. I'm a practice nurse and I have a patient to take bloods from. Could I call you back in an hour when I've finished work?' the woman asked hesitantly.

She sounded so apologetic and nervous, Devlin felt sorry for her despite her irritation at not being able to get to the bottom of the matter. Whatever this was about, it was clearly an ordeal for this Nenita Santos woman.

'Look, would you be free to meet and talk about this in person?' Devlin said impulsively. 'I'm on the Northside if that's any use.'

'Oh! I'm in Glasnevin. If that's handy for you.'

'Great. How about I meet you in the Botanic Gardens, it's a nice day. There's a seat on the path up to the big Palm House, or I could meet you in the restaurant,' Devlin suggested.

'Oh . . . oh thank you so much. I love the Botanics. I'll be there about ten past three, if that's OK. The seat on the pathway would be fine.'

'Perfect. I'll see you then,' Devlin agreed and hung up.

She was glad she'd taken the bull by the horns and suggested meeting. Get whatever it was over and done with, as Luke had advised, and then she could put the whole episode out of her mind and get on with her life.

She was sitting, with her eyes closed, listening to the birds singing, the breeze whispering through the trees, the heat of the sun on her face, when a gentle voice said, 'Ms Delaney?'

Devlin's eyes shot open. She saw a petite, dark-haired woman with molten brown eyes and a harried expression looking back at her.

'Sorry, I was in another world,' Devlin exclaimed. 'Are you Nenita Santos?'

'Yes, that's me.' Nenita nodded, a smile lifting the stress from her face. 'I'm so grateful to you Ms Delaney—'

'Please, call me Devlin.' Devlin smiled, moving along the seat to make room for the other woman. 'Would you like a coffee? I can run over to the restaurant and get us one.'

'I'm too nervous,' Nenita confessed. 'If I don't say what I have to say now, I'll run away.'

'Ah, don't do that.' Devlin laughed. 'I was tempted to run away myself. It's about Colin Cantrell-King, isn't it?'

Nenita nodded, sitting down beside Devlin. 'Yes,' she said heavily. 'It's about that bastard, for sure.'

CHAPTER FOUR

Devlin/Nenita

Devlin took a deep breath. 'Why do you need to see me about him?' It felt surreal to be talking about a man who had caused her so much heartache with a complete stranger.

'Forgive me, maybe I shouldn't have got in touch.' Nenita bit her lip, seeing the expression of pain cross Devlin's face. 'It was inconsiderate of me. I didn't mean to cause you distress, but of course how could it not? I read an interview ... em ... Sorry, maybe I should go,' the other woman said agitatedly, standing up.

'It's OK. Please stay. It does bring back unhappy memories, I can't deny that,' Devlin said. 'How can I help you?'

'Well, it was just ... you see, I'm a nurse ... I was his nurse once ... and ... ' Nenita burst into tears.

'Oh Nenita!' Devlin instantly forgot her own misery and put her arms around the sobbing woman. Heart sinking, remembering her own experience, she had some idea of what she was going to hear. 'Look, it's not very private here.' She could see people walking past, looking at them. 'Why don't we grab a coffee and let's sit at one of the outdoor tables in the tearooms behind the restaurant?' she suggested gently.

'I'm terribly sorry, Ms Delaney.' Nenita gulped. 'I—'

'Please call me Devlin. You go and get a table and I'll get the coffee, or would you prefer tea?' Devlin asked kindly.

'Coffee would be fine. An Americano, please,' Nenita said shakily as they began to walk towards the restaurant.

'I got us a couple of cupcakes, they do nice ones,' Devlin said ten minutes later, placing the coffee and buns on the white table Nenita was sitting at, in a sheltered nook away from prying eyes. The outdoor seating area was almost empty, just an elderly couple, and a man reading a newspaper, a few tables away.

'This is better.' Devlin sat opposite the younger woman and reached across the table and squeezed her hand. 'What did CCK – that's what I call him – do to you?'

'It happened about fifteen years ago. I came to Ireland from the Philippines when there was a lot of recruitment going on. I did agency nursing three days a week and I worked for Mr ... em ... CCK on Thursdays and Fridays when he saw patients in his private rooms.' Nenita took a sip of her coffee and shook her head at the memories that engulfed her.

'Go on,' Devlin encouraged.

'After a while he sort of began ... began ... invading my space, I suppose you could call it. Leaning over me when I was writing my notes, or standing very close if I was at the supplies cabinet getting rubber gloves or lubricant or whatever. Touching me on the arm and shoulder. He started paying me compliments, telling me it was wonderful to have a pretty, lively girl working for him because his first nurse had been a bit cranky and serious—'

'That would have been Nurse McGrath. I worked with her. She was somewhat dour to say the least.' Devlin grimaced. 'Sorry, I interrupted you.'

'Well, one day, when the last patient was gone, I was in the examining room taking the paper sheet off the couch and I had my back to him and he came in and . . . and . . . ' Nenita swallowed hard. 'He grabbed me, put his hands under my breasts and began rubbing himself against me. I was so shocked . . . I literally froze. He was groaning and breathing heavily and he told me I was so beautiful I was making him come. He'd unzipped his trousers. I tried to struggle but he was very strong and then he . . . he . . . rammed his fingers inside me, it was so painful and then . . . then he was . . . well, I felt the wetness . . .' Nenita closed her eyes and wept.

'I'm so sorry . . . So . . . so sorry.' Devlin felt tears dampen her own eyes and they sat holding hands, weeping.

'He told me he thought he was falling in love with me, and I had been driving him crazy with desire, and that he would buy me some beautiful jewellery – as if that made everything all right,' she added bitterly. 'I was so shocked I could hardly speak, but I managed to say, "You assaulted me!" Oh Devlin, he changed completely. He was vicious. He said if I *ever* said anything about what had happened he would make sure that I would never work in Ireland again. That I'd be deported. That it was his word against mine. To think very carefully about what I was doing. And then he asked me why would I not like to be his lady friend. He would be very generous with me. His wife didn't love him and only stayed with him for the lifestyle he provided and that he was very lonely.' It all poured out of Nenita in a torrent of anger and grief.

'I said I'd think about it. All I wanted was to get out of there. I was afraid of him. He told me to go home and he would see me the following week and that he was going on a golf trip to Portugal for the weekend. I said OK. Grabbed my coat and bag and got out of there as quick as I could. I never went back. I was petrified that he would damage my reputation as a nurse, and get me deported. For years after, I worried about what he might do to me. I never told anyone what had happened, not even my boyfriend whom I married five years later. I was *so* ashamed—' Nenita buried her face in her hands. 'I carried that shame for so long, and finally I told my husband and he wanted me to go for counselling. He wanted me to report it to the guards and the medical council but I said no. I had a baby girl by then, I couldn't face any of that.'

'That's very understandable,' Devlin consoled. 'Can I ask why you contacted me?'

Nenita drank some of her coffee and nibbled on a piece of cupcake. 'I'm on a Facebook group chat with other nurses and we talk about everything. Covid took up a lot of our conversations, but we also discuss who's nice to work for, what GP clinics have a bad name, that kind of thing. It's great really because we all look out for each other. Anyway, one nurse said she was going for an interview with CCK. He still maintains a private consultancy but doesn't operate anymore. She wanted to know did anyone know what he was like to work for? Two other nurses told her to stay well away. One said he had a 'creepy vibe'. The other one said he was more than creepy, and he was very 'hands on' – she put an angry emoji beside. I said

I had a bad experience with him and wouldn't advise her to work for him. Anyway, I got a private message from the 'hands on' nurse asking could she get in touch with me, and we spoke, and the same thing that happened to me happened to her too. She's originally from Estonia. So then we Googled him and your name came up in some newspaper articles—'

'Ah, yeah, the interviews,' Devlin said heavily. 'I'll never forget that bitch of a "journalist", and I use the term lightly. She was a sleazy hack from a shitty redtop, setting my mother up and getting her drunk, and another one of her slimy colleagues going out to Ballymun to question my old neighbours about when I lived there as a single mother. They were planning a big reveal. My mother took an overdose after it.'

Even decades later Devlin could still remember the terror of her mother's overdose, and the burning rage and betrayal she had felt at the seedy exposé the rag of a newspaper had planned, and how she had scuppered it by giving an interview herself to a rival broadsheet and telling her own story of getting pregnant and ending up at an abortion clinic.

'That was a terrible thing for you. Did he ... did he rape you, Devlin?' Nenita asked hesitantly.

Devlin grimaced. 'Technically, legally, I'm not sure. I thought I was in love with him. I was a foolish, naive twenty-year-old, barely out of my teens, who had read too many romance novels.' Devlin threw her eyes up to heaven. 'When I see twenty-year-olds now! So clued in! Anyway, I believed him when he told me he loved me. I was flattered when he said I was driving him wild, but *now* I know he was grooming me all along. He'd even put me on the pill for my painful periods, and when we had sex – it was my first time – it was in the surgery, it happened very quickly – like it did with you. It was *very* painful. I believed him when he said he was overcome and the next time it would be better. I got pregnant. That was it! He turned on me. Cold and vicious, like you said. He organised for me to go for the termination. I didn't have it in the end. To answer your question, I don't know if a court of law would find him guilty of raping me, Nenita,' Devlin replied. 'Are you and the other nurse considering taking him to court?'

'We've talked about it. It would be our word against his, and he's highly respected. I don't know if I want to open this can of worms. She's not keen to do it. Should I let the past stay in the past?' She looked so unhappy Devlin felt an impotent fury engulf her. Colin Cantrell-King had got away with ruining young women's lives for years. If Nenita and her colleague took him to court they would face all the trauma of reliving their assaults in the glare of publicity that would certainly accompany a case of such notoriety.

'I don't know how to advise you,' Devlin admitted. 'If you go to court it will all be in the public eye, you'll have to relive it and that will be horrendous. On the other hand if you stay quiet about it, you have to live with that too. Your choices are difficult either way.'

'I know.' Nenita shrugged. 'We say nothing, he wins. We say the truth, we suffer. It's much easier to say nothing but, Devlin, I have a daughter. I don't want anything like this ever to happen to her, or any other women out there. If we go to court, we will certainly help other women.'

'Look, Nenita, whatever you decide, I'll support you,' Devlin said firmly. 'I will go to court with you if that's of any help—'

'Oh my God, would you?' Nenita looked astonished.

What am I doing? Devlin thought in dismay. But she knew she couldn't turn her back on the other women.

'Yes, I will,' she reiterated. 'But either way whatever you decide, you *must* go for counselling, Nenita. I have a wonderful friend who specialises in counselling abused women – she was abused in her own marriage – she knows all about coercion. Counselling is the *most* important thing for you right now.'

'I know! It's time.' Nenita sighed. 'I will go to your friend. I've put it off for far too long. I didn't want to bring back the memories but, until I deal with it, I'll never be free of it, or him.'

'I'll text you the contact details, and I'll make sure you get to see Caroline herself.' Devlin rooted in her bag for her phone and began to scroll through her address book.

'Devlin, there's one other thing . . .'

'What's that?' Devlin asked, absently, tapping away on her phone.

'I em . . . well, you remember Monica Lewinsky kept the dress with the stains on it from the Bill Clinton thing?'

Devlin's head jerked up. *Yes!* She stared at Nenita.

'I kept my uniform. I shoved it in a plastic bag that day. It's in the back of my wardrobe. I have the proof!'

CHAPTER FIVE

Maggie

'He's not walking me down the aisle, Mom.'

'He's your father!'

'He's a bollix!'

'Shona, stop that,' Maggie chided, observing the stubborn jut of her eldest daughter's chin. Shona was so like Maggie had been at her age. Stubborn, passionate, living life to the full.

'He is, you know he is.' Shona scowled, pouring more tea into their mugs.

They were sitting in Shona's dockland apartment, or the 'egg box' as she called it, before Maggie drove back home to Wicklow after her day in the city. Her daughter had just informed her that she was getting married. Privately, Maggie thought she was mad. Why would a young woman with her life before her tie herself up in the bonds of marriage? Were young women of Shona's generation still hung up on having the ring on their finger? They could have it all and still not be tied.

Admittedly Maggie had a coloured view, she thought sourly, remembering the disaster of her marriage to Terry.

'Are you sure this is what you want, Shona? It's a huge step for you and Aleksy. What's wrong with what you have now?' She changed the subject.

'He's the one, Mom,' Shona said simply, smiling at her mother. 'We really love each other.'

Maggie smiled back, reached across the table and squeezed her daughter's hand. 'I know you do. He's a lovely fella.' It was true: Aleksy Laska, her daughter's Polish boyfriend, was sound. They had been going together for three years, and Maggie had been sharply observant of his treatment of Shona. Everything she saw made her like him all the more. His humour; his discreet, mindful tenderness in the small ways he treated her daughter. And he was no pushover. When Aleksy put his foot down, which was rare, it stayed down. Just what her exuberant, wild daughter needed sometimes. And Aleksy was kind to *her* too, Maggie thought gratefully. Unpacking the groceries from the car when she shopped, fixing a bunged-up loo, mowing the grass sometimes when he and Shona came down to Wicklow. Not in any lick-arsey way, just matter of fact, practical. 'A very decent chap,' Maggie's mother, Nelsie, had declared and *that* was all the endorsement her future son-in-law needed, Maggie decided, amused at her mother's imprimatur.

'What are you smiling at?' Shona cocked an eye at her, before popping a large chunk of Maggie's banana bread into her mouth.

'I was just thinking that your granny thinks Aleksy is a "very decent chap"! You can't get higher praise than that!'

'It took her a while.' Shona laughed. 'She wasn't at all sure about me going out with a "foreigner" at the beginning. Remember she said there were plenty of farmers in Wicklow looking for a wife, and what did I need to be hobnobbing with Polish blokes for?'

'The day he rescued Sooty from the apple tree was the day she changed her mind. Now he can do no wrong.' Maggie slathered butter onto her bread. 'She loves that little cat.'

'Who couldn't love Sooty?' Shona remarked. 'Another reason we want to get our own place. We're not allowed pets here. And, anyway, we want to get on the property ladder soon, or we'll never get on it. If we're married it will be easier, tax-wise and all of that.'

Shona and Aleksy were living in an apartment Maggie had bought as an investment, at the start of the millennium, with one of her writing advances. Her pension, she called it. It was little use to her as a rental property anymore, seeing as Shona and Aleksy were paying a minimal rental that covered the maintenance fees and property tax, and not much more. She was trying to help all her children out in the current accommodation crisis. Fortunately the twins had no notion of getting married anytime soon. Mimi, working in a graduate placing agency after gaining her degree, was enjoying her freedom after so many years of studying, and Michael had just gone back to sea to get his time in, after a year in marine college in Cork studying for his master's ticket.

'So when are you planning on getting married?' Maggie asked, trying to let on she was pleased. The thought of having to referee between Terry and Shona filled her with dismay.

'As soon as we can—'

'You're not pregnant, are you?' Maggie's jaw dropped at the notion.

'*Mom!* No, and would it matter even if I was?'

'No, no, of course not,' Maggie spluttered. 'It's just I don't want to see you tied down so young.'

'We want a small wedding. Immediate family and a few friends. We don't want to spend a fortune. And that wagon, who's married to Dad, and their spoilt little brat are *not* coming!'

'*Shona*—'

'I mean it, Mom! It's *my* wedding.'

God, what did I do to deserve this? Maggie took a slug of tea and wondered gloomily if she could persuade her daughter to elope.

Terry would go ballistic, Maggie fretted as she headed towards the East Link an hour later. She didn't think his second wife, Denise, would be that keen on going to Shona's wedding, or their teenage daughter, Chloé. But façades had to be kept up.

It wouldn't bother Maggie, seeing her ex's second wife there. She rarely thought about them. Any feelings she'd had for Terry were long gone, but he was her children's father and she had always tried not to disparage him to them. Shona had never forgiven him for his betrayal, though. Maggie could still remember as though it were yesterday that awful moment when her children's innocence had been taken away and the true state of their parents' marriage had been revealed.

She, Shona and the twins had been on their way to visit Nelsie in Wicklow for an overnighter. She'd been happy at how they loved going to stay in the country with their gran. It was a glorious summer's day, and she was looking forward to the jaunt herself. They were about to drive through the Glen of the Downs when her son said, 'Mom, I feel sick.'

Heart sinking, she'd just about managed to pull in to the

side of the road before Michael had puked spectacularly into the ditch, accompanied by the cries of, 'Eeewww! Gross!' from his siblings.

He'd been to a birthday party, and it seemed that one mother whose child had a tummy bug the previous day had brought him to the party to 'get him out of her hair'. Maggie and the other mothers had been horrified when they'd heard of it.

If Michael had it, the others could get it. She could get it. There was no way she could bring them to visit Nelsie. Amid howls of dismay she'd cleaned her son up as best she could and turned back for Dublin.

They had barely made it home before Michael barfed again, fortunately making it in time to the downstairs loo. Maggie was holding his head when she heard Shona squeal *'Mom!'* The loo door was open and she saw her daughter pointing across to the sitting room where a horrified Terry was sitting half-naked on the sofa with a busty blonde, in a white bikini top, astride him.

It was as though time stood still, as she stared at her husband and then her devastated daughter, unable to speak. Gathering the remnants of her wits about her she hurried across the hall and slammed the door shut, to block out the scene.

'What's going on?' Mimi came barrelling through the front door, hearing the commotion. She'd been dawdling outside until the puking episode was over.

'Go upstairs the two of you, please, I'll be up in a minute,' Maggie said as calmly as she could, her heart thumping so loudly she was sure they could hear it.

'I hate him,' yelled Shona. 'He's a . . . a dirty sleazebag!'

'Who's a dirty sleazebag? He only puked, Sho. He couldn't help it.' Mimi defended her twin.

'I'm talking about Dad. He's in there with a nudey woman sitting—'

'Go upstairs, *now*!' Maggie ordered and the tone of her voice was so grim her children did as they were bid.

She took off her son's stained T-shirt, washed and wiped his face and told him to join his siblings upstairs.

'I'm going to get you some Dioralyte, sweetie, I'll be up in a minute,' she said, pointing Michael in the direction of the stairs. When he'd trudged off forlornly, she'd marched into the sitting room where Terry was standing up, adjusting his clothing. Maggie could see the blonde out on the patio, stepping into a pair of white cut-offs.

'Did you have to bring her here? To our home? To our children's home? Have you no decency in you at all, Terry? Pack your stuff and get out. It's over. We're done,' she said coldly.

'I thought you were going to be away,' her husband muttered.

'You should NOT have brought her here, Terry! To MY space. To our CHILDREN'S space. They know now. No more pretending for their sake. It's over so get out.' She walked out of the room, went into the kitchen, grabbed a glass and a sachet of Dioralyte from the medical supplies she kept in a cabinet and went upstairs to join her distraught children. I'll never forgive you for what you've done to them, she thought bitterly, gathering a sobbing Shona into her arms, knowing that what she had just seen had ruined what was left of her childhood, and her relationship with her father.

'Mom, why is Daddy with another woman? Is he having an affair?' Mimi's lower lip wobbled. Michael, pale as a ghost, stared at her speechless.

What could she say? There was no denying it. Maggie

swallowed hard, knowing this was a life-changing moment for all of them, knowing that her children's lives were going to be disrupted in a way no parent would wish for. The family dynamic they had taken so much for granted, never thinking it would change, was shattered.

'Look, Dad and I have fallen out of love with each other. It doesn't mean we don't love you. He loves you and I love you. We've stayed together until now, for you. But it's time now I think for us to make other arrangements—'

'Are you going to get a *divorce?*' Mimi was appalled.

'Not immediately, no, pet. Probably in the future. But Dad's going to get his place, so he can be with ... em ... his new friend,' she said lamely.

'I am *never* speaking to him again. That was *disgusting!*' Shona spat.

'Like were they having actual *sex*?' Mimi was still gobsmacked at what her older sister had told her going up the stairs.

'Look, it doesn't matter now,' Maggie said hastily. 'What we have to do is make a plan to go forward and make the best of things. And we will, don't worry.'

I hate your fucking guts, Terry Ryan, she swore silently as Mimi's face crumpled and she burst into loud sobs. Maggie ended up with her arms around her three precious children as their tears drenched her face and dress.

What a year from hell that had been. Maggie frowned, remembering the trauma of trying to persuade the twins to spend time with their father in his new apartment. Shona refused point blank to have anything to do with him and, as Maggie pointed out to a gutted Terry, he only had himself to blame. Their oldest daughter had seen him in flagrante, a vision she would never forget, and Maggie had no intention of forcing her to spend time with him. The twins hadn't seen the actual episode so they weren't quite as traumatised.

The detached house had been sold, the proceeds split between her and Terry, and she and the children had moved to a smaller three-bed redbrick semi in Ranelagh.

A fresh start, she'd told her children, the first night they had stayed in their new home. But their mournful faces had tugged at her heart and she'd known there was a hard road ahead to get them back on an even keel.

Time had eased their trauma and, as the years passed and they'd settled into their new way of living, it was no longer anything they gave much thought to ... *until now*, Maggie thought glumly, waiting for the traffic lights to change at Cornelscourt, to join the N11.

Shona's forthcoming wedding would bring the great divide back to the fore, and she'd be slap-bang right in the middle.

CHAPTER SIX

Maggie

'She sent me a bloody text, Maggie. That's the way my own daughter tells me she's getting married. It's outrageous. I'm very hurt, and I'll be having words with her.' Maggie's heart sank as her ex-husband ranted down the phone at her. Trust Shona! Could she not at least have *phoned* her father? 'How long have you known? She didn't even have the manners to take my call when I rang back.'

'I only found out yesterday evening, Terry,' Maggie said evenly. 'And at least she *did* text you. I happened to be in Dublin so I had tea with her in the apartment.'

'Lucky you, being invited to the Holy of Holies. I suppose she'll expect me to pay for the big day,' he grumbled.

'I'd hardly think so,' Maggie said dryly. 'She's having a small wedding.'

'*What?*'

'I said she's having a small wedding—'

'By God, I'm not going to have people saying I'm too mean

to pay for a big bash for my daughter. You can muck in too, you've plenty of lolly,' Terry exclaimed. 'The McIntyres had Wendy's in Powerscourt. No expense spared.'

'I wouldn't know. I wasn't invited. It was you and Denise went,' Maggie reminded him drily.

'Oh . . . oh, yeah well,' Terry blustered. 'Anyway, no one's going to get the chance to say we wouldn't put on a good show for Shona. She's our eldest and the first to be married, even if it is to some yoke from Poland. Don't ask me why she couldn't settle down with some Irish fella.'

'*Terry!* Don't be such a racist prick!' Maggie exclaimed. 'It's no wonder Shona doesn't want you to—'

'To what?' he demanded angrily.

'To . . . to have a big wedding,' Maggie lied. She wasn't going to be the one to tell Terry that he wouldn't be walking their eldest daughter down the aisle. 'You need to cop on about Aleksy; he's a fine man. A lot better than some of the Irish men I know,' she added pointedly. 'Bye. I have to go. I'm working.' Not waiting for his reply she hung up, furious.

'The cheek of him, the absolute cheek,' she muttered, marching in to the kitchen to make herself a cup of tea. She'd been writing when he phoned: she was too mad now to go back to it. Maggie needed to calm down. And his smart gibe about having loads of lolly . . . *If only*, Maggie thought crossly, filling the kettle. The days of big writing advances were gone. Thank God she'd had enough saved from the good times to buy a small house in Wicklow, during the pandemic, and be near her mother when she needed her most.

Maggie stared out the window. Across the treetops at the end of her garden she could see the chimneys of her mother's house. The house she'd grown up in. Left to her own devices she wasn't sure if she'd have chosen to come back to live in the countryside. She'd liked the handiness of city life and it had been much easier to meet up with Caroline and Devlin. Bloody pandemic, she scowled. It had brought the best out in some, but it had certainly brought the worst out in others. Never in a million years had she thought her own brother would insinuate his way into their mother's home and feck her out of her own bedroom into the smaller double room at the back so that he and that wagon of a wife of his could have the bigger one.

'They're doing a bit of revamping, as they call it,' Nelsie told her one day after her brother and sister-in-law had moved in with her, when Maggie had FaceTimed her from Dublin to see how she was, and could hear hammering going on in the background.

Maggie felt her hackles rise. 'When did this start?' She kept her tone neutral. She didn't want to agitate her mother.

'At the weekend. They've decided to put in laminate upstairs. They said it's easier to keep clean and the carpets were getting threadbare,' Nelsie said. 'I'm across in your room until my one is done.'

'But no one's working because of Covid.'

'This fella's doing a nixer. He's wearing a mask and I'm staying put in the sitting room. God, I hope he's not wrecking the place,' she added as a particularly loud bang made her jump.

'I'll give Tony a ring later,' Maggie said.

'You better not ring until after five. The pair of them are working from home, you know. They won't want to be disturbed. They've set up the dining room as an office.'

'As soon as we're allowed to travel beyond the two kilometres limit I'll come down and see you, and see what's going on,' Maggie assured her.

'I'll be looking forward to seeing you and the children. It's a terrible time we're living in,' Nelsie replied, sounding so woebegone Maggie had wanted to jump in the car and drive straight down to Wicklow.

'What's going on with the house? Mam said you're revamping and putting laminate down. How come you've someone working there? That's not on, Tony.' Maggie came straight to the point when she rang her brother later that evening.

'Ah keep your hair on, he's not near her,' Tony retorted tetchily.

'And what are you revamping exactly?' Maggie enquired.

'That carpet in her bedroom is frayed. She nearly tripped a while back. The house needs to be made safe for her. It's gone old and shabby. This is the perfect time to do it.'

'And how much is this costing?' Maggie demanded.

'It's not that much, Maggie. Look, if it wasn't for me and Ginny coming to live with her while Covid is going on, she'd have ended up with you so stop giving out and be a bit grateful,' Tony snapped.

Maggie had said no more. When lockdown had started Nelsie had refused point blank to come and stay with Maggie. 'I don't like Dublin. There's no view except houses in that guest bedroom of yours,' she'd declared. 'You can come and stay with me.'

Maggie's heart sank. Even though Nelsie was a sprightly woman for her age, she needed help with her shopping and housekeeping. She had a woman who came to clean once a week and do her 'big shop', as she called it, but now that lockdown had come so suddenly and unexpectedly, Nelsie was on her own. If she didn't like the view from Maggie's guest room perhaps she'd like the view down towards the Dublin Mountains in Tony and Ginny's townhouse, in Carrickmines? It had the added advantage of being nearer to Wicklow. It certainly was more picturesque than the Southside suburb Maggie lived in.

'We'd be on top of each other,' Tony had protested when Maggie put the proposition to him. 'We're working from home now, we'd *need* that second bedroom.'

'I'm working from home too,' Maggie wanted to say, but there was no point. No one ever thought she actually worked! The words in her books just magically floated onto the pages with no effort whatsoever. The following day she'd been surprised when her brother had phoned. 'Look, Ginny and I will go and stay with Mam for a while. We can use the dining room for work.'

'Really! God that would be great.' Maggie was astonished. She hadn't thought Ginny would ever be the type to put herself out and certainly not go and live in Culchie land as she referred to anywhere beyond Dublin. Maggie didn't like her sister-in-law. Ginny had, as Nelsie astutely perceived, 'notions about herself'. She worked in a big insurance company in actuarial analysis and investments and her team were the best in the company, she boasted to Nelsie. She wore sharp business suits, designer shoes and sunglasses, and had a Gucci bag that had 'cost well over a thousand euro,' Nelsie had informed Maggie, aghast!

'How do you know that's what it cost? Did she tell you?' Maggie asked.

'No, she didn't,' snorted Nelsie. 'I wouldn't let on I was that interested. I Googled it.' Maggie laughed. Her mother was a great woman for Googling. 'It's far from Gucci handbags she was reared. She maintains she's from Killiney, but she's from Loughlinstown and not the coast side either!'

Maggie loved to see empowered women succeeding but Ginny's superior attitude was hard to take. 'I don't read soppy romance novels,' she'd said disparagingly to Maggie when Tony had first introduced them, 'so I've never actually read any of yours.'

'You wouldn't find much romance in mine, Ginny, I write about the nitty gritty stuff of real life,' she'd said amiably. 'But to each his own. I hate book snobbery.'

Ginny's eyes narrowed. Maggie eyeballed her back and they took stock of each other. Instant mutual dislike. Ginny had said nothing, just given a sweet little smile and taken a sip of her cocktail.

In the years that followed they had maintained a polite façade whenever they were at family gatherings or one of Maggie's book launches, which she felt obliged to invite her sister-in-law to, always hoping that Ginny and Tony would say no. She smiled remembering her last launch and Ginny – dressed to the nines in a stunning pink Joseph Ribkoff strapless pencil dress – scanning the large gathering in Fallon & Byrne, seeing other well-known authors nattering away to each other. 'I suppose you have to ask them for form's sake,' she remarked, adding slyly, 'it must be hard to be gracious knowing that Sheila Kelly knocked you off the number one spot with her last one. Do you *loathe* her?'

'We're actually great friends.' Maggie laughed at the idea. 'I couldn't be knocked off by a better woman. All the writers here are good friends, believe it or not. We're always delighted for each other when we chart.' Maggie knew Ginny genuinely couldn't fathom that there was no competition between her writing colleagues. Business for Ginny was cut-throat. No room for friendship in the actuarial analysis and investments department, she thought in amusement as another author friend, Claudia Cassidy, breezed over and hugged Maggie warmly.

Everything with Ginny was competition - out to impress, see and be seen – so why on earth would she want to spend lockdown in Wicklow with her mother-in-law?

'Look, you do a lot of the looking after of Mam,' Tony said when she questioned him. 'We can take our turn and do this while lockdown's happening.' Maggie had felt bad about thinking that her brother didn't put himself out, stepping up to the plate as Nelsie got older and needed more help. Truthfully she had felt utterly relieved to relinquish the role of primary minder to their mother, for a while, and hadn't put up any argument. With her other brother Rick and sister Niamh living in Australia and America respectively, Maggie sometimes felt resentful that she was left to do everything.

The early months of the pandemic had been so weird. Given the time and space to write without having to juggle family responsibilities should have been a gift but, to her dismay, Maggie couldn't bring herself to sit at her computer and immerse herself in her characters' lives. The weather in late spring and early summer had been so fine and warm she'd sat in her garden listening to the chorus of birdsong and the lazy hum of bees as they gathered their pollen, and felt as though she was releasing a huge exhale of weariness and worry. It had been a strangely enjoyable and liberating time, and she'd embraced her reclusive state until – on one of their FaceTime calls – Nelsie had told her about the renovations.

As soon as the driving restrictions had been lifted Maggie had driven down to visit Nelsie, feeling the yoke of responsibility settle heavier on her shoulders the closer to home she got. Her mother greeted her at the door, her hair an unruly white halo around her head, her blue eyes lighting up at the sight of her daughter. Maggie knew, behind the blue face mask, Nelsie was smiling.

'I suppose we can't hug, but I've missed you giving out to me,' Nelsie declared, ushering Maggie into the homely farmhouse kitchen where Sooty was languorously grooming himself on the windowsill, bathed in a beam of sunlight. Maggie tickled him under his chin and he purred ecstatically. 'Sooty's missed you too. That other one doesn't like cats,' Nelsie murmured, casting a glance over her shoulder to check that the kitchen door was closed. 'The squawks of her one night when Miss Joy went in and jumped up on the bed in my room, where they are now—'

'They're in your room *still*,' Maggie said sharply. 'When are you moving back in?'

'They've asked me can they stay there as long as they're here. Your room's a bit too small for the two of them, especially with all the clothes and shoes she has.'

'I must go up and have a look at the renovations,' Maggie said, filling the kettle.

'You go on up, I'll make the tea. I've fresh scones made.' Nelsie shooed her towards the door, delighted that Maggie was back again and feeling like she was in charge in her own house once more.

After the initial novelty of having her son and daughter-in-law move in with her, she'd begun to feel like a stranger in her own home. Their inexorable, insidious appropriation of her home had got underway in the early days and, before she knew it, she'd been moved into Maggie's old room while they redecorated the bedroom Nelsie had shared with her beloved husband. They'd bought a big queen-sized bed in place of the double she and Ted had shared. Her chintz curtains were gone. Ginny had one length of white muslin voile draped artistically, and held by a gold tieback, on each window. Nelsie hadn't been allowed to see the room until it was finished, because it was a 'surprise'. She had cried when she'd seen what had been done to her lovely comfy bedroom with all her treasures – her wedding photo, the picture of Our Lady that had been one of her mother's wedding gifts to her and Ted, their burnished mahogany dressing table, with their hairbrushes side by side – all out in the shed.

Nelsie hadn't wanted any changes, only a lick of paint perhaps to freshen up the house, but Tony had somehow talked her into it and Ginny had assured her she'd love the new contemporary look she was planning. Nelsie hadn't let on to Maggie how drastic the changes were, because she was ashamed of how she'd been steamrolled, and worried that Maggie – who had a short fuse – might get in the car too soon and break the travel restrictions, and get into trouble if she was caught by the police driving to Wicklow to confront Tony and Ginny. Nelsie had felt trapped and isolated during the lockdown. Now that her daughter could come and visit again, she was going to tell Tony that she'd be fine living on her own, and he and Ginny could go back to their 'minimalist design' townhouse.

For the first time since that awful day when lockdown had been declared, Nelsie felt some of her old spirit reassert herself. When the pair of them were gone, she was going to repaint her bedroom, get rid of the voile, and get her dressing table and pictures brought back to their rightful places.

Maggie ran up the wooden stairs, her jaw dropping when she saw the new grey laminate floor and the white painted walls of the landing. It looked so bare and cold. She walked down to her parents' bedroom and stood open-mouthed, surveying the massive bed, dressed in white broderie anglaise, the white voile curtains on the two sash windows and the two rolling clothes racks with Ginny and Tony's clothes hanging neatly. The walls, doors, skirting and ceilings were all white. The only splash of colour three purple cushions resting against the pillows. It looked like something out of an interiors magazine.

She walked down to her old bedroom where Nelsie was now ensconced and her lips tightened when she saw the two rectangular storage boxes under the window with her mother's shoes in one and items of clothing in the other. A clickity-clack of footsteps up the stairs made her turn.

'I didn't know you were coming. You should have let us know,' Ginny exclaimed breathlessly.

'Why?' Maggie said tightly.

'Well, well ... we could have got something tasty in for lunch,' Ginny stuttered, noting her sister-in-law's stern visage.

'Why is Mam in my room still? Why isn't she back in her own room? And did you take into account her wishes and requirements when you were "revamping"?' Maggie's questions came thick and fast.

'We wanted to surprise her,' Ginny retorted, collecting herself. 'We felt the floors needed updating and we—'

'"We"!' snapped Maggie. 'That's what I'm hearing: "*We*". What about what *Mam* wanted?'

'I don't like your tone, Maggie. You can discuss it with Tony when he gets back,' Ginny said coldly, 'and that room needed doing up and revamping, this whole house does, it's outdated and—'

'It's my mother's *home!*' Maggie tried to contain her fury.

Ginny gave a dismissive wave of the hand. 'Talk to Tony, I've to go back to work. I'm not a lady of leisure unfortunately.' She marched back down the landing and clattered down the stairs, leaving Maggie incandescent at her snide, superior attitude.

'Well, what do you think?' Nelsie asked, placing a mug of steaming tea and a plate of buttered scones and jam at the far end of the table. 'You stay down there, and I can stay at this end, and we can take our masks off: it's more than two metres.'

'It's different,' Maggie removed her mask and sat down. She didn't want to launch into a tirade, preferring to hear what her mother had to say first.

'I'll be repainting it, and getting rid of those nets—'

'I don't think Ginny would describe them as nets somehow or another,' Maggie interjected wryly, biting into a scone.

'Everything white: did you ever? Could you imagine that in the winter when the snow's on the ground? You'd never feel warm in it. Anyway, I'm going to tell the pair of them I can look after myself now that the worst of the restrictions have been lifted. Sure you'll be able to pop down and see me every so often,' Nelsie said briskly, removing her mask.

'Are you certain you don't want them to stay for another month or two until we see how things go?' Maggie asked.

'Not really. No. I'd like to have my house back to myself. It's a bit unsettling having them here, to tell the truth.' Nelsie bit her lip. She looked worried and vulnerable, so unlike the feisty woman Maggie knew. 'Maggie, I haven't said anything and I'm sure it's an oversight but they have my debit card and, even though I've reminded Tony to give it back to me, he keeps forgetting. Now that I can get out and about myself, I'll be able to do my own shopping and pay my own bills. He's spent quite an amount on the upstairs.'

Maggie's stomach lurched. What the hell was her brother up to?

'Don't worry, Mam, we'll get things sorted. I'll get your card back. As you say I'm sure he's just forgotten.'

'I was thinking, Maggie, I know I've been afraid to do that online banking in case my account was hacked but I think I'll give it a bash if you'd set me up on it. I believe it's very easy once you get the hang of it.' Nelsie eyed her thoughtfully.

'Great idea, Mam. There's nothing to it. Just don't give anyone your password when you're set up.'

'Well, I'll give it to you of course in case I go doolally and forget it.' Nelsie chuckled, feeling relief flood her bones that Maggie was going to look after things for her just like the old days.

'Mam's debit card please, Tony.' Maggie eyeballed her brother. They were standing in the drive outside Nelsie's house.

'I took it because it was easier than having to ask every time she wanted shopping done,' Tony said irritably, taking his wallet out of his pocket.

'Well she'll be able to do her own shopping from now on. It's good for her to be as independent as possible,' Maggie said coolly. She was determined not to start a row because she knew her temper would get the better of her.

'Here,' Tony said sulkily handing her the bankcard. 'There's no need to make such a big deal about it.'

'If I was making a big deal about something you'd know about it,' Maggie retorted. 'See ya!' She turned and went back into the house to the kitchen where her mother was making an apple tart.

'There's your bank card, Mam.' She handed Nelsie the card and saw an expression of relief cross her mother's face.

'Thank you, Maggie,' she murmured slipping it into her apron pocket as Tony walked into the kitchen scowling.

'Ginny and I'll be moving back home at the weekend,' he said curtly.

'I'll make a tart for you so,' Nelsie said brightly, ignoring the frosty atmosphere between the siblings and Maggie felt a barb of irritation that she'd had to do her mother's dirty work, because Nelsie wouldn't ask her son to return her debit card.

Grumpy and tired she loaded the dishwasher and felt the yoke of responsibility land firmly back on her shoulders.

CHAPTER SEVEN

Caroline

'I just can't believe our marriage has been a complete lie. I never guessed. We had kids so quickly and, both of us having such demanding jobs, our sex life dwindled. I put it down to both of us being wrecked most of the time. It never crossed my mind that he was gay.' The woman sitting on the comfy two-seater sofa in front of Caroline burst into tears.

Caroline picked up a box of tissues and offered them to her client. Her natural instinct was to sit beside her and hug her – who knew better than she did what it was like to discover your husband was gay? – but therapists didn't hug in sessions and clients were better off expressing their emotions, rather that suppressing them.

'God, I feel *such* a fool! Such a stupid, idiotic mug!' Anger replaced grief.

'You have nothing to reproach yourself for, Rita,' Caroline said firmly. 'Your husband wasn't honest with you at the beginning. You were given no choice about entering into your marriage contract with a gay man. That's on him.'

'Oh Caroline, I'm so gutted and so conflicted. I love him. We get on really well. He's been a great father but I always felt there was a place I couldn't reach in him. A sadness I could never fix and now I know why. I don't know what to do.'

'You don't have to do anything until you're ready to. You need time to adjust. It's been a seismic shock. But coming here for counselling is a great first step. And when the time is right, if it's what you want, you can have family counselling sessions for you, your husband and your children,' Caroline said calmly. She felt for her client with all her heart as memories flooded back of finding herself in a similar situation, upon discovering that her own husband was gay, all those years ago. Nothing had prepared her for the revelation, and unlike Rita she'd had no one to counsel her.

'At least he waited until they were almost out of their teens to tell me,' Rita said bitterly.

'It's good that your children are of an age to understand the situation,' Caroline pointed out gently. 'It will be a shock, of course, but our experience here shows us that children can be very accepting of such situations, especially when they're older.'

'Do you have many clients in my situation?' Rita wiped her eyes and blew her nose.

'We do. We have men whose wives come out as gay, too, and we deal with a lot of transgender people, and families who have to deal with all these issues. I've seen great healing and acceptance when our clients and their families engage in counselling, and people get to the point where they can move on in their lives.'

'Move on! Huh! Where am I going to move on to? Who's going to look at a menopausal middle-aged woman with kids.

I'll end up on my own and he'll probably end up with some toy-boy!' Anger resurfaced and Rita dissolved into tears again.

'Look, we're almost finished here for today: why don't I bring you to one of our relaxation rooms and get you a tea or coffee, and you can compose yourself and mull over what we've spoken about?' Caroline stood up, signalling the end of their session. She led her client down the landing to a small airy room with a large sash window overlooking a pretty garden. Two comfy armchairs and a coffee table sat on a rug, a candle burned on the mantelpiece and soothing music played in the background.

'This is nice.' Rita exhaled, slumping down into one of the chairs. 'Peaceful.'

'We like for our clients to be able to gather themselves before having to face the world again,' Caroline said, giving her a kind pat on the shoulder. 'Tea or coffee?'

'Coffee, strong,' the distraught woman said gratefully.

'I'll have it brought up and, if you feel you'd like to come again, make an appointment down at the front desk. Take care, Rita.' Caroline smiled and closed the door behind her.

She ran lightly down the stairs and almost collided with a man coming onto the stairs from the first floor. He seemed upset. 'Are you OK?' Caroline asked.

'It's nonsense! It's all nonsense. She's my *daughter*! She's not a bloody boy. I'm not going to lose my daughter.' The man was furious but Caroline could also see his bewilderment.

'Could I get you a cup of tea or coffee? You could sit in one of our relaxation rooms and unwind a little,' she offered.

'Oh! Oh, OK then. I just can't cope with all this he/him/she/her/ pronoun shite. And of course I can't say that at home or I'm the worst in the world. One of her friends is saying she's a 'They'! A *They*! What's *that*? Did you ever hear such rubbish? Binary, non-binary! And what the fuck is *'Pansexual'*?' Wild-eyed, he stared at Caroline and shook his head. Utterly perplexed.

'In here.' Caroline put her hand gently on his back and opened the door to a room similar to the one she had left her client in.

'Sorry. Sorry for cursing. I ... I'm at my wits' end. And it's all causing terrible stress at home and with my wife. She and my ... my ... they're with a counsellor.' He jerked his thumb in the direction he'd come from. 'I just couldn't take any more of it.'

'Look, you're here with your child and your wife. That's a start and a good one,' Caroline said reassuringly. 'And the fact that you're here shows how much you have your child's interest at heart. We see a lot of families with similar issues and being able to talk about it with someone who isn't involved really helps. Stay here for a while: I'll let your counsellor know you're here. Now, tea or coffee?'

'Oh, right! Thanks. You're very kind,' the man muttered, his anger dissipating. An expression of weary resignation crossed his features. 'I'll have tea, thanks.'

Caroline hurried down to the small coffee shop, ordered tea and coffee to be sent up to the distressed clients and then headed for the staff room to grab a cuppa for herself before her next appointment. Following that she had a meeting with her office manager scheduled and then she was heading home to a long, lingering bath with the latest *Vanity Fair*, she promised herself.

Caroline filled the kettle and opened her locker to get her phone for a quick scroll.

A message made her smile.

> Just giving you advanced warning, Dee is coming home at the weekend so I'll be organising an Abu Dhabi Group get together. We haven't had one in ages. I'll send you the date as soon as I have it. R.

'Oh lovely,' she murmured, tapping in a reply. She had kept in touch with the friends she'd made while living in Abu Dhabi and Rachel was great for keeping everyone in touch and organising gatherings.

Something to look forward to. She could do with a lift, Caroline acknowledged, and she'd be able to tell Dev and Maggie she was socialising and not being a total workaholic, as they often teased.

Ten minutes later she was welcoming a woman who wanted to become a parent and who was devastated that her partner didn't want children – *'ever!'*

CHAPTER EIGHT

Caroline

Caroline strode briskly along the seafront at Clontarf, turning left onto the Alfie Byrne Road pathway. She was late doing her walk. It was dark. It had been a long day and her mind was frayed from full-on sessions with her clients. Thank God it was Friday she thought gratefully, the week seemed to have gone on forever. She breathed deeply and made herself focus on her steps and the landscape around her.

The moon was full: sailing joyously over the top of the ESB chimneys in a velvet, star-studded sky, silvering the glimmering sea with sparkling moonbeams. It was such a glorious sight, Caroline paused to drink it all in. Taking her phone out of her gilet pocket she aimed it at the view in front of her and took some photos. She'd post them on the Facebook page that kept her connected with her friends in the Emirates.

It was so peaceful – the sea whispering softly against the shore, a light breeze perfumed with the scent of summer – she decided to sit for a while and let nature's balm soothe her. A memory flashed across her mind and an old heartache instantly resurfaced. Caroline's heart sank. She didn't need to think of sad memories and what-might-have-beens right now. It was the moon shimmering over the sea that brought her back to a night on the Claddagh in Galway, with the man she had fallen in love with, after the disaster of her marriage to Richard, her descent into alcoholism and her subsequent hard-won sobriety.

She'd loved living in Galway, loved overseeing the opening of the City Girl gym for Devlin, in those heady days of expansion and the Celtic Tiger. And she'd fallen head over heels in love with Matthew: a calm, patient, handsome West of Ireland widower who'd made her laugh, shown her the sights of the beautiful West and made her think she had met someone to share a future with, something she never thought she'd have after Richard.

That moonlit night on the Claddagh, watching the full moon rising pink over an iridescent sea, Matthew had kissed her for the first time and she had responded with joy and desire, happier than she could ever remember as his firm mouth had touched her lips so tenderly and she had felt years of *uaigneas* – that loneliness beyond description – drift away on the breeze.

And then . . . and then . . . Even now, years later, Caroline could remember the utterly overwhelming despair and heartache when he had raised his head and looked into her eyes and said slowly, 'Caroline, I'm sorry . . . I can't. I don't think I can do this, much as I'd like to. I thought I could, with you. I thought I'd be able to move on but I can't forget my wife. She was and is still the love of my life. What I had with her I'll never have with anyone else. I can't lie to you, Caroline, I'm so sorry.'

Why didn't you think of that when you befriended me? she'd wanted to shout.

Do you know what it took for me to give you this level of trust?
You're not the only one who's hurting!
To hell with you and your dead bloody wife!

But, looking at him engulfed in melancholic despair, she'd swallowed hard and managed to say, 'It's OK. I understand.'

'Caroline, I—'

'Matthew, please, just go and leave me my dignity. I need to be on my own for a while,' she'd said firmly, standing up from the wooden bench they'd been sitting on.

'I'll walk you home,' he'd said miserably, standing up. In the moonlight she'd seen the haunted look in his eyes and known he was feeling as wretched as she was and her anger had evaporated. Caroline cried while he held her in his arms and she felt tears that had rolled silently down his cheek mingle with her own.

Caroline had left Galway soon after and returned to Dublin. She attended intensive counselling that had shaken her to her core but set her on a path of study and self-exploration in the following decade that had led her to become a skilled and compassionate psychotherapist.

In an irony that always made her smile wryly, considering how much her late mother-in-law had loathed her, Caroline had inherited Richard's family home, which she'd converted into a counselling clinic. Caroline often felt, with a degree of satisfaction, remembering how cruel her mother-in-law had been to Richard – denying vehemently that he was gay and blaming Caroline for his 'behaviour' – that her ex-mother-in-law must be spinning in her grave at the desecration of her home and the comfort it now gave to 'degenerates', as she had called the LGBT community.

Richard would have been pleased, Caroline knew. She was so glad they had made their peace with each other before he died.

Her work gave Caroline immense satisfaction and she immersed herself totally in it, even though Devlin and Maggie told her she needed to get out there and socialise and meet someone special.

'Don't give up on finding the right person,' was what she would tell her own clients, Caroline acknowledged ruefully, but she was never going to risk heartbreak again. She'd had enough of that and so she'd buried the longing for companionship, love and sex and the unbearable desire to be a mother, and ploughed a busy, if often lonely, furrow.

Looking at the moon shining luminously over Dublin Bay, Caroline felt deep regret. Perhaps she *should* have taken the gamble and tried to find love again, given herself a chance to experience motherhood. It was far too late for that now.

'Oh for God's sake, get over yourself,' Caroline muttered crossly, getting to her feet and resuming her walk. I might be a lonely singleton but at least I'm a very fit lonely singleton, she thought, breaking into a jog.

She was laying out her clothes for the next day, a couple of hours later, when her phone pinged. It was Rachel reminding her of the Abu Dhabi night the following evening. She'd forgotten about it.

I'll be there! Looking forward to it. X

Caroline *was* looking forward to it, she thought later as she lay in bed, looking at the moon peeping in at her through her Velux skylight. Her boobs ached and a sudden rush of horny desire flooded her. 'Bloody full moon, bloody surges,' she cursed. A doctor friend had told her it was her ovaries having their last fling, knowing that their purpose was coming to an end.

She reached out and opened the drawer in her bedside table, rooting for her Rampant Rabbit. Devlin and Maggie had bought it for her fortieth. 'I'd be lost without mine.' Maggie had grinned. 'Far, far superior to what I had with Terry!'

She turned it on and thought of Hugh Jackman's hard muscular thighs wrapped around her. Might as well make the most of it, Caroline thought with a sigh, making herself comfortable. A sad little putter then silence as the battery died.

'Feck's sake!' she swore grumpily, shoving the vibrator back in the drawer and pulling the duvet over her head to shut out the unquenchable moon.

CHAPTER NINE

Caroline/Mick

'Long time no see!' Caroline turned to see a tanned, middle-aged, grey-haired man smiling at her. She gazed at him blankly for a moment and then recognition dawned.

'Mick!' she exclaimed. 'I didn't know you were going to be here. I haven't seen you on the app for a while.'

'Haven't been on it much, to be honest, a lot going on,' he replied as they hugged warmly. 'You look great: you've hardly changed since all those years back.'

Caroline laughed. 'Ah Mick, that's kind, but thanks for the compliment. Let's grab a seat and have a catch up.'

'I'd love that. What will you have to drink?'

'A glass of tonic for me, thanks.' She smiled.

'Still on the dry?' He asked, leading her to a table which already had a pint of Guinness awaiting his attention.

'I sure am,' she said lightly.

'Good woman.' He winked. Caroline laughed. She'd always felt very comfortable with the good-humoured Kerry man. She watched him make his way to the bar, stopping here and there to greet people. There was a good crowd at the Abu Dhabi reunion evening and she was enjoying catching up with her old friends. Meeting Mick unexpectedly was an added bonus. He'd been one of her great pals when she'd lived in the Emirates. Fun, dependable and supportive, he'd been very kind to her when she'd been finding her feet. He was always kind to the newbies, she'd observed, as were many of the friends she'd made all those years ago. She gazed around looking to see if Sally, his wife, was around or if he was here on his own. He might have come back to see his elderly parents. Mick had mentioned on one of the group chats that his mother was having a hip replacement.

If Sally were here there'd be more than a pint of Guinness on the table, she surmised. Sally had always liked her cocktails – she had always been a chirpy, outgoing party-girl, the complete opposite to her more restrained and laid-back husband. A real case of opposites attract, Caroline mused, as Mick arrived back with her sparkling, cold tonic.

'Thanks, Mick. Is Sally with you?'

'Nope!' He took a glug of his pint. 'We got divorced,' he said flatly.

'Ah no. I'm sorry to hear that.' Caroline reached across the table and patted his hand. 'Always difficult. Are the kids OK?'

Mick shook his head. 'The eldest two are. Ciara's working in property sales in France and she loves it. Conor's in Melbourne working in IT. But Dervla . . .' He sighed and grimaced. 'She's sixteen, three months pregnant and as bolshie as hell. I'm at my wits' end, to tell you the truth. Bad enough being single and pregnant at that age, but being an under-age unmarried mother in the Emirates is not the ideal situation to be in.'

'Oh cripes, Mick, that's a real bummer.'

'Tell me about it.' He exhaled and eyed her despondently. 'I might need your counselling skills yet.'

'You've got them and I'll give you a good discount,' she assured him, feeling very sorry for her old pal.

'I'm bringing her back to Ireland. I've wanted to come home for a long time – that was one of the reasons for the divorce. I don't like the Emirates. It was a great place to make money and I did well. I worked damn hard. You did too when you were there,' he acknowledged, taking a long draught of Guinness. 'Sally loves the lifestyle: the parties, the social scene, the Botox and fillers and all that stuff. She'd never come back home. She met someone else too.' Mick shrugged.

'Oh dear,' Caroline murmured.

'Oh dear, indeed. She's living with an Iranian guy on his second divorce. He won't stay on the scene. Of course, Dervla's opted to live with Sally although she spends every second weekend with me. She's got in with an older, more sophisticated set, late teens. I'm not laying all the blame on Sally. She was out socialising with the new man so much she … ' He paused, unwilling to be disloyal. 'I took my eye off the ball too. Allowed Dervla far too much freedom. I was the worst in the world when I tried to set ground rules. I should have been more forceful. It's my fault that I didn't put my foot down.'

'It's hard to negotiate that tricky path, especially when parents are living apart.' Caroline took a sip of her tonic. 'Am I right in thinking the law in the UAE has changed concerning unmarried mothers?'

'Yep, it's not the horrendous drama it was when you lived there. Sheikh Mohamed introduced a new law that recognises the rights of single mothers to register their children without the requirement of a father or a marriage certificate. But even if she *was* eighteen, marriage is out of the question. The fella doesn't want to know. It could get very awkward if I went after him to admit paternity and pay maintenance. You know what it's like over there. My poor child is pregnant, heartbroken and completely messed up.'

'That's terrible, Mick,' Caroline said sombrely.

'And to add insult to injury, I'm having trouble getting the tenants to leave the house in Drumcondra. They wouldn't go when their lease was up, so we've had to rent an apartment. It's a bloody nightmare and the Residential Tenancies Board are so slow following through. Once they're out I'll *never* let the house again.'

'But that's your family home in Ireland!' Caroline was horrified. 'I've property rented to an elderly lady. She's lovely but I'm reluctant to rent it out again when she goes. You hear so many stories like yours.'

'Ah, it'll work out somehow.' Mick sighed. 'Sorry for dumping on you. I haven't said anything in the group about Dervla being pregnant. It's her business, after all. She's entitled to her privacy.'

'Hey you two. How ya doin?' A laughing, effervescent woman kissed Mick on top of his head and leaned in to hug Caroline.

'Maura, how are you?' Mick stood up and returned the kiss.

'All the better for seeing you pair. Schoosh up there, Caroline, and let me in. I've loads to tell ya. Oh look, there's Féile. Come over here, missus!' Maura called out to the attractive, svelte blonde who was heading to the bar.

Before they knew it, two more friends had joined Maura and Féile and hugs were exchanged and high-spirited conversations flowed as the party really began in earnest.

'Mick, get in touch with me and let's have a natter on our own again,' Caroline said several hours later, when she got up to go. A lot of people were giddy and tipsy – even after all these years of sobriety, it was sometimes a trigger point for Caroline, making her think that perhaps it would be OK to take just one drink.

'Ah, don't go,' he said expansively, his eyes bright from the few drinks he'd lowered.

'Have to,' she murmured. 'I've got a longing.' She indicated a balloon glass of fizzing gin and tonic on the table.

'Of course, sorry! I'm a bit pissed. I wasn't thinking.' He was instantly apologetic.

'No worries.' She shrugged. 'We'll talk soon.'

'Are you getting a taxi?'

'No, I parked just around the corner.'

'I'll walk you to it,' he offered instantly.

'Stay where you are. It's literally a minute's walk and I've a few people to say goodbye to. Mind yourself.' She gave him a hug and he hugged her back.

'*Ma Salama*,' he offered her the Arabic goodbye. 'And *shukran*.'

'*Afwan*, or *tá fáilte romhat*, even.' She laughed, adding on the Irish response to his thanks.

'Ah, don't go, Caroline. We're going to Coppers,' Maura begged.

'Good for you, Maura. I'm booked in for a few sessions in the morning, so I need to have my wits about me.' Caroline smiled at her.

'But it's Saturday!' The other woman protested.

'Sometimes I have to see clients on Saturdays, if they can't get time off work. I'll take Monday morning off instead.'

'Aw.' Maura took a swig of her Cosmo and swayed slightly on her feet. She was pissed and she'd get even more drunk at the nightclub. If Caroline went clubbing with the gang she'd end up driving half of them home and she wasn't in the mood for that tonight.

Caroline made her way out of the pub and walked briskly to her car, glad she wouldn't have to hang around waiting for a taxi. Revellers were standing outside pubs and restaurants, smoking, laughing, enjoying the Friday night vibe, but she felt heavy-hearted. The overwhelming urge to have a drink had taken her by surprise. She hadn't felt that in a long time.

She got into her car and threw her bag on the floor. Caroline knew what was behind her low mood: listening to the other women talking about their children and what they were doing or hearing them make plans to travel with their husbands, now that their offspring were grown. Seeing those contented couples whose marriages had lasted the course, and comparing her own childless, manless self, had made her feel lonely and unfulfilled. It wasn't a new feeling but it had become more acute as she'd become perimenopausal. The aching sadness of knowing her time to be a mother had slipped away.

All her life she'd longed to be happily married and a mother. To have her own family unit. Caroline knew that losing her mother in her early teens, and being expected by her father and brothers to step in and take over the running of the household, had led to years of unexpressed grief and resentment. None of her family had ever acknowledged her shock and trauma at losing her beloved mother. She'd just been expected to get on with things. That suppressed grief was one of the reasons she'd rushed into marriage with Richard. A marriage that had been a disaster from the start.

Now making her way home to the cosy cottage she'd bought, just off Kincora Road – near the apartment on the seafront in Clontarf she'd lived in during her marriage – she dreaded going into it alone.

CHAPTER TEN

Caroline

Caroline yawned, weary after a busy day at work. The aroma of mint and rosemary when she opened the drawer of the air fryer made her mouth water. The rack of lamb was crisping nicely: a few more minutes while she set the table would finish it off. The creamy, cheesy potatoes were bubbling enticingly and the ding of the microwave told her the petit pois were ready.

She'd had a stressful day. Her clients, full of trauma, anger and despair, seemed stuck in a mire of negativity. Caroline felt most of them had made little progress in their sessions and wondered whether she was at fault somehow. After she'd got home from the Abu Dhabi booze-up she'd slept badly the previous night. It had been a hot, airless, muggy day and – even though she had a fan blowing in her consultation room – she'd had several hot flushes, which hadn't helped.

Her phone rang. She saw Frances Hennessy's name come up. Frances only rang when she wanted a shoulder to cry on. Caroline scowled, ignoring the call. It had taken years for her to cop on that syrupy sweet Frances was a leech and a drain, not interested in the slightest in Caroline's problems because her own were so much more absorbing.

Frances was an interior designer Caroline had employed to work on the clinic when she'd turned her ex-mother-in-law's house into her therapy practice. Caroline had been going to one of Maggie's book launches and had mentioned it to Frances who had gushed breathlessly, 'I absolutely *adore* her books. I'd *love* to go to that.'

'Come with me,' Caroline had offered generously and Frances had been thrilled to encounter so many authors and well-known people at the event and had been effusive in her compliments to them. She'd posted a plethora of photos on her Facebook and Insta accounts.

'She's pushy. Watch her, Caro,' Maggie warned in her usual direct manner, seeing Frances, with plenty of business cards in her bag, work the room with a focussed intensity and make a determined effort to corner Devlin at an art exhibition they'd been invited to.

'It's good for her to get out and about,' Caroline said airily, unable to see, for many years, what Maggie had swiftly intuited.

As Frances's interior design business had grown, and she'd acquired a list of moneyed clients and new society friends, the daily phone calls had lessened, the weekly lunches had become monthly, and gradually Frances had latched onto others and only rang Caroline when she had a problem. She had a new man in her life but it wasn't going smoothly.

This evening Caroline was not in the mood to listen to the other woman's narcissistic whingeing, so she ignored the phone and plated up her dinner and one for the next day.

She ate her meal with one eye on the news and one eye on Insta. Lately she was finding it hard to relax as she usually did after a hard day's work, preparing her meal and eating it in her bright, airy kitchen. There was a tension in her shoulders, an agitation in her that she hadn't felt in many years, and it unnerved her.

Caroline chewed on the lamb chop bone, thinking she could have eaten the whole rack and chastising herself for being greedy. An hour later, she stepped out into the glowering evening hoping the rain would hold off until her run was over. She did her stretching exercises and jogged down to the seafront where she began to run in earnest.

Gradually the tension eased out of her shoulders as she kept a steady pace, dodging strollers and dog walkers, pushing herself until she reached the Wooden Bridge, then turning to run along to the end of the sea wall. Breathing heavily, when she reached it she stopped and took a sip of water from the small bottle she carried. Grey skies merged with grey sea on the horizon and the moody dark clouds over the Sugar Loaf in the distance were rapidly sweeping north. If she ran back the way she came she'd get home dry. Taking a few deep breaths, Caroline jogged to get back into her stride and when she got to the Clontarf Road she didn't even glance over towards the Port but turned right and headed towards Howth.

A feeling of triumph and fleeting happiness overtook Caroline. She was in control now, finally. No longer agitated and tense. Relief flooded her and she ran hard and fast even as drops of rain began to flatten her hair and run down her cheeks. Tonight she was going to run further than she had the previous evening. It was good to challenge herself even though her legs ached and her chest hurt. She was in control.

An hour and a half later, soaked, she let herself into the hall, stepped out of her runners and dripping tracksuit, and ran upstairs and stood under her power shower. Caroline let the hot water soak away the sweat, the aches and the tiredness. Nothing could beat the satisfaction she felt after her run. *Well, perhaps one thing could*, Caroline thought guiltily, drying herself. She was on thin ice, she knew, but nevertheless, wrapped in a soft terry-towelling robe, she ran downstairs to the kitchen, opened the fridge door, reached in and took out the plate of dinner she was going to have tomorrow. She ripped off the cling film and took the remaining rack of lamb and bit into it, stuffing her mouth with as much of the meat as she could. She grabbed a spoon and dipped it into the cold cheesy potatoes and filled her mouth to bursting. She had the plate cleared in two minutes.

Sated, Caroline scraped the bones into the bin, opened the dishwasher and deposited her plate and cutlery. She turned out the kitchen light, walked to the small downstairs loo, shoved two fingers down her throat and threw up every morsel that she had just eaten. She drank a mouthful of water from the tap, wiped her mouth, avoided looking at herself in the mirror and went up to bed. She never turned on the light, just pulled her night shirt over her head, slid into bed, stuck her head under the pillow and was asleep in minutes.

CHAPTER ELEVEN

Devlin

'I'm not convinced your pain is coming from gynaecological issues. It sounds more like IBS. Have you had tests—'

'Excuse me?' Devlin couldn't believe her ears. 'I have endometriosis not IBS.' She stared at the urbane middle-aged man sitting, doodling on a pad, across the desk from her. Her GP had told her he was an excellent gynae – her old one had retired – but sitting here in front of him, heart sinking to her boots, she felt the years had rolled back and once again she was a young woman desperate to be listened to. To be believed that she wasn't imagining the constant pain she was in or the nausea or bloating.

'Yes, yes, I've read your GP's letter,' he said smoothly, 'but there are other factors that can contribute to your symptoms.'

'But ... but I had terrible pain when I was ovulating and I still have pain in my ovaries,' Devlin stuttered, wondering if she was having a bad dream. This was the twenty-first century, wasn't it?

'How do you know you were ovulating?" He eyed her over his bifocals.

Because I'm a woman,' she said tartly.

'Hmm,' he pursed his lips. Thin and unkissable. She couldn't imagine him romping uninhibitedly. 'Perhaps you have a low threshold of pain.'

When she heard that she knew she was getting nowhere fast and had just wasted a morning to come and be patronised by a Neanderthal.

'Look, Dr Clark, I *want* to have a hysterectomy. I'm off the pill because of my age, my periods are excruciating, my childbearing years are over. I want to be finished with all this sickness: it's had a terrible impact on my life,' Devlin said coldly.

'That's very radical at this stage. You're perimenopausal, clearly. You've only another few years to go.' The gynaecologist shook his head. 'I feel the Mirena coil would benefit you greatly. It's made a huge difference to many of my patients.' He stood up and said crisply, 'Let my secretary make an appointment for you to come in for a day procedure. I'll have a look around, scrape the womb and we'll see how it progresses.'

'I don't *want* the coil,' Devlin retorted as he escorted her to the door. He picked a leaflet out of a display stand on the wall and shoved it into her hand.

'I want you to read this. It's an information leaflet: it will answer any questions you have.'

'But—'

'I'll see you in theatre.' He opened the door and made a shooing motion, calling over to his secretary in the outer office – 'Book Ms Delaney in for a Mirena and D&C, please.' – before closing the door behind her.

Dismissed like a silly schoolgirl, Devlin fumed. *Nothing* had changed. Men were still not listening, not hearing; thinking they knew more about her own body than she did. She felt like she had felt all those years ago – when she had struggled to find out what was wrong with her – powerless and dismissed.

'The fucking cheek of him! How *dare* he! *"How do you know you're ovulating?"* I swear to God if men ovulated, suffering from endo, they'd be squealing like pigs and a cure would be found yesterday!' Maggie raged when Devlin relayed the details of her disastrous encounter with yet another gynae who had pooh-poohed her.

'Yeah and *"you've only another few years to go"*. How dismissive is that? *Just put up with it until the menopause is over.* How long will that be? Why *should* you have to put up with it?' Caroline shook her head in disbelief.

'I know.' Devlin was exasperated. 'Honestly, I felt like I did back in those dark ages when I was struggling to get a diagnosis. I was waiting for him to say the pain was all in my head!'

'Arsehole!' Maggie scowled, spearing a prawn from the starter selection they were sharing and devouring it with relish. They were having an early lunch in Lemon & Duke: a lunch at which they thought they'd have been celebrating good news for Devlin who had, after years of pain and misery, decided to bring an end to the cause of it all.

'Are you going to get the coil in?' Caroline asked.

'Nope! I'm certainly not going to put myself in the care of that arrogant prat. *"I'm* not convinced. *I* feel … *I* want. I.I.I."* That's all I heard.' Devlin forked a piece of smoked salmon and avocado into her mouth but hardly tasted it, she was so pissed off.

'Leave it with me.' Maggie patted her arm. 'I think I have just the chap for you. A friend of mine dated him, didn't work out but they're still great friends. He's very pro-woman. Very sympathetic—'

'No! I'm not going to another man,' Devin said firmly.

'Huh! Some of the women are worse. I knew one years ago who wouldn't give young women the pill in case they did anything "untoward"!' Maggie scoffed. 'Trust me, Dev. I wouldn't lead you astray.'

'You've been leading me astray for years.' Devlin grinned.

'Me too,' teased Caroline.

'And don't you both love it,' Maggie retorted. 'Now wait until I tell you the latest. I heard that Niall Finlay is suing Carla for maintenance.'

'The absolute *leech!*' exclaimed Devlin, disgusted. 'She's kept that show on the road, and practically reared those kids on her own, and runs a successful business.'

'I know! He's got no shame,' Maggie observed.

'She's a really strong woman. I hope she fights it in court, even though it's the last thing she needs,' Caroline remarked.

'Some men have no pride, no sense of decency, and I speak as someone who's been on that particular roundabout,' Maggie said.

'And how *is* Terry?' Devlin raised an eyebrow.

'Shona's meeting him this week to tell him she's no intention of having a big wedding and he's not walking her down the aisle. He'll go ballistic.'

'Go Shona, I say.' Devlin laughed. 'My godchild knows her own mind. I don't give much for his chances of getting her to change it.'

'I'll keep you informed. In fact, why don't the pair of you come down to Wicklow for a gals' night? It's been a while.'

'Deal,' agreed Caroline.

'Say when,' Devlin chimed in, her equilibrium restored somewhat, as it always was when she was with Maggie and Caroline. 'And I'm not going into it here because we're pushed for time, but I met someone recently and what she had to tell me would make your hair curl.'

'That's not fair! You can't leave us hanging,' Maggie remonstrated.

'I really *do* have to go, I've to do an interview. A podcast thing I promised to do ages ago and there's too much to tell you to rush it. Then I've a meeting with the events manager about the reunion party.' Devlin stood up. 'Let's sort our Wicklow night as soon as we can: I need it. Bye, lovelies, I'll see you soon.'

CHAPTER TWELVE

Devlin

Sorry now that she'd agreed earlier in the month to take part in the *Empowering Women* podcast, Devlin was fed up as she sat in bumper-to-bumper traffic. She felt far from empowered and quite grumpy. She wasn't sure exactly *why* she was grumpy. You have no business being grumpy, she chastised herself. Even though it had been lovely having lunch with the girls, she hadn't let on to them how bloated and sick she felt. The constant nagging pain she endured was wearing, as was the nausea. Since coming off the pill, the endo symptoms previously kept at bay had come roaring back.

People had this impression that she was a high-powered, successful business woman. If only they knew what a physical wreck I am, she reflected as the traffic crawled at a snail's pace along Baggot Street. She'd spoken about having endometriosis in interviews but only sufferers of the debilitating disease truly understood what it was like to live with it. That was why she'd agreed to take part in the discussion 'Periods. Power.

Patriarchy', to try and bring awareness to the mainstream. She'd certainly had a rude awakening that the patriarchy was alive and kicking, Devlin fumed as the anger that she'd kept buried deep in her psyche had come roaring back after her disastrous consultation with Dr Smarmy Clark.

Twenty-five minutes later she was sitting at a round table meeting her fellow panellists: Debbie, a counsellor and psychotherapist who specialised in women's health and couples' counselling, and Pam, a former nun, who'd become a therapist and who worked with the Divine Feminine Energy. *All a bit woo woo*, Devlin thought privately, as she shook hands with the smiling, petite middle-aged host, before being mic'd up and sitting down.

'If you've listened to the previous podcasts, you'll know that after I've introduced you all, and you've shared your stories, the conversation will take its own course. It's very relaxed and I just want you to remember the reason you're here is to share, encourage and nurture all the women out there who follow *Empowering Women*. Please feel free to say anything you want to about today's topic. It's incredible to think that in the twenty-first century 176 million women suffer from endometriosis yet millions struggle to get diagnosed,' Michelle Lieffes, the host, said warmly, pouring coffee into mugs before sitting down and putting her headphones on. She nodded to her soundman, looked at the three women and said, 'Let's go, ladies!'

In spite of herself, Devlin was fascinated as Pam told of her journey and her complete disillusionment with the Catholic Church and its treatment of women, which led her to leave holy orders and begin her own journey of empowerment.

When it came to her turn to speak, Devlin took a deep

breath and said, 'I thought I was finally a woman in control of my body, and my needs for my body, until I went to a gynaecologist recently looking to have a hysterectomy. I was plunged right back to my teens and twenties: I couldn't believe that decades later I *still* wasn't being listened to.'

'Exactly!' interjected Debbie. 'I was told to go and have a baby – I was in my very early twenties and single, by the way – but as it turned out my endo was so bad I couldn't have children.'

'I told that gynae I was diagnosed with endometriosis,' Devlin cut in, 'but he said *he* wasn't convinced that it was the cause of my pain. I remembered all those years of trotting around to consultants, feeling I was the biggest hypochondriac ever. I was lucky, though— I was able to have children.'

'*He* wasn't convinced? That consultant made it all about *him*,' interjected Pam. 'A typical patriarchal response.'

'And why, in your work, Pam, do you think there's such a huge prevalence of endometriosis in young women?' Michelle asked.

'Let me say from the start this won't be for everyone who suffers from endo, but a lot of women who come to me have resonated with an explanation I give them. So to all our listeners, if it resonates with you fine, if it doesn't, that's fine too.' Pam smiled at Devlin. 'I work with past-life therapy if clients care to go down that road. I believe that what we've lived through in other lives can have a major impact in our present life. Only recently one of my clients had a past life as a Cathar where she was a preacher or *bonnefemme,* as they were called. At the siege on Montségur she wanted to pretend to recant, so she could keep the knowledge and the Word alive. Her husband was adamant. He wouldn't recant, even knowing that he would be burnt at the stake as a result. In the past life she was shouting at him, "Why is it always about *you*?"

'Her punishment for recanting was to watch her children walk to the pyre with their father and burn to death. She hanged herself afterwards, unable to live with what she had witnessed.' Pam took a sip of her water, clearly moved. 'In *this* life she has chronic endometriosis, and couldn't conceive. I could see her womb, in our session. It was burning. When, after years of trying to be diagnosed, she had her surgery, she was also told she had adenomyosis – endo in the womb – very, *very* painful. She too had had her symptoms dismissed,' Pam explained.

'That's *fascinating*!' Devlin exclaimed, intrigued.

'Not for everyone,' Pam said. 'Mainstream medicine has no truck with metaphysical healing, though I do have doctors and nurses as clients.'

'I see a lot of couples where one emphatically doesn't want children and the other does,' Debbie remarked. 'Perhaps that's linked to their past lives? What an interesting concept, Pam, let's chat afterwards.'

'Sure. Love to,' agreed the other woman.

'I wonder were you a Cathar, Devlin?' Michelle joked. 'And now you're back empowering women with your City Girl gyms. Tell us about your Giving Back project,' the presenter invited.

Devlin put her coffee mug down. 'I'm very aware that our brand can be seen as exclusive and is out of reach for many struggling women. I remember when I was a single mother with not a penny to my name: a session in a gym or a facial was far beyond where my finances would stretch. So we factor in gym slots and beauty slots at a very, very reduced price for women with low incomes. We have baskets in reception where our members can donate a gift of products, or beauty treatment vouchers they can buy in our shop, and our coffee bar has a Suspended Coffee initiative. You can buy a coffee for someone that really needs it. Our members are very generous,' she added, 'and we match donations.'

'And Debbie and Pam also have reductions for low-income women. It's truly wonderful that you three extremely successful women devote such energy to empowering others,' Michelle declared.

'A rising tide lifts all boats,' Debbie said matter-of-factly and Devlin was suddenly very glad that she'd taken part in the podcast. It was always satisfying to hear other women's experiences and to reassure herself that she wasn't a neurotic, hypochondriacal, demanding diva, as she'd been made to feel on the quest for a diagnosis.

CHAPTER THIRTEEN

Maggie

'... seemingly one of the relatives is married to a criminal, and they were laundering money—'

'NO! Are you *serious*?'

'That's where they got the big holiday home from. It's been sold pretty smartly I believe.'

'And that's not all ...'

Snippets of conversation floated through the window into the kitchen where Maggie was making tea for Nelsie and two of her close friends who had been invited to lunch. Nelsie was wearing a wrist splint because of tendinitis and had needed extra help for the past week.

Maggie busied herself taking the cling film off the selection of dainty triangle sandwiches she and her mother had made earlier. A serving dish of smoked salmon garnished with chunks of lemon, frilly fronds of dill and a scattering of black pepper was ready to go and she had just finished buttering fingers of brown bread. She placed them all on a tray alongside a laden charcuterie board and carried them outside to the big round table on the patio.

'All right, ladies, tuck in,' she invited, smiling at her mother's friends.

'Maggie, you're a treasure,' Cora Doyle exclaimed warmly, unwrapping her knife and fork from her napkin. 'I'm peckish after catching up with all the news, scandal and gossip.' Cora too was in her eighties and had always had a hearty appetite as long as Maggie had known her.

'I have to take a photo of this for WhatsApp, to send to Deirdre and Anita,' Lil Walsh declared, rooting for her iPhone. 'My daughters think they're the only ones who are Ladies-Who-Lunch. They wouldn't get this in their fancy bistros up in Dublin. Come on, girls, let's take a selfie,' she urged, positioning herself between Nelsie and Cora and taking the photo.

'I'll take one of the three of you,' Maggie offered and the trio of elderly women raised their chins and flashed beaming smiles for her photo.

'If you wrote a book about us three goddesses, you'd have a bestseller,' Cora smirked, holding up her glass for the Prosecco Maggie was pouring, and they all hooted laughing.

Listening to their laughter and chat outside while she tidied up the kitchen before leaving, Maggie was glad that her mother had two such good friends. A bit like myself, Devlin and Caroline, she thought, suddenly seeing the trio of elderly women in a new light. Nelsie, Lil and Cora had shared a lifetime of experiences, had been friends long before Maggie was born, had stuck with each other through thick and thin and still, decades later, enjoyed being with each other as much as Maggie loved being with her gals.

Would *they* be like this in years to come? The thought of it sent a dart of dread through her. Nelsie told her that Bette Davis had once said 'getting old ain't for sissies'. 'And she was right,' Nelsie declared. Maggie had laughed when she'd heard it but watching her elderly mother slowly losing her physicality was dismaying.

Nelsie had been in bad form lately, Maggie had observed. She'd looked troubled that very morning as she studied a bank statement that had arrived in the post. 'Everything OK, Mam?' she'd asked. 'Anything on your mind? You seem a bit down.'

'No, I'm grand. Would you mind getting me a couple of pounds of sugar the next time you're in the shop? I forgot to get it and I want to make my marmalade,' she'd said, changing the subject pretty quickly and shoving the statement into her cardigan pocket. Maggie refrained from pointing out that she'd need help making marmalade with a brace on her wrist.

'Sure,' she'd said easily. 'I'll get it tomorrow. If you need anything else, let me know.' She wondered what was in the statement that had made her mother frown but Nelsie was private about her finances and Maggie had no idea what her savings were. Nelsie's pension went directly into her bank account and Maggie knew she had some bonds in the Post Office but not what their value was. That was her mother's private business. Maggie wouldn't dream of asking about it but she did have her mother's password to her online account. Nelsie had taken easily to online banking when Maggie had set it up for her, and had given her the password. Maggie could have a snoop, to see if everything was in order, she supposed, but it felt like a betrayal to go behind her mother's back like that.

She knew she needed to have a chat with Nelsie too, about

her final wishes, DNR, power of attorney and so on. She'd been putting it off, hoping Nelsie would bring it up in conversation, especially after the terrors of the pandemic. A few of her mother's elderly acquaintances had died during Covid and she'd had to watch the funerals online.

Maggie refreshed the water in the jug holding a glorious profusion of sweet peas and placed it back on the centre of the kitchen table, folded the tea towel neatly on the oven door as Nelsie liked it folded – ends level with the oven gloves – and picked up her tote.

'... and she got those filler things. Looks like a chipmunk, if you ask me,' was the last snippet she heard before, chuckling to herself at her mother's acerbic wit, she left the women to enjoy their 'Ladies' Lunch'.

CHAPTER FOURTEEN

SHONA/TERRY

'So what will you have? Order whatever you want, lunch is on me,' Terry declared expansively when Shona sat down opposite him at an outdoor table at the Bailey.

'I'll have the Caesar salad,' she said briskly.

'But you haven't even seen the menu,' her father protested.

'I looked it up online.'

'But aren't you going to have a starter?'

'I don't have a lot of time. We're filming.'

'Tsk. You'd think you could have made a bit of time to have lunch with your old dad. We don't see each other that much,' Terry complained, waving imperiously at a waiter. 'And we've a lot to talk about. You're my first child to get married. We've plans to make.'

Shona's lips tightened as the waiter handed her a menu and asked what they would be having to drink.

Terry raised an eyebrow at her. 'Pouilly-Fumé or Chablis?'

'Water for me, thank you.' Shona smiled at the waiter.

'Oh for goodness' sake, have a glass of wine. It might relax you,' Terry said irritably.

'No thanks, water's fine.'

Terry shook his head, exasperated. 'I'll have a pint, Carlsberg. Thanks.' He handed back the drinks menu. 'So,' he said, sitting back in his chair, when the waiter left them. 'You're getting married. It would have been nice to have heard the news in person rather than in a text. I was hurt, Shona.'

'Why?' She stared at him noting that he'd started to dye his hair. Her father had always been anxious to keep ageing at bay. She thought it was pathetic.

'*Why?* You're my daughter! I'll be walking you down the aisle.'

'Em . . . no, Terry, that won't be happening. Even if we had a good father-daughter relationship, which we don't, I wouldn't be having that nonsensical patriarchal crap. You wouldn't be giving me away. I'm not a possession to be handed from one man to another—'

'I suppose that's your mother's notion,' Terry scoffed.

The waiter arrived with their drinks, interrupting his rant, and took their order.

'Nothing to do with Mam. It's how I feel and you won't be walking me down the aisle. I'm not having a church wedding: I'm having a handfasting ceremony,' Shona said calmly.

'A *what*!' Terry stared at her, horrified. 'What the hell is that?'

'Don't worry about it, Dad. You can come if you like . . . on your own.'

'Shona, do you not think it's time to let bygones be bygones? It's years since your mother and I separated.'

'Since you cheated on her, you mean. In *our* home.' She didn't try to disguise her disgust.

'Shona, grow up,' Terry said wearily. 'These things happen. You're an adult now. You've been in relationships that haven't worked—'

'True, but I've ended them with a modicum of respect and dignity,' she retorted.

The waiter arrived with their orders, giving her a chance to cool down. She wanted to tell Terry to get lost and to dump his beef and Guinness stew over his head. Shona forked some chicken into her mouth, trying to keep a lid on her temper. She wanted to roar at him that she hadn't ended a relationship by riding someone in the family home. That he hadn't cared enough about them to make sure that he wouldn't be caught with his side chick by his wife and children.

All the roiling rage that she thought she'd let go of engulfed her again as she remembered walking into the sitting room and seeing that woman having sex with her father, on the sofa. That image was seared into her subconscious and she'd never be free of it. Not only had it brought an end to her parents' marriage, it had brought an end to her relatively carefree childhood and it had broken the special father-daughter relationship that she had so treasured. Shona had been her father's pet. She always knew that. She'd adored Terry, her protective, generous fun dad who'd always been her mainstay.

That awful, never-to-be-forgotten day had torn Shona apart and, as she reset her young life from 'before' to 'after', she had shut Terry out. It didn't matter how much Maggie told her she was OK with Shona spending time with her dad and actively encouraging her to do so. Terry had tried to make amends, buying her expensive gifts – she was the envy of her school friends when she got an iPad, when they were only new to the market.

Shona had taken the gifts and written polite thank-you notes to *'Terry'* rather than *'Dad'*, which she knew cut him to the quick. She realised even at that young age that she was now the one with the power in the relationship and keeping Terry at arm's length was her way of punishing him.

'Where are you having this hand-thing?' Terry shovelled gravy-soaked pastry into his gob.

'Possibly Mam's garden.'

'So your mother knew about this and never told me?' Terry glowered before taking a slug of beer.

'We haven't completely made up our mind about the venue yet, so there's nothing to tell.' Shona shrugged.

'It all sounds a bit cheap and tacky. What does the boyfriend think?' Terry sneered.

'My Aleksy is very happy to have a small, intimate ceremony. He's not a flashy, shallow dude who cares about what equally flashy, shallow acquaintances think, thankfully.' Shona pushed her half-eaten salad away and stood up. She took a twenty from her purse and dropped it on the table.

'That will cover my lunch, see ya!' she said and walked under the canopy onto Duke Street, before Terry had time to react.

CHAPTER FIFTEEN

Maggie

'And then she walked out, Maggie. How bloody childish is that? I was very nice. Told her to order whatever she wanted from the menu. Offered to buy expensive wine. And what does she do? Tells me she's having some handfasting malarkey, if you don't mind, and not – and I use her words – "nonsensical patriarchal crap". It's a bit much, Maggie. I'm her father, I deserve much better than that.' Terry oozed self-pity down the line.

Oh Jesus in the tabernacle, Maggie thought in exasperation and then became even more exasperated to think she was turning into her mother. That was Nelsie's favourite expression when she was irritated.

'Look, Terry.' With some difficulty Maggie kept an even tone. 'Shona's an adult now. She's entitled to have whatever type of wedding she wants—'

'Not if I'm bloody paying for it,' her ex-husband argued.

'But does she *want* you to pay for it? Has she *said* that she does?'

'I'm her father, *of course* I'm paying for her wedding,' Terry bristled.

'Terry, I'm not sure that's what Shona expects. She certainly hasn't expressed any notion like that to me. I'll have a chat with her and see what she's thinking and get back to you, but to be honest I wouldn't hold my breath. Shona's her own woman and I certainly won't be interfering with her wedding plans. I'll support her all I can. Turn up on the day and do my mother-of-the-bride duty and that's the best I can do. You're going to have to sort this out between you,' Maggie said impatiently. 'Bye.' She hung up, cutting off Terry's plaintive reply.

No doubt Shona would be ringing Maggie with her own version of events later. Maggie was fed up being the referee between them. Her daughter was filming a series where well-known writers showed their workspaces and places that brought inspiration to them. 'I never truly realised what hard work the writing process was,' Shona had remarked after filming the first segment.

'Did you think the words just floated onto the page when "inspiration" hit?' Maggie had queried dryly and her daughter had laughed.

That was the impression most people had, Maggie acknowledged, picking up the pages that had just slid out of her printer. She was scheduled to do the voiceover for the latest episode in a series about the goddesses of Ireland, that they had filmed, on the following Tuesday. She cleared her throat and read aloud, 'The land of Ireland is named after the ancient Goddess Éire. She is a sovereignty goddess from the mystical light race of people called the Tuatha Dé Danann.'

She'd have to be careful with her ts and ths. '*Tuatha Dé*

Danann, Tuatha Dé Danann,' she repeated several times until she was happy with her pronunciation.

She worked steadily, revising and timing her script until hunger nagged her belly. It was after seven and she hadn't eaten much, except for nibbling on some of the canapés Nelsie had served for her Ladies' Lunch. Once the pandemic had ended and she had her house to herself again, Nelsie was delighted to entertain her friends and was inclined to forget Maggie was working, expecting her to organise everything.

Wearily, Maggie shut down her computer. She had a salmon steak in the fridge. She'd have it with some asparagus and a couple of the Wexford Queens she'd bought from the farmer in Ashford. It wouldn't take long to prepare.

Maggie went out to her herb garden and cut a bunch of chives, loving that she had her own fresh herbs to garnish her meals.

She brought her dinner outside to the round ceramic table on the patio and felt some of the tension she'd been carrying drift away. The evening sun still had warmth; the scent of lavender and orange blossom wafted around her on the soft breeze. The birds sang in full-throated chorus in the trees and hedgerows surrounding her garden. The fields in the distance, with their tapestry of green and gold, were bathed in a soft ethereal light that brought balm to her fraught spirit.

Maggie sprinkled a scattering of salt and daubed Kerrygold butter on the two floury new potatoes and took a mouthful. 'Food of the goddesses,' she murmured, relishing their yumminess. She took a sip of her chilled Pino Grigio, wishing she could stay put for the rest of the evening but she'd have to go over to her mother before ten, when Nelsie would be preparing to go to bed.

How wonderful would it be to have no responsibilities, to be as free as a bird to take off and go wherever the fancy took her? Like Caroline could, if she wished. Just when Maggie's children had flown the nest, and Maggie had felt it was her time at last, Covid had intervened, knocking her travel plans on the head and, after her brother and sister-in-law's behaviour, making Nelsie more dependent on her than she had ever been.

Don't think about it. Maggie exhaled, trying not to let frustration and regret spoil her tasty meal.

She was clearing away the dishes when Shona rang.

'Hi, I heard you walked out on your dad, over lunch,' Maggie said matter-of-factly, forestalling the outburst that she knew was coming.

'Oh, he rang, did he? Getting his story in first. Typical,' jeered Shona.

'Shona, it's like this. I told your father you're an adult. You can have whatever wedding ceremony you choose. I will support you as best I can and be there on the day for you but I'm not going to be stuck in the middle of you two. I've enough going on in my own life,' Maggie said calmly.

'What's going on in your life that's so difficult?' Shona asked sulkily.

'Your grandmother. Changes wrought by damn menopause. My career, for starters, Shona,' Maggie retorted sharply. 'Life's not all about you.'

'I know that, Mam. Look, apart from the disgusting fact that he's a racist, who looks down on Aleksy, I don't see why I should have to invite that man, his simpering cow of a wife and his spoilt brat to my wedding. And I want to be loyal to *you*, Mam,' Shona said heatedly.

'I appreciate that, lovey, and I thank you for it, but honestly there's no need to factor me into the picture. I've let go of all of that long ago and rarely give it a thought. Bitterness is not a thing for me anymore. That man is your father; the spoilt brat, as you call Chloé, is your half-sister. Deal with it, Shona. Make your peace with it or you'll be angry and revengeful all your life. That's an awful baggage to carry and I think you've carried it long enough. Don't let it ruin your wedding day. Talk to someone. Talk to Caroline and get an unbiased perspective on it. For once and for all, confront it and put it behind you. You have a whole wonderful life ahead of you: don't let it be poisoned by this shite,' Maggie advised wearily.

'That's easy for you to say, Mam. I lost my childhood and my idol because of Terry and that wagon.'

'I'm not denying that, Shona. I'm just saying you can be victim to that reality all your life, or be victorious with a new reality. There: I sound just like Caroline,' Maggie said crossly and Shona laughed.

'I suppose so. It's hard though.'

'I know. We love hugging our dramas to us, and feeling sorry for ourselves, but the freedom of letting go of something is exhilarating, I promise. Now I have to go over to your grandmother's. I'll be in studio doing voiceovers on Tuesday, if you're around to have a coffee.'

'OK, that would be nice. I'll be editing in the morning and filming in the afternoon, so let's catch up then.'

'Sure I'll look forward to it. See you then, sweetie,' Maggie agreed and hung up before her daughter could drop any more drama-bombs on her. She slipped on her loafers, closed the back door behind her and walked across the garden towards her mother's house. It was coming up to ten but she was surprised to see Nelsie already undressed and ready for bed.

'Although it was great to see the girls,' Maggie hid a smile at the description of the eighty-year-olds, 'I'm tired after it. I'm having an early night.' Nelsie yawned and eased herself into bed.

'Good idea, Mam. Entertaining can be fun but tiring.'

'Speaking of entertaining, your brother and herself are coming down tomorrow. He's coming early, she'll be down in the evening. He said they'd bring food and they're taking me out to lunch on Sunday.'

'Oh! Right!' Maggie was surprised. Tony and Ginny weren't in the habit of staying for an entire weekend. They usually called every six weeks or so to take Nelsie out to Sunday lunch.

'Seemingly some friends of theirs are staying in the Powerscourt Spa and they want to meet up with them. Herself is going to have some treatments.'

Too mean to pay for a stay in the hotel, Maggie thought, amused at how Nelsie always called her daughter-in-law 'herself'.

'You should go up to Dublin and see your friends and have a bit of a break for yourself, while they're here.' Nelsie pulled the duvet up over her and snuggled under it.

'I might, I'll see.' Maggie smiled at her mother and bent down to give her a kiss. 'I'll take the bag of clothes for washing with me, while I'm here,' she added, going into the bathroom to the linen basket.

'Ah, you're a great girl. Don't forget to put the alarm on,' Nelsie murmured sleepily, as Maggie closed the bedroom door behind her.

Might she go to Dublin and see if Devlin and Caroline were

free? It would be fun to spend time with them, now that she had an unexpectedly free weekend. She'd give them a call in the morning and see what their plans were, Maggie decided later, while locking up her own house and going upstairs with a glass of wine to read for a while out on her balcony.

Her book, about the young Anne Boleyn's time in France before coming home to marry Henry VIII, was absorbing. Maggie switched on the outside wall lamp, settled onto her recliner and opened up where she'd left off.

She'd love to explore Occitanie someday and research all those amazing women. Maggie took a sip of wine, enjoying the stillness of the countryside and the velvet black sky speckled with sparkling stars. Those women would make great subjects for a documentary too. She could do some research on them tomorrow, seeing as she'd have time on her hands. Her jaw dropped as a thought struck her. 'Why not?' Maggie asked herself, sitting up, galvanised. 'Why not? *Carpe diem.*'

CHAPTER SIXTEEN

Maggie

A blast of heat hit Maggie as she made her way down the steps of the Ryanair jet and walked across the concourse to the arrivals hall in Carcassonne Airport. Exhilaration swept through her as she made her way through Customs Control in the small, busy provincial airport. She could hardly believe she was in France. Could hardly believe she had, to all intents and purposes, run away from all her responsibilities and actually put herself first. Maggie almost had to pinch herself to see that she wasn't dreaming.

She had no baggage to collect, having packed enough for the three days in her carry-on and tote. There was a small queue at the car hire counter but twenty minutes later she was tapping in 36 Rue du Port, 81500 Lavaur to her sat nav and heading south. 'I did it,' she exclaimed, opening the window and letting the hot, lavender-scented breeze blow through her hair. That moment of madness, when she'd suddenly realised she was free for an entire weekend and could do what she pleased, had coalesced into a frantic two hours of activity on the Internet when she'd booked her Ryanair flight and a car, researched her points of interest, booked a night in a pension in Montségur, and one in Carcassonne, located her passport, thrown a few clothes and toiletries into a carry-on case and set her clock for a very early start.

There'd been very little traffic on the M50 and she'd reached Caroline's cottage in less than an hour, a few minutes before the taxi she'd ordered to take her to the airport had arrived there. Once she'd gone through security and arrived at the gate in T1, she'd bought coffee and sent Caroline a text to say she'd parked in her drive, would collect the car on Sunday evening and tell her all then. She texted Nelsie, Shona and Mimi to tell them she was researching for the weekend and would get in touch on Sunday evening.

Three whole days of freedom, and no one knew she was in France, Maggie grinned, her heart leaping when she saw the awe-inspiring sight of the medieval castle and walls of Carcassonne in the distance.

Much as Maggie had enjoyed writing fiction, she loved the new path her career had taken her on, writing about the women history had brushed aside. The satisfaction of researching and presenting documentaries was a door that had opened for her thanks to Shona's career as a producer, when she had asked Maggie to front a TV series about famous Irish women writers. It had been so successful that Maggie had, over the years, filmed several more documentaries for the production company her daughter worked for.

An hour and ten minutes later she was driving through the narrow winding streets of Lavaur, which were lined with colourful houses with pastel shutters. Small cafés, their awnings flapping in the breeze, were full of people sitting relaxed and happy, chatting, laughing and drinking strong coffee. The boulangeries with their sinful offerings were calling to Maggie. I'll start my diet on Monday, when I get home, Maggie assured herself. She was going to eat fresh crusty bread, croissants, cheeses and pastries and not feel guilty. She was, after all, in La Belle France.

She parked outside a Bar Tabac where a wide leafy tree shaded the outdoor tables from the brilliant sun. *Perfect*, she thought gaily.

Sipping the strong, sweet coffee while she waited for her savoury Gruyère and ham croissant, Maggie felt the pressure of burdens and responsibilities melt away and she sat listening to the rich cadence of the French language and watched the world go by. An hour later, revived and eager to begin her research, she Google-Mapped her destination. It wasn't far and soon after she drove past the blue-shuttered house she'd seen on the Internet and parked the car.

As she strolled up towards the commemorative stele, on the site of an old castrum on Esplanade du Plô, she could see the Cathar dove in the centre – an allegory of peace. The stele was ringed by a stone wall, overlooking the river, and Maggie thought how peaceful it was now, surrounded by forests, the trees stippled with sunlight, the birds singing and the river flowing serenely below. So different from the days of horror during the siege by Simon de Montfort when Dame Guiraude, a revered Cathar preacher, had been tortured before she was thrown down the well and stoned to death by de Montfort's soldiers. Maggie took her photos and sent them to her location folder before strolling back to the car for the next part of her journey.

Driving to Montségur, Maggie was entranced by the stunning scene ahead of her and the beauty of the French countryside. The sharp outline of the Pyrenees piercing the azure sky in the distance. What a shot for the documentary, and so much more to come, she thought happily, driving into the small village where she was staying.

Maggie parked outside her *chambres d'hôtes* and took out her camera to photograph the teal-shuttered house with glorious waterfalls of lilac wisteria tumbling down the walls.

Her room was modest, furnished with a double bed and side lockers with pretty lamps, an old-fashioned wooden wardrobe and a blue-tiled ensuite with a walk-in shower. A comfy chair was placed in front of the window, through which Maggie could see houses with red-tiled rooftops nestling into the hillside and woodlands overlooking the gorge.

She turned on the fan, relieved when the welcome breeze began to cool the sweltering heat of the room.

Tiredness overwhelmed her. Maggie yawned, remembering she'd been up since 5am. She undressed, stuffed her hair under a shower cap and stepped into a cascade of delightfully refreshing lukewarm water that eased away the weariness of travel and the stiffness in her limbs after the drive from Lavaur. The bath sheet was soft and a decent size. Built for womanly women, Maggie thought, gratefully wrapping it around herself. She hated the postage-stamp-size towels that wouldn't meet in the middle that some hotels offered.

She washed her underwear, the light cotton cut-offs and T-shirt she'd been wearing and hung them on the towel rail. The heat would have them dry by the morning and she'd wear them again for her journey home. Twenty minutes later she was sitting outside a café she'd found, on a narrow winding street a short walk from her *chambres d'hôtes*. The height of the three-storey houses and the narrowness of the street provided welcome shade from the sun, although the sweltering heat of earlier had cooled as the afternoon lengthened towards evening. The espresso and a croque monsieur revived her and she set off to find the path up to the castle.

From the base, it looked inaccessible and forbidding but she made her way through the thickly wooded mountainside and wondered awestruck: how had the castle been built up on that rocky outcrop and how had it been besieged?

'Thirty minutes my hat,' she puffed an hour later, when she swigged greedily from her bottle of water and wiped damp tendrils of hair from her face. It was a steep climb and she'd had to stop several times as she neared the top, breathing heavily, dripping with perspiration, horrified at her lack of fitness and acknowledging ruefully that her left hip was in rag order.

A wind swirled around the ruins of the castle, cooling her overheated body, and Maggie gazed out over the ramparts at the stunning views over the forests and mountains.

By the time she reached the foot of the mountain, the evening sun was streaking the sky a flaming orange. Her hip was aching as she made her way back to the village and she was grateful to sit outdoors at a restaurant close to where she was staying and tuck into a cassoulet de Castelnaudary, the slow-simmered stew of white beans, sausage, duck confit and pork that was a classic Occitanie dish.

After a leisurely meal Maggie walked back to her guesthouse as darkness dropped gently on the village, inhaling the scents of the voluptuous blossoms of perfumed flowers. She showered again, slathered night cream on her face and fell into bed, lulled to instant slumber by the soft whirring of the fan above her supremely comfortable bed.

The following afternoon, having visited the thought-provoking museum in the village and driving to Foix, Maggie drove through the winding roads of Occitanie to Rennes-le-Chateau. She'd long been interested in visiting the mysterious village, with its church dedicated to Mary Magdalene. Studying the exquisitely detailed bas-relief of the revered saint that decorated the altar, Maggie wondered would the real truth of the place ever be discovered beneath the rumours of secret societies and esoteric practices. She meandered through the knots of tourists, along to the belvedere where the neo-gothic square tower stood, and climbed the narrow spiral staircase to gaze in awe at the stunning vista in front of her.

A multi-coloured tapestry of vineyards, forests, bucolic pastures and the river Aude spread as far as the eye could see. In the distance the Corbières Massif: their peaks assaulted by great spears of lightning, the black clouds on the horizon a threat of bad weather to come. Maggie felt a frisson of anxiety. She didn't want to be driving down French hillsides in a thunderstorm. Listening to the distant rumbles of thunder, Maggie hastily made her way back down to the main street and had a mosey around the shops before stopping at a restaurant to have a light meal and open her phone messages, which she'd ignored thus far. One from Caroline saying she was looking forward to seeing her on Sunday evening and dying to hear where she'd been researching. One from Nelsie telling her to enjoy her research, a thumbs-up emoji from Shona and a message from

Mimi telling her to have fun. She paid her bill and hurried back to the car.

Less than an hour later she drove into grounds of her hotel. Her room, more luxurious that the one of the night before, had a view of the imposing ramparts of Carcassonne and was only minutes away from the centre of the walled city. She'd only booked bed and breakfast, wanting to dine in the city, so she showered and changed into a light sundress and unpacked a neatly rolled pashmina she'd brought, in case it was chilly later in the evening.

The tourist office was a two-minute walk away and she collected leaflets and maps for her research, before walking through the narrow shop- and café-lined streets over to the archway with the pointed orange-roofed towers, which she'd seen from the car. It led to the medieval city. She wandered along the winding cobbled streets soaking up the atmosphere, not finding it hard to imagine life in medieval times, as she walked part of the three kilometres of ramparts that circled the old town.

Her hip was aching and she was hungry so she made for the centre of the city, which was dotted with restaurants, many of them with terraces for outdoor seating. There were several unoccupied tables outside one and she sat and eased her feet out of her shoes. She'd walked more in the past twenty-four hours than she'd walk in a week at home.

'*Toute seule?*' A young waiter appeared at her table with menus.

'*Oui?*' She smiled at him. He grinned, gave a Gallic shrug and handed her a menu.

'*Vin? Bière?*' he enquired.

'*Un verre de Chardonnay s'il vous plait*,' Maggie replied, glad indeed to be *toute seule*. Being all alone in a restaurant in France was no hardship. Buttering the crusty bread that the waiter brought with her wine, Maggie tried not to think of the massive number of calories she'd consumed in her two days in France. Tomorrow was Sunday and her great escape would be over. She'd be back to real life.

CHAPTER SEVENTEEN

Maggie

How could Maggie's three days have gone by so fast? There was still so much to see and do in the Languedoc. She'd had breakfast in a shady courtyard in the hotel, listening to church bells ringing and birds singing. Oh, to be able to stay in her Carcassonne bubble and never have to go home, Maggie daydreamed.

She left her bag with the concierge before going back to the city to walk the cobbled streets. She watched a performance of troubadours and their ladies dancing and singing and re-enacting medieval times. The music had been uplifting and she sat drinking a coffee and writing down her impressions of the ancient city. A novel about a middle-aged woman leaving behind her responsibilities and moving to France might be interesting to write sometime. The notion amused her.

Maggie's heart sank when she saw DEPART on the large red sign over the departures area. The airport was in the distance, as she was driving to the car-hire offices. It had taken less than fifteen minutes to get from the hotel to the airport and as the Ryanair jet roared down the runway into the sapphire sky a couple of hours later, Maggie was torn between gratitude for the privilege of being able to take an unexpected, unplanned mini break and regret to be leaving a unique cultural region, where she'd felt so carefree and at home.

'Hey missus, where were you? You were in the sun, anyway: you've a great colour.' Caroline hugged her warmly, delighted to see Maggie when she finally arrived in Clontarf. It had taken over three-quarters of an hour to get a taxi at the airport and she'd had to listen to the taxi driver pontificating about politicians ruining the country. In desperation to shut him up, she'd phoned Caroline to tell her she'd be with her shortly to collect the car and to stick the kettle on.

'I ran away to France, to the Languedoc. Oh Caroline, it was *magic*,' she burbled, following her friend into the kitchen. 'It was spur of the moment. Tony and Ginny were staying with Mam so I took my chance and skedaddled.' Over a chicken korma that Caroline had prepared for them, Maggie regaled her friend with her adventures.

'It sounds *amazing*. I'd love to go there. I've only been to the French Riviera.' Caroline offered her more salad.

'It was perfect. Short flights, which gave me much more time to travel and suss out filming locations. Researching Margaret of Austria, and Matilda of Tuscany will take more time.'

'Oooh Tuscany! Lovely! I'd love to come when you're doing that research,' Caroline exclaimed.

'Matilda of Tuscany was badass, Caroline; she founded the first law school in Europe. And folklore has it that when

Queen Maeve had her period the battles were halted until she was finished menstruating. I *love* researching these women. Margaret was a powerful ruler as well as being the mistress of Pope Gregory *who*, if you don't mind, had the absolute cheek to label Mary Magdalene a *sinner*! The hypocrisy! I can't wait to film a segment about her.'

'I could come and be your bag carrier and all-round dogsbody,' Caroline offered, laughing.

'Take a holiday and come anyway, whenever it's happening.' Maggie's eyes gleamed. 'Maybe Dev would drop everything and fly over for a few days. She's not in great form, have you noticed?'

'I have, now that you say it.'

Maggie's phone rang and she sighed when she saw her mother's number come up. 'Hi, Mam. I'm leaving Caroline's shortly. I'll be home before ten,' she said.

'I was wondering where you were, seeing as you never lifted the phone to me the whole weekend,' Nelsie said crossly.

'I was out of range a lot. I'll tell you all when I see you,' Maggie fibbed, feeling a familiar surge of irritation that only her mother could induce. 'See you soon, bye.' Putting down her phone, she groaned. 'Back to real life. I better get going, Caro. We really should have a girls' night for a catch-up. We could try and find out what's bugging Dev.'

'I'd love that. We need it. Something's bothering her for sure.' Caroline followed her outside.

'Could be after going to that fecker who told her he wasn't convinced she should have a hysterectomy,' Maggie replied, unlocking the car. 'But you're right: she's not herself. You sort a night that suits you both. I'll be available. My wings are well and truly clipped again.' She kissed Caroline and sat into the car. 'Thanks for dinner. It was scrumptious. It's been such a treat not having to cook for myself. I'd say I've put on a stone since Friday. I'll see ya!'

Caroline laughed and waved her off.

Maggie decided to take the East Link, seeing as she was closer to it than the M50. She thought of Carcassonne, and how the French so valued their cultural sites, when she drove past the monstrosity of modern offices that had been built in front of the Point, as the beautiful old rail terminus was known before it had become a concert venue. The city manager and the planners who allowed that ugly office block to be built were utter philistines, she scowled. Though driving across the toll bridge and down the R131 reminded her how beautiful the Liffey was with the sun setting, sprinkling orange light onto the gently flowing river.

The traffic was heavy when she joined the N11 at Deansgrange, because of roadworks, but she knew it would disperse once she got past the Bray slip road, so she stayed put in the middle lane. Avicii was singing 'Waiting for Love', and she sang uninhibitedly, swaying to the music. She happened to glance sideways and saw two guards in an adjacent police car, stopped in the fast lane, grinning at her. Maggie laughed and winked at them as the traffic in their lane started to move. A middle-aged woman singing to loud music was obviously entertaining to them.

Maggie didn't feel middle-aged, apart from an aching hip and a thickening waist. In her head she was still in her thirties – early thirties, she thought gloomily. Where had the years gone? Now that her children were reared and had flown the nest, she should have been free to live an unimpeded life. Much as she loved her mother, Maggie couldn't help feeling resentment that she was Nelsie's main carer, left to it by her siblings who were free to live their own lives. It was time to have a chat with them. Rick and Niamh could do feck all from Australia and America but Tony and Ginny could come and stay one weekend a month. It wouldn't kill them.

The thought cheered her and when she walked into her mother's sitting room and found her watching the weather forecast, Maggie leant down and kissed Nelsie affectionately.

'You're home,' Nelsie said snippily.

'I am.' Maggie was determined to remain serene.

'A phone call would have been nice.'

'I knew you were with Tony and Ginny. I didn't want them to think I was checking up on you, either,' she said equably, 'and I didn't have signal sometimes.' This was not a lie, she comforted herself: she'd lost signal in some of the mountainous areas in the Languedoc.

'Hmm. Where did you go?' Nelsie gave her a side-eye, unimpressed.

'Em ... the wilds of Sligo,' was the first fib that came to mind. If she'd said she'd gone to France, Nelsie would have wanted to know how long had she planned her trip and why had she said nothing about it. Then she'd do her martyr act and say she was holding Maggie back and being a burden. Her mother was an expert at passive aggression. Maggie's equanimity was quickly turning to irritation. She was a grown woman, telling fibs to her mother. It was ridiculous.

'What would you be going there for?' sniffed her mother.

'I was looking for film locations as well as researching for my next project.' That at least was true. She changed the subject. 'I called into Caroline on the way home. I'm trying to get her and Devlin to come for a visit. They haven't been down in ages.'

'That would be nice, I'd look forward to seeing the pair of them.' Nelsie brightened.

'It would. I hope they can get a date to suit them soon. Would you like a cup of tea?'

'I would. Will you have one with me?'

'Of course I will.' Maggie tried not to yawn. All she wanted to do was to fall into bed.

'So how were Tony and Ginny?' Maggie asked when she handed Nelsie a cup of tea and a cream cracker with cheese – her mother's favourite supper.

'Well, of course they were having lunch at that posh hotel up near Enniskerry and then Herself stayed to get her toes painted and have a facial. Tony came down earlier and took me into Wicklow and we had coffee and cream cakes in The Coffee Shop. Such delicious cakes, Maggie, I do like going there. On Saturday we went into Arklow, to Bridgewater, and Ginny treated herself to a sundress in River Island. Honestly, I've never seen anyone like her for buying clothes. They took me to lunch in the Chester Beatty on Sunday and off she went again, spending all round her in Wardrobe. Maggie, she bought *three* pairs of trousers and two tops and they weren't cheap!' she declared. 'No wonder Tony's strapped for cash.'

'What?' Maggie looked at Nelsie, surprised by this revelation.

'Ah... Well, he must be, with that kind of spending.' Nelsie flushed. 'Now tell me what date the girls are coming down, won't you? I'll bake one of my cream sponges.'

Good deflection, Maggie thought crossly. It was most likely

Nelsie who'd paid for lunch in Chester Beatty. 'I'm going to head home. It's been a long day. I've a wash to do and I'll put yours in with it, before I go to bed.' Maggie took the empty plate and cup from her mother's side table to put in the dishwasher.

'I could do with a good shop. Would you bring me to Supervalu tomorrow? I need to stock up. I know you're going to Dublin on Tuesday to do your voice thing.'

'Right.' Maggie tried to keep her tone civil. Why hadn't Nelsie asked Tony to do her shopping with her when they were in Wicklow at the weekend? The supermarket was right beside the car park. Maggie had planned to spend tomorrow typing up her notes. Real life was back with a decisive bang.

At home, she unpacked her case, threw her clothes into the washing machine and emptied the linen bag of Nelsie's clothes she'd left on the utility room floor before she went away. She picked up the cream cardigan to check the pockets and was relieved she'd done so when she took out a crumpled-up document. The last thing she needed was a wash flecked with bits of wet paper. She glanced at the wrinkled page on the counter-top and saw it was her mother's bank statement. An entry caught her eye. Three thousand euro. That was a lot of money to come out of Nelsie's current account.

Curious, she smoothed out the page and saw the entry properly. Maggie's eyes widened when she saw the account it had gone to. What was her brother up to taking that amount of money from their mother? Then she remembered Nelsie's remark about Tony being strapped for cash.

The bastard, she swore. Sponging off their mother. How long had this being going on? And how was she going to deal with it?

Even more importantly: how was she going to put a stop to it? How was she going to ask her mother what was going on, without invading her privacy? Nelsie was of sound mind. Mam can be a bit forgetful, but so can I, Maggie acknowledged ruefully. Their mother was entitled to do with her money whatsoever she liked but if Tony was putting on the poor mouth and inveigling money from her that was nothing less than elder abuse.

Furious, concerned and disgusted, Maggie went upstairs to take a shower, all the highs of her weekend in France fading away like a dream.

CHAPTER EIGHTEEN

Devlin/Caroline/Maggie

'I'll drive, Dev. I can come and collect you, no problem!' Caroline offered as they made plans to spend a weekend down at Maggie's.

'No, I'll drive us. I can come and pick you up and carry on from yours.'

'But if I drive you'll be able to have a drink at lunch on Sunday,' Caroline pointed out. 'And anyway, you know me, I like to be in control.'

Devlin laughed. 'OK. You win! But don't bother coming out to Howth and then having to go back. I'll take the Dart to yours. What time are you free to leave?'

'I'm taking a half day on Friday. It would be great to miss rush hour, so will we leave around lunchtime?'

'I'll take a half day too. A perk of being the boss. Let's have lunch on the way.'

'Perfect,' agreed Caroline, her spirits lifting at the thoughts of spending a weekend with the girls.

'You're not having a lunch without me,' Maggie protested, when Caroline rang her to tell her of their plans.

'We might want to talk about you,' Caroline teased.

'Feck yis, I'm coming too. I'm *living* for this weekend after the week I've put in. We could meet up in Jack White's or Chester Beatty's in Ashford. It can be the start of our weekend shenanigans. On Saturday afternoon I've booked us in for massages, reiki healing and afternoon tea in the Latin Quarter in Redcross.'

'Oooh lovely,' enthused Caroline.

'It's fabulous. It's so relaxing I go once a month. If it wasn't for those sessions I'd be a basket case down here,' Maggie declared.

'What's up?' Caroline was instantly alert.

'A long story. I'll tell you all when I see you. Ring me when you're coming off the M50 and we'll decide where we're going.'

'Will do, see ya. Can't wait.' Caroline hung up, turned her phone to silent and went to collect her next client from the waiting room. *The weekend can't come fast enough*, she thought, ushering in a man whose wife had left him and their children to explore her sexuality.

'Isn't it just typical? The weather's turned. I had plans for us to go down to Brittas and go for a swim, after a stroll around Mount Usher,' Maggie tutted as the rain hurled itself against the windows of the restaurant they were lunching in.

'It's a horrible day. It was hard driving across the M50 for Caroline. I was glad I wasn't driving.' Devlin shuddered.

'Well, we'll just bunker in when we get home: I think it's only to last for the day.' Maggie dipped some crusty bread into the creamy lemon, garlic and butter sauce that accompanied her mussels and ate it with relish. She'd gone on a diet when she'd come home from Carcassonne but she was giving herself a dispensation for the 'Girls' Weekend' and she was going to enjoy every morsel of sinful deliciousness that presented itself. They were having their coffee when a man walked past their table, turned and walked back.

'Maggie! Long time no see, how's life?'

She stared up at him and her heart sank. A former neighbour who lived a few doors down from the house she'd shared with Terry when they were married. She'd never particularly liked him and he and his wife had dropped her after the divorce.

'Life's good. How are you and Anna, Jon?' she asked with pretend civility. 'This is an old neighbour of Terry's and mine,' she said to the girls.

'We're fine. Hello ladies, are you enjoying your girls' lunch?' He pulled out the vacant chair and sat down. *The absolute arrogance of him, gate-crashing our lunch*, Maggie fumed and was about to say something when he went on, 'So, are you still churning out the romantic novels or have you given it up to prance around our TV screens instead?' he asked smarmily, grinning at his own wit.

'Let me correct you there, Jon,' she said coolly. 'I don't *churn* anything out. I don't write *romantic* novels.'

'Really? I thought you did. That's all Anna reads and she devours yours.' He looked surprised.

'I write books about real life. Births, deaths, marriages and the universal experience. Sometimes,' she smiled sweetly at him, 'I even write about misogynistic, sneery, tax-dodging, golf-playing arseholes. Nothing romantic about them! Give my regards to Anna and, if you'll excuse us, we're having a working lunch putting together a programme of events from which several charities will benefit. Cheers.' She turned away from Jon and said to Devlin, 'You were saying, Devlin, which women's charities you'd like to involve in the reunion festivities?'

'I was,' Devlin said smoothly, not even looking at the ignoramus. 'I have a list of women's aid charities and I'd like to focus also on young women who are struggling to get an education.'

Jon stood up. 'Sorry for interrupting. You were all having such a good laugh I never assumed it was a *business* lunch,' he drawled sarcastically.

'You know the old saying about making assumptions.' Caroline arched an eyebrow at him. '"When you assume it makes and ass out of you and me."'

His face darkened and he stalked off towards the exit to the sound of their laughter floating along behind him.

'He was always an arrogant, narcissistic prick,' Maggie raged. 'Sitting down as if we were *delighted* to have his company.'

'That was a terrific putdown when he said you churned out romantic novels.' Devlin grinned. 'That wiped the smirk off his puss.'

'He never lost an opportunity to try and belittle me when I became well known. He's one of those smug D4 types: an ex-banker who salted away a lot of money in offshore accounts and was, unfortunately, never caught. I think they live in a big pile in Newcastle, not too far from here, and they've a holiday home in Donegal and a place in Portugal. Terry used to play golf with him.'

'I still can't believe he actually had the bad manners to pull out the chair and sit down,' Devlin said.

'I'd say you're not far off the mark calling him a narcissist. That trait of having an unreasonably high sense of your own importance is a red flag for sure,' Caroline observed.

'You're off duty, Caro, you don't have to analyse him.' Maggie laughed. 'Let's get ourselves home and get into lounging gear and start relaxing. I might even light the stove. It's much cooler today than it's been for the last week.'

An hour later they were gathered in Nelsie's kitchen drinking tea and tucking into her specially made strawberry cream sponge.

'Nelsie, it's as light as a feather.' Devlin wiped a crumb off her dress and licked the cream off her lips.

'It's yummy as always. I was hoping you'd have one made when Maggie asked us down.' Caroline smiled at the older woman who was delighted to see them and basking in their praise.

'When I heard you were coming I said to Maggie, "I'll have to make a sponge for the girls", didn't I, Maggie?'

'You did,' her daughter affirmed.

'And isn't it a terrible shame about the weather? It's been so fine until today.' Nelsie glanced out the window where the rain was dancing off the patio tiles. 'It hasn't stopped all day; you'll be swimming across the field to Maggie's house. No sunbathing in the garden for ye.'

'I'm going to light the stove and we're going to flop and have a good catch-up. There's a dinner in the fridge for you and I'll pop in on the way home from Latin Quarter with one of their pizzas tomorrow—'

'The four cheeses one,' Nelsie reminded her.

'I know.' Maggie tried not to be irritated. Her mother said that *every* time.

'I have my own tin of pineapple pieces. They're purists down there, and wouldn't insult a pizza with a pineapple, but I *like* pineapple on a pizza. It gives it a bit of added flavour,' Nelsie said.

'I'm the same. In my local pizzeria they won't put pineapple on their creations so I have my tin of pineapple too,' agreed Caroline.

'You could do with a few extra pounds, miss.' Nelsie eyed her. 'I hope you're not on any faddy diet. Have another slice of sponge.'

'Mam!' reproved Maggie. 'That's very pass-remarkable.'

'I'm not on a diet. I jog and walk a lot. I just couldn't fit another morsel, thanks, Nelsie. We're not long after lunch.'

'Just as well we didn't have a dessert after it,' Devlin said, forking the last strawberry into her mouth. 'Remember we used to have the "Sin Bag" when we were young gadabouts? We used to fill it with chocolate goodies whenever we were going on a jaunt,' she laughed, catching Maggie's eye.

Maggie's frown was replaced with a grin. 'Oh yeah. Remember we cruised down the Shannon, and it was always replenished wherever we stopped for the night? I have a few goodies for us over yonder. We'd best make a move.'

'Ah, stay for a while,' Nelsie urged. 'Sure I haven't seen the girls in ages.'

'I haven't seen them either, Mam. I want to get them settled in and relaxed, it's half three already,' Maggie said firmly, standing up and bringing her plate and cup over to the dishwasher.

'Always rushing,' complained her mother, tutting.

Maggie ignored the comment and carried on clearing the table.

'We'll see you before we go,' Devlin assured Nelsie, standing up to help.

'It was lovely to see you and thanks very much for the flowers and the chocolates.' Nelsie hugged the two women and stood waving at the window as they raced across the rain-drenched yard to Maggie's car.

'She'd have kept you there for the afternoon,' Maggie said grouchily, reversing to turn. 'And of course I'm the worst in the world for rushing you out the door. We were there for over an hour. She does my head in she's so demanding sometimes.'

'Old people get like that. My dad was the same. It's loneliness,' Caroline said gently.

'She looks well though, if a bit frailer than the last time I saw her,' Devlin said.

'She's in good health, thankfully, although I'm always driving her to the optician, dentist, and chiropodist. Just as well I don't have to drive from Dublin to do it. The Greens would be giving out at my carbon footprint,' Maggie grumbled.

'Yeah, they make me laugh. Telling us to use public transport: ha! I would if it was any way decent,' Devlin groused. 'We don't even have a rail link to the airport. Luke and I were in London last week and we were waiting ages for a taxi at Dublin airport.'

'I was waiting three quarters of an hour the afternoon I came home from Carcassonne.' Maggie demisted the car window.

'Was Nelsie fascinated with your research? It sounded like such an interesting trip.' Caroline shook the raindrops off her.

'Listen to this and how sad is it? I chickened out of telling her I went to France on the spur of the moment. She was in a snit with me for not ringing until Sunday. And could you imagine if I told her I'd gone to France for the weekend without letting her know? Girls, I just didn't have the energy for it and then to completely ruin my buzz I discovered something disturbing that has really rattled me.'

'Oh no!'

'What?'

Maggie pulled into her drive and switched off the engine. 'Let's go in and get into our loungy gear. I'll put a match to the stove and I'll tell you all then you can see what you think.'

When the girls came down from settling into their rooms, dressed in casual leggings and tops, Maggie had the Prosecco ready to pour and a non-alcoholic sparkling wine for Caroline. The flames from the stove cast a warm glow around the room: the rain pelting against the windowpanes adding to the snug, cosy ambiance.

'I've needed this time with my gals.' Maggie handed around the drinks. 'There's naughties in the dish so help yourselves. That's my hostessing done.' She grinned.

'I think we all needed this weekend.' Devlin held up her glass. 'To the best of friends.'

'Always and forever.' Caroline clinked.

'My tribe. The Goddesses,' Maggie added her toast.

'Now, what's rattling you?' Devlin settled into a comfy armchair and tucked her feet under her. Caroline sat into the opposite one and cast a quizzical look at Maggie who was flopping onto the sofa.

'I think ... no, let me rephrase that,' she said distractedly,

'I *know* Tony's finagling money from Mam. Remember when they moved down to mind her during Covid? I thought it was a very unexpectedly kind gesture but I heard afterwards they'd let their own house on a short-term lease. Win win for them. Living rent-free in Mam's. Anyway, they kicked her out of her bedroom and did up *her* house to *their* taste, with *her* money, and were buying their groceries with her debit card as well. If I hadn't have moved back to Wicklow they'd still be there, living off Mam and getting rent for their own place, I'd *swear* it.'

She took a swig of Prosecco. 'The thing is, Mam is private about her finances: she does her own banking online. I'm happy she's able to but I've noticed something's bothering her lately and, more fool me, when the pair of them said they were coming to stay for the weekend, I was delighted because it gave me three days to myself. But when I came home and was putting my washing into the machine, I threw in hers as well. I went through her cardigan pocket and found a bank statement. I didn't look at it deliberately,' Maggie added hastily. 'I just uncreased it to fold it. Anyway, I saw that she had transferred three thousand euro into Tony's account. I know it's her money to do what she likes with and I know he's always been her favourite but I think he's putting pressure on her,' Maggie said agitatedly. 'I suppose I'm also going to have to have a conversation with her about power of attorney, and DNRs and all that stuff, and I just *dread* it. What do you think?'

Caroline made a face. 'That's awful, Maggie, and to be honest I did feel when you told me about the Covid carry-on that it could be verging on elder abuse. I think you definitely have to talk to him.'

'I don't want to take Mam's agency from her. She has all her marbles and is a determined woman – and stubborn,' she said. 'But what if she ever needs to go into a nursing home or even have some homecare? She'll need her savings for it and he's dipping into them with no consideration for what's to come.'

'That's horrible what he's doing. Good luck with the DNR chat, Maggie. Luke had to have it with his parents. His mother wasn't too happy with him for, as she said herself, "making her feel old"!' Devlin chipped in.

'It makes people face their own mortality and it's scary for some,' Caroline said. 'There's always something, isn't there?'

'Just when I thought I was going to have time to myself. I hadn't factored in mammy minding,' Maggie said dolefully. 'Am I a bitch?'

'No, not at all!' exclaimed Devlin. 'All the times I resented my "minding" duties wasn't because I didn't love my parents but because I was stressed, worn out with all my other responsibilities, and being a working mother. We're only human, Maggie, and tragically,' she made a face, 'we're getting older and don't have the energy we used to have. Well, maybe not Caro here,' she amended fondly. 'She goes for 5k jogs and works out three times a week and it doesn't knock a feather out of her.'

'I was thinking of you when I was puffing and panting up the mountain to Montségur.' Maggie laughed. 'Caroline, you'd have hopped up to the summit like a gazelle.'

'You're very hard on yourself, Maggie. And I don't know if my jogging and gym work isn't just my way of running away – literally – from my own problems,' Caroline said quietly.

'What are you running away from, Caro?' Devlin shot her a look of surprise.

'I don't know exactly. Loneliness. A feeling of being a failure.

Grief for not having a happy marriage and children. I'm angry with myself.' Caroline gulped and tears welled in her eyes.

'Caroline!' Maggie was on her feet in an instant to go over and hug her friend. 'How long has this been going on? Why didn't you say anything to us?'

'I'm the psychotherapist, allegedly. I should be able to sort out my problems.' Caroline sniffled.

'Don't be ridiculous. Haven't you enough to be doing trying to sort out everyone else's?' Devlin scolded. 'Typical of you to keep it to yourself. We're friends. Your *best* friends, Caro: that's what we're here for. The good *and* the bad.'

'I know, Dev. You've both got enough going on yourselves though,' Caroline pointed out.

'What's brought it on? You've been cutting back on your grub too, haven't you? I noticed you did a bit of pushing food around your plate at lunch today—'

'I *did* eat a good bit of it, Dev!' Caroline snapped indignantly. Devlin stared hard at her and Caroline dropped her gaze.

'Yeah, I've been flirting with bulimia. I really wanted to go and make myself sick after eating Nelsie's beautiful sponge. I didn't, though, and I won't,' she added hastily.

'You better not, or I'll tell Mam and then you'll certainly get an earful! For Christ's sake, Caroline, *why* on earth would you go down that road again, after the nightmare you had with it?' Maggie was so shocked her voice sounded sharper than she'd intended.

'I'm not doing it on *purpose*, Maggie. Some of us aren't as good at dealing with stuff as you are,' Caroline retorted, hurt. 'You have children to come to your aid if you're having difficulties.'

'Sometimes they *are* the cause of my difficulties,' Maggie bit back.

'Oh boo hoo, poor you,' muttered Caroline. 'I resent that, Maggie. Just because you have problems with your kids doesn't negate my grief for not having any. Don't be so bloody smug.'

'Girls, girls, calm down,' Devlin intervened as Caroline and Maggie glared at each other.

'Well, she's very judgemental, Dev, *and* insensitive,' Caroline griped.

'I was and I didn't mean it. I'm sorry, Caroline. I just got a bit of a shock. I hate to see you struggling.' Maggie was immediately contrite. 'And you know the kids adore you like a second mother. You can have them and their problems with a heart and a half.'

Caroline gave a watery smile. 'Thanks.'

'So what's going on with you, tell us?'

Caroline bit her lip and shrugged. 'Life, I suppose.'

'Come on now, Caro, spit it out.' Maggie was not to be fobbed off.

'I know everyone sees me as very successful, having my own practice, employing people, not having to worry about money, when so many people are struggling,' Caroline said slowly. 'I mean I know I'm very lucky...'

'You are not *lucky*, Caroline, you *worked* your ass off and studied hard to achieve what you've achieved, and you damn well deserve your wealth after what Richard and his cow of a mother put you through,' Devlin declared.

'I know but—'

'"But" nothing. Stop feeling guilty about feeling miserable,' Maggie said sternly and in spite of herself Caroline laughed.

'You should be a therapist, I've said that a few times to clients. Hoist by my own petard.'

'Exactly!' Maggie gave her a hug. 'What ails you, darling?'

The kindness in Maggie's tone brought tears to Caroline's eyes. 'I'm so lonely and I feel such a failure,' she blurted. 'No relationship. No children. I longed so much to be married to a lovely man and have babies. When I met up with all the gang from Abu Dhabi again and heard them talking about their lives, their children, their grandchildren even, I went home that night to an empty house and no one to share my life with. I wanted to drink so badly – I didn't,' she said quickly when she saw the dismay in their faces. 'I rang my sponsor and went to a meeting the next day and I've been going every couple of days. So I haven't drank but I *have* made myself sick. I'm not going down the anorexia route again, that was all about being in control, bulimia is about anger, *and* I'm running too much and doing too much gym work. "Control! Avoidance!" I know the behaviour very well,' she said wryly, 'but it gives me some comfort.'

Maggie, who was about to declare that having kids and a husband could be a load of hassle and wasn't a panacea for loneliness, prudently kept her mouth shut. She realised that such a comment might not be the best one to make right at that moment, especially after their little tiff. 'Don't be angry with yourself, lovie. You're so *not* a failure, Caroline. But loneliness is hard to combat and I know you have your various social outlets but I understand what you mean about not being in a relationship. The comfort of loving arms around you cannot be underestimated. I miss that myself.'

'Would you go to counselling again?' Devlin ventured.

'Hmm.' Caroline made a face. 'I know the tricks of the trade;

I'd be doing my best to avoid the hard questions. And then there's the thing of another psychotherapist knowing my business. A bit childish I suppose but I do have my professional pride.'

'I get that,' Devlin agreed. 'Always having to put the façade on at work, when three weeks out of four I'm in rag order and swallowing Ponstan by the handful.'

'Look, even talking to you and not keeping it inside anymore is such a help.' Caroline wiped her eyes. 'I actually feel better having admitted I'm heading for real trouble if I'm not careful. I was literally running away from it.'

'How lucky are we?' said Devlin, raising her glass. 'We know the ins and outs of each other, the ups and down of each other. We don't need counsellors or therapists: we just need more weekends like this.'

'Speaking of ups and downs, are you going to get that damn womb out, Dev?' Maggie demanded bluntly. 'I thought of you and that conversation with that lady on the podcast, about the woman with the burning womb, when I was in France, in Cathar country.'

'I'm just putting it off, after going to that yoke who was so dismissive. I don't want to go through that again.'

'Look. I told you about the guy—'

'*Nope!* Not going to a man.' Devlin shook her head.

'This man is so pro-woman, he might as well be one,' Maggie assured her. 'Honestly, would I send you to someone dodgy? I still keep in touch with friends from my nursing days and he's the go-to for hysterectomies.'

'The thought of going, having to explain this endometriosis rigmarole again: I don't think I've the energy for it.' Devlin groaned.

'I'll come with you!' Maggie said firmly. 'It's time to get you sorted, once and for all. And while we're at it,' she glanced at Caroline, 'is there anything else up with you apart from the gynae stuff? You're not yourself lately.'

'Did you ever think you should have been a PI?' Devlin said crossly.

'Sarcasm will get you nowhere. Would that be called "deflection", Caroline?' Maggie queried.

'It would,' her friend agreed.

'Ah, feck off you two,' Devlin said truculently.

'It's too wet to feck off anywhere,' Maggie smiled sweetly. 'We're all ears.'

Devlin gave her a look of exasperation and laughed. 'I suppose it would be good to talk about it. I said very little to Luke about it and I tell him everything.'

'Wow! It's a biggie then if you can't talk to your beloved about it.' Maggie frowned, concerned. 'What's going on? Is Finn OK?'

'He's fine, living his best life, loves Barcelona, and he's the least of my worries,' Devlin assured her. 'No, remember when we had lunch in Lemon and Duke? I said I had something to tell you, about someone I met, but I had to go and do the podcast.'

'Yeah, we never did get around to it,' Maggie said.

'It's about someone I never wanted to hear about ever again and nor did I expect to.' Devlin gave a deep sigh. 'It's CCK.'

'Colin Cantrell-King! What does he want?' Maggie couldn't hide her shock.

'It's not what he wants, it's what he did to someone else,' Devlin said quietly. 'It seems I wasn't his only victim.'

'Oh God, Dev! What's happened?' Caroline was equally dismayed.

Maggie got up. 'Let's have our Prosecco later. I think we could do with a cup of tea. I could, anyway. I'll put the kettle on and you can tell us what's going on.'

'Good idea. Tea is such a comfort.' Devlin gave a shaky smile.

'I have some of those pretend teas for you too, Caro,' Maggie winked at Devlin.

'Excuse you, my herbal teas are very healthy.' Caroline followed them into the kitchen and, sitting at the kitchen table, Devlin told her friends about Nenita Santos's disturbing phone call and their subsequent meeting.

'What an abhorrent, amoral man. He should have been struck off,' Maggie raged.

'I don't really want to get involved. I don't want all those memories coming back. I was at one of Luke's niece's engagement parties a while back, a gorgeous girl, and I just couldn't stop thinking of Lynn and what she might have been doing if she'd lived. She's in my thoughts a lot lately. I feel such a huge sense of loss, which is kind of shocking: I thought I'd done my grieving for my baby,' she said sadly.

'Ah Dev, that's hard. Milestones are very difficult. Birthdays, graduations, engagements, weddings: it's only natural for you to feel like this.' Caroline reached across the table and squeezed her hand. 'And menopause makes it worse. I see that often, with clients.'

'I can't even imagine,' Maggie said sombrely. 'It's like the waves, dearest. They'll come strongly and then recede again. You know that better than any of us.'

'I know, it's just this wave seems to be swamping me. I always hoped I'd have another daughter for Luke, as well as for me. Because of the progression of the endo I know I was very lucky to have had two children. But I still always secretly hoped it might happen. I'd come off the pill every so often and now that I'm starting menopause I have to face reality and let go of that dream.'

'Yep, it's a real time of letting go of dreams, isn't it?' Caroline nodded. 'I'm letting go my one of being a mother and it's hard.'

'What are you going to do about the CCK thing?' Maggie asked, topping up their tea.

'I couldn't live with myself if I didn't stand with Nenita. She's doing it for her daughter. I had a daughter, once; I'd have done anything to protect her from a predator like Colin. The more that kind of grooming, predatory behaviour is exposed, the more abused people will come forward with their stories. I'm pretty sure Luke won't want me to go down this route, because he'll be worried about me, that's why I haven't said much to him about it.' Devlin took a sip of tea, relieved that, as always, she could speak so easily to her friends.

'He'll back you up whatever you decide. You know that,' Maggie said reassuringly.

'I know. He always has my back even if he doesn't agree with what I'm doing. I'm a lucky woman to have him.'

'Yep, you are, don't rub it in.' Maggie grinned at Caroline. 'We're relying on our Rampant Rabbits.'

Devlin spluttered out her tea and the three of them laughed heartily as the rain bucketed down outside and they sat snug in their bubble of companionship, confiding worries and woes as only the best of friends could.

CHAPTER NINETEEN

Devlin/Caroline/Maggie

'Oh this is gorgeous,' Caroline exclaimed when Sandra, the owner of Latin Quarter, led the trio through a cosy lounge area with a wood burner and paintings and *objets d'art* spread around. People were sitting at tables or on sofas, having coffee or lunch, and a hum of laughter and conversation followed them upstairs to the rooms the reiki and massage therapists worked in. Further along the landing, Sandra led them into a dimly lit oriental-themed room with a low table, big cushions on the floor, and with flickering candlelight and soft music playing.

'This is your relaxation room, ladies, and when your treatments are over we will serve you a light meal. Remember to drink plenty of water after your sessions and if you need anything just ring the bell.' She pointed to a small brass bell on the table. 'Enjoy!' She smiled and closed the door behind her.

'I love this room,' Devlin enthused, gazing around her at the smudge-painted green walls and the exotic floor lamp that cast warming shadows all around. 'I could do something like this in City Girl.'

'It's ideal for a small group, isn't it?' Maggie sat on the fat, cushioned sofa. 'Sandra does afternoon tea parties too, for older women ... like us.' She smirked.

A knock at the door interrupted their laughter and Maggie opened it to find Caitríona the reiki therapist and Rodrigo the masseur outside.

'Please fill out the forms and decide who's doing what first, reiki or massage. I'm in room one and Rodrigo is in room two. I'll see one of you in five minutes. Put the names in a hat, if you can't decide who gets to go first,' the young woman said good-humouredly.

'I have sessions with both, regularly, so this is all about you two. Why don't you go first,' Maggie suggested. 'I'm happy to just lie here and chill for a while and flick through some magazines.'

'I'll do the reiki first. I've never had it but several of my clients have and swear by it,' Caroline agreed. 'You have the massage, Dev, and then we can swap'.

'Perfect,' agreed Devlin, beginning to fill out her information sheet.

'All you need to do is lie on the plinth, close your eyes if you wish and let me do the work, Caroline,' Caitríona said kindly, as Caroline hopped up onto the treatment bed without having to use the step provided. The therapist made sure she was comfortable before covering her with a soft throw and placing calming hands on her shoulders. Caroline closed her eyes and felt herself relaxing as gentle Buddhist chants filled the room and Caitríona called in her spiritual guides.

Caroline was aware of the young woman placing her hands on either side of her head, and a burst of colour and heat enveloped her as the therapist explained she was going to work on Caroline's heart chakra. As she did, it was like a dam burst and Caroline found herself sobbing as years of pent up sadness and loneliness seemed to be released in a tidal wave of emotion. 'I'm so sorry,' she wept, struggling to control herself, wiping her eyes. But the tears wouldn't stop.

Caitríona handed her tissues and said calmly, 'Don't be sorry. It means you're allowing the reiki to work for you. Be glad that you are releasing all that trapped energy that's been holding you back and stunting your growth. Now take some deep breaths and let's start working on your control issues and the unhealthy habits you struggle with.'

Caroline was stunned. 'How did you know? Were you talking to Maggie?'

Caitríona laughed. 'Not at all. This is completely private and confidential, just between us. But this is where my guides assist me. I'm led to areas that need working on. Sometimes clients cry and release like you do. Sometimes they fall asleep. It's different for everyone. Are you happy for me to continue the session?'

'Oh, yes ... certainly.' Caroline swallowed hard. 'I need all the help I can get.'

'You'll get it, Caroline. Sometimes you just need that first step to acknowledge you need help and the way will be shown to you.'

'I know: I'm a psychotherapist, believe it or not,' she said deprecatingly.

'Sometimes people who work in counselling and therapy are

the last to seek help for themselves.' The other woman smiled down at her. 'But here you are and well done you.'

'Wow, this is fabulous.' Devlin gazed at the trays of food the waitress had brought up from the bistro downstairs. A charcuterie board, hummus, salads, dates, melon, nuts, a cheeseboard, fresh crispy breads with honey and jams: it all looked so tempting. 'This has been *such* a relaxing afternoon. How did you get on, Caro?'

'Oh my God! It was *amazing*.' Caroline tried not to be dismayed at the sight of the banquet laid out for them. 'I just burst into tears when she was working on me.'

'I did too,' Devlin confessed. 'She knew I had gynae issues and she told me I carried grief for a child, who is around me always.' Sadness darkened her eyes. She glanced over at Maggie. 'She said I should see another gynae. I need to do something to take away a lot of heavy energy I'm holding onto. Maybe I *was* one of those Cathar women.' She forked a selection of cold meats onto her plate. 'Or maybe I'm just a woman who needs a hysterectomy,' she said dryly. 'How did *you* get on?'

'I fell asleep and woke myself up snoring,' Maggie laughed. 'She spent a lot of time on my left hip and told me to use heat and ice and have Epsom salt baths. I fell asleep in the massage as well. Rodrigo always laughs at me. He's my saviour. I'd be as rigid as a poker if it wasn't for him. I go to him every month.'

'Oh, he's brilliant. He really got into my shoulders. I was yelping a few times, I can tell you.' Devlin wriggled her shoulders. 'It was sore, but I feel so much looser.'

Caroline spread some hummus and a small portion of smoked salmon onto a cracker. She felt a knot of tension as she took a bite. *Enjoy this food*, she ordered herself silently. She would do everything in her power not to make herself sick later. She was at the top of the slippery slope. After today's experience of reiki she vowed she would not hurtle down it towards disaster.

They chatted and ate and relaxed in their small hideaway, reluctant to have to leave and face real life. But Maggie had one last treat planned for them and that evening found them on a quiet beach further along from the main Brittas strand, with the sunset softening the sky into dusky hues. The sea shushed softly in front of them and the trio undressed and walked into the sea just as a golden glow on the horizon heralded the rising of an enormous full pale lemon moon that slowly darkened to orange, throwing a shimmering golden Jacob's ladder where they swam.

The tide had come in over sands heated by the afternoon sun that had banished the rainclouds. The sea was warm and tranquil, almost womb-like, as they floated in its silky waters under the light of the moon and stars, feeling utterly at one with the Universe. They swam and floated and chatted in the undulating sea for an hour as the moon ascended to the heavens, before drying off, slipping into their dry robes, and going back to Maggie's to drink hot chocolate and star gaze on her patio under the moon's benevolent gaze.

They hugged each other tightly when it was time to leave after a long lazy brunch the following day.

'Right, let's get ourselves sorted and deal with the shite and we'll have another weekend to ourselves when we're all back on the straight and narrow. I'm ringing Anthony Lane to make an appointment for you, Dev. Start clearing your desk to take six weeks' recovery. Caroline, you make an appointment to sort out the bulimia carry-on, and cut down on the jogging and gym, and I'll get the mother sorted, power of attorney and all that stuff, and try and get to the bottom of what my brother is up to,' Maggie said briskly.

'You always were such a bossy boots.' Devlin laughed.

'I like it when she bosses me around,' Caroline admitted. 'I have to make all my decisions for myself, so sometimes it's actually nice to be told what to do. I *will* make an appointment with a counsellor, Maggie. And thanks for this weekend. I was able to resist the urge to make myself sick and that's a huge step. And sorry for snapping at you when I did. I was being oversensitive.'

'I'm glad the weekend helped, Caro, and don't give it a thought. You were right. You weren't being oversensitive. I was thoughtless and too sharp with you. It was because I was concerned. But at least we can say things to each other and not take the hump.'

'We're too long in the tooth and know each other too well to take the hump,' Devlin commented as they strolled to the car. 'We're lucky to have each other. I don't know about you but as I get older I copped that there were people around me who just wanted to be in my circle because of City Girl. They drifted away when I stopped giving them freebies.'

'Yeah.' Caroline nodded. 'And sometimes friendships are just a habit. Like Frances Hennessy who only rings me when she's in trouble—'

'*Exactly!*' interjected Maggie. 'One good thing about getting older is you stop putting up with bullshit. Ya just don't have the energy or the patience for it.'

'Steady on, we're not geriatrics yet. We've a lot of living to do, madam. We're women in our prime!' Devlin said indignantly.

'We *are*! And we better start having more fun like we had this weekend; we've been letting things slide. We've all worked our asses off, it's time to step back a bit and start enjoying ourselves in ways other than our work.' Caroline opened the car door. 'Get in, Miss Daisy. Let's hit the road.'

Maggie waved them off, sorry to see them go. It had been a splendid weekend. Just like the old days when they were younger and relatively carefree. Caroline was right: they had worked hard, very hard, she acknowledged. It was time to take the foot off the pedal but first they had things to sort. For her part, the conversation with her mother was going to have to be had sooner rather than later. She watched the car disappear around the bend in the road and hoped fervently that the next time she saw her girls they would all have sorted the problems they had to deal with.

PART TWO

PARAGRAPH TWO

CHAPTER TWENTY

Devlin/Nenita

'I want to do it, Devlin, but I'm scared. After all, he's a respected consultant and I'm just a nurse from the Philippines. It's his word against mine and you know what those barristers are like: they could say I tried to seduce him and wanted to blackmail him or something and the jury would believe him.'

'No, no, Nenita. As well as having DNA proof – which is undeniable! – I'll be a witness for you. That will show that he has form.' Nenita sat across from her at a table in the restaurant in the Botanic Gardens, their usual meeting place. She looked so miserable Devlin's heart went out to her. 'Look, if it's too much of an ordeal don't go through with it,' she advised, trying not to feel guilty about the relief she felt at the prospect that Nenita might not go to court.

'But that's how they get away with it, Devlin,' Nenita raged.

'I know!' Devlin agreed.

They sat in silence drinking their coffee.

'Do you think I'm being a coward?' Nenita asked hesitantly.

'No ... Not at all. I never reported him and I don't beat myself up about it. You must do what's right for you. Whatever you decide I'll support you.'

'That means a lot, Devlin. I'm very grateful to you.'

'No need to be grateful, just be at peace,' Devlin urged.

'Thanks. I better go and collect my daughter from school. Thanks for meeting me again.' Nenita stood up to go.

'Do what's best for you and put him out of your head. Don't give him your energy.' Devlin hugged her.

'I won't. You take care.' Nenita turned to walk away. Devlin saw the glitter of tears in her brown eyes and silently cursed Colin Cantrell-King with all the venom she could muster.

Relieved as she was that Nenita wasn't going to take the matter any further, she doubted that the other woman would ever be able to put the trauma of what had happened to her completely out of her mind. And even more distressing was knowing that that despicable man had got away with his depraved behaviour.

But maybe his life could be made a misery in another way, she thought. Why *should* he get away with it? At least he could be made *aware* that his past could come back to haunt him. Why should he have peace of mind, when they hadn't? It was time for a reckoning of sorts one way or another.

Devlin grabbed her bag and hurried out of the restaurant after Nenita, who was walking rapidly towards the car park.

'Nenita, Nenita, wait,' she called, panting and running after her. 'Jeepers, I'm not fit,' she gasped, when she caught up with her. 'Listen, I have an idea I want to run past you,' Devlin said. 'Maybe we can do this another way.'

'Oh! Really?' Nenita's eyes widened.

'Oh yes,' Devlin said emphatically. 'CCK's past is finally going to catch up with him.'

CHAPTER TWENTY-ONE

Devlin

'Thanks so much for seeing me so quickly,' Devlin said to the tall, thin man who was piloting her into his consulting room.

'When Maggie Ryan commands something be done, I obey. It's as simple as that,' he said drolly, indicating a seat opposite his own.

'She does have that effect on people,' Devlin laughed.

'Now, Devlin, what's the problem?' he enquired.

'Em... er... I have endometriosis: it's excruciatingly painful and sickening and it's making my life a misery. I want a hysterectomy.' Her voice shook as the words came tumbling out and she braced herself for the refusal she was sure would come.

'Right. Well let's get a date sorted,' Anthony Lane said calmly.

'*What?*' Devlin couldn't believe her ears. 'You mean you're going to do it?'

'Well, that's what you want, isn't it?' He raised a bushy grey eyebrow.

'Yes. Yes, I do . . . I just thought I'd have to argue the toss with you.'

'I heard what you said, Devlin. It's what you want. It makes sense to me, having heard what you've just said, for you to have a hysterectomy. Your symptoms are only going to get worse. Whether we remove both of your ovaries and fallopian tubes depends on what I find when I look. If it's radical surgery you'll be plunged straight into menopause, just to be clear, but we can discuss HRT post-surgery if that's what you want,' the consultant explained.

'I know I'll be straight into menopause. The other guy said I only had another few years to put up with my symptoms but I can't hack it anymore. Menopause can't be any worse than what I'm enduring at the moment. I've already had a couple of hot flushes. I've had gynae problems all my life, except during my two pregnancies. I've done my time.'

Anthony pushed his chair back and stood up. 'Let's go make a date. If you think Maggie's bossy, I can assure you my secretary is even more so.'

Devlin could hardly believe that not only had she been listened to but she had also *finally* been heard.

Ten minutes later she was walking along Merrion Square, heading back to Stephen's Green, exclaiming to Maggie, 'He's doing it! I'm having the hysterectomy. I can't believe it, Maggie. He was lovely.'

'Told you,' replied Maggie smugly. 'He's brilliant and he won't let them throw you out of the hospital too soon, either. You'll get at least four days. A friend of mine had a hysterectomy in a private hospital. She went in at 6am on the Monday, was operated on at 12pm, was asked by the consultant if she was well enough to go home the next day but her nurse ... her *nurse* told him she should stay another day. She was fecked out early on the Wednesday morning and told to change her own dressings. I'll tell you Devlin, I'm glad I'm not nursing anymore. That guy would have got a kick in the goolies from me, although it's the hospital managers that are putting the pressure on to throw people out. It's all about the beds and the money now.'

'Two and a half days, for a hysterectomy! That's bloody shocking, Maggie.' Devlin was horrified.

'But sure people are being sent home the same day after all kinds of surgeries. Remember Dorothy Young was sent home the same day after getting her gall bladder removed, and got sepsis and nearly died. It's actually scary. But let's think positive. You're going to be fine and I'm going to stay with you for a few days after you get out of hospital.'

'Maggie, that's so kind of you.' Devlin felt a lump rise to her throat.

'I'm not being kind, I fancy a jaunt to Howth and a sleep in that very, very comfortable guest-room bed,' Maggie replied gaily. 'I'll be able to write all day while you sleep. Tell Luke I want him to cook one of his fabulous chowders.'

'You're on.' Devlin laughed. 'I better ring him, he's in London. I rang you first.'

'Natch.' Maggie smirked.

'He wanted to come with me but I didn't want him to. There was no point in him cancelling his meetings in London.'

'Little Miss Independence. But at least it's sorted now and you can get the op over and done with and reclaim your life. You won't know yourself. I'm delighted for you.'

'It wouldn't have happened without you. I love you dearly.'

'Love you too, mind yourself,' Maggie said warmly before hanging up.

Devlin walked briskly along the Green, feeling as though a huge weight had lifted from her shoulders. One problem almost sorted, problem number two was getting dealt with. She and Nenita were going to show CCK that his karma was coming for him, big time. Devlin was no longer stuck in the mire.

CHAPTER TWENTY-TWO

Devlin

Devlin sat in her car, tucked into a gateway, watching the entrance to the enormous three-storeyed redbrick house on Merrion Road. A Merc and a Series 5 BMW were parked on the large gravel drive. A neatly manicured high hedge blocked the rest of the mature garden from view. It was 8.30am. She'd been spying for the last fifteen minutes.

She'd remembered Colin's address from the old days and needed to make sure that he still lived there. If anyone saw me they'd think I was a looper, she thought ruefully as the rush-hour traffic whizzed past. If Luke saw her he'd be horrified. This was one little episode she'd be keeping to herself.

Colin had always been an early riser. His hospital rounds would start at seven-thirty before he began his surgeries or his clinics. He'd liked to play golf two afternoons a week and at the weekends. She'd place a bet that even after all these years his routine was still the same. He was in his seventies now but she'd Googled him and found a recent photo of him at an

RCSI event looking as straight-backed as ever, tanned and fit. His once-handsome face had turned jowly and his hair, white now, had receded but she would have known him immediately if she'd met him on the street.

To think he was the father of her daughter. A daughter he'd never seen or wanted to see. It all seemed like a dream now. Another life, when she'd become pregnant and kicked out of home by her furious, alcoholic, snobby mother. Worse still that her mother had been enabled by the father Devlin loved, who had never stood up to his wife. And then Devlin finding out that she was adopted. The child of her mother's sister. Colin paying for her to have an abortion in a private clinic in England and never wanting to see her again. One horror after another. But she had overcome them all, had her precious baby and turned her life around. And then Lynn had died in a car crash.

How did I survive it all? she wondered. How different her life would have been if her boss, a man she trusted, and was utterly besotted with, had not taken her virginity in a sleazy, opportunistic, unwanted coupling that made her pregnant.

He had carried on with his successful career, had an affluent lifestyle and, no doubt, never gave her a thought. Well, he would be giving her lots of consideration now, Devlin vowed grimly, hoping he wasn't holidaying in his Algarve villa. Maybe she was wasting her time, she fretted, as the clock on her dash showed her it was 9am. Perhaps he didn't live here anymore. Ten more minutes and she was gone, she decided. If the worst came to the worst she could hire a private detective, even though that seemed a bit OTT. She was just about to start the ignition when she saw Colin emerge from the basement entrance and cross the drive to the Merc. There was no mistaking him, despite not having seen him for decades. He got into the car, started the engine, drove through the high wrought-iron gates and nosed out into the traffic.

Devlin glanced at the neatly typed envelope, ready to be posted, on the car seat beside her as she switched on the ignition and drove in the opposite direction. CCK would be getting a registered letter from her that was going to turn his smug life upside down.

He hoped it wasn't a summons for speeding. Colin frowned, two days later, when the housekeeper who came three mornings a week handed him a registered letter in the sunroom where he was having breakfast.

'Thanks, Norah,' he said before taking a bite out of his avocado on toast and ripping the envelope open. He read the typewritten single page, on headed notepaper, and blanched.

'Christ almighty, what the fuck?' he swore, shocked.

He read it again to make sure he wasn't dreaming.

Colin,
  To advise you, I'm taking legal advice about having you charged with a historic sexual crime against me.
  Yours etc.
  Devlin Delaney

His toast and avocado turned sour in his mouth. Colin Cantrell-King thought he was going to puke.

'Devlin, there's a Colin Cantrell-King on the phone for you. Do you want to take it?' Madalina said after buzzing her.

'Put it through, Madalina, thanks.' Devlin's stomach knotted. Even though she'd been expecting his call, it was still a shock to realise she was going to be talking to him after all these years. She took a sip of water and composed herself. You're in control now, she told herself, picking up the receiver.

'Colin,' she said coldly. 'I presume you got my letter.'

CHAPTER TWENTY-THREE

Caroline

'Your window boxes are lovely,' Caroline remarked to the tall grey-haired woman who handed her a cup of green tea and offered biscuits from a pretty tin, which she refused politely. She was sitting in a side room, with a small cane sofa stuffed with cushions, off a galley kitchen, opposite what she assumed was her psychotherapist's consulting room.

'I love gardening. It's one of my retreats from the noise and bustle of city life. I took it up when my children were teenagers and I had to get away from the sulks and the attitude and the dramas,' the woman laughed. 'Do you garden, Caroline?'

'No, I had no children to get away from. I mow the lawn and get a young chap to put flowers in the planters, every season, and that's about it.' Caroline took a sip of her tea and wondered when the psychotherapist would bring her into the consultation room to start her session. But Aideen Hemsell seemed in no hurry as she gulped a mouthful of coffee and bit into a chocolate teacake.

'I was gasping for a coffee,' she confessed. 'An addiction I have yet to cure myself of. Well done you with your green tea.'

Caroline shrugged. 'I love coffee too but I allow myself one cup in the morning or I'd drink it all day.'

'I'd love to have that degree of self-control,' Aideen sighed. 'I'm addicted to Tunnock's teacakes as well. What are you addicted to, if anything?' She cocked an eye at Caroline.

Here it comes, thought Caroline, admiring how Aideen had tried to lull her into conversationally revealing a truth as she segued so casually into her first question.

'I suppose my running is important to me,' she replied equally casually, 'not sure if it's an addiction though.'

'My knees would give up the ghost if I ran, not that I'd have any inclination to. I'm far too lazy.' Aideen made a face. 'I like swimming. Easier.'

'Me too,' Caroline said politely, wishing the session could get properly underway so she could go back to her own clinic.

'My dream is to have a swimming pool at home, someday. Wouldn't that just be fabulous? I might as well dream here as in bed. Do you have an unrealised dream?'

'Em . . . I suppose we all have.' Caroline was not ready yet to admit that her dream of being a loved wife and mother was never going to happen.

'True.' Aideen drained her coffee and put her mug down. *At last*, thought Caroline with relief, putting her own cup on the small coffee table and expecting Aideen to invite her to follow her to her room. Instead the psychotherapist lifted up the sash window and began deadheading the geraniums in the window boxes. Caroline's shoulders tensed with exasperation.

'Why did you become a counsellor, Caroline? Do you like it?' Aideen asked casually, glancing at her over her shoulder.

'I suppose, after all I'd been through with my husband and having got so much help myself, I found it interesting and I wanted to help other people who found themselves in stressful or traumatic situations. It's very satisfying work, for me anyway.'

'Hmm. I went into it because I got some sort of satisfaction knowing other people had problems like I had, too, and by helping them deal with theirs I didn't have to face my own. I could run far, far away from them. Needless to say they eventually caught up with me and I had to face them. When I did was when I really became a good counsellor, especially to others who did the same sort of work. It was hard facing up to that but such a relief when I did.'

She turned and looked Caroline straight in the eye. 'We can get straight to the nub of things, if you're willing, or you can pussyfoot around me, trying to avoid giving me honest answers and trying to control the session. But you know that I know all the tricks people use not to confront their true selves. You can waste my time and yours, and pay a hefty fee for it, or you can gift yourself with a chance to stop running physically and metaphorically and move forward. Your decision, Caroline.'

Caroline swallowed hard, staring at her peer whose blue eyes stared back into hers: not without compassion but with a steely glint that unnerved her. It wouldn't be easy. She knew that she would be shaken to her core and she was afraid. But Caroline knew too that she instinctively trusted this woman and would be in safe hands.

'My dream was to be a mother, have a husband who loved

me and have a family life that would nourish and sustain me. I'll never have a child of my own now: it's too late. I can't see me ever being in a relationship again, at my age, and I'm alone. That's why I fill my life with work and with running and trying hard not to drink or to slip back into bulimia and it's all such a struggle and I'm weary of it,' she blurted. 'And I feel guilty because I know I'm very privileged, and there are people in such dire straits – and I see clients with much worse problems than I have, and so do you, I'm sure – so I feel I'm being self-indulgent, by being here, but I need some help.'

The words gushed out of her but the very unleashing of them was such a relief that Caroline burst into tears.

Aideen gave her a light pat on the back. 'Well done, Caroline,' she said kindly, handing her a box of tissues. 'Where would we be without our tissues? We must add considerably to Kleenex's profits.' Caroline wiped her eyes and managed a watery smile. 'Now let's get to work after that courageous and very good start and, who knows, I might even manage to persuade you to break your rule of one cup of coffee per day. It can be our little reward during our sessions.' Aideen closed the sash window and walked towards her room.

Taking a deep breath, and grabbing a handful of tissues, Caroline followed the psychotherapist, myriad emotions engulfing her, the strongest of which was gratitude.

CHAPTER TWENTY-FOUR

Shona/Chloé/Maggie

'So, just to clarify, you're saying she doesn't want us to film her at home, now, and she's filming in Galway and we can do the interview there?' Shona tried to keep the irritation out of her tone. She was speaking to an agent whose actress client was being a diva about appearing in a segment of a documentary honouring a well-known Irish playwright.

'Yes, I'll email you the details of where the interview can take place,' the agent replied brightly.

'Grand, thanks,' said Shona and she hung up. They'd been due to film the diva the following day, in Dublin, now they were going to have to travel to bloody Galway and schedules were going to be messed up. She spent ten minutes texting the crew to let them know there'd be a change in plans and she'd get back to them. She'd have to let the presenter of the show – Orla Breen, a fellow playwright – know as well. They had most of the programme filmed and she knew Orla was due to appear at a literary festival in Edinburgh at the end of the week. Scrolling through her contacts she found the number and rang it.

'Hiya, Shona,' Orla answered cheerily. 'What's happening?'

'The diva has cancelled filming in Dublin. She wants us to go to Galway where she's on set filming—'

'*Galway!* She can feck off, Shona, this is the second time she's mugged us off. What happens if we arrive in Galway and she puts us off again? I've a feeling she doesn't want to do it.' Orla's exasperation mirrored Shona's.

'I know. It mucks everything up.'

'Do we have to use her? Is there someone else we could ask? I'll find it hard to be civil to the old bat when I'm interviewing her, the way she's behaving.'

Shona laughed. She'd enjoyed working with Orla, who was easy-going and fun. 'I suppose we could. It's just time is of the essence now. We need to wrap it up ASAP. It's due to air next month, so who do we look for? Another actor, actress, a fellow playwright?'

'Do you know who's great? Peter Sheridan. He's a director, screenwriter, playwright. He directed Imelda May in *Mother of All the Behans*. He's a lovely man and he'd be a great interviewee.'

'Oh yes! *Brilliant* suggestion, Orla. Let me talk to the team and I'll get back to you,' Shona agreed, just as the office landline rang. 'Better go, Orla, thanks.' She hung up and picked up the landline. 'Hello Galaxy TV, Shona Ryan.'

'I think you're very mean to our dad. He's very upset and you're not treating him very nicely,' a young woman's voice floated crossly down the line. Shona's jaw dropped.

'Is that you, Chloé?'

'Yes, it's me.'

'It's none of your business really, if you don't mind my saying so,' Shona said coolly.

'It is if my dad's upset. He's a good dad and he's very kind and you're not one bit nice to him and I just wanted to say that to you, so goodbye. We don't want to go to your crappy wedding,' her half-sister raged, before hanging up.

'That's telling me, then,' Shona muttered. How dare that little brat ring me up and speak to me like that. And ringing on the landline, too. She should tell reception to block that caller ID. Chloé didn't have her mobile number.

'The absolute cheek of her, Aleksy,' Shona fumed later that evening when she and her fiancé were preparing dinner.

'Mmm. I suppose she's standing up for her dad. Her experience of him is different than yours.' Aleksy paused from slicing peppers for their stir-fry to look at her.

'Yeah, she didn't ever have to walk into their sitting room when he was riding another woman: that little entitled bitch's mother.' Shona gave the chicken breast she was dicing a vicious chop.

'You know your mom's right, *kochanie*. You need to move on and let the past go. It poisons everything, even our wedding.'

'Don't "honey" me, Aleksy,' she snapped. 'I do *not* appreciate being phoned at my workplace by a spoilt little madam.'

'Perhaps if you got to know your half-sister – who is much younger than you – you might find her neither spoilt nor entitled but someone who has the courage to stand up for her father,' Aleksy pointed out, calmly.

'I don't want to talk about it,' Shona retorted.

'Fine. What will we talk about as you massacre our chicken?' Aleksy joshed, peeling an onion.

'Ha ha, very funny.' But she couldn't help but laugh. Her fiancé could always stop her in her tracks with his astute observations and he could always make her laugh. She was being childish to a degree, she admitted. It wasn't Chloé's fault that Terry was her father and, before that life-changing occurrence when she was a child, Shona had loved her dad with every fibre of her being. *And* she had to agree with her half-sister: Terry had always been a most generous father. Mimi and Michael had a good relationship with him; they had let bygones be bygones, a long time ago. Chloé's timing was crap: Shona was up to her eyes, she didn't need to have to deal with this stuff right now. And being told off by her half-sister stung, she thought crossly, heating up the wok to stir-fry the dinner.

'She's not a bad kid. She's a teenager. It's all *me, me, me* but she can be quite funny and she *adores* Dad,' Mimi remarked as she and Shona sat in Chorus café, a small bistro on Fishamble Street, near Mimi's office. They sometimes treated themselves to breakfast there before going to work, if Shona was working in town.

Shona dipped a piece of muffin into her eggs Benedict. 'I find her sulky and snarky whenever I've had dealings with her.'

Mimi picked up a crispy rasher of bacon drenched in maple syrup and crunched on it. 'Maybe it's because she senses your hostility when you're together,' she said mildly. 'There's no one like you for radiating hostility when you want to.' Mimi grinned at her older sister.

'I'm not *that* bad,' Shona said defensively. 'And is it so awful not to want them at my wedding? I want it to be a happy day.'

'It could be a happy day with them there if you made the effort.' Mimi eyeballed her. 'And to be honest, I *like* that Chloé had the guts to ring you and call you out on your behaviour and stand up for Dad. It shows that she's a decent kid at heart.'

'Oh for God's sake!' Shona hadn't expected this from her sister.

'All I'm saying is what everyone else is saying, even Aleksy. But you stay in the past if you want to and keep hugging your wounds to yourself if that's what you need to do.' Mimi shrugged and devoured a piece of her syrup-soaked pancake with relish.

'It's all right for you, you—'

'"You didn't see what I saw." That tired old refrain, Shona. Like I said: hold on to the past tightly. But guess what? If you could let it go, and lighten up and meet up with Chloé like I do every so often, you might even surprise yourself and like her. It's called being a grown up.' Mimi wiped the last of the maple syrup with her pancake and shoved it in her mouth. She stood up and said, 'I better go: I'm opening up today. You pay and I'll Revolut you what I owe. Love ya, sis, see ya.' And then she was sprinting out of the courtyard, with a wave.

Shona glowered after her, annoyed at being more or less accused of being childish by her own sister. Mimi was far more pragmatic the she was, she reflected sourly, draining her coffee mug. And she didn't hold grudges, Shona acknowledged dispiritedly, rummaging in her bag for her wallet.

Walking along the quays, with a Liffey breeze caressing her face and the morning sun dappling the river, Shona pondered her sister's words and had to admit the truth of them. Her behaviour *was* childish. She had projected her disgust at her father onto Chloé, who had nothing to do with his past behaviour. That wasn't very mature or kind. And there was something else, something she wouldn't admit to anyone, not even to Caroline who had once, a long time ago, broached the subject when Shona had been venting about Terry and his new family. 'Are you jealous of Chloé?' she'd asked. 'It would be a perfectly natural emotion if you were.'

'No, I'm not!' she'd protested heatedly. 'I just don't want to have anything to do with *any* of them. Him especially.'

'That's OK too,' Caroline had said gently and hugged her tightly.

But Caroline had been right, even though Shona wouldn't admit it. Chloé had the type of relationship Shona had once had with her father. Shona had always been Terry's pet. He'd known her nose was out of joint when the twins had been born and the fuss that had been made of them. He'd more than compensated for her utter sense of discombobulation when her new brother and sister had arrived and taken all the limelight off her. Terry had always been her champion when she was naughty and Maggie would chastise her. Terry would come to her rescue and she'd loved the feeling that she was special to him. And then her father had broken up their family, shattered her childhood innocence and replaced her with Chloé.

Tears slid down Shona's cheeks. Jealousy, rage, hurt and grief had been her companions since that unforgettable day all those years ago. They'd accompanied her into adulthood and she had to deal with them now. She couldn't run away from them any longer.

Struggling to regain her composure, before she linked up with her film crew on the Halfpenny Bridge where they were shooting a promo for a city centre hotel, Shona wanted to run as far away as she could from family friction.

'My mom suggested I have a session with you, she enjoys hers so much,' Shona said to the reiki practitioner sitting across from her.

'I love to hear that. They were a lovely group, it was great to see them relaxing and having fun. There was a lot of laughter that day over in the relaxation room. Now, why don't you lie up on the plinth and relax and let me do all the work,' Caitríona said kindly.

Even though they were around the same age, Shona judged, the young woman helping her onto the plinth had a calm, reassuring air that made her feel less tense. She didn't know what to expect but as she lay on the comfortable treatment bed with a soft cushion under her head, candles lit in the background and soothing music softly playing, Shona felt the stress begin to ease out of her.

'I'm just going to place a crystal on your heart chakra, Shona, and call in my guides,' the therapist murmured and as Caitríona placed her hands gently on her head, Shona felt as though a knot had begun to unravel in her breastbone, where the crystal lay, and she began to sob. Years of pent-up emotions released from her and that young girl inside that had been so hurt and traumatised was finally set free.

'God, it was powerful, Mom. The heat from her hands was unbelievable. I really feel different. Something's changed. When she put that crystal on me I felt that knot in me opening. Thanks for treating me to it and driving me down.' Shona leaned across the sofa they were sharing and hugged her mother.

'Caroline cried in hers as well and she's booked another session.' Maggie bit into her four cheeses pizza. They were sitting outside in the courtyard of Latin Quarter, in Redcross, after Shona's reiki session on a sunny Saturday afternoon. Shona was staying overnight so they were in no rush to leave.

'This place is lovely.' Shona looked around the welcoming space. 'It's so relaxing and they do Nutella crêpes, too. I'd be here every weekend if I lived close by.'

'I bring Mam here regularly; she loves the trad music on Sunday afternoons. It's the coffee that does it for me. Sandra, the owner, is Brazilian and she serves Brazilian coffee to die for.'

'It would be a lovely venue for a wedding with a difference,' Shona remarked, looking around at all the different seating areas.

'Shona, it would be *perfect!* They do all kinds of parties here.' Maggie grabbed her daughter's hand excitedly. 'What do you think?'

'Oooh Mom! I'm getting a shiver,' Shona gasped. 'We could have the handfasting ceremony under the trees there! I'll tell Aleksy to come down tomorrow. I think he'll love it.'

'Well, who would have thought having a reiki session would solve where to hold your wedding? The Universe sure works in strange ways,' laughed Maggie, extremely relieved that she didn't have to put a marquee up in the back garden. Now to get Terry onside; he and Shona being at least civil to each other was the next hurdle. And she really had to have the 'talk' with Nelsie. Devlin had got her hysterectomy sorted. Caroline was having counselling. They were being very proactive since their 'Girls' Weekend'. She needed to get her skates on. Definitely this week, Maggie promised herself. Before Michael came home on his shore leave. She wanted to spend carefree time with her beloved son.

CHAPTER TWENTY-FIVE

Maggie/Nelsie

Nelsie closed the front door behind them and locked it. 'Did you get me one of those prepaid envelope things from the Post Office to send a parcel?'

'I did,' Maggie said.

'Did you book me in with Alana?'

'I did.'

'She's a lovely girl. Very patient. I never mind going to her.' Nelsie settled herself into the front seat of Maggie's Peugeot and clicked in her seatbelt. They were going into the Clearwater Shopping Centre for Nelsie's annual eye check-up. 'I don't think I'll need new glasses. I'm hoping I won't, anyway. Now, have you got the shopping list?'

'I have.' Maggie looked right and left before emerging onto the narrow winding country road that took them down to the slipway to the M11, thinking all the while that she should make an appointment for herself. She could do with new glasses, especially for her computer work. She'd had to increase her font size.

'I had a FaceTime with Niamh last night. What's rare is wonderful.' Nelsie compressed her lips in a thin line.

'How is she?' Maggie didn't let on that she'd been speaking to her younger sister earlier in the week.

'You know her, busy with this that and the other. Too busy to bring her children over to visit their grandmother,' Nelsie sniped.

'Mam, it's expensive to fly them all over from New York: she's not made of money.'

'They went to Disneyland in Florida for a week, so they had to fly down there. I'm sure *that* cost a pretty penny.' Nelsie was unimpressed. 'Why she can't come home and rear her children here I can't fathom. Did you see in Florida they're banning children's books in school libraries? Have you ever heard the like from a so-called democracy in the twenty-first century? They might have a fine big house in America but it will all end in tears. That country's not what it used to be.'

Maggie said nothing. Niamh and their mother had never got on and she'd always been piggy-in-the-middle trying to keep the peace. It was wearing.

'You were mad to come home from America all those years ago because Mam had a hysterectomy and expected you to nurse her,' Niamh had said to Maggie on one of their FaceTimes.

'I know. It was six months before Mam stopped her invalid act.'

'We were just little slaves to her, even before she had it. "Do this; clean that", while she spent her time doing ICA stuff. Baking for this sale or that Bring and Buy. Chairing meetings, being treasurer. Running the parish council. She was *never* at home. We had to keep the house spotless and woe betide if we didn't polish the silver properly,' her sister grumbled. 'And Tony and Rick got away with doing nothing. Tony was always her pet. I thought I'd never get away after you left the first time.'

Niamh had been the last to leave home; Maggie had left Ireland to continue her nursing career in America a couple of years before Niamh took flight. Unlike Maggie, Niamh had found herself an American husband and had never returned to Ireland except for the occasional holiday.

Rick their youngest brother had gone to Australia, much to their father's disappointment. Neither of his sons were interested in the farm so in his later years he'd rented his land to a neighbour.

'It was just as well Mam had the ICA when Dad died: it kept her going,' Maggie pointed out. Nelsie had still been active in the Irish Countrywoman's Association until her eightieth birthday.

'Poor ould Dad, he was such a softy. She got her own way in everything. He never got a look in,' Niamh said sadly. 'I really miss him.'

'You were his pet. He expected a lot from me. I was the eldest who had to get on with things. The eldest is the responsible one. *Moi!* The sons are the princes of the family and can do no wrong. And you, the youngest, are ungrateful for all that was done for you and you're not repaying it back by coming home to live in Ireland. We all have our assigned roles. Mam's not going to change at this stage of her life. I'm going to have to have the "chat" with her about her wishes, her will and if she wants a DNR directive. It has to be done in case anything untoward happens. She's fine now but who knows what's around the corner?'

'If you want to do a Zoom with the others, I'll do it with you so it's not left to you. Because why should it? She needs to have her plans made if she wants nursing home care, or care at home if it ever gets to that stage. And it would be good to know if she wants to be resuscitated or not should it ever arise and good for there to be a witness when she decides what she wants. Things can get heated at a hospital bedside. I saw it with my in-laws,' Niamh advised.

'Thanks, Niamh. I appreciate that advice. Tony can't accuse us of anything when he hears it coming from Mam herself. We just can't trust him after the Covid carry-on.'

'I couldn't believe it when you told me what he was up to, taking money from Mam. *Disgusting.*' Niamh frowned.

'I know. I'll broach it with Mam and then all of us can have a Zoom with her: Princes Tony and Rick included.'

'Right, let me know how it goes and good luck with it. Do try and come over for a couple of weeks, I'd love to see you,' Niamh urged.

'I'll see how it's going. I have a lot going on filming-wise in the next few months. Maybe I might come over late autumn. I could write in peace and quiet over there and Mam could go and stay with Tony.'

Niamh laughed. 'Good luck with arranging that. I'm sure our darling sister-in-law will be delighted to have her.'

'Hmm.' Maggie shrugged. 'They owe Mam big time; they can step up to the plate as far as I'm concerned. I'm not looking after her solo anymore,' she said firmly. 'I've done it for long enough. I've my own life to lead too, while I still can.'

'No arguments from me. You do what you must. I know I'm no help to you but as far as I'm concerned let her spend her money on herself, and whatever money Dad left, and raise equity for her care from the house if she needs it. I won't be standing beside her coffin with my hands out looking for my share, Maggie. You make her spend what she needs to so you're not stuck being her carer.'

'Easier said than done, but we'll see how it goes.' Maggie was grateful for her sister's attitude. She was straight about the fact that she wouldn't be involved in their mother's old age care, and Maggie had to suck that up, but at least she wasn't like Tony, looking to see what he could get from Nelsie on what seemed like a regular basis. The chat needed to be had. She couldn't put it off any longer, Maggie acknowledged.

After the optician's appointment and the shopping was done, she'd bring Nelsie to lunch in Jack White's on the way home and get down to the nitty gritty of what needed to be done to safeguard their mother's last years.

An hour later, Maggie had the shopping packed away in the boot of the car and was sitting outside the consultation rooms waiting for Nelsie to emerge from her eye check-up. She scrolled through her emails and had responded to a few when Nelsie emerged, smiling, followed by the optician.

'My eyes are grand, Maggie. I don't need new glasses,' she said proudly.

'Great eyesight, nearly as good as my own,' Alana, the optician, approved. 'No macular degeneration, no cataracts. All well in the eye department.'

'Thanks a million, Alana.' Maggie was relieved to hear the news. Some of her friends had parents with failing eyesight, necessitating regular visits to opticians and to hospitals for eye injections. Thankfully she wouldn't have to give away her precious writing time for eye-care visits. 'I'll make an appointment myself while I'm here,' Maggie said.

'The girls will sort that for you. I'll see you when I see you,' the optician said, smiling at her next client before leading him into her room.

'Wasn't that great news?' Nelsie said chirpily. 'Bring me to that new café that's opened, here in the centre. I was reading about it in the *Wicklow People*. We'll give it a try and see what the coffee's like.'

'I was thinking we might have a bite of lunch in Jack White's on the way home, then neither of us would have to worry about what to have for dinner,' Maggie suggested.

'Well now, that would be an idea all right. You always get a tasty bit of food in Jack's.' Nelsie was delighted with the offer. 'I just want to have a poke around in TK Maxx. You get great bargains there sometimes.'

Maggie's heart sank. She was up to her eyes in work. She had a script to work on for her next filming and she wanted to progress a novella she'd been asked to write for the Open Door Literacy initiative. The way Nelsie was going, they'd be here all morning and it could easily be three by the time they got home because she was not one to rush when having a meal out. Nelsie had no conception of what Maggie's writing entailed.

'I've a business Zoom at two-thirty,' Maggie lied. 'So we need to be gone from here by 12pm because otherwise we'll hit the busy time in Jack's and we'll be waiting to be served.'

'Tsk, *always* in a hurry.' Nelsie threw her eyes up to heaven as she preceded her daughter into TK Maxx.

I'm a working woman, Maggie wanted to shout. *You wouldn't expect Tony to trot around TK Maxx after you in the middle of the day.* But she swallowed a retort down and followed her mother into the shop.

They were having their post-lunch coffee in a small snug in Jack White's, where they were on their own, when Maggie finally got to begin the long put-off discussion she'd been so reluctant to broach.

'Mam,' she began, trying not to fidget in her chair. 'I've been meaning to have a chat with you about a few things.'

'Oh, what kind of things?' Nelsie looked at her sharply.

'Well, we need to discuss matters that will be of importance in the years ahead,' Maggie said delicately. 'We never know what's in store for us so I just want to make sure what your wishes are.' She paused and took a sip of coffee. 'Em ... we need to know, for example, if you have a serious illness, do you want to be resuscitated if you have heart failure? Is your will up to date? Do you want to make an appointment to see Garrett Fitzpatrick? You should designate one of us to have power of attorney should you become mentally incapacitated and not be able to conduct your own affairs—'

Nelsie put her hand up. 'There's no need to worry about any of that stuff, it's all sorted,' she announced.

'Oh!' Maggie was taken aback. 'Did you go to see Garrett about it all? Does the person doing power of attorney not need to be with you?'

'I didn't go to Garrett. I went to a different solicitor, during Covid.'

'What? Who?' Maggie frowned. Something didn't feel quite right, her gut was telling her.

'I can't remember his name now,' Nelsie said testily. 'Tony organised it for me. He's my power of attorney. You don't have to worry about a thing.'

CHAPTER TWENTY-SIX

Maggie

Maggie stared at her mother trying to disguise her shock, dismay and hurt. Since she'd come back to Wicklow to live close to her she'd ended up being the family member who did everything for Nelsie. Never once had her mother said anything about Tony bringing her to a new solicitor and becoming her power of attorney. It was almost sly, she thought, disgusted.

She noted her mother's defensive expression and knew Nelsie was waiting for an outburst.

Not today, Maggie decided grimly.

'That's great,' she said calmly, thinking she should win an Oscar. 'Kudos to Tony for organising it.'

'Oh, em ... yes he was very helpful.' Nelsie eyed her suspiciously.

'It's good that you have everything in place,' Maggie continued chattily, 'should anything untoward happen and you have to go into a nursing home or need someone to conduct your business.'

'I'm hoping I can stay away from those places.' Nelsie shuddered. 'Anyway, haven't I got you to nurse me if anything goes wrong?'

Maggie's jaw dropped. 'Sorry?'

'You were a nurse, you can look after me if needs be. You're only across the garden, Maggie.' Nelsie sipped her coffee nonchalantly.

'Let's be clear here, Mam, I'm going to be travelling to Europe a lot with my work in the future. I have my commitments to my children and want to be there for grandchildren if I'm blessed with them, so it would be wise for you to make sure you have money for home care should you need it.'

Nelsie blinked. 'You mean you *won't* nurse me?'

'I'm just saying you need to make provisions for home care if you don't ever want to go to a nursing home, Mam. And I couldn't help but notice when I took something out of your cardigan pocket there was a bank statement. I wasn't being nosey but I saw a transfer of three thousand euro to Tony and you did mention he was short of cash—'

'That's between me and your brother, Maggie. It's none of your business,' Nelsie retorted sharply.

'I know that. It's your money. You can do what you like with it. I'm just advising you to make sure you have enough to look after yourself if you need it in the future.'

'Don't worry, I won't be troubling you, miss,' Nelsie snapped. 'Now we better get home so you can have your meeting. I'll pay for lunch.'

'I invited you, I'll pay.' Maggie took her credit card out of her wallet and slid off the banquette she was sitting on before Nelsie even had her handbag open.

They drove home in silence, Nelsie bristling with umbrage that radiated from her with an intensity that Maggie was well aware of.

'Drop me off at the gate. You don't need to come into the drive,' Nelsie ordered as they drove up to the house.

'Fine,' Maggie agreed coolly.

The slam of the car door left her in no doubt of her mother's annoyance. 'Be annoyed, Mother,' Maggie said crossly, driving towards her own cottage. 'Because it's *nothing* to how annoyed *I* am.'

'Imagine,' she ranted to her sister later on FaceTime. 'She gives Tony power of attorney but is reserving the honour of *me* being her personal nurse if she needs one, because she's not going into a nursing home. Say she has a stroke or gets dementia? And that cute little bollix didn't bring her to the solicitor who made Dad's will, he brought her to a different one. I don't know what sort of a will she's made. She's probably left everything to him.'

'Can she change Dad's will? He left the house to the four of us to be divided equally after he and Mam are both gone,' Niamh reminded her.

'I'll have to ask Garrett about it. All I know is that she's put herself in Tony's care and I hope she doesn't live to regret it. And I can tell you one thing, I'm going to go travelling and live my life and the pair of them can work out her care between them,' Maggie spat. 'If Tony's in charge he can damn well get his ass down here and do everything I've been doing for the last couple of years. I've had it, Niamh.'

'Let's hope nothing awful happens, Maggie. I know it's easy for me to say over here. But you know you're welcome to visit any time.'

'I know that. Talk soon, sis. See ya.' Maggie closed down the session. It *was* easy for Niamh to talk, thousands of miles away across the Atlantic. If anything went wrong with their mother, she'd be no help whatsoever. Neither would Rick, who wasn't great at keeping in touch, Maggie thought resentfully, staring out across the field that separated her from Nelsie. Not today, when she was angry, but soon she'd be having a chat with her brother Tony and letting him know in no uncertain terms that he and Ginny were going to be taking a lot more responsibility than heretofore, because she was damn well stepping back.

'So what did she say when you told her?' Tony's voice rose an octave. Nelsie could hear his dismay at the other end of the line.

'To be honest, I thought she might get a bit annoyed but she didn't seem to put much pass on it,' Nelsie said. 'But then she told me she wouldn't be looking after me if anything went wrong, which I wasn't expecting. She was quite resolute about it. And that hurt, Tony. She's a nurse. You'd think she'd be the one to nurse her own mother.'

'Maggie's always sure to suit herself,' Tony said.

'Indeed. And she found my bank statement and saw that I'd transferred that three thousand euro you asked me for. She gave me a lecture about keeping enough money to look after myself if I needed home care,' Nelsie said indignantly.

'Nothing will happen to you,' Tony assured her.

'How do you know? Who knows what's waiting for us down the road? Don't come looking for any more money, Tony. I need to have some savings at my back,' Nelsie said crossly.

'OK,' he muttered. 'I have to go. I'm at work. Bye.'

Nelsie heard the click and wondered had she made a big

mistake giving Tony power of attorney. He'd been very persuasive when he'd been living with her. Frightening her with talk of what Covid might do to her. Telling her that Maggie wouldn't be able to come down to Wicklow because of lockdown and she needed to have her affairs in order.

And now Maggie had the hump. *I'm more to be pitied than laughed at*, Nelsie thought sorrowfully, gazing at the wedding photo of herself and her husband when they were young and fit and healthy and happy, with no thought of the trials and tribulations to come.

Perhaps he was the lucky one to have gone before her, Nelsie reflected, studying the smiling face of her deceased husband. He'd never had to worry about power of attorney and suchlike. Suddenly weary, Nelsie scooted Sooty off her armchair and sat down. Her elderly cat, Miss Joy, rubbed herself against her owner's leg. Sighing, Nelsie picked her up and tucked her into her lap murmuring, 'Let us two elderly ladies take a well-deserved nap and forget about all our woes. At least you won't have to worry about who'll look after you in your dotage because I will, never you fear.'

Miss Joy stared at her with wise old eyes and, purring loudly, nestled into her and soon they were both fast asleep.

Every time the phone rang Tony expected it to be Maggie launching a broadside. He was lucky, he supposed, that he'd got away with the little handouts his mother gave him without Maggie knowing. Niamh didn't give a hoot. She was in her ivory castle in Boston with no intention of ever coming home. Rick was practically a stranger. Why should either of them even get a penny of their mother's estate, he'd asked Nelsie, who'd agreed with him. And Maggie was loaded. She didn't need more money, he'd speculated, although his mother had swiftly assured him that wasn't the case.

'Sure she sells thousands of books,' he'd argued. 'Twenty euro a pop when someone buys one of 'em.'

'That's what everyone thinks. I'd thought so myself,' Nelsie explained. 'But she only gets a percentage, because the publishing people have to get paid. And she told me something about discounts and the like that the shops look for. In some shops they charge for shelf space. Could you credit that? And she has to pay her agent, so it's not as much as you think,' Nelsie put him straight.

Maggie had clearly been doing the 'poor me' to their mother. She had plenty of money, Tony was sure. Hadn't she bought that cottage next door to their mam, as well as having the apartment Shona was living in, in Dublin? Who could afford to do that in this day and age? Only someone with plenty of money. And the way she'd driven down to Wicklow and practically ordered him from their mother's home, after he and Ginny had been so good as to stay with her during lockdown. His bossy older sister had thought she was in charge of everything. Today she'd learned she was in charge of nothing and no matter what she said to him, whenever she phoned, there was nothing she could do to change that.

Nevertheless he'd be glad to have that phone call done and dusted. The sooner he had to deal with his sister's undoubted wrath the better.

All that week, Tony waited in nervous anticipation for a phone call that never came.

CHAPTER TWENTY-SEVEN

Devlin

Devlin checked her reflection in the mirror and was satisfied with what she saw. A classy, elegant businesswoman of indeterminate age, dressed in a lightweight single-breasted Dior jacket of purple wool and silk, worn with a black pencil skirt, sheer black stockings and high-heeled black pumps. Nothing ostentatious: just a simple classic outfit accessorised with a Yves Saint Laurent black pouch. A gold locket nestled in the vee of her jacket, her only jewellery.

If only she hadn't had to wear the damn Spanx but she was so bloated she looked pregnant without them. The sooner I have the hysterectomy the better, she thought dolefully, wondering if her nausea was because of meeting Colin or her endo. Probably both.

'OK, Delaney, get your act together. This has been a long time coming. The day of reckoning is finally here,' she said aloud to her image in the mirror before walking out of her small private bathroom into the outer office. 'I should be back in an hour or so, Madalina. I'll have my phone on silent in the Shelbourne.'

'No worries, Dev. See you later,' her PA replied.

Devlin walked rapidly towards the iconic city-centre hotel where she'd arranged her meeting with Colin Cantrell-King. She was making sure to be there at least fifteen minutes before their scheduled time. She wanted to claim ownership and be seated at the table. She wanted to be in control.

Devlin hurried up the steps and through the swing doors, hardly noticing the gleaming tiled foyer filled with massive vases of fresh flowers. She was disgusted with herself that she had butterflies in her stomach and her heart felt as though it was doing flip-flops. She'd booked a table by the window. Devlin wanted to see Colin coming into the hotel. It would give her a few moments to prepare herself. Perhaps he would stand her up. Part of her hoped he might.

Ten minutes later, seated and with a pot of tea in front of her, Devlin thought back to their phone conversation. Her stomach had lurched when he'd growled, in a voice she remembered well, 'What the hell are you up to, Devlin? Are you trying to blackmail me? It won't work—'

'Don't be ridiculous,' she'd said coldly, managing to control her emotions. 'And I've no intentions of discussing it over the phone. I have two windows where I'm free to meet this week. 10.30am on Tuesday or 10.30am Thursday. In the Shelbourne. The Lord Mayor's Lounge. Take your pick.'

'Eh ... eh ...' he stuttered, clearly taken aback by her sharp proposal.

'Tuesday or Thursday, Colin, make up your mind, I have a meeting to attend,' she'd said briskly.

'Very well, tomorrow then,' he snapped. 'And just so you know—'

'Fine. I'll pencil it in,' she cut him off. '10.30am it is. If you don't turn up I will go straight to my solicitor to tell him to take my case further. Bye.' She hung up, glad that her erstwhile boss couldn't see the tremor in her hand or hear the thudding of her heart.

Devlin was glad Luke was in London, unaware of her meeting with Colin. She'd tossed and turned in their king-sized bed the night before, half-sorry she'd decided to support Nenita and come up with this plan.

The arrogance of CCK on the phone, though. The way he spoke to her. 'Bastard,' she swore. The nerve of him thinking she wanted money from him. That he was angry was not in question, or that he was mystified that she'd got in contact after all these years, but was he worried? Did he think she'd follow through with her threat to take a case against him?

She'd decided, after some thought, to meet in a public place. She remembered Colin's temper. If they were in public he'd have to restrain himself from letting loose at her. The Shelbourne was near work and a place he definitely wouldn't cause a scene.

Devlin glanced at her watch: it was almost 10.05am. She'd wait ten minutes after his allotted time, she decided, sipping her tea out of a fine china cup and thinking how surreal it was to be sitting at a window in the Shelbourne, looking out onto Stephen's Green watching people hurrying past, tourists taking photos, and limos and taxis drawing up to the entrance to discharge their passengers. At a discreet table in the far corner she recognised a journalist and a well-known media personality doing an interview. At the window table ahead of her, two American tourists were oohing and aahing over the coffee and scones they'd just been served. She'd had many business meetings here, especially in the early days of City Girl. She'd given interviews at the very table she was sitting at, but never in all that time did she think she would end up meeting the father of her dead child, who, she'd discovered, was an even more vile and despicable human than she'd imagined.

A taxi drew up outside and, dry mouthed, tense with dread, she saw Colin emerge from the rear door, look around him and walk up the steps of the hotel. He was still a commanding presence with his white hair, tanned jowly face and tall, lean physique. He wore a light navy jacket and cream trousers and looked as though he had just come from watching a polo or cricket match.

Devlin took a deep breath, the Spanx cutting into her waist, as he disappeared from view, only to appear at the entrance of the lounge. He scanned the room. Their eyes met and he made his way towards her.

Silently she indicated the chair in front of her, relieved she didn't have to stand up. She was so nervous she was afraid her legs would buckle under her. She had asked the waitress to place a third chair at the table and had put her bag on the chair beside her, not wanting Colin to sit there.

'A table for three? Are we expecting someone else? Your husband no doubt, or your solicitor?' he sneered.

'Sit down, Colin,' she said coolly, ignoring his question.

'Quite the well-known business lady, aren't you? You look great.' He pulled out the chair and sat down.

'For your information, Colin, I don't need my husband to fight my battles. I'm very able to fight my own.' She was proud of the icy distain in her voice.

'What's this all about? You know you haven't a leg to stand on if you take me to court. It's your word against mine. And I'll say you were an infatuated young woman who threw herself at me. You were, you know. Everything was consensual.' He stretched languidly and sat back in his chair, never taking his hooded eyes off her, as though he was having a patient-doctor consultation.

'Is that right, Colin?' Devlin could feel her anger rising and was glad of it. 'Perhaps if I was doing this on my own I might think twice.' She looked across the room to where another woman was sitting drinking tea and nodded. Nenita picked up a carrier bag and stood up. 'But the fact that there are *two* of us taking a case against you might change a jury's opinion.' Devlin took her bag off the chair so Nenita could sit down.

Colin glanced at her, sat up straight and paled. 'What the *fuck* are you doing here?' he hissed in a low voice, shocked.

'Taking you to court for sexual assault,' Nenita said quietly but very firmly.

'You pair of bitches. This is a set up. You have no proof of anything,' Colin raged. 'I'm out of here.' He made to stand up.

'Sit down,' Devlin said icily. 'We *have* proof, if that's what you're looking for.'

Nenita lifted up the carrier and took out a plastic bag, with a set of nurse's whites in it. 'Your semen is on this, Dr Cantrell-King. I think you'll find that a perfect DNA match will convict you.' She calmly replaced the uniform in its wrappings.

Devlin caressed the locket around her neck. 'There's a curl of our daughter's hair in this,' she said flatly, 'that will determine her paternity.'

'I'm admitting nothing. You'll have to prove it. What do you want? Money?' Colin was puce with fury.

'We want justice,' replied Devlin contemptuously.

'We're doing this for our daughters and our sons. Let them see that men like you cannot treat women the way you treated *us*!' Nenita's eyes sparked with anger and disgust and her voice rose slightly.

'Keep your bloody voice down, you,' Colin swore.

'It's like this, Colin; you can go to court and deny everything and have the whole circus that a court case will entail. Paps and journalists at your door. Film cameras at the steps of the court. You can have every tawdry detail laid bare. Or you can plead guilty and spare yourself the embarrassment. We don't care. We'd actually like our day in court. We're not young women to be cowed by the likes of you anymore.' Devlin stared hard at him and his mouth tightened into a thin line.

'I will fight you tooth and nail. I will get letters testifying to my good character from judges, business men, medical colleagues and politicians—'

'Fine. Get your golf buddies to write their letters.' Devlin shrugged. 'DNA is DNA. And you'd better hope that there are no more victims out there because once this gets into the papers you might just find there are more than just us two. Would I be right?' It was a guess but it hit its mark. Dismay replaced anger as he stared at them in shock before rising to his feet and striding from the room.

'Jesus, Mary and Joseph: Devlin, I'm shaking. But I think you hit the nail on the head. I wonder how many women *did* he abuse?' Nenita whispered, as all around them the hum of laughter, chat and the clink of cutlery on china seemed utterly bizarre, after what the two women had just experienced.

'It really rattled him when I said about others coming out of the woodwork. Whether we go ahead with this or not we've ruined any peace of mind he'll ever have, for the rest of his life. We did good,' Devlin said warmly, gripping the other woman's hand. 'I'm *so* proud of you, Nenita. You did well by your children.'

'And you also, for your little girl. We did it together.'

'We did,' agreed Devlin, taking a welcome sip of tea.

'You know something? Seeing him there all arrogant and dismissive, deriding us, sickened me and brought back all the disgust I feel.' She sat up straight. 'Let's go after him. Let's follow this through. I'm not afraid of him anymore.' She stared at Devlin, her face hard and determined.

Devlin stared back. 'Let's lawyer up then. I'm with you all the way, Nenita.' Devlin caressed the locket at her throat. Luke wouldn't be happy but this was something she had to do. 'Let's put Colin Cantrell-King where he belongs. Behind bars.'

CHAPTER TWENTY-EIGHT

Devlin/Luke

'I would have come with you, you know that.' Luke hugged his wife tightly when he got home from his fortnightly overnighter to London.

'I know that,' she murmured against his chest: loving as always when his arms were around her, even after years of being married to him.

'Always so independent,' he observed, shaking his head.

'Ha! Maggie said the same thing to me. Sure I was able to walk from the Green. What was the point in you rescheduling your London trip and driving into town and trying to find parking when I was able to walk to my appointment?'

'Just so you could have had some support, maybe?' He murmured into her hair. 'The way you'd want to come with me if I was going to a consultant.'

'Sorry,' she replied, abashed. 'I was afraid he might say no and then I'd be upset, and I didn't want you to be upset too. But it doesn't matter now, he's doing it – yay!' Devlin raised her head to look up at him. 'So we need to ride each other ragged because I'll be out of action for six weeks.'

Luke burst out laughing. 'Devlin, you're incorrigible.'

'And you're a sexy ride,' she murmured, cupping her husband's beloved face and raising her lips to his. Even after all these years the feel of his lips on hers was always a turn on and she kissed him passionately and pressed herself against his lean, muscular body, delighting in the fact that she could always arouse him. 'Mister Ever-Ready,' she purred.

'Be gentle with me, I'm not as young as I used to be,' he kidded as hand in hand they walked upstairs to their bedroom.

Later as she lay snuggled up against him, she observed regretfully, 'These fabulous perimenopausal surges will be gone forever after the surgery. The sex is so satisfying now. I'll be a dried-up prune after it.'

'You! Never!' scoffed her husband reassuringly. 'Anyway, there's always that KY stuff.'

'We're lucky, aren't we, that we're still mad about each other?'

'Mad being the operative word.' Luke grinned and squeezed her hand, which was nestled in the dark tangle of hair on his chest. 'We *are* lucky. We're able to talk to each other, argue with each other, laugh with each other and support each other and we have a wonderful son.'

'Do you know what we should do?' Devlin raised herself on her elbow and stared down at him, eyes sparkling. 'Let's surprise Finn with a trip to Barcelona and have a minibreak. We could go for dinner at Perla Del Mar and have the maître d' ask Finn to come out to our table. He'd get *such* a surprise.'

'That's a good idea, Delaney! You're not just a pretty face.' Luke looked pleased.

'You charmer, you.' She grinned. 'While you're making din dins, I'll see if our favourite hotel has rooms and book our flights.'

'And bossy as well.' Luke yawned, throwing his leg over her. 'Let's have forty winks first: you've worn me out.' He was asleep in minutes and, as she lay drowsily with her arms around him, she thought how fortunate she was to have been blessed with a man like Luke. Caroline and Maggie had found no joy in their marriages and for Caroline especially Devlin knew it was a source of unhappiness that was always with her.

She needed to be more mindful of her friends, Devlin thought guiltily. Sometimes she was so consumed with what was going on in her own life, she didn't think about what was going on in theirs. She lay listening to Luke's deep, even breathing.

Luke: her beloved. He loved her deeply, as deeply as she loved him, and she knew when she told him about what she and Nenita had decided he would worry for her and she hated that. She would have to tell her darling son, too, why she was taking a case against a man for sexual abuse. And that would be very, very hard.

Devlin would say nothing until the end of their little holiday. Let them have this precious family time together before all hell broke loose.

CHAPTER TWENTY-NINE

Maggie/Niamh/Tony/Rick

It had taken a week before Tony had finally agreed a date and time for a family Zoom call. Maggie had, with enormous difficulty, kept her cool until finally Niamh – knowing full well the reason for the Zoom and knowing that her brother knew the reason – had had a terse WhatsApp call with him, telling him to get his act in gear and agree a date.

'I told him to cop on to himself; he wasn't the only one of us up to our eyes in work. I have your back, sis. Say what you have to say. In fact give him hell,' Niamh advised crossly.

It was easy for her sister to say 'give him hell' from the other side of the Atlantic. She wasn't the one who might need back-up if anything happened to their mother, Maggie reflected as she sat at her laptop, at the kitchen table, ready to invite her three siblings to their first face-to-face meeting since Nelsie had made her gobsmacking revelation.

One thing she was clear on: Tony would be left in no doubt that he would be called upon to muck in. Now he wouldn't have a choice. He was going to be involved whether he liked it or not. With a determined set to her jaw, Maggie keyed into Zoom and started the meeting.

'Hiya, Niamh, Tony, Rick,' she said matter-of-factly as her siblings came into view. 'I know we're all very busy, and we have big time differences, so great to finally get a date for our catch-up. The reason I called is Mam, obviously. I need to get a few things settled.'

'Sure, Mags. Shoot. Not that I can do much from Australia,' Rick said easily.

'Is everything OK? Nothing wrong with Mam, is there?' Niamh pretended innocence.

'She's fine,' Maggie said calmly. 'When I say it's about Mam, I should also add it's about me too.'

'What's wrong with you?' Tony eyed her suspiciously, awaiting her onslaught.

'Physically nothing, apart from being tired, very busy at work and having a wedding to organise.'

'Brilliant! So Shona's named the day.' Niamh beamed.

'She hasn't decided the exact date yet, sometime in the early autumn.' Maggie eyed her younger brother and he couldn't hold her gaze. 'Anyway, the thing is, I've done all the caring for Mam, ferried her to all her appointments, done her shopping, sorted plumbers, electricians and the like when they were needed, kept her garden as well as my own and now I've decided I'm not doing it on my own anymore. Tony, you have to step up. I'm going to work out a schedule of her requirements and send it to you.'

'I can't take time off work!' he exclaimed testily.

'I have to, all the time, since I moved down here after Covid.'

'That's different,' he derided.

'How so?'

'Well ... well, you're more of a free agent than I am!'

'Tony, let me tell you, when I have to bring Mam to an appointment I have to work late into the night to make up the time I've lost. I give up a good chunk of my weekends running after her. My work is as important to me as yours is to you. I've managed to put my children through college and kept a roof over their heads and my own.'

'You're not short of a bob or two,' he said snidely.

'Because I work hard: very, *very* hard. So you just cut that out.' Her eyes were like flints. 'I have to travel for research and my TV work too, not that that's any reason I should have to *ask* for help to look after our mother. I know you're in the US, Niamh, and you're in Oz, Rick, and that's my hard luck. But you're here, Tony. It's time to buckle up and do your bit. It would be good for you to have some idea of Mam's day-to-day requirements when I'm abroad or should you ever have to exercise your power of attorney. Mam's still sprightly but she's getting older and needs more assistance, so if you want to organise more home help, or a gardener, feel free to discuss it with her. After all, that's what her money's for. She should spend it on making her last years as easy as possible, don't you agree?'

'Absolutely,' Niamh intervened. 'If she needs to she can always get an equity release deal on the house with the bank.'

'Excellent idea, Niamh. I'd be all for it,' Maggie approved. 'That's what her money and her assets are for. You can take that under consideration too, Tony, if it's something that will be needed in the future. I know she's not mad about the idea of going into a nursing home. We could get home nursing for her if she needs it. She expects me to nurse her if anything happens, but I won't be doing that. I have to look after my own needs, too. Mam has enough money and assets to see her out.'

'Go for it, Mags. Get a gardener and homecare for Mam. Do whatever you think is right,' Rick concurred.

Maggie looked at Tony on the screen. 'I'll email you the schedule. Ginny might be able to help out. And I suggest we all Zoom for updates every couple of months, or whenever is required, from now on in. OK?' He remained mute, while Niamh and Rick agreed.

'Right, gotta go. I'd love to stay and chat but I'm on a tight schedule. I'm recording a podcast with Ciara Geraghty and Caroline Grace-Cassidy, two terrific authors. It's called *Book Birds*, if you want to catch it online. Cheers!' She fibbed. She'd recorded the podcast the previous week. She waved at her siblings and left the call.

'Put that in your pipe and smoke it, dear brother.' Maggie scowled, closing the laptop with more force that was necessary, proud of herself that she'd not let loose on him when he'd sneered at her work. 'Superior, ignorant, arrogant little prick,' she ranted. Her WhatsApp tinkled and she saw Niamh's number pop up. She didn't answer. She wasn't in the humour to talk to her sister right now. It's well for Niamh that she doesn't have to put up with what I have to, Maggie thought resentfully, opening the fridge door and pouring herself a hefty glass of chilled Chardonnay. If anything happened to Nelsie tonight that was her tough luck, because Maggie had had enough of her family for one day.

CHAPTER THIRTY

Shona/Chloé

How entitled her half-sister looked, Shona thought, looking across the concourse in Dundrum Shopping Centre. Chloé was sitting at a table in Bakers + Barista, DKNY bag slung casually over the back of her chair, sunglasses – designer, no doubt – perched on her head, an expensive-looking top over her leggings. She had her head stuck in her phone and didn't see Shona observing her.

Don't be hostile. Be kind: you're the adult here, Shona reminded herself, walking over to the table.

'Hiya, Chloé,' she said guardedly.

Her half-sister's head shot up and a mutinous scowl flashed across her features. 'Why are *you* here? I'm meeting Mimi,' she said truculently, hardly able to hide her distaste.

'I know that. She'll be here shortly. Do you mind if I sit down?'

'Suit yourself.' Chloé gave a sullen shrug and bent her head to her phone again.

Shona tried not to be annoyed at the teen's rudeness. 'Look, I know I haven't been very friendly in the past and I'm sorry about that, Chloé. I have issues with my dad and I took my anger out on you. I'd like to apologise.'

'*Oh!*' Chloé looked at her, astonished, and Shona noticed what beautiful hazel eyes she had. Like their father's.

'Not very grown-up of me, I'm sure you'll agree,' Shona continued, wishing she could apply her eye make-up as perfectly as Chloé did. 'And I also wanted to say I thought it was great that you phoned me to em ... give me a piece of your mind about the way I ... I ... walked out on Dad at lunch that day. I always stood up for him too, when I was young. We're actually quite alike in some ways, I think.'

'Well, you were *very* rude to him. He's a very kind father,' Chloé admonished her crossly. 'He gets really upset, you know, whenever he has to meet you. He's not like that with Mimi and Michael because they're nice to him and me,' she said sulkily.

Shona met her young half-sister's accusatory gaze. 'They're nice people. I'm the family biotch.'

Chloé's jaw dropped. 'Oh! Well, like ... ya.' Her D4 accent got even more pronounced.

'It's all right, Chloé, I'm owning it.' Shona grinned and Chloé gave an uncertain smile. 'So I was wondering perhaps if we could put the past behind us and make a fresh start? And I'll be nice to our dad,' she offered.

'Em ... like, that would be really nice, Shona. Dad really loves you, you know. He's so proud when he sees your name on the TV on one of your programmes. He always makes sure to record them if he's not able to watch,' Chloé informed her eagerly, dropping her faux sophistication. Shona was touched at how keen Chloé seemed to let bygones be bygones.

'Really? That's nice to hear.'

'Like, I know divorce is hard and all. Some of my friends at school have parents who are divorced and they hate their step-parents but some of them get on OK and, like, it would be good to get on with you like I do with Mimi and Michael. Like, he's *so* cool in his uniform. You should hear my friends when I show them the photos of him on the bridge of his ship. They think he's hot.'

'Do they?' Shona laughed. 'Don't tell him or he'll get a big head.'

'He brought me a beautiful jewellery box from Japan,' Chloé confided.

'Michael's got a very kind heart: he's a great brother.' Shona smiled at the younger girl's endearing hero worship. A raucous laugh from a small group of teens at a table across from them brought a flush to Chloé's heavily made-up face. She flashed them a glance and bit her lip. 'You keep looking at them, do you want to join them?' Shona asked, about to stand up, happy that a reconciliation of sorts had been reached.

'No, I just know two of them,' she muttered. 'They're in my class.'

Two of the teenagers stood up and walked past their table towards the concourse, bursting out laughing as they passed by. Chloé's phone pinged and she glanced down at it and opened the message that had arrived. Her lower lip wobbled and Shona was dismayed to see the glitter of tears in her eyes. 'Did they send you a text?' she asked, concerned.

'It doesn't matter. They're mean girls.' Her half-sister's sigh came from the depths of her.

'Let me see it,' Shona demanded.

'It doesn't matter.' Chloé was about to delete whatever it was she'd seen but something – some protective urge that surprised Shona – made her grab the phone. Her eyes widened when she read the message aloud. 'Fat Cu— Hey, Chloé that's not on!' she said, not finishing the vile word. Shona picked up her own phone, snapshotted the message and stood up from the table and hurried after the pair who had stopped to look in a shop window.

'Hey. You two.' Shona stood behind them, blocking them. They turned and looked at her in surprise. 'That disgusting message you sent Chloé. Do you realise you've broken the law by sending that?'

'Get lost,' the older one said cheekily.

'None of your business,' drawled the other.

'Really?' said Shona, taking a photo of the pair of them. She almost laughed at the outraged expression on their faces.

'You can't do that.'

'You can't take photos of us without our permission.'

Their fury and indignation did make her laugh. 'I just did. And let me tell you if you carry on with your mean girl behaviour, this photo of your disgusting message,' she waved her phone under their noses, 'is going to your school principal *and* my fiancé who's a detective garda *and* your parents will be getting a call from the guards *and* you may end up in juvenile court. Now get your mean, nasty little asses over to Chloé and apologise.'

'No!' answered one defiantly while the other one chewed the inside of her mouth, not sure what to do.

'Your choice, missy. Principal, parents and guards or an apology.' Shona eyeballed her.

'OK,' she muttered, backing down.

'Get over there and apologise!' Shona pointed to where Chloé was sitting and they trudged over, mortified and gobsmacked.

'Sorry,' mumbled the defiant one.

'Sorry, Chloé,' stammered the other.

Chloé ignored the first one and stared at the second girl, who couldn't look her in the eye. 'You and I were best friends until *she*,' she gave a dismissive nod at the other teen, 'came into our class. But you know something, Avril: you're welcome to each other because you don't know how to be a proper friend. So sod off.'

'You heard Chloé: sod off. And if either of you pair of horrible girls ever make my sister miserable again you'll have me to deal with,' Shona assured them.

'You're not her sister. I met Mimi,' Avril blurted.

'I'm Chloé and Mimi's *older* sister, madam. And just hope you don't get to meet *me* again. Now buzz off, little wasps, and take your horrible mean girl stings elsewhere.'

'Everything OK?' a voice behind them asked.

'Hi Mimi.' Shona was delighted to see her sister. 'Just telling these mean girls who sent the most vicious, horrible text to Chloé not to mess with our sister again or they will be dealing with their parents, the school principal and my fiancé, the detective garda.'

'Right. He's one detective I would *not* want on my case.' Mimi made a face. 'I thought you were a nice girl, Avril, the few times we met. Chloé told me about your nasty betrayal, trying to turn her classmates against her because of this one.'

She jerked a thumb towards the teens in the café. 'Fortunately they have much more backbone and integrity than you, and are much nicer girls. So you've ended up with the perfect so-called friend. Now scram, you horrible little wagons!' Mimi gave them a filthy look and they scurried away with the older one turning to give them the finger. Shona waved her phone at them and they hurried off and melted into the throngs of shoppers.

'So you're engaged to a detective garda since we last spoke: what does Aleksy have to say about that?' Mimi laughed, slinging her bag onto a chair and taking out her wallet. 'I'm getting coffee and a cake. What are you gals having?'

'Same for me, unless you want to talk to Mimi on her own?' Shona looked enquiringly at her half-sister.

'Oh . . . no. It would be, like, nice if you stayed,' Chloé said hastily, feeling that she was having the weirdest afternoon. 'Em just a latte for me.'

'Sure I couldn't tempt you to a little celebratory cupcake?' Mimi urged.

'They said I was fat, I better not.'

'Don't mind those little bitches. You're not fat, you're *fabulous*,' Mimi declared.

'How about you and I share a cream slice, if that would make you feel more comfortable?' Shona suggested.

'OK, that sounds good.' Chloé brightened.

'Excellent. Go get them cakes, sis.' Shona winked.

'Your ring is lovely.' Chloé eyed Shona's diamond set in a gold Celtic knot.

'Would you like to make a wish?' Shona took it off and handed it to her.

'Oh ya,' she agreed enthusiastically, sliding it on to her wedding finger and twisting it around. 'Your fiancé has good taste.'

'He has.' Shona grinned. 'Didn't he choose me? Oh and by the way he's not a detective. I just said that to worry that pair. Although as far as I know it *is* a crime to send threatening or abusive messages from a phone.'

'That gave them a bit of a shock,' giggled Chloé.

'And well done for saying your piece to the Avril one. That will give her something to chew on. Do your mum and dad know they're bullying you?'

'Not really.' Chloé bit her lip. 'I don't tell them stuff cos it upsets them, especially Dad. He'd go around to their houses and cause a row.'

'That would be Dad all right,' laughed Mimi, who'd overheard the last bit of the conversation as she set a laden tray down on the table. 'Remember when Michael was getting bullied by the little Wallace thug on our estate and Dad got him boxing gloves and taught him to box, and Michael flattened the guy on the green one day. Big Daddy Wallace came out and started giving out to Dad and Dad said, "Unless you want to suffer the same fate as your little brat I'd advise you to shut up" and he did!' Mimi and Shona laughed at the memory. 'Anyway,' Mimi cut their pastry in two and handed them a plate each, 'if you get any more of those texts or WhatsApps just let me and Shona know. Your sisters have got your back, lady.'

Chloé blushed to her roots and smiled as she took a sip of her latte. 'Thanks,' she said shyly. 'Actually they're Snapchats and they disappear.'

'Take a photo, like I did,' Shona warned.

'Ya, like, I will but anyway I won't be seeing them at school next year. They're not doing transition and I am. They think it's a doss year for saddos. They want to get to Trinity fast.'

'Are you serious? Sad little feckers,' Shona scoffed, licking some cream off her fingers. 'Transition year is brilliant! You get to do so much that you wouldn't in an ordinary term year. We get transition students looking for their work experience with our company. I love them: they're so eager and anxious to learn.' She eyed Chloé. 'What are you doing for work experience?'

'Um I was, like, hoping to get some experience in a bookshop or a pet shop. I love reading and animals.'

'If you want a placement in a TV production company with me as your boss, let me know.' Shona bit into her cream cake.

'Oh! My! God! Like, *really*?' Chloé spluttered out her coffee.

'Sure. Then you'll really see how bossy and bitchy I am. Isn't that right, Mimi?'

'Run a mile, Chloé. She bosses me around terribly,' joshed Mimi. 'Seriously though, it's great experience. You meet all kinds of people. I've gone on a few shoots with Mam and Shona, when my Mam's presenting one of the documentaries they make, and there's a great buzz. And Shona's brilliant at her job,' she added loyally.

'Transition's gonna be MEGA!' Chloé exclaimed and Mimi gave Shona the tiniest wink and a thumbs up under the table.

'That wasn't so bad, was it?' Mimi and Shona headed for the car park having left their half-sister happily perusing cosmetics counters.

'She's not half as confident as she appears. She's a bit of a softy behind that façade, isn't she?' Shona observed as they stood at the exit before saying their goodbyes.

'Yep. You really made her day telling that pair not to mess with "our sister". You didn't see her face because you had your back to her. She was as proud as punch,' Mimi said.

'Was she? Ah, that's nice.'

'And when you said about doing the work experience I thought she was going to choke with excitement. Well done you, missus.'

'No, well done *you*, Mimi, for showing me what a horrible person I was and for helping me to let go of grudges. Thanks for arranging the meet-up. I owe you one,' Shona said gratefully.

'You sure do.' Mimi grinned.

'To tell the truth I'm ashamed of myself for my behaviour. I guess I should try and mend some fences with Dad. How come you're the younger one but you've always been far more grown up than me?'

'Ah, don't beat yourself up *too* much! We had different experiences growing up. You had the worst of the break-up because you were older. Michael and I adapted to it quicker. And you're a hot head, like our beloved mother.' Mimi hugged her. 'Give Aleksy my love. We must have a barbecue soon. Michael's coming home on leave. Let's have a family get together.'

'Perfect! I'd love that. Mind yourself.' Shona hugged her back warmly and went to her car feeling as though a weight had been lifted from her shoulders.

'Dad, she was *really* nice. We had such a laugh with Mimi and she's said I could do work experience at her TV company.

Like, how cool is that?' Chloé was fizzing with excitement. Terry hadn't seen his youngest daughter so carefree and happy in ages. Not since before the falling out with her best friend.

'That's great to hear, sweetie. Shona is a sound person and I'm so glad things are good between you at last. It's what I've always wanted.'

'Yeah, me too, and Dad,' Chloé popped a kiss on his head, 'she told me she thought it was great how I rang her up and gave out to her for being so rude to you.'

'You rang her up and gave out to her?' Terry was astonished.

'Yep, like, she was mean to you and I told her so.'

'Aren't you my little pet?' Terry was touched at Chloé's loyalty. 'Thank you, sweetie. What did she say on that call?'

'She, like, told me it was none of my business before I hung up and then Mimi must have said something to her cos I was supposed to meet Mimi in Dundrum and Shona came first and she apologised to me, Dad. Imagine,' Chloé said in wonderment.

'Rightly so,' Terry declared.

'Anyway, Mimi came later and we had a great laugh and I'm just so happy and I'm going to do work experience for transition year in her TV company. They get loads of transition students applying. Like, how cool is that?'

'Very cool indeed,' agreed Terry, hardly able to believe what he was hearing. *Mimi is one good daughter and sister to have brokered this détente*, he thought proudly.

'Shona told me to tell you she'd be in touch. I think she wants to make up with you, too. And she let me try on her engagement ring to make a wish and she showed me a photo of her fiancé. He's *gorgeous!*' Chloé chattered on and Terry had to blink hard and swallow several times as emotion threatened to overwhelm him: one of his greatest wishes had finally came true.

CHAPTER THIRTY-ONE

Caroline/Mick

'I let my secretary pay all the bills – rent, electricity, wages, everything – while I concentrated on the business. I'm a physiotherapist and I've two more working for me. Anyway, I've just discovered after what I thought was a twenty-year friendship that my secretary has been creaming off thousands over the years: even managed to pay off an extension that she had built. And she has landed me with a fine fat tax bill for Covid payments, even though the clinic was open. I ... I just can't get my head around it.' The woman opposite Caroline shook her head in bewilderment. 'I've been defrauded by someone I thought of as a friend. Irene, my secretary, even babysat my children. I'm a widow, single parenting two kids, trying to get them through college. I only discovered it when she was off work for two months and my temp had me check every day's takings. My God, I was *fleeced*.'

'Why would you hand over your financial power like that to someone?' Caroline probed.

'What!' the client exclaimed indignantly.

'Why did you not take responsibility for your finances?'

'I'll have you know I was working all the hours I could get. I didn't have the time or the energy to do what I was paying my secretary good money for. Why are you blaming me for what she did?' The other woman's eyes sparked with fury.

'I wasn't blaming you. I was merely asking why you, as a business woman, were content to let someone else have control of your financial affairs?'

'I just told you. Are you *deaf* or something?' The woman stood up, grabbed her bag and raged, 'Don't think I'm paying you for this . . . this waste of my time. Some psychotherapist you are. I was told you were good. You're bloody crap,' she vented before slamming the door behind her.

'And you're a crap businesswoman,' Caroline muttered, annoyed with herself that she had fitted the client in as a favour to another client and seen her on a Saturday morning. She was used to people getting annoyed with her questions. It went with the territory, especially when the questioning got too close to a truth the client couldn't handle. Oftentimes after storming out of a session there'd be a phone call afterwards to apologise and the client would ask if they could come back. But there'd always be the ones who couldn't accept what was said to them and preferred to blame Caroline for the anger that was really directed at themselves.

Caroline glanced out the window. It had been raining when she'd come to work but the sun was out now and a little breeze kissed the leaves on the rowan trees in the park. She typed up her notes, closed down the computer and adjusted the blinds on the window. A tinkle on her phone as she walked downstairs alerted her to a notification and she sat on her receptionist's chair and scrolled to find a WhatsApp from Mick.

> How's things? I'm in your neck of the woods, had to get a computer problem sorted. Would you be free for a coffee?

Oh, what a treat. Caroline's heart lifted. A catch-up with Mick would be just the thing after the morning she'd had. She guessed he was at the computer place in Fairview so she typed back:

> Perfect timing. How about Surge on the seafront? You can park in the car park opposite.

> I'll be there in less than 10.

Caroline replied to his last message with the thumbs-up emoji, dropped her phone into her bag and went to lock up and set the alarm.

Ten minutes later, she was reversing into a space when she saw Mick walking away from the parking machine. She beeped and he turned in her direction and a grin spread across his face. Caroline grinned back and got out of the car.

'Hiya, that was good timing. How's things?'

He threw his eyes up to heaven, gave her a hug and replied, 'Don't ask. How's things with you?'

'Don't ask,' she echoed, hugging him back before he walked towards his car with the disc. Caroline paid on her phone.

The café was buzzing with Saturday morning customers but as they reached the entrance an outdoor table became vacant.

'Grab that, Caro. What would you like?' Mick asked.

'An Americano's fine.' She plonked her bag on the chair. She hadn't had her daily coffee yet so there was no issue about what to order.

What difference would it make if you had two coffees in a day, once in a blue moon? she thought crossly, remembering what Aideen Hemsell had said at their first meeting. She was trying to control her addictive behaviour and Aideen was pushing her hard at their sessions.

'You don't need to work so hard: why are you still working five and sometimes six days a week?'

'Have you taken a holiday this year?'

'Why have you never let yourself get into another relationship after what happened with the widower in Galway?'

'If I was presenting to you with your same issues what would you say to me?'

Aideen was like a dentist drilling relentlessly and Caroline knew exactly why. She had some sympathy for the client that had bailed out on her this morning. She'd been looking for some sympathy and got none, Caroline thought ruefully.

'I bought us a couple of croissants. I'm starving and they were calling to me,' Mick announced, placing her coffee in front of her and a selection of croissants and Danish.

'I'm fine with coffee,' she said although her mouth watered at the aroma of almond tantalising her nostrils.

'You're too much of a skinnymalinks, Caroline. Are you starving yourself again?' Mick said bluntly, sitting down opposite her.

'Stop it,' she murmured, mortified. 'That's very rude.'

'You told me you had anorexia before you came to Abu Dhabi, remember?'

'I should have kept my mouth shut.' She scowled.

'Well, you can open it now and eat one of these. They're delish.' He was completely unfazed by her glowers. 'I, on the other hand, am comfort eating my way to obesity so it would be a real help if you had one.'

Caroline laughed. Mick always had a great sense of humour.

'All right then.' She reached over and took one of the Occasions of Sin and broke off a piece. 'Why are you comfort eating your way to obesity? Is it because of Dervla?'

'Yeah,' he sighed, taking a drink of coffee. 'This is good,' he said appreciatively.

'What's happening?' Caroline could see the stress lines etched in his forehead.

'Everything's my fault. For leaving Abu Dhabi and bringing her home to Ireland, a "backward hole where it rains all the time and where she knows no one". Her words. My heart goes out to her, Caroline, but I'm at my wits' end. Her laptop's acting up so I brought it in for repair. We've both agreed that there's no point in enrolling her in a new school yet because the baby's due in October and she'd only be settling in when she'd have to leave, until at least Christmas. She wants to put the baby up for adoption. But I think she's in such a heap she doesn't really know what she wants. She won't even FaceTime Sally, who's blaming me for alienating her. I can't win with either of them.'

'Does she talk to her brother and sister?'

'She does, yeah. Ciara has said she'll come to Ireland when the baby's born, to be with her, so that's a comfort of sorts.' He exhaled deeply.

'The poor child and poor you.' Caroline reached across the table and squeezed his hand.

'Sorry for unburdening all that lot.' Mick squeezed back. 'Tell me what's up with you.'

'I fell into a black hole but I'm climbing back out of it. And it's not anorexia this time: it's bulimia. Menopause tipped me over the edge. One of my great sadnesses is not having ever had a child and now it's too late. Life's full of ironies, isn't it?'

'You can say that again and it damn well doesn't get any easier. I'm sorry for your sadness, Caro. I won't diminish your feelings by saying children can be a pain in the neck but for what it's worth I think you would have made a great mother,' Mick responded kindly.

'I might have been too neurotic,' Caroline admitted.

'You're not really neurotic. Lorna Keating is neurotic.' He grinned and Caroline giggled.

'Stop it, Mick,' she chided, chuckling. Lorna was married to a wealthy Abu Dhabi businessman and she'd liked to lord it over their set. She was forever having lifestyle crises.

'Well, she is. Good God, I've never seen anyone with so many dramas in her life. Choosing which friggin' bikini to wear is a drama.'

'Remember when she invited us to the "Taj Mahal" for St Patrick's Day and her elderly father-in-law was staying with them? She was making her welcome speech, dressed to impress in Dior and wearing a ton of jewellery, and he got up out of his chair and let off a rasper that went on for about five minutes and stank to high heaven,' Caroline recalled. 'Lorna turned forty shades of puce and nearly got lockjaw.'

They whooped, laughing at the memory.

'We had some great fun there, didn't we?' Caroline wiped her eyes, wet from laughter. She'd very much enjoyed working in Abu Dhabi after the trauma of her marriage break-up.

'We sure did,' Mick agreed. 'I'd forgotten we used to call her gaff the Taj Mahal.'

They sat for an hour reminiscing about the good times and when they parted at the car park each felt the better for their unexpected meet-up.

A run would be just the thing, Caroline decided when she got home five minutes later, delighted that Mick had got in touch so unexpectedly. Their interlude had put her in good form and she changed into her running gear and felt ease flood her as she did stretching exercises in the front garden before jogging out onto the street. She was only going to run as far as the Bull Island statue, she promised herself. No more pushing herself past her limit.

She enjoyed her run, the breeze blowing the hair off her face and the scent of salty seaweed invigorating her as the waves crashed against the seawall. She did some calisthenics on the Street Workout machines on the promenade and then carried on jogging, turning right onto the Wooden Bridge that led to the Bull Island. She passed the coffee van and, seeing customers sitting outside enjoying lunch, a madness came over her and impulsively she joined the queue.

'A cappuccino and a tuna melt,' she ordered when it was her turn.

After she was served, Caroline strolled towards one of the seats facing the Sugar Loaf and the Port. The calm, sunlit sea lapped the rocks and a ferry and a cargo vessel steamed towards the Port, the steady thrum of their engines adding to the holiday atmosphere.

Relaxed, calm about the delicious sandwich she was eating, Caroline felt happier than she had in ages. It had been such a lovely day so far. She'd go home, shower and lie out in the sun for the afternoon. Aideen would be so pleased for her when Caroline relayed her little triumphs at their next session. She sat for ages, enjoying the view and smiling and being smiled at by the walkers and joggers passing her by. She noticed, surprised, that she'd enjoyed her second coffee without feeling guilty. She might have a smaller portion of dinner later, after having the tuna melt, but that was OK too, Caroline assured herself. It had been a big sandwich with lots of bread. That was her carbs eaten for the day.

She walked back to the café, binned her rubbish and jogged towards the main road. When she reached Vernon Avenue, Caroline slowed to a walk on the narrow path: the parked cars and people coming in the opposite direction left little room for manoeuvre.

She stopped to let an elderly couple coming out of Picasso pass. Perhaps she and Mick could go have lunch there someday. Their slow-roasted pork belly was delicious.

Caroline moved ahead, felt her foot hit something and suddenly she was falling. As she twisted to try and save herself she felt a rip and an excruciating pain in her upper arm. *Something bad's happened*, she thought in horror, as a woman gave a little scream from behind her, before Caroline hit the ground with a sickening thud.

CHAPTER THIRTY-TWO

Devlin/Luke/Finn

Devlin stood on the balcony of her Barcelona hotel room gazing out at a leaden, windswept Mediterranean sea. 'I can't wait to see Finn. He's going to get *such* a surprise. I just hope the weather improves.' She yawned. They'd been up since 4am to catch their early morning Aer Lingus flight to Spain. Devlin, who was not a morning person, was having a hard time trying to stay awake. 'Wasn't it great they had the room ready for us? We can have a teeny little nap to freshen us up.' She closed the floor to ceiling balcony door against the rain that had started to fall. 'I won't feel a bit guilty about missing the sun because it's raining. Perfect weather for that gorgeous bed. Let's have a cuppa.'

Luke rooted in their case for the teabags his wife always insisted on bringing with them when they travelled, while she filled the kettle with bottled water. She took a packet of Chocolate Goldgrain out of her tote, shucked a few onto a plate and brought it and the cups and saucers to the coffee table between the two very comfortable blue-and-white bucket chairs.

'I love this hotel. I love the bookshelves on either side of the bed. So civilised and homely and not at all generic. Plus, the beds are so comfortable.' Devlin sat happily into her bucket chair, delighted at the prospect of a few days rest and relaxation, as well as seeing her adored son.

'Hmm, we've had some good times in these beds.' Luke busied himself making the tea.

'Yep, we better make the most of it while we can. This time next month I'll have gone under the knife and there'll be no rumpy pumpy for six weeks.' Devlin yawned again.

'For heaven's sake have your tea and get into bed,' her husband ordered, amused at her prodigious yawns.

Twenty minutes later Devlin was in bed, fast asleep, with Luke's arms around her as an easterly wind hurled the rain against the balcony.

It was just after one when Devlin drowsily opened her eyes, confused for a moment as to where she was. Luke was still asleep beside her and she lay contentedly listening to his slow, even breathing. She could see an aura of light around the top of the curtains and hoped that the sun was out. After they'd had lunch, Luke would stroll over to where the cruise liners were docked while she would lie by the pool having a read. But first, she smiled to herself, as she slid her hand up between his hard muscular thighs, there was another treat in store.

Her husband gave a soft groan as she caressed him and when he hardened to her touch she straddled him and leaned down to kiss him awake.

'Devlin.' He murmured her name huskily, his hands reaching for her, thrusting into her until she moaned with pleasure.

'Luke, Luke,' she whispered into his hair when he rolled her over onto her back and they came together, waves of pleasure washing over them.

'A great way to start our mini-break, isn't it?' He raised his head to look down at her, his eyes crinkling with the smile she loved.

'The best way. I'm so glad we managed to get away for the few days. We need it.'

'We do,' Luke agreed, kissing the tip of her nose. 'But I need something to eat to get my energy levels back up.'

'Ha!' Devlin laughed as he got out of bed. 'Sexy ass,' she complimented, sitting up and pushing her tousled hair off her face. She heard the shower running and lay back against the pillows. She was hungry herself. She'd have a light lunch so as to be able to enjoy her meal in Perla Del Mar later.

An hour later they were sitting outside, under the shade of a large umbrella, sharing a selection of tapas dishes and drinking chilled white wine. The sun had come out, chasing away the sullen clouds, and the Mediterranean shimmered below them, white crested waves caressing the shore.

Devlin sighed with pleasure and felt herself relax. She'd been tense since the encounter with Colin but had forced herself to put it out of her head as soon as she began to pack the case for their trip abroad.

'You never relax at home the way you do abroad, sure you don't?' she observed, savouring her crispy chicharrones. The pork belly, slow-cooked and flash-fried, was out of this world.

'I'll do my best to relax until I get jumped on again,' Luke said straight-faced and she laughed.

That night, hand in hand, they strolled along the seafront to the restaurant where Finn worked as a chef. He'd always loved cooking as a child and when he told them he wanted to be a chef, after his Leaving Cert, they had supported his choice. Devlin and Luke had been delighted when, after his two-year Commis Chef apprentice course was over, he'd passed his exams with flying colours and gone to work in a five-star hotel in London for a year. After getting his degree Finn moved to a restaurant in Menton in the south of France before ending up in his current job in a seafood restaurant in Barcelona. He loved living there. Devlin and Luke had been to visit several times and could see what he liked about the buzzing, vibrant city.

Devlin had booked their table and when they arrived the maître d's smile of welcome lifted her heart. 'He does not know. We tell him nothing,' Pedro revealed, leading them to a window table overlooking the sea. 'Now, the gin and tonic for you and the beer for *el Señor. Sí?*'

'*Gracias*, Pedro: you always remember.' Devlin gave him a hug before she sat down.

'I tell him the customer is not happy with the fish and wish to speak to him.' Pedro was always up for a joke and he strode off to the kitchen, chuckling, to prank his colleague.

'I bet Finn will barge through the doors with a face on him,' Luke predicted and laughed as their son did just that, looking annoyed, in his chef's whites. He turned inquiringly to Pedro, who had followed him straight-faced, and the maître d' pointed in their direction. Finn strode over but halfway across the room recognised who they were and a beam of delight crossed his face.

'What the heck are you doing here?' He swept Devlin into a bear hug, squeezing her tightly before turning to hug his father. 'Pedro *tu zorillo*.' He punched his friend lightly in the arm, grinning.

'You better go in and cook the prawns para *tu madre*, how she like them.' Pedro was highly amused. 'And the bream para *tu padre, sí?*' He raised an eyebrow at Luke.

'*Sí*, Pedro. *Sí, gracias. Mi favorito.*' Luke approved.

Svetlana their favourite waitress arrived with their drinks and there was more hugging and kissing and laughter and chat. Devlin was always delighted for her son that there was such a warm, friendly atmosphere in the restaurant. He was clearly very happy working there.

'I'll cook you the best meal *ever*,' Finn assured them. 'I can't wait to finish up and have a drink and hear all the news. What a surprise. How long are you staying?'

'Three nights, four days.' Devlin gave his hand a squeeze, thinking how tanned and healthy he looked. His eyes gleamed with delight as he stared at her, chuffed with their surprise arrival.

'There's someone I'd like you to meet, too,' Finn said. 'I think you'll like her.'

'No wonder you have a sparkle in your eye,' Devlin teased. 'You can tell us all the news tonight.'

When Finn had gone back into the kitchen and they were alone, Devlin murmured, 'I hope this one's better than the last one,' to her husband.

'She was a bit of a disaster all right.' Luke took a draught of beer.

'Very "me me me". Or should I say *moi moi moi*.' Ines Arnaud had not impressed Devlin when they'd met. Her air of French superiority, her faux charm, her passive-aggressive manner and the way she allowed Finn to run around after her had all grated on Devlin. She'd tried to tell herself that she was just being overprotective of her son, and was being too critical. So she'd done her best to be nice to the tall, chic, young Frenchwoman the few times she'd met her in Menton, when they'd gone to visit Finn. But in her heart of hearts Devlin knew they would never be kindred spirits. Ines had given Finn an ultimatum when he'd told her he was considering a move to Barcelona: if he left Menton it was over between them. Fortunately for Devlin, her son didn't take kindly to ultimatums and he'd bid his French girlfriend *adieu*, much to his mother's delight.

She liked Alicia Garcia immediately when they met her the next day. With her jet-black straight hair, expressive brown eyes and vivacious personality she made Finn laugh and Devlin liked that very much. She chatted away to Luke in Spanish when he told her his mother was from Seville and he could speak the language fluently.

The trip passed all too quickly and on their last morning Finn came to the hotel to say his goodbyes.

'Alicia's a lovely girl, Finn. She's fun. Ines was a bit too serious,' Devlin observed. They were having a coffee in the room, while Devlin was doing some last-minute packing and Luke had gone to get petrol for their hire car.

'I really like her, Mom. We have a lot of fun.'

'Finn, while we're on our own, there's something I want to tell you,' Devlin said quietly.

'What's that?' Finn stretched his long legs out in front of him.

'You know I had a little girl, before I met your dad. Well, I never really told you the full story, I just told you that she died in a car accident. I didn't tell you anything about her father.'

'That's OK, Mom. I figured if you ever wanted to say anything about him you would. I kinda felt he didn't feature in your life once you met Dad.'

'And you would be very right, darling.' Devlin smiled. 'Your dad's the love of my life.'

'As if people didn't know that,' her son kidded.

'Anyway, something's happened with this man and I just want you to know the background, so you're not sideswiped.' Devlin refilled their coffee cups and as unemotionally as possible she told her son about Colin and his past behaviour and how she and Nenita were taking him to court.

'*Cabrón*,' Finn cursed when she was finished. 'Jeez, Mom, that's *awful*.' His black brows drew together in a frown and she thought how like his father he looked. 'I'd like to have five minutes on my own with him.'

'It's been a long time coming but his past is going to catch up with him, Finn. It's his turn to suffer like we did.' Devlin stood up and went over to where he was sitting and put her arms around him. 'I'd prefer not to have told you all this but it will be in the news, I'm sure, and I needed you to know.'

'What does Dad think about it all?' He looked up at her.

'Well, he knows about Colin of course but he doesn't yet know that Nenita and I are taking it further. I wanted him to have our little trip to Barcelona, untroubled,' she explained.

'Oh! He'll be worried about you.' Finn looked concerned. '*I'll* be worried about you.'

'There's no need for either of you to worry,' Devlin said firmly. 'It will bring closure to Nenita and me and let predators like him out there know that women are not keeping silent anymore and there are consequences for their behaviour.'

'I think you're very brave, Mom, as well as being a brilliant mother.' Finn stood up and put his arms around her.

'And you're a great son, the pride and joy of my life.' Devlin ran her fingers through his hair. 'Remember I used to do that when you were a teenager and you used to get mad because you'd have had it gelled just so? And then you got too tall for me to reach and you could hold me at arm's length instead.'

She smiled at the memory and he laughed and said, 'That's because you're a little titch, Mom,' just as Luke entered the room.

'Your son has just called me a little titch,' Devlin informed him. 'That's a fine way to talk about his mother.'

'You *are* one, *querida*,' her husband joked. 'But you're *our* little titch.'

They laughed and Luke said, 'We better get a move on, Dev. I've settled our bill at reception.'

'OK. It's your turn to come and see us, mister.' She poked Finn in the chest.

'Yup, it's happening. I was talking to Michael. He's coming home on shore leave soon so I said I'd come home when he's there. Shona and Mimi are organising a barbie. It would be nice to see the gang.'

'Brilliant!' Devlin perked up. 'That will be something to look forward to. Let me know when you're coming and I'll have your room freshened up and I'll collect you from the airport.'

'So spoilt.' Luke put his arm around his son and hugged him. 'Your mother will be in great form now. Thanks for that.' He winked at Devlin.

Finn picked up the suitcase and Luke picked up Devlin's carry-on. '*Hora de decir adiós.*' Finn nodded towards the door and Devlin, knowing that he hated goodbyes, pasted on a bright smile and led the way to the lift. When Finn had loaded the luggage into the boot, he opened the car door for Devlin. 'Safe home, Mom. Dad, see you soon.' He waved as they drove off and Luke, glancing over at Devlin, threw his eyes up to heaven as he saw tears roll down her cheek.

'Softy,' he said patting her knee.

'It's hard.'

'He's happy and he'll be home soon,' Luke comforted.

'Luke, there's something I need to tell you and you're not going to like it but it's something I have to do.'

'Ah no, Dev. Don't tell me you're going ahead with the Cantrell-King prosecution.' Luke's face hardened and a muscle jerked in the side of his jaw. 'You know what a circus it will turn into. When did you decide this?' he asked in a stern tone he rarely used with her.

'Nenita and I met him last week—'

'You *met* him and you didn't tell me?' He looked over at her, stunned.

'I knew how you'd react and I didn't want to spoil our trip,' she protested. 'It's not something I want to do, Luke. It's something I *have* to do to have peace of mind and some sort of closure. Lynn deserves it. Abused women whose lives are ruined by predators deserve to know there's justice for them. You're a man. You'll never understand,' she said bitterly.

'All I know is that I don't want you to suffer at that bastard's hands ever again, Dev,' Luke said grimly. 'I'm trying to *protect* you, not *obstruct* you.'

'I know that, Luke, and I appreciate it and I know this isn't something you want in our lives. We're hoping that he'll plead guilty so we won't have to endure the ordeal of a trial.'

'OK,' he said tersely, privately thinking the odds of that were slim.

They sat in silence for the remainder of the journey, lost in their own thoughts, relieved when El Prat airport came into view.

Luke studied his sleeping wife. One thing about Devlin: she never took the easy path. Not only was she now facing major surgery that would have life-changing repercussions but she was also determined to bring Colin Cantrell-King to justice. While he understood her reasoning behind it, he wondered had she really thought it through. If she'd at least talked to him about it he would have had a chance to point out the huge negatives of pursuing the path she was set on.

It hurt, too, that she'd gone and met that man without telling him. But that was Devlin all over: self-sufficient to the last. It was a trait he had hugely admired when he'd met her first but it could be a little wearing after all these years of marriage. She was annoyed with him that he'd argued with her when she'd dropped the bombshell. Dev must know that it was because he loved her. There was no need for her to get thick with him.

They'd hardly spoken on the flight home and she'd gone straight into work mode once there and spent the evening answering emails. They'd ordered a Thai takeaway for dinner. She'd gone to bed before him.

It hadn't taken her long to fall asleep, although when he saw the blister pack of painkillers on the top of her locker Luke guessed she'd taken 'the big guns', as she called them. The ones that knocked her out.

He slid under the duvet, switched off his lamp and wondered how long the coolness between them would last. At least their son was far enough away and wouldn't have to endure what was coming. That's a comfort of sorts, Luke thought tiredly as he listened to Devlin's deep breathing as she slept beside him.

CHAPTER THIRTY-THREE

Caroline/Mick/Dervla

'Will you reschedule my appointments and give my apologies to my clients? I'll take the week off and hope, even if I'm not driving, I can walk to work after that,' Caroline said wearily to her secretary. 'I can arrange Zoom consultations if the worst comes to the worst and anyone is in dire need.'

'Sure, no problem. Mind yourself, Caroline. If there's anything you need let us know. Are you OK for shopping?' Maria asked.

'I'm fine, my sister-in-law did a shop for me. I have everything that I need,' Caroline assured her. 'If I'm stuck for anything, I'll give you a shout. I promise.'

'Make sure you do,' Maria said firmly and Caroline smiled at her colleague's bossy tone.

'I will. See you.'

It was the day after her fall and with her right arm in a sling and a torn rotator cuff confirmed after a scan, Caroline was in pain and feeling utterly pissed off. After the initial shock of the fall, and trying hard not to puke or pass out with people all around her, all she had wanted to do was to get up and escape the mortification of face-planting on the pavement. After assuring the concerned group who had gathered around that she was fine, she'd managed to limp into Beshoffs and order a Coke. She drank it slowly sitting on the red banquette, her right arm dangling by her side, agonising pain shooting up into her shoulder. She'd walked home and collapsed onto her sofa, crying in pain and shock, knowing she needed to go and get herself seen to but dreading a trip to an overcrowded A&E.

The horror stories she heard about people being left on trolleys or, worse, sitting in chairs for hours, were frightening. A client had told her that her sister had been brought into an A&E and had her bag and phone stolen. The poor woman was desperate to ring her family. She had died the next morning.

A shroud of apprehension enveloped Caroline as she tried to get her panties down to pee. Her right arm was useless. She could do nothing with it. In desperation she rang her brother Declan who arrived with her sister-in-law, Eileen.

'Cripes, Caroline, we'd better get you seen to,' her brother exclaimed when he saw the state of her. 'I'll bring you to the Mater.'

'I really don't want to go there. If it's a broken arm I'll be waiting for hours. It wouldn't be considered important.' Caroline was sick at the thought.

'Why don't we go to the VHI Clinic in Swords?' Eileen suggested. 'They're brilliant. Are you in the VHI, Caro?'

'Yeah, yeah I am.' Caroline brightened up. 'That's a much better idea.'

Two hours later, she was back home with her arm in a sling, a prescription for painkillers and a letter for a consultant. Caroline couldn't believe her luck. She'd been triaged and seen within twenty minutes and had a thorough examination and a scan.

Eileen stayed the night with her, helped her to shower, did a shop and had left strict instructions for Caroline to phone *any* time if she needed them. 'You could come and stay with us and have the joy of squabbling teens, a mad dog and an antisocial cat who thinks we're all there to serve Her Highness.' Eileen laughed.

'Ah, I'll stay put and lie on the sofa and catch up on my Netflix stuff, but thanks for asking.' While Caroline loved her nieces and nephews, the Stacey household was noisy and chaotic and not what she needed right now. She'd stood at the door waving her kind sister-in-law off, grateful to know that Eileen and Declan always had her back if she needed them.

After she had made her work phone calls, Caroline went into the kitchen to make herself a cup of coffee. Even that simple task was difficult and water spurted out of the tap when she held the kettle the wrong way, soaking her dressing gown sleeve. Trying to open her milk carton caused more irritation. It was immensely frustrating. She'd been told it could take months to get her range of motion back to what it had been.

The following few days were a nightmare. Showering was difficult. Wearing a bra was impossible. She struggled to pull tops over her head and even putting on her tracksuit bottoms was hard.

How was she going to get dressed to go to work? She'd have

to type on her computer with one hand. Clearly she was going to have to stay at home longer than the week she'd planned. *I'll go off my rocker,* Caroline thought glumly as a text pinged on her phone.

> Hi Caro, any chance we could meet up for a coffee? We're filming a segment about Bram Stoker, so I'll be in Marino on Thursday? S XXX

She placed the phone in her right hand and managed to scroll up to the top of the message, to phone her godchild.

'Hiya, godmammy,' Shona's cheerful voice came down the line.

'Sorry I couldn't text back, I've torn my friggin' rotator cuff and I'm in a sling. I can't manage to text,' Caroline explained, trying not to sound too pissed off.

'Oh no! Sounds painful. How did you do that? Mam never said anything when I was talking to her.'

'I didn't tell her. She has enough going on and you know Maggie: she'd want to be nursing me.'

'But if you're in a sling how are you managing? Look, I can't talk now, I'm in studio. I'll come over after work and bring some dinner. I can get us something nice in Wrights, OK?'

'Are you sure? I don't want to put you out, Shona.'

'Don't be daft. I'll see you later. Make out a list of anything you need,' her godchild responded good-naturedly and Caroline felt warmed by her loving kindness. She had a great bond with Maggie's daughter. She had a great bond with Mimi, Michael and Finn too, she acknowledged gratefully. They'd all had giddy sleepovers at Caroline's when they were children, much to the delight of their mothers, who had enjoyed their occasional childfree weekends.

Caroline hadn't said anything to Devlin about her injury, either. She couldn't remember what day she was coming back from Barcelona and she didn't want to spoil her friend's mini-break.

Caroline hauled the duvet up over the bed with her left hand. It was heavy at the best of times but she made the bed as neatly as she could, gave her ensuite toilet and sink a clean and dragged the linen basket down the hall to the utility room and managed to put on a wash.

Wrecked after her exertions and with her right arm and shoulder throbbing painfully she made a cup of green tea and took two painkillers. It was cloudy outside but sultry, so she threw some cushions onto her lounger and went to sit outside with her book. The birds were singing, nibbling at her birdfeeder, and a couple of goldfinches splashed merrily in the birdbath. It was entertaining to watch and it calmed her agitation a little. It was so weird to be sitting in her garden on a weekday. If she were counselling a client in the same predicament she would be telling them to try and enjoy the enforced time off.

Caroline felt she should be up *doing* something. She wondered wildly might she be able to go for a jog.

'Oh cop on,' she muttered crossly and picked up her book. There was a small library in the clinic for clients and she'd gone into Chapters, one of her favourite bookshops since she'd been a teenager with meagre pocket money, to replenish the stock. She'd asked the helpful bookseller for recommendations for young adults and he'd given her *Not My Problem*, with high praise. Seeing that the author, Ciara Smyth, worked in social services, Caroline had been intrigued, especially by the title, and kept it to skim through herself. Settling herself as comfortably as she could, she picked up the novel and began to read, trying to dispel the notion that she was being lazy.

Twenty minutes in, Caroline was guffawing, hoping that her neighbours couldn't hear her. The author had the rare gift of bringing a lump to the reader's throat and then a hoot of laughter, all on the same page. And how superbly she wrote about teenage angst and loneliness, especially if you were gay. A book Caroline would be adding to her list of recommended reading that she often gave to parents and young adults.

She read until her eyelids drooped from the effect of the painkillers and she fell into a drowsy half-sleep. The ping of a text awakened her.

> Hi Caro, I won't make it to the next reunion night. Dad's had a fall and I've to go to Kerry to try and sort things out for Mam. M x

Aw, she thought, disappointed. She'd been planning to ask Mick for a lift into Neary's where the gathering with their Abu Dhabi pals was being held.

She scrolled up with her thumb to the call icon.

'Hi, it's me. Sorry to hear about your dad. Is he OK?' she asked when Mick answered the phone.

'He's crocked his knee and sprained his wrist and he's as grumpy as hell. Poor Mam's at her wits' end. She's hardly able to look after him when he's in the whole of his health.' Mick sounded totally fraught.

'That's bad luck. At least you can work from home, so you'll be able to work down there,' Caroline comforted.

'Yeah, that's a plus I suppose but Dervla's losing it and giving me guff about having to go down to "the back end of nowhere" to quote herself. So then I lost it and roared at her, because I was up to ninety, and now the atmosphere's so icy the North Pole would be warm in comparison,' Mick confided. 'And I completely understand, of course, and I know she gets carsick on long journeys but I'm not leaving her up here on her own, here in the apartment, especially being pregnant. Does life ever get any easier, Caroline?' he asked dejectedly.

'Tell me about it. I fell last week and tore my rotator cuff and am absolutely banjaxed. I'm going around like the Hunchback of Notre-Dame, in a sling. It's a damn nuisance.'

'That's a real bummer. Are you OK?' Mick sounded concerned.

'Yeah, it's just trying to do everything with my left hand and being home from work is doing my head in.'

'That's rough.'

'Not as rough as your situation,' Caroline said. 'When are you going?'

'I'd go this evening if I could but Dervla's got a hospital appointment in two days' time so I've to hang on for that. It's just unfortunate timing.'

'She could stay with me and I could bring her,' Caroline offered. 'We could get a taxi.'

'God no, I wouldn't impose her on you but thanks all the same. I *really* appreciate it. You're a pal.'

'Look, why don't I WhatsApp you a photo of the bedroom she'd be in. If she'd do a few light bits and pieces for me – not heavy-duty cleaning, I've a woman who comes once a week – I could give Dervla a few bob and that would give you some leeway with your parents. Do you think she'd be up for it?'

'I don't know, to be honest, but I could put it to her. Are you sure, Caroline? She's all over the place with her hormones and as moody as hell.'

'I deal with lots of moody teenagers.' Caroline laughed. 'And, God love her, she's got it hard, coming home to Ireland where she knows nobody, and being pregnant to boot.'

'If you're absolutely sure, I'll say it to her and I'll be forever in your debt if she says yes,' Mick said doubtfully.

'I'm going in to take the photos now. Give me a minute and tell her there's a TV in the room as well as an ensuite,' Caroline said before hanging up.

She hauled herself off the lounger and went into the guest room, which she had decorated in shades of lilac and cream with a deep pile grey carpet underfoot. A comfortable grey velvet chair dressed with lilac cushions sat under the big window that overlooked the garden. Fitted cream wardrobes lined one wall and a double bed with a lilac throw and masses of fluffy pillows lined the opposite one. It was a room that was calming to the spirit, Maggie had once told her, and she loved sleeping in it when she stayed over.

Caroline managed to take a selection of photos and sent them off to Mick. Ten minutes later she got a text:

She said she'd stay, are u ABSOLUTELY sure?

ABSOLUTELY

Caroline texted back with a smiling emoji, suddenly wondering whether her impulsive, ill-thought-out invitation was one she'd come to regret.

CHAPTER THIRTY-FOUR

Caroline/Mick/Dervla

Caroline saw Mick's car reverse up the driveway. He'd phoned for her to open the gate. She stood at the door to greet them and to get a look at her new lodger. Mick looked weary to his bones when he got stiffly out of the car and, on the other side, a small, plump, blonde teen got out, her pretty face sullen and antagonistic as she stared around her before her glance rested on Caroline.

'Hi, I'm Caroline. You're very welcome,' Caroline said warmly and was rewarded with a muttered 'Thanks'. Mick was taking Dervla's luggage out of the car and, at the amount of it, Caroline wondered was she staying for a year.

'Dervla doesn't travel light,' Mick joked.

'I *need* my stuff, Dad. You never know how to dress here. It's freezing and scorching all in the one day.' Her withering looks and response caused Caroline's heart to sink. It must have been the effects of the painkillers that had influenced her to make her offer of assistance. Facing the actual reality of what awaited her was somewhat disconcerting.

'Come in, let me show you to your room, and make yourself at home in it,' she invited.

'You *are* in the wars, Caro! How long will you need the sling?' Mick was careful hugging her.

'A couple of weeks at least. There's so much I can't do it's such a nuisance,' she said over her shoulder as she led the way to the guest room and opened the door.

'Here you go, Dervla. Why don't you settle in and then come and have tea with us in the kitchen?'

'I only drink green tea or coffee,' Dervla responded but she looked pleased as she took in the pretty bedroom, which would be her refuge for the next few days.

'Me too, although I allow myself one coffee a day,' Caroline said lightly. 'Here's your wardrobe and there's your ensuite.' She indicated the door into the small, marble-tiled bathroom with a walk-in shower. 'There's a bath in the house bathroom if you prefer one.'

Mick placed her luggage onto the chair and remarked, 'Bigger and brighter than the bedroom in Kerry. Smart choice, Derv.'

'Yeah, well, I love Gran and Granddad but I don't like where they live,' Dervla said defensively. 'It's so far away from everything.'

'You liked your summer holidays there when it was too hot to stay in Abu Dhabi. You liked helping out on the farm,' he reminded her.

'I was a kid then. And I wasn't expecting a kid of my own, Dad.' Dervla looked at him as though he'd just crawled out from under a rock.

'True. Settle in, we'll be in the kitchen,' Mick said resignedly.

*

'I can't do anything right. I can't say anything right. It's a nightmare. Are you sure about having her to stay? My brother and sister-in-law are here but she's adamant she doesn't want to stay with them. Valerie's a bit judgemental and her cousins are much older,' he said when they stood in the kitchen waiting for the kettle to boil.

'Could your brother not go down to your parents?' Caroline asked, taking some mugs out of the dishwasher.

'I was let know in no uncertain terms by Valerie that it was my turn to muck in with the parents, having in her words "got off scot-free" all the years I was living abroad. I think Tim was a bit embarrassed. She's very much the boss in that household.'

'I guess I was lucky I never had any in-laws, except the mother-in-law from hell and fortunately she's no longer with us.' Caroline popped a green teabag into a mug for herself and teabags into the pot for him. Mick poured the boiling water.

'Valerie always enjoyed her trips to the Emirates with the kids when they were small, loved lounging around the pool while our maid took care of the little ones.' Mick grimaced. 'I always gave Tina, our maid, extra money when they went home. She more than deserved it. When I look back on it, Valerie was actually a rude, superior, racist woman. I had to call her out on it a few times when she expected Tina to do way more than was reasonable and was impolite and discourteous to her.'

They were sitting at the table chatting when Dervla made her appearance. 'Dad, can you Revolut me some money for extra credit on my phone, for the Internet?'

'Please,' he reminded her.

'Don't worry about the Internet. I'll give you the password for here and you can use it, no problem,' Caroline assured her.

'Thanks,' Dervla said and walked out of the kitchen to go back to her bedroom.

'She'll probably live in her room, if you're lucky.' Mick frowned. 'Are you sure—'

'Don't ask me again. Now get going so you'll miss the rush-hour traffic and give my best to your parents,' Caroline said briskly, standing up. 'I'll make sure she FaceTimes you after the hospital appointment.'

'Thanks, Caroline. I really appreciate—'

'Feck off out of here, will ya?' she commanded and he laughed.

'Do you need me to do a shop or anything?' Mick asked. 'You can give me a list, I saw a Supervalu over on the Howth Road.'

'No, I'm grand thanks. Shona, my godchild, did a shop for me when she was over. We can stroll up to Nolan's to get groceries and Dervla can choose what she likes.'

'I've given her extra money.'

'Mick, will you stop fussing? It's only for a couple of days. It'll be fine. Dervla: come and say goodbye to your dad,' she called, and there was firmness in her tone that ensured that the teen came down the hall pretty quickly.

'See ya, Dad, tell Granddad I hope he gets better soon and tell Gran I was asking for her.' Now that her father was actually leaving, Caroline could see the girl's stroppiness melt away and uncertainty cross her pretty face.

'We'll be fine. It will be great for me to have Dervla here to help me out. Safe travels, Mick,' Caroline told him as he hugged his daughter tightly and Caroline saw her lower lip wobble.

He gave a toot on the horn as he drove out the gate. Caroline and Dervla looked at each other.

'I've never been pregnant, sadly, but I believe the tiredness is horrendous, so why don't I give you the Wi-Fi password and you can go and rest yourself for a while. Then we can have a natter about your wages.'

'My wages?' She looked surprised. 'You *really* want me to work?'

'That was the agreement, wasn't it? You staying with me instead of going to Kerry. Answering some emails, chopping up veg, cutting my meat. Things I can't do.'

'I didn't think I'd have to do anything,' Dervla said sulkily.

'I'll pay you the minimum wage of course, Dervla, plus a few extra euro. I'm sure it will come in handy for you.' Caroline stared at her, taken aback by her attitude. 'We'll start properly tomorrow. Get used to being here today and we'll take it one step at a time from tomorrow. OK? And we'll go shopping for food you like.'

'Whatevs.'

'Are you hungry now? Help yourself to what's in the fridge. I thought we might have a chicken kebab tonight if you'd like. I'll marinade the chicken now.'

'Are you serving toum with it? Tina, our maid, use to make a brilliant one.'

'Well, unfortunately we have no maids here and as you can see I'm a bit afflicted so, if you want to make it, fire ahead. I have the ingredients, otherwise we'll just have to use garlic mayo,' Caroline said calmly. 'If you would just get me the casserole dish in the press over the oven that would be great. I can't reach and keep the door open with one hand.'

Silently Dervla opened the press door and took out the casserole dish. 'Do you need anything else?'

'Could you chop an onion and some peppers and peel some garlic please?' Caroline pulled an onion and a clove of garlic from her vegetable basket under the island. 'I'll manage everything else,' she said, placing a chopping board and sharp knife on the island beside the vegetables. 'Give them a rinse first,' she said before getting the peppers from the fridge.

Dervla's eyes widened in dismay.

'Haven't you ever chopped veg before?' Caroline asked, surprised.

'Um, we had servants in Abu Dhabi and Dad cooks here,' the teenager muttered, rinsing the veg under the tap.

'OK! Well, try not to chop your fingers and you don't have to be too particular. Try and keep everything the same size.' Caroline handed Dervla the knife, hoping her charge wouldn't cut herself.

Gusty sighs and then a frigid silence accompanied the awkward preparation of the veg. After the onion had slid across the counter and tears began to stream after it was retrieved and cut in half, Caroline could contain herself no longer.

'Look, you go and have a rest and settle in. The Wi-Fi password's on the box beside the TV. We'll have dinner around six. There's some crackers, cheese, cold meats and grapes in the fridge, if you'd like something to nibble on to keep you going until dinner.'

'I'm OK,' sniffed Dervla, making her escape as fast as she could.

Caroline watched her go, half exasperated, half sorry for her. She slowly managed to slice the onion into haphazard chunks with her left hand.

By the time she had the chicken marinating, and had

swallowed some painkillers, Caroline was ready for a nap herself. She manoeuvred herself into as comfortable a position as she could with her injured arm resting on a cushion on the sofa. She hoped that her new lodger's attitude might improve after she had settled in, because right at this moment Caroline was massively regretting her impulsive invitation to put Mick's daughter up.

CHAPTER THIRTY-FIVE

Dervla

Dervla connected her iPad to Caroline's Wi-Fi and lay on the bed, scrolling through her social media. Most of her friends from Abu Dhabi were spread throughout Europe to escape the sweltering Emirates' summer heat. She wondered where Amir had gone this year. Last year he'd spent the summer in Sardinia. Dervla had thought he loved her. He'd been so charming and attentive, much more so than the other boys in their group.

Amir was nineteen, divinely handsome with limpid brown eyes and lashes to die for. All the girls in her group flirted with him but he'd paid her extra attention. Dervla thought he was being kind, because she was the youngest of them, but one weekend after an afternoon spent swimming and lazing on the Cornice beach, they had all gone to Chakh Kebab and her card wouldn't work. She'd been mortified and had been about to ring her mom when Amir had tapped his card on the machine and said, 'It's sorted.'

He was the wealthiest of their group, a third cousin of a

member of the royal family, he'd boasted, and he always seemed to have plenty of money.

'I'll pay you back,' she assured him, knowing she only had enough dirhams left in her purse to pay for her taxi.

'It's my gift to you.' He smiled at her and she'd basked in the warmth of it.

'I think Amir likes you,' Cesca, her best friend, remarked enviously when they travelled home in a taxi after their meal.

'No, he likes Karla Malone better than anyone, he's always putting his arm around her.'

'You mean he's always sneaking off somewhere with her so she can give him a BJ. Doesn't mean he *likes* her,' scoffed Cesca. 'She's gobby in more ways than one. Would you give him a BJ if he asked?'

'I suppose.' Dervla eyed her friend. 'Would you?'

Cesca made a face. 'I don't really like doing it, do you? I don't know why they like it.' She and Dervla had practised many times, sucking on lollypops before actually preforming the act for real, but had both agreed privately after several encounters with the boys in their group that they didn't like doing it. Unfortunately it was expected and, if they wanted to stay with the older group it was a chore that had to be done, occasionally.

Dervla had lost her virginity in an awkward fumbling in a Dutch boy's bedroom. He had a free house. Her parents had thought she was at school. It was painful and messy and the Dutch boy never asked her to his home again. Cesca had fared no better with the son of her mother's friend. They were relieved to have shaken off the shackles of their unwanted virginity but couldn't understand what all the fuss about sex was.

'Karla and that big gob of hers has given BJs to half of the

Dhabi. Did you hear her saying she was going back to England to audition for *Love Island*? With that weird accent of hers, she'd need a translator,' Dervla quipped and the two girls had burst into giggles in the back seat of the taxi. They were always comfortable in each other's company and could drop the faux-sophisticated façade they embraced when they were out with their group.

It was more than a BJ Amir had wanted, Dervla thought sadly, lying on Caroline's guest bed. The endearments he'd murmured, kissing her, cuddling her when he came to pick her up to drive to Yas Island to meet the others. Cesca had not been allowed go. Her Portuguese parents were quite strict and she'd stayed out later than her curfew and was grounded for two weekends.

When Amir had called to collect her and found that Sally – Dervla's mother – and her partner were at an Irish Society bash, and the maid was on her day off, he'd suggested they take a swim in the pool and do a line. Dervla had never done cocaine before. She'd smoked weed a few times but it made her sick.

She'd watched him inhale the line of white dust from the kitchen counter top and then he'd rolled up a hundred dirham note and handed it to her. With his brown eyes melting into hers and not wanting to appear unsophisticated, she'd copied him and felt an exquisite rush of euphoria envelope her.

'Wow!' she'd exclaimed, astonished.

'Good, isn't it?' Amir enthused, setting up another line each.

After the next hit, they'd ripped off their clothes and dived into the pool laughing their heads off as they splashed each other. Dervla had never felt so happy in all of her sixteen years.

When he'd pressed her up against the cool tiled wall she'd returned his kisses ardently and when he'd pulled off her bikini bottom and his speedos and entered her the pleasure had been overwhelming.

Later, when she'd come down off the high, on the beach at Yas Island, she'd whispered to him. 'Next time bring a condom, I don't want to get pregnant.'

'For sure,' he'd murmured back. 'For sure.'

He had worn a condom the next time she was home alone but by then it was too late. She was already pregnant, although she did not know it.

Tears prickled behind Dervla's eyelids as she remembered how cold and cruel Amir had turned when, a month later, she'd told him she thought she might be pregnant.

'How do you know it's mine? You fucking slutty Irish girls give it away to anyone.' His face was contorted with anger, his eyes black beads of sneery distain.

Dervla had been stunned, almost speechless. 'It . . . it *is* yours, Amir,' she stammered. 'I don't sleep around.'

'Not what I've heard. Get an abortion and don't talk to me again,' he snapped before walking away. The pain of her heart, sliced in bits at his callous rejection, was nothing to the terror she'd felt. Who could she turn to? What would she do?

'OMG!' shrieked Cesca, horrified, when Dervla confided her sorry plight after school the next day. They were sprawled on Dervla's bed. 'My parents would *kill* me if I came home and told them that.' Cesca's parents, both doctors, were Catholics and went to Mass every Sunday. If they knew how she behaved with boys she would be sent straight back to her grandmother in Lisbon. 'What are you going to do?'

'I don't know,' sobbed Dervla. 'I might save my parents the bother and kill myself.'

'Oh no, don't do that,' Cesca exclaimed. 'What did Amir say? Have you told him?'

'He's mugged me off, said that how did I know it was his, that us slutty Irish girls gave it away to everyone,' she said dully.

Her friend's sharp inhalation of breath as Cesca's hand went to her mouth in horror made her burst into more anguished sobs.

'Don't cry, Derv,' she pleaded. 'Look we better get you a test to be *absolutely* sure. We need to look as old as we can, and you need to wear a wedding ring.' Cesca took charge. She was always good in a crisis.

'Where will I get a wedding ring?' Dervla asked, panicked. 'Sex outside marriage is illegal, *and* I'm underage. They won't give me a test. They could report me.' Paranoia crept in.

'Just turn a ring around so the band is on the top of your finger, it doesn't have to be gold, silver's fine.' Cesca rooted through Dervla's jewellery and found a pretty silver Pandora shooting stars ring. 'This is perfect,' she approved, sliding the ring onto Dervla's wedding finger. 'Borrow one of your mom's bags – they look more grown up than yours. And you know the way she wears a pashmina draped around her shoulders, do that too. And wear sunglasses. We'll go to the pharmacy in the Mall. It's big.'

They'd set about preparing Dervla for the trip to the pharmacy. She certainly didn't look sixteen, they agreed, looking at her appearance in the long mirror in her mother's walk-in closet. Wearing tailored black jeans, a white, high-collared, long-sleeved Tommy Hilfiger shirt with a multi-coloured Ferragamo silk scarf knotted loosely at her neck and a Gucci tote slung over her shoulder, her eyes hidden behind her sunglasses, she looked like a young woman in her twenties. 'We better get going, Cesca, Mom will be back from her tennis over in the Country Club, in time for dinner.' Dervla's heart was thumping so fast she felt she might faint.

They walked to the end of the street and hailed a passing taxi on the main road. Cesca, noticing that Dervla's hands were trembling as they sat in the back, rubbed her arm reassuringly. 'Maybe it's a false alarm because you're worried and it's stopping the period from coming,' she murmured. 'Stay calm.'

An hour later, back at the house, the test kit secured, Sally's clothes safely back in the closet, Dervla thought she was going to puke when she held the wand that said **Pregnant** in unmistakable black letters.

'My life is so over, Cesca,' Dervla whispered as she heard her mother's car crunch into the gravel drive.

It was when she'd refused scrambled eggs and bolted from the breakfast table, puking in the downstairs loo one morning a week later, that her mother began to suspect something was going on and, after another puking episode two mornings later, Sally had followed her into her bedroom and produced a pregnancy test.

'*Mom!*' protested Dervla, flushing a bright pink before turning pale.

'I hope I'm wrong. I *really* hope I'm wrong, Derv,' Sally said grimly. 'Mariam Gamal's mother told me the other day that you were seen with Amir Al Mazroui and his crowd. He's got a bad name. When did you and Cesca start hanging around with that lot?' Sally demanded.

'We only go to Yas or the Corniche with them. Loads of us go,' she muttered.

'Did you have sex with someone? Are you pregnant? Don't lie to me.' Sally's blue eyes bored into hers, sharp as lasers, her Botoxed forehead unable to frown.

What is the point of lying? Dervla had asked herself, standing in front of her irate mother. The morning sickness was a dead giveaway. Her boobs were starting to swell like balloons. She wasn't showing in her tummy yet but that would come as surely as the sun rose every morning.

'Yes, I am pregnant. I'm sorry, Mom, really sorry.' Her voice faltered when she saw the expression on her mother's face.

'Ah Jesus, Dervla. Ah *Jesus*!' Sally swore. 'Your dad is going to give me hell for allowing you too much freedom. We better arrange for an abortion. Say nothing to your father. We'll have to go abroad. I know a place in Spain.'

Relief had swept through Dervla. An abortion would be so simple. Wipe the slate clean. Pretend it had never happened. Her dad would never know.

Two days later her sister Ciara FaceTimed her from Nice. 'Mom told me your news. She said she's taking you to Spain. She wanted me to pretend you were coming to see me. I said no. Derv, you *have* to tell Dad. It's not fair to keep it from him. He loves you. He's really good when you're in a fix and you're in a big one.'

'I can't, Ciara. He'll be gutted,' Dervla protested.

'Well then, you're going to have to tell him a whole load of lies about going to Spain in termtime. When I said no to Mom she freaked and told me to mind my own business and said she was sorry she'd told me. But you *are* my business, Derv. You're my little sis and I love you and I'll tell Dad for you, if you like. Please don't go behind his back,' Ciara entreated.

In her heart of hearts Dervla knew her sister was right. It would be a really mean thing to do to their father. What she couldn't face was his disappointment in her. Mick loved her: he was always so glad when she went to stay in his small, two-bed apartment that he'd moved into when he and her mom had divorced.

They had fun together going bowling or to their favourite cinema. Sometimes they went camping in Al Ain, lying under the millions of stars glittering in the blackest sky she'd ever seen, so vast it seemed unending. Dervla loved that it was their special place. Just her and her dad.

He would be disappointed for sure but even more devastated if she had an abortion behind his back and he ever found out.

'Will I tell him?' her sister pressed.

'No,' Dervla said sadly. 'No. I'll tell him myself.'

Mick hadn't shouted or cursed when she told him. He'd said nothing: just hugged her tightly while she'd sobbed against his shoulder, drenching the crisp blue shirt he was wearing.

'Did he force himself on you, this chap?' he asked.

'No, Dad,' she wept. She wasn't going to say she was high on coke when it happened.

'Well then, we should go and talk to this young man and his parents. You're underage, Dervla. What age is he?'

'Dad, no,' Dervla exclaimed heatedly. 'He's a third cousin of one of the princes, he said, and you know what they're like. They'll make it my fault. It would cause trouble for us. He's saying it's not his. But it is. He told me I've never to speak to him again.'

'Ah, Dervla.' His eyes flashed with anger. 'I'd like to get my hands on him for five minutes. Do you *want* an abortion?' he asked in a resigned, weary tone that tore at her heartstrings.

'Yes, I think so.' She started crying again, more with relief that now both her parents knew of her predicament.

'OK then. But I'm just going to say one thing. When your mother found out she was pregnant with you – a pregnancy we hadn't planned – she considered having one. I'm glad she didn't because I wouldn't have the most loving, amazing, wonderful daughter in the world.' His arms had tightened around her and she'd felt his tears on her cheek. 'We can work this out together, you and me, if you change your mind.'

Later that evening sitting out on her dad's balcony, she'd gone into her social media. Shazza Burnley had messaged her.

> Amir's just told me you're up the duff and claiming it's his, he's saying bad things about you. Just thought you should know.

Dervla's cheeks flamed. She checked Amir's Insta and all his other accounts. He'd blocked her. So had half their set. Just like that she'd been wiped from their lives. Even if she had the abortion, those people would still know Amir had got her pregnant and that she'd had a termination. If Cesca's parents found out, she wouldn't be allowed to pal around with her. Dervla was in a no-win situation.

OK thanks Shazza she answered back with trembling fingers. Shazza was nice enough. It was through palling around with her that she and Cesca had got with Amir and his crowd. Shazza's sister Emma had dated Amir for a while before leaving Abu Dhabi to work in their father's office in Jordan.

Dervla wished from the bottom of her heart that *she* could leave Abu Dhabi and work in Jordan and never have to see any of her so-called friends again.

She'd heard her parents arguing about her. Her mother shouting that an abortion was the best route to take, especially as Dervla was underage and Amir would not accept that he was the father.

Mick had retorted harshly. 'Typical of you. The short-term solution is the way you've dealt with every problem we've ever had. What about Dervla's peace of mind when she's older? What if she has regrets—'

'She *won't* have regrets: no one wants an unwanted baby.'

She'd been unwanted by her mother, Dervla knew. Sally was forever saying that having Dervla had ruined her figure, pretending it was a joke, but Dervla knew her mother meant it. Sally had been much stricter with Dervla's older siblings. They would never have been allowed go to Yas with a crowd like the ones Dervla mixed with.

Once, after Ciara and Conor had left home to work abroad, Dervla had heard her mother say to her friend, sipping drinks by her new partner's pool, that becoming a mother again in her forties had been the biggest shock of her life. There was a ten-year gap between Conor and Dervla and an eight-year one between her and Ciara.

When her parents' marriage ended, Dervla had thought she was so lucky living mostly with her mom and Faisal. Apart from having a bigger swimming pool and her own bedroom with an ensuite, she had freedom. Far more than Ciara and Conor had had and certainly more than Cesca had. Now Dervla realised with deep sadness that giving her freedom to do more or less as she liked, socially, gave Sally the chance to do the same. Her mother often changed outfits three times a day to go to various events. Apart from enquiring whether Dervla had done her homework, Sally wasn't really around much. Dervla mostly ate whatever meal Faisal's housekeeper prepared.

Sally was far more concerned how Dervla's pregnancy would ruin *her* life, rather than her daughter's. It was this more than anything that convinced Dervla that it was her father, as always, who would be her protector and champion.

'Dad?' she'd asked, when Sally had marched off in a strop. 'If I don't have an abortion, what will I do?'

'Come home with me to Ireland. I've been thinking I'd like to go home for a while anyway. Your grandparents are getting old: I'd like to spend time with them.'

'Live in *Kerry*!' she'd exclaimed, horrified. Her grandparents' farm was in the country; there was only a small village close by.

'No, no. We'd live in Dublin in our house,' he'd laughed. 'I can work from anywhere there's Wi-Fi, don't forget.'

'Oh! Phew!' Dervla liked Dublin. Her friend Mona Saleh's mother was from Dublin and when Sally came home from the Gulf in the summer they would spend a lot of time with the Salehs, who also summered in Ireland. Mick and Sally had a house in Drumcondra and it was Dervla's summer home. She could have her baby, get it adopted and start afresh back in Abu Dhabi – well, maybe France with Ciara, she thought.

'Dad, I'll come home with you and have the baby and get it adopted,' she'd said and had seen a look of relief cross his tired face.

The relief on her mother's face when Dervla told her of

her decision had been for herself, Dervla knew. No pregnant daughter to worry about and no grandchild, either. Adoption would solve *that* problem.

Leaving Cesca had been the worst. They'd gone to the Lake Park to feed the swans and say their goodbyes. Only Cesca knew the real reason Dervla was going home to Ireland. Cesca too would be leaving the Emirates to spend the summer in Portugal but she'd be back in the autumn. Dervla wouldn't.

'Look, we can Snapchat and WhatsApp every day,' Cesca said comfortingly as they leaned against the green railings and threw frozen peas to the swans floating serenely past. It was one of their favourite activities, not that they'd let on to the others, who would view it as childish and uncool.

'Do you think your mom and dad might let you come to visit us in Ireland again this year?' Dervla asked eagerly.

'I don't see why not. They don't know you're preggers. It would be great, wouldn't it? We had such fun the last time. The Academy was cool.'

'Not sure if I'll be going to the Academy, I guess my bump will be showing by then, but we can go to McGowans. Just don't forget your fake ID.'

'I won't,' Cesca assured her.

'If you hear anything about Amir let me know, won't you?' Dervla's lip wobbled and tears slid down her cheeks.

'Sure. Of course I will and I'll let you know all about Gobby Malone and whether she gets on *Love Island*,' Cesca promised. Dervla managed a giggle at the mention of Karla.

'Shazza's keeping in touch too. She's kind. She Snapchatted me at the weekend to say she was at the airport. Her mam and her younger sister were with her. They're going back to

Manchester for the summer. They left a week early. Her school's not finished yet.'

'I have to fly to Lisbon by myself. Mãe's coming for the end of July and August. She couldn't get any more time off this year.'

'Oh, your poor mom. It will be scorching here in July.'

'Will your mom go home again this summer?'

'If Dad's gonna be there I don't know and I don't care. They had a big row about me. All she thinks about is herself.' Dervla flung her last handful of peas into the water and watched glumly as they were gobbled up.

'Let's go get some *aish el saraya*. It's going to be a while before you taste it again,' Cesca suggested. The mention of their favourite sweet treat almost lifted Dervla's spirits.

'Good thinking. Who knows when I'll be back in the Dhabi again? I hope it doesn't make me feel pukey, though. Maybe I'll just have baklava. Goodbye, swans,' Dervla said sadly. 'It was nice knowing you.'

Dervla had been almost buoyant on the flight to Ireland, just after Christmas, until she discovered she and Mick would be living in an apartment in Drumcondra until the tenants in their house vacated it in July when the lease was up. July had come and they had refused to leave, because of a shortage of rental properties in Dublin. So now Mick was in the process of trying to persuade them to go, which was causing him enormous stress. Dervla's bedroom in the two-bed apartment was small and she just wanted to get back to the roomy, high-ceiling bedroom that had been hers in the house in Drumcondra. Half her stuff was still in cases on top of the wardrobe in the apartment.

And now, months later, here she was in a strange woman's house in Dublin who she was having to *slave* for, feeling sick and scared, wondering had she made the second-biggest mistake of her life. Tears dripped down her cheeks and Dervla buried her face in the pillow to muffle her sobs.

CHAPTER THIRTY-SIX

Caroline/Dervla

'Why didn't you ring me?' Maggie said indignantly down the line. 'Shona said you're in a real heap.'

'Stop fussing, Maggie,' Caroline replied, trying to stick the phone under her ear so she could butter a slice of toast.

'I'm coming up to collect you: you're coming to stay with me,' her friend declared.

'I can't, nice and all as it would be.' Caroline gave up on the toast and held the phone properly.

'Why not?' Maggie demanded.

'I have a guest staying with me for a few days so she's going to help out,' Caroline explained, although the helping out bit was something of an exaggeration seeing as Dervla had yet to make an appearance and it was ten-thirty in the morning.

'Who?'

'Nosey parker,' admonished Caroline.

'Sorry, Caro. I didn't mean to—'

'I'm joking. It's Mick's daughter. She's staying with me for a few days. Mick's dad took a tumble and he's had to go down to Kerry to sort out home help and stuff.'

'Oh right, OK. But do NOT struggle there on your own, I mean it now,' Maggie said firmly.

'OK, bossy boots. What's happening with you?'

'Loads to tell you but I'd prefer doing it face to face. Michael's coming home on shore leave next week, so I'll be up to see him. The girls have a barbie planned, as you know, so why don't I collect you? Shona said you were coming.'

'No! That's putting you out of your way to come over here and then to drive to Ranelagh. Dev and Luke will bring me,' Caroline assured her.

'Oh! That makes sense I suppose.'

'It does.'

'But then either Dev or Luke won't be able to drink. It's usually you that drives,' Maggie pointed out.

'We'll manage, stop worrying about it.' Caroline broke off a piece of toast with her afflicted hand and grimaced as a dart of pain shot along her inner arm.

'Right, I better get going. I'm having a Zoom with my editor at eleven. This Zoom thing is such a gift. I don't have to get dressed up and drive up to Dublin. I had a swim at eight and it was divine but my hair needs attending to and I should slap on a bit of lippy. You can go feral down in the country. My roots are as grey as a badger,' Maggie said ruefully.

'Put a bit of that root spray on them. It's a lifesaver. Good luck with the Zoom and thanks for the offer to come and stay. You're the best,' Caroline said before hanging up.

She strained her ears to see if she could hear anything from the guest room and felt a frisson of relief when she thought she heard the sound of running water. Dervla had appeared in the kitchen the previous evening when Caroline had called to say dinner was ready. Her red-rimmed eyes were streaked with mascara.

'Are you OK?' Caroline had asked.

'Fine,' muttered the teenager. 'Could I take a tray to my room?'

'Sure,' Caroline agreed. 'Could you just do me a favour and cut up my chicken for me first? I can't hold a knife and a fork. One or the other, unfortunately.'

'Oh! Yeah. Sorry, I forgot you're injured.' Dervla had cut the chicken and roast peppers into pieces. 'Will I cut the wrap in half?'

'That would be great. Thanks so much. Help yourself to dressings. There's some Magnums in the freezer if you'd like one for afters.'

'OK. Thanks.' The tone was a little less surly and Dervla helped herself from the dishes on the table, putting her plate and a glass of milk on the tray Caroline handed her.

'See ya,' she mumbled and scurried back to her room.

Caroline had knocked on her door at 10pm and said she was going to bed but for Dervla to help herself to anything if she felt like a snack.

'Thanks,' came the response and an hour later, propped up with pillows in her own bed, Caroline heard movement in the kitchen and was relieved that her guest had emerged from her burrow and wouldn't starve. She'd sent Mick a text.

Hope your parents are OK. All fine this end. Night. C

> Thanks, Caro. Dad's a bit banjaxed but they were delighted to see me. Hope to get assistance for them up and running. I can't thank you enough. M

Caroline was filling the dishwasher when Dervla walked into the kitchen the next day. 'Morning. I hope you slept well,' she greeted her young guest, who was wearing black leggings and a Ralph Lauren pink, white and black sweatshirt. 'You look lovely.'

'Thanks, I slept OK,' Dervla said awkwardly.

'There's cereal, porridge and fruit or you can have eggs, boiled, scrambled or fried and toast or brown bread,' Caroline offered.

'I don't eat much in the morning. I was em . . . a bit pukey for the last while. I'll just have toast if that's OK.'

'Have whatever you want and when you're finished let's go to a supermarket nearby and stock up.'

'I'll only be staying until the weekend: Dad hopes to be home by then,' Dervla reminded her.

'I know but we can get a few bits and pieces. It's not far. I'm just going to my home office to make a few calls. Would you help me pull the duvet up over my bed before we go?'

'Sure,' Dervla agreed unenthusiastically.

'And after we've done our shopping, we'll sit down and discuss your work schedule. Your *light* work schedule,' Caroline said, crisply marching out of the kitchen.

God she's lazy, she thought, disgruntled, closing the door of her small home office behind her. Having maids certainly did not encourage teens to muck in and do housework but surely Dervla could see how hamstrung Caroline was. Was she that self-absorbed? Poor Mick certainly had his hands full with his youngest daughter.

An hour later, duvet straightened on the bed, they walked along Kincora Road towards Nolan's supermarket in silence. Dervla had ear buds jammed in her ears. It suited Caroline, who was trying not to be disheartened at not being able to drive, work or live her life as normal. Who could believe that one minute she was walking along, as she did every day, and the next her independence was so severely diminished, her pain so incapacitating, that she wanted to burst into tears of self-pity and frustration. *You can cry when Dervla's gone back to Mick's*, Caroline promised herself.

'I'll push the trolley: I can lean on it,' she said to Dervla when they got to the supermarket's entrance.

'Sorry, what?' Dervla took one of her ear buds out.

'I'll push the trolley,' Caroline repeated, trying not to show her irritation.

'Fine.' The teenager's disinterested tone made Caroline want to slap her. *Stop it*, she reproved herself silently. She wasn't usually so irritable. She'd had lots of experience dealing with surly teens at work. The pain, loss of sleep and feeling out of control certainly was making her grumpy.

'If you see anything you like put it in.' Caroline hung her shopping bag on the trolley and manoeuvred it out of its row, leading the way along the first aisle. She stopped at the pasta section.

'Anything here?' she enquired.

'Um ... I like macaroni cheese.'

'Chuck in some macaroni so. How about rice?'

'Basmati's nice with chicken korma or biryani.'

'Go for it.' Caroline nodded.

They meandered around to the next aisle and came to the fizzy drinks and chocolate section. Caroline paused and looked at Dervla. 'I suppose we better go easy here: you need to have a reasonably healthy diet, I expect.'

'I love chocolate,' Dervla said longingly.

'One bar, perhaps. I'm sure they've told you about gestational diabetes,' Caroline said sympathetically.

'Yeah, the doctor I saw in the Rotunda told me to watch it. She's the one I'll be seeing tomorrow.'

'Throw in a bar. You can have a couple of squares a day; that shouldn't be too much.'

Dervla plucked a bar of Lindor milk chocolate from the display. 'Are you having one?' she asked.

'Hmmm, it can be a bit of a trigger for me: I'm just coming out of a recent relapse with bulimia. I might give it a pass today,' Caroline said ruefully.

Dervla's head whipped around in astonishment. '*Really?*' she exclaimed. 'But you're ol— em . . . eh.'

'Old,' Caroline finished, amused.

'No . . . I don't mean. I mean . . .'

'It's not just a young person's disease,' Caroline said, moving around to the next aisle. 'Eating disorders can affect any age group.'

'I didn't know.'

'Why would you? I'm an alcoholic too, thankfully sober for many years,' Caroline announced cheerfully, reaching up to get some McCambridge's sugar-and-yeast-free brown bread.

Dervla's jaw dropped as she digested *this* piece of information.

'We all have our problems,' Caroline remarked. *That will give you something to think about.*

'Does Dad know?' She gazed at Caroline in astonishment.

'Indeed he does. When I went to Abu Dhabi all those years ago, I was recovering from alcoholism, an eating disorder, a failed suicide attempt and a failed marriage. He was a very kind friend to me.'

'Dad *is* very kind,' Dervla affirmed, as they headed towards the deli and meat counters.

'He is. He took me under his wing and I'll always be very grateful to him. I'm so glad we stayed in touch down the years and I'm delighted to repay his kindness in some way by having you to stay,' Caroline said, putting some chicken breasts and thighs into the trolley.

'I didn't know you were such good friends. He knows so many people. I've only one really good friend,' Dervla confided in a moment of weakness.

'One good friend is worth a thousand fake ones. Why don't we go into the Bistro and have a cup of tea? Maybe you could eat something now and I'll tell you of some of the things I got up to with your parents in Abu Dhabi. We had some great laughs.'

This elicited a smile from her young charge and Caroline saw how pretty and youthful she was behind the surly, bored façade.

'I *am* a bit hungry now,' Dervla admitted.

'I might even eat something myself.' Caroline winked and Dervla gave a delightful, shy little giggle, which was music to Caroline's ears.

CHAPTER THIRTY-SEVEN

Shona/Terry

Shona stared out the window of the Dart as it clacked its way out of Booterstown Dart station. The tide was in. Dublin Bay glinted ethereally in the early Saturday morning sun, silver effervescences dancing atop the white tipped waves as they embraced the shore. She could see the church spires of Dun Laoghaire in the distance. She'd arranged to meet Terry at the fountain in the People's Park. It was handy for her to take the Dart and meet him on the Southside so he wouldn't have to drive too far.

So this was it, she thought as they sped towards Blackrock. A day of reckoning? A day of reconciliation? It was up to her. Her father had tried many times to make amends, to put the past behind them, but she had dismissed them all. Her siblings, her mother even, had all moved on with their lives. She alone had held onto her hurt, pain, anger and grudges. What did that say about her? *Not a lot*, Shona admitted.

> Thank you so much for meeting up with Chloé and being so nice to her. I've longed for the day that this would happen. And thank you for asking to meet with me. I hope we can resolve things between us. Dad.

Shone reread her father's text. The one he had sent after she'd asked to meet him to talk things over.

Tears pricked her eyes and she was glad no one was sitting in the seat opposite her. She hoped she wouldn't disgrace herself by crying. That would be absolutely mortifying. But as the church spires drew closer Shona feared she might not be able to put on the aloof armour that had always protected her in her encounters with her father.

'Don't give in to her emotional blackmail, Terry.' Denise Ryan sat propped up against the pillows of their bed, watching her husband pull a blue Boss cotton polo shirt over his head. She made a mental note to not buy light colours for him in the future. The belly bulge would be better disguised by darker tones. No matter how hard she tried to keep him on the straight and narrow, Terry's love of sugary treats and takeaways defeated her efforts.

'I think it will be different this time, Denise. I think Shona's meeting up with Chloé has made a difference.' Terry slipped his wallet into the pocket of his chinos.

'She's all talk about Shona now but don't get your hopes up too high. You know what Shona's like.' Denise pursed her filler-enhanced lips. 'I hope she's not all talk about Chloé doing work experience with her TV company and that she'll follow through.'

'One thing about Shona: she's very straight, Denise. She wouldn't go back on her word,' Terry said touchily. He didn't like it when his second wife criticised his first family.

'If you say so,' she said acidly. 'We're going to an early afternoon barbecue at the Nolans' later. Don't eat too much if you're going for coffee with her.'

Terry scowled. The Nolans were friends of Denise's and he didn't particularly like them. Bill Nolan was a bumptious know-it-all who was even more overbearing when he was pissed, which he invariably was at the weekend. 'Do we have to go? Billy-boy's such a pain in the ass.'

'I know but they know everyone and it's good for us to keep a high profile. Good for your business. It was hard-going during Covid,' his wife pointed out.

'OK. I don't know how long I'll be with Shona. I'll see you when I see you.'

'Take no nonsense,' was her parting shot as Terry left the bedroom.

For some reason he didn't think his eldest daughter was going to be as belligerent as she usually was. He sat into the car and opened her message on his phone once again.

> Hi Dad. I was just wondering if we could meet up for a chat. If it suits could you meet me in the People's Park in Dun Laoghaire around 9.30 on Sat morning. It a good half way mark and I can take the Dart. Shona.

For the first time in *years* she'd called him Dad instead of Terry and therein lay the difference.

Hopeful, apprehensive and uncharacteristically unsure of

himself, Terry turned the key in the ignition and headed for his rendezvous with his oldest daughter.

Shona watched her father walk towards her and felt a knot in her stomach. He looked younger in his casual clothes. *The dyed hair helps, of course,* she thought acidly and then chided herself for being bitchy.

She stood up from her wooden seat to greet him. 'Hi,' she said uncertainly. 'Thanks for coming.'

'Of course I'd come, Shona. I'm your father, despite all that's happened between us. I'll always meet with you when you want me to,' Terry assured her earnestly. 'Do you want to walk or sit?'

There was only one elderly dog walker, feeding treats to her equally elderly dog, on a seat at the other side of the fountain so Shona said, 'Let's sit for a while.'

'I just wanted to say thanks to you, again, for arranging a meeting with Chloé.'

'It was actually Mimi who did that,' Shona divulged, not able to take the kudos for being magnanimous when she hadn't always been.

'I know that. But you made a connection with Chloé that's made her very happy. She's been having a hard time at school lately. She told me what you said to those little bitches. It made her day when you called her "my sister". Terry reached out and squeezed her hand. It was the first time since she was a teenager that Shona had permitted her father to touch her without withdrawing.

She left his hand where it was on top of hers and said quietly, 'It was good to confront those bullies. I'm glad they won't be in her year for transition. And ... I was glad to get to know her a little. She's a nice girl.' Shona raised her head and looked at her father. 'Dad—'

'Shona.' He spoke at the same time and then took her two hands in his. 'Shona, I would give *anything* to turn back time so that you didn't see what you saw that awful day. I know it haunts you and I'm so, so sorry. It haunts me too. I can never forgive myself for it. You know I've always loved you.' His voice cracked and to her astonishment she saw that his eyes were bright with tears.

In all the years since that life-changing day, Shona had never given much thought to how horrified and mortified Terry had been when she'd walked in on him and Denise. The barriers had gone up between them and, no matter how hard he tried, Shona had never allowed him to own his feelings of shame or accepted his protestations of apology.

She knew she could revisit the moment of finding him in flagrante with Denise, tell him yet again how it had traumatised her, but in the face of his tears – seeing him broken, his face crumpled in misery – Shona felt her anger towards him fade. Her mother, Caroline and the reiki therapist were all right. Holding on to that horrible memory only embittered her. She'd had enough of it.

Shona swallowed hard. 'Let's leave it in the past where it belongs, Dad. Let's see how we do moving forward. We can discuss the wedding when Aleksy and I have made our plans. I love him very much, Dad: he's a wonderful man.' She eyeballed him.

'If you love him then he must be,' Terry conceded, wiping his eyes and holding her gaze. 'I look forward to meeting him again.'

This time it was her eyes that brimmed up and father and daughter made their peace, their tears intermingling as they held each other tightly.

PART THREE

CHAPTER THIRTY-EIGHT

Devlin

'Right, the builders are booked to put the stud walls in the attic space to make two rooms and the painters are booked to paint them. We have the artist MH Hensley lined up to paint the mural. I'll ask Maggie to ask Sandra in Latin Quarter where she got her Persian rugs and tapestries.' Devlin tapped in a note on her iPad. 'The DJ's booked, the guest list is partially compiled, the sponsors are on board and the design for the invite is to be finalised. It's going to be a great reunion party.' She smiled at her team gathered around the oval table in the small meeting room next to her office. 'We're doing great. You're mighty. And the good news is you won't have to put up with me for a couple of weeks. I'm having my hysterectomy next week. Madalina will be taking over so, if you've any urgent business to deal with, go to her. And as you all know she's a much tougher cookie than I am,' Devlin teased affectionately, smiling at her PA. Everyone laughed as they stood up and began to offer her their heartfelt good wishes.

When the team had left, Devlin stacked up the dirty plates and mugs tidily for one of the café staff to collect. It had been a working breakfast and she'd been so busy outlining plans for the City Girl anniversary celebration that she'd only taken a few sips of coffee and a nibble of a Danish. She bit into a pain au chocolat and licked her fingers as the chocolate oozed out. She felt as though she was expecting a period: bloating, niggling pains – which she knew would worsen if she didn't take some painkillers – and a craving for chocolate and salt. All the symptoms of PMT. A packet of crisps would sort the salt craving, she decided, popping two pills out of a blister pack she kept in her bag. She swallowed them and took a glug of water from her bottle. Dev needed to keep her pain at bay. Shona and Mimi were having their barbecue that evening and she wanted to enjoy it and not have it ruined by friggin' endo. She shoved the tablets back into her bag. This day next week hopefully she'd be sorted.

'Devlin, there's a Colin Cantrell-King on the phone for you,' Madalina called from the office. 'Do you want to take it in there?'

Devlin tensed, longing to say no.

'OK,' she called back and went to the landline on the wall.

'Yes?' she said curtly.

'I'll pay that Santos bitch thirty thousand and if she thinks she's getting any more dosh from me she can go—'

'I'll pass on that message,' she snapped and hung up.

Speaking to him made Devlin's skin crawl. She wasn't sure what Nenita might do when she heard about his offer. Both of them had decided to hold off making a formal complaint to the gardaí until Devlin had undergone her surgery. She took out her mobile and sat on the deep window ledge, looking out at an azure sky as the morning sun dappled the verdant leaves of the treetops in Stephen's Green. Thirty thousand euro.

'Cheapskate!' she muttered, scrolling through her contacts for Nenita's number. A derisory, insulting offer for all the trauma she had endured. How typical of Colin, a multi-millionaire with a mansion in D4 and a villa in Portugal.

The call went to voicemail. Nenita was probably at work, Devlin reckoned, leaving a short message explaining Colin's offer.

She checked her watch. Eight-thirty: she needed to get her skates on. She was speaking to a class of students about entrepreneurship, in the NCI across town, and then she was scheduled for her pre-surgery checks.

'I'm off. I'll keep in touch, although I'll be on silent for a couple of chunks of the day,' she mouthed to her PA, who was on a call.

Madalina gave her a thumbs up and Devlin hurried out of her office.

She was driving across the Liffey when her phone rang and she saw Nenita's name pop up in the console.

'Hi, Nenita. You got my message.' Devlin flashed a 'go ahead' to a motorist who was indicating to get into her lane.

'I did, Devlin, thank you. And, to tell you the truth, part of me was tempted to agree to it,' the other woman sighed. 'But then he wins, and he makes me complicit in his crime, and I couldn't live with myself if I did that. I won't enable him to salve his conscience by buying me off.'

'I actually don't think he has a conscience, Nenita. He has a supreme sense of entitlement and he's totally misogynistic,'

Devlin replied, turning right along the quays. 'So are you saying to me that you're going ahead to press charges?'

'I am,' Nenita said firmly.

'I'm by your side, you know that. I'll ring him and tell him, and I'll say never to contact me again. His next contact from us will be a garda at his door.'

'Thank you, Devlin. I don't think I could have done this without your support.' Nenita sounded so earnest and heartfelt Devlin couldn't but smile.

'You would have but two is easier than one and this is for our daughters and for women everywhere. There's a great comfort in that.'

'For sure. Listen, I'm on a quick break: I have to get back to work. My next patient is due in for a smear.'

'After next Thursday I may never need one of them again. Mind yourself,' laughed Devlin before hanging up. She drove along the quays, cursing the bollards that prevented her from parking. She was about to nip into the set-down space in front of the Spencer to ring Colin when a thought struck her. *Let him stew.* Let him sit, waiting by his phone, wondering if he was going to get away with it or if he was going to face the worst ordeal of his life.

Knowing him, he'd imagine that Nenita would jump at thirty thousand. He'd think he was off the hook but he wouldn't be *quite* sure. Revenge was a dish best served cold. It would be freezing by the time they were finished with him, Devlin promised herself as she turned onto Clarion Quay and drove into the NCI car park. She hoped her nausea would subside before she faced her student audience. She popped a mint into her mouth – they always helped – and, taking a deep breath, assumed her best 'Successful, entrepreneurial business woman' façade. As she got out of the car, Devlin wished she could go home and hide under the duvet until her surgery was over.

Colin Cantrell-King picked up his phone for the umpteenth time to see if he'd by any chanced missed a call from that Delaney bitch. No missed calls, his phone unhelpfully assured him.

What was talking so long? No doubt they were hoping to spook him out so that he'd offer more. Forty was his absolute limit. He wasn't going to be blackmailed. The next time she rang him he was going to record their conversation to *prove* that he *was* being blackmailed. That might put a halt to their gallop.

For God's sake, what was wrong with them? All this 'woke' nonsense was giving women ideas. A little bit of slap and tickle and you were behind bars, now. And, worse luck for him, they could go after men for 'historical' charges. *Hysterical* was more like it. He glowered at his phone, willing it to ring.

He stared out the window at his sun-drenched garden and took no pleasure from the sight of the pots of voluptuous multi coloured begonias and petunias tumbling over the sides of their massive planters in riotous profusion.

His life had been going so smoothly, so enjoyably pleasurable since he'd semi-retired. He still lectured occasionally. He loved the faint awe, the gravitas, his presence brought to a lecture hall, where students absorbed the wisdom and knowledge he bestowed upon them.

When his wife had died, drinking herself into an early grave, he'd felt nothing but relief. Jessica had never forgiven him for the little mishap that had occurred before the Devlin Delaney episode, all those years ago. But all that had faded away, eventually, and when Jessica had died from cirrhosis he had been free to have liaisons without the binding ties of marriage.

He had a 'friends with benefits' partner in Dublin, Gayle, and a lady friend in Portugal. Viagra was a godsend as he'd grown older. Both women thought they'd trap him into marriage, eventually, but that wasn't going to happen. His housekeeper was as good as any housewife, even better, he reflected, because she knew her place and didn't talk back to him. He had no need for a wife.

Colin's golf was his greatest relaxation. The banter in the clubhouse his entertainment. But since that dreadful letter Devlin had sent him, digging up the past, he took no pleasure in it. It was as though a yoke had settled on his shoulders, enveloping him in a pall of apprehension that, today, seemed even more oppressive than previously. Was no news good news? Colin couldn't tell.

CHAPTER THIRTY-NINE

Caroline/Dervla

'Do you want to WhatsApp your dad and tell him everything's OK?' Caroline asked when they walked out of the Rotunda after Dervla's prenatal visit. 'Would you like a decaf latte before we get the taxi home? You could message him from the café. I know he'll be anxious to hear how it went.'

'All right,' Dervla agreed. She was just glad the ordeal was over. The doctor had been nice enough, though, telling her that the baby's heartbeat was strong and healthy and her own blood pressure was fine, and answering her questions about when Dervla would have a scan to know the sex of her baby. She'd advised her to take her folic acid, eat plenty of greens and get plenty of exercise. Dervla had asked if her boobs would ever stop feeling sore and was horrified when the doctor suggested she start wearing maternity bras. But her boobs were getting *enormous*. She'd gone up a bra size and it looked like she was going up another one again. What would she be like when she was nine months pregnant?

'I've to get a maternity bra,' she said to Caroline as they stood at the busy junction waiting to cross.

'Let's get it today then,' Caroline suggested. 'We can go to Dunnes in the Ilac or M&S in Mary Street. They're very close by. Let's have our coffee and Google them and see which one you'd prefer. It would be better than ordering online. I'm not sure what the returns policy on bras are if they don't fit.'

'Oh, that's a good idea.' Dervla brightened up, relieved that Caroline had made it all sound easy.

'Let's go to Chapters Bookshop first. They have a café upstairs and a gorgeous arboretum with a crystal garden in it. When I went for reiki the therapist told me to get some selenite: it's good for clearing energy.'

'Sure.' Dervla liked the sound of a crystal garden.

'This is one of my favourite shops ever,' Caroline confessed as they walked into the iconic Dublin bookshop. 'Don't let me buy any books today, though. I have a huge pile to read. You might have to drag me out of here, squealing.'

Dervla giggled. She was relieved that the hospital visit was over and, to her surprise, she found Caroline surprisingly easy to be with and talk to. She wasn't at all stuffy – which she thought a psychotherapist might be – and she was amazingly honest about her bulimia, which astonished Dervla. She'd never realised older women could suffer from eating disorders. She'd thought it was just her age group.

They walked up the stairs to the big airy café that was humming with the sounds of chat and conviviality. 'OK, I'll grab us a table. You take my Revolut card out of my wallet and will you get me an Americano and I suppose I could go wild and have a Danish. You get whatever you want.'

'I'll get them: Dad said I was to treat you,' Dervla said hastily.

'That's kind, thanks. I'll get a table so.' Caroline saw more people coming up the stairs and moved towards a table she had earmarked for them.

The cream cakes at the counter looked deliciously inviting but, remembering that the doctor had said about minding her weight, Dervla reluctantly bypassed them and asked for a granola bar instead. It was bad enough having big boobs without having a fat ass as well.

'She's out in the garden, hooting laughing at a book I gave her to read,' Caroline murmured, not wanting her voice to carry and for Dervla to know she was talking to Mick about her.

'She's supposed to be helping you,' Mick protested. 'I hope you're not running around after her.'

'We were going to attack my office this afternoon but it's such a cracker of a day it would be sinful to stay inside, honestly. So we're going to do it tomorrow,' Caroline explained.

'I can't thank you enough for what you're doing for us, Caroline. It's great she was able to get to her hospital appointment and not have to cancel. My parents were disappointed she didn't come down with me but I'm just as glad, to be honest. It's been a bit stressful but I've got home care in place for Dad for a couple of hours a day, so that's sorted. I'll drive home late Friday night and collect her early on Saturday, to take her off your hands.'

'She's fine. Don't be worrying. It's been handy having her here while I'm afflicted. Go and sit out yourself, if you get a chance, and relax. Being in a sling is liberating in some ways. I'm not able to do much so I'm going out to sit in the garden too. Something I'd never do in the middle of the week. I think I'm learning to go with the flow!'

Mick laughed. 'That's saying something for you! Enjoy it. See ya.'

'See ya,' she said back with a smile before hanging up. Caroline took two cans of wild berry kombucha out of the fridge and went out to the garden and handed one to Dervla. She was stretched out on a lounger in a pair of shorts and a boob tube, reading *Not My Problem*.

'Oh thanks,' she said gratefully when Caroline handed her the cold drink. 'This book's *really* funny! I don't read a lot but I'm definitely going to get more of this author's for sure.'

'I know, I loved it myself.' Caroline sat down on her lounger and cracked open her can. 'I was just thinking . . . ' She looked at Dervla.

'What? Do you need me to do something?'

'Not yet. I was wondering should you do a WhatsApp with your mom? Mick mentioned that you haven't been taking her calls and I'm sure she's worried about you too.'

Dervla's face darkened. 'She only worries about herself. You know she wanted me to have an abortion behind my dad's back? That's the kind of mother she is,' she added bitterly.

'Perhaps she panicked and thought it was the best option for you?' Caroline said gently.

'She just couldn't wait to get me out of Abu Dhabi.'

'Well, it is difficult being in your situation there, don't forget. When all's said and done, it's not a liberal country for women despite the façade.'

'I suppose,' Dervla said sulkily.

'Think about it.' Caroline dropped her sunglasses onto her

nose and lay back against her lounger cushion and closed her eyes. She had emails to answer and phone calls to return but her arm ached, even though she'd taken painkillers, and she was tired after trotting around town with Dervla earlier. She just couldn't summon up the energy to start working. Most unlike me, Caroline admitted ruefully. That fall had knocked the stuffing out of her. If she worked in the public service she'd be on sick leave. I'm giving you a sick cert until next Monday, she told herself, as her eyelids grew heavy and a delicious lethargy overcame her and she drifted off into slumber in her garden oasis.

CHAPTER FORTY

Caroline/Mick/Dervla

'Caroline, I'm terribly sorry: I have bloody Covid.' Mick's groggy voice came down the line as Caroline sat sipping her morning coffee at her kitchen counter the following Saturday. There was no sign of Dervla, no sounds from the bedroom, so no doubt she was still fast asleep.

'Oh no, Mick. That's awful. When did it hit? Are you in Kerry or Dublin?'

'I felt a bit off last night when I was driving home and then around three this morning I woke up with a sore throat and a temperature. I did a test just now and it's positive. I can ask my brother if Dervla could stay with them for a few days: I don't want to put you out any longer.'

'You're not putting me out, Mick. If she doesn't want to go to her uncle's she fine to stay here, honestly. We've managed quite well actually, once she settled in and relaxed a bit,' Caroline assured him. Her heart hadn't sunk at the prospect of having Dervla stay for a few more days, she realised with surprise. She, who was so used to her own company, had adapted quite well to having a moody, pregnant teen around. 'Look, don't say anything to your brother. Let me ask her what she'd prefer and I'll ring you back. Have you got hot drinks and paracetamol?'

'Yeah, there's stuff like that here in the bathroom cabinet. I'll dose myself.'

'Right, I'll get back to you.' She got off the kitchen stool and went down to Dervla's bedroom and knocked on the door.

'Mmmm?' came the drowsy response and Caroline opened the door to see Dervla sitting up, half-asleep, blonde hair tousled around her shoulders.

'Is Dad here?' She yawned and stretched.

'No, unfortunately your Dad's tested positive for Covid. He just phoned me.'

'Oh, poor Dad.' Dervla looked startled. 'Is he OK? Is he still in Kerry?'

'No, he drove back last night. He said he was going to ring your uncle to see if you could go and stay with them—'

'Oh no!' Dervla wailed. 'My uncle's decent, but my aunt's a bit grim. She'll think I'm a slut for getting pregnant. I know she will. I can go home and wear a mask, and Dad can lock himself in the bedroom.'

'Or you can stay here,' Caroline said calmly.

'What?' Dervla's head shot up.

'If it hasn't been too much of an ordeal, you can stay here.'

'Oh Caroline, thank you, thank you *so* much,' Dervla exclaimed fervently. 'I'll do anything you want me to,' she added dramatically.

'Great! Breakfast in bed every morning at 8am and dinner on the table at 6pm,' Caroline said with a straight face. Dervla looked a tad shocked.

'Oh! OK!'

'I'm teasing you but there is something I was going to ask you to do today. Would you blow-dry my hair for me? I've to go to a barbecue. You might like to come. You've met Shona. It's her and her twin brother and sister who are giving it. It would get you out of the house and Shona has a half-sister around your age who'd be there. You could wear that lovely floaty top you bought in Topshop.'

'You mean the *tent*!' Dervla sighed.

'It's not a tent: it camouflaged your bump beautifully. Come on,' she urged, seeing a doubtful expression cross the teen's face. 'Finn, my friend Devlin's son, is doing the cooking. He's a chef in Barcelona. He makes *fabulous* food. Let's get our glad rags on and you can do my make-up for me too. I hate trying to do my eyeshadow with my left hand and you do yours so beautifully.'

'I won't really know anyone,' Dervla demurred.

'You know me and you know Shona. Plus, you're used to meeting people: how could you not be, in Abu Dhabi? You'll be fine. Make your bed, tidy your room and come on down and have your breakfast. Then you can make my bed,' Caroline said briskly, opening the curtains. 'And ring your dad and make a fuss of him. Tell him you're staying here until he's OK. And don't forget to take your folic acid.'

Dervla blinked at the rapid-fire instructions. 'Right.' She yawned again. 'I think my Bobby Brown Disco Drama would look great on you. You have such beautiful brown eyes.'

'Thank you.' Caroline was touched at the matter-of-fact compliment. 'I look forward to being a disco drama queen.'

She chuckled to herself going back to the kitchen. Two weeks ago she'd been working away, exercising, jogging, living her – she had to admit – slightly dull life. Now she was living with a teenager, who was anything but boring, Caroline reflected, throwing caution to the wind and making a second cup of coffee, before texting Devlin to ask if it was OK for her to bring Dervla to the barbecue too.

'There, I'm just going to add some kohl to the side and some eyeliner – open wide – that will really make your eyes pop!' Dervla instructed, concentrating intently on Caroline's make-up. Caroline had never had so many creams, serums, foundations, powders and blushers applied to her skin. Dervla worked like an artist, with her selection of make-up brushes.

'Just a teeny bit more blusher,' Dervla declared, lightly dusting Caroline's cheeks and standing back to admire her handiwork. 'Perfect! I'm going to dry your hair now. What product do you use?'

'Er ... Gliss, it's in the bathroom cabinet.' Caroline went to stand up to look at herself in the mirror.

'Stay! No peeking!' Dervla ordered.

'Yes, Dervla,' Caroline said meekly and the teenager laughed. Her own make-up was flawless. It had taken a while but no professional beautician could have done a better job. Caroline was often in awe at the young women who came for counselling who looked as though they'd just stepped out of a beauty salon.

'How did you learn all this?' Caroline asked as Dervla rolled a length of hair onto a brush and aimed the hairdryer at it.

'There's loads of tutorials on YouTube. Me and my best friend, Cesca – that's short for Francesca – spend hours practising,' Dervla said airily. 'We all do.'

'You do a terrific job but you have young dewy skin, not wrinkly old leather like mine.'

'You've great skin, Caroline. You really look after it and all that water you drink is so good for hydrating it,' Dervla assured her kindly. 'And you have a perfect bob because you hair is so straight. My hair is too wavy, even with a straightener. I used to have the six-week blow-dry. I have to watch what products I use now because of being pregnant.'

'It's good that you are being so responsible, Dervla. Well done you. Lots of women aren't as careful.' Caroline smiled up at her.

'I wouldn't like to do any harm to the baby, even though I'm having it adopted.'

'Is that your plan?' Caroline asked.

'Yes. I think it's the best thing for the two of us, even though Dad said we'd manage fine if I kept it. I want it to have a good mother. I'm too young. I wouldn't know what to do with a baby.'

'You must do what's best for both of you.' Caroline patted her arm. 'And I'm sure you will.' *The irony*, she thought as Dervla fussed with her fringe. She who had longed for a child and never been blessed with one and Dervla who had been and didn't want it. *Life was a funny old cocktail*, she thought wryly.

'You can look now!' Dervla whipped the towel from around her neck. 'What do you think?'

'Wowza! You did a brilliant job.' Caroline stared at her

reflection in the mirror. Her skin was glowing and creamy, her chocolate-brown eyes looked wide and alluring with the dusky colours Dervla had used and her hair framed her face like a silky curtain.

She was wearing a pair of white cotton cut-offs with a La Redoute Breton striped boat neck T-shirt and white mules. She looked the epitome of chic sophistication, even with her arm in a grey sling. Dervla had helpfully fastened her bra for her: another intimacy that Caroline couldn't have imagined possible in the first few days after Dervla had come to stay.

Dervla was wearing a pair of black Seraphine straight leg maternity trousers that she'd ordered online and a crushed cotton sleeveless orange top that floated gently over her bump. A pair of glittery black sandals finished the look.

'Look at us! Two gorgeous gals looking ever so summery. Just as well it's a peachy day for the barbecue. FaceTime your dad and let's see how he's doing. You could show him your handiwork with my hair and make-up,' Caroline suggested, hoping her pal wasn't feeling too grotty.

'Do I know you two glamorous ladies?' Mick croaked.

'Ya poor ould thing, you sound awful,' Caroline sympathised. 'Will I do an online shop for you and get it delivered?'

'I'm fine. I actually did some shopping in the Applegreen on the way home. I've enough to keep me going. I'm not hungry, to be honest.'

'Keep hydrated anyway,' Caroline advised as the doorbell rang. 'Our chariot awaits. We'll ring when we get home.'

'Enjoy the barbecue. Caroline told me you were going to one. Have fun, babes,' Mick said to his daughter.

'I will but if you feel really bad I *will* come home to you,

Dad,' Dervla told him, feeling lonely and sorry for him when she saw his watery eyes and heard his hoarse voice.

'I know that. I'll be fine,' he assured her before hanging up. Mick felt more grateful than he could say that he had a friend as sound as Caroline.

CHAPTER FORTY-ONE

The Barbecue

The late afternoon sun was still high in the sky as Maggie raised her face to it, loving the feel of heat on her skin. She was sitting in the shelter of the ivy-covered wall at the end of the long narrow garden, the mature trees and shrubs affording invaluable privacy from her neighbours on each side and to the rear. It was the garden and its southwest facing aspect that had been the deciding factor to buy the mid-terrace redbrick house in Ranelagh, long ago when her marriage to Terry had broken down. When she'd finally paid off the mortgage, years later, Maggie had felt a deep satisfaction that she'd leave behind a valuable asset that would give her three children a decent inheritance.

It had been strange coming from an ultra-modern detached house with ensuite bathrooms and an 'all mod cons' kitchen to the period house with sash windows, big fireplaces and a dark, poky kitchen. The kids had been unimpressed, to say the least. That first year after the move had not been easy as she tried to deal with her children's resentment, her own fury and keeping her feelings hidden so the kids could have as good a relationship as possible with their father. Today was evidence that she'd done well in that regard, Maggie thought with gratitude, and she was glad Mimi and Michael were still happy to live there.

Over the years she'd revamped the house and now sliding doors opening out to the garden ran the width of the house. They were open today and guests were wandering in and out while Michael and Finn barbecued a feast. Shona and Mimi had set up big platters of food, bowls of salad and dips on the island in the sleek modern kitchen. The sound of music and the buzz of chat and laughter filled the air and it did Maggie's heart good to see Chloé laughing at something Finn was saying to Michael. Terry and Denise were chatting to Nelsie. Maggie had told her mother about the truce between Shona and her father and had asked her not to be snooty with Denise, if she could possibly help it. This barbecue might just pave the way for easier blended family relationships all round that would carry on to Shona's wedding.

'I'll "zip it", as the young ones say,' Nelsie agreed reluctantly. She liked having the moral upper hand over the tarty Jezebel who had stolen Terry away from Maggie. She had always had a fondness for her son-in-law. 'But she's a little trollop nevertheless.'

'Mam, the only issue I have with Denise is that she was with Terry in our family home. We were only putting on a façade for the kids at that stage of our marriage. It was over between us by then. Don't forget that, just in case your tongue runs away with you,' Maggie reminded her as they drove up to Dublin at lunchtime.

'Hmm.' Nelsie sniffed. She was convinced that Terry and Maggie had just been having a hiccup in their marriage and that they'd have worked it out had it not been for the 'blonde bimbo'.

'Here, Mam, have a couple of cocktail sausages to keep you going.' Maggie's son broke her reverie and she opened her eyes to see Michael standing in front of her, blocking out the sun. He was six foot two, broad shouldered and handsome and sometimes she wondered how her adored son, who had been such a carefree, easy-going child, had turned into this fine young man who carried the responsibilities of his demanding career so easily on his shoulders. The years seemed to have gone in the blink of an eye and a mixture of pride and sadness filled her.

'You always were such a kind boy, lovey.' She took the paper plate and bit into a sausage, enjoying its crisp tastiness. Maggie was peckish, having just had time for a banana and a cuppa that morning.

'You're easy to be kind to, Mam,' he said affectionately, sitting beside her on the small wall that edged a raised herb bed. 'It's great to be home and it's fantastic that Shona's made up with Dad. I always felt a little bit disloyal to her that Mimi and I were OK with him and she wasn't. I wanted us to be on the same level. I always felt it was all because of me and that it was my fault that she saw what she saw—'

'Ah no, Michael!' Maggie protested, horrified. She felt gutted at his matter-of-fact admission. 'You couldn't help being sick. That was just the way it panned out that day. Why didn't you *tell* me you felt like that?' Her heart went out to him: that he'd carried that guilt through his childhood into adulthood. What sort of a failure of a mother was she, that she'd never copped it?

'It doesn't matter now, it's sorted,' he said easily.

'It *does* matter, Michael. That was not your burden to carry. I wish I'd known how you felt.' She strove to keep her composure and not upset him but she was nearly undone and it was a struggle not to break down in tears.

'Mam, you were the best mother a guy could wish for. You had so much on your plate. Do you know how lucky I feel to have you for a mother? Forget it. Let's have a fun family day. To have Dad and Shona on speaking terms again, here this afternoon, is just brilliant. Look at Chloé: she's thrilled with herself that she finally has another big sister onside.' He gave a wave to his young half-sister who gave a huge grin in return.

Maggie swallowed. Hard. 'That *is* great, Michael. I'm happy for her.' She forced herself to sound cheery.

'Mimi organised that getting together with Shona thing. My twin is so cool, just like our mam. I better get back to the barbie. Finn is playing a blinder over there. It pays to have a chef for a buddy.' He had just stood up to move away when Devlin, Luke, Caroline and a pregnant teen came out onto the deck.

'Yay, the godmothers. Who's the girl with them?' He waved at the group.

'A friend of Caroline has moved back from Abu Dhabi with his pregnant daughter. She's only sixteen. She's staying with Caroline at the moment.' Maggie stood up to go greet her friends.

'Aw, the poor kid. That's tough,' Michael said sympathetically, as their guests walked down the garden towards them.

'The gang's all here.' Michael grinned, hugging Caroline and Devlin enthusiastically and punching Luke on the shoulder. 'Hiya, I'm Michael. Welcome to our barbie,' he said to Dervla.

'Thanks,' she murmured, obviously uncomfortable with all the strangers she was thrown among.

'You lived in Abu Dhabi, Mam told me,' he went on.

'Yeah.' Dervla seemed strangely tongue-tied.

'Right. Well then, you don't want to get stuck down here with the City Girls gang. You'll never escape. Come on over to the grill with me and meet my sister and give us a hand.'

'Oh!' She looked at Caroline.

'I'll come with you and introduce you to Finn, Devlin and Luke's son,' Caroline offered, acutely aware of Dervla's discomfort. 'He's the chef I told you about.'

'And I'll get Dev and Luke a drink,' Maggie said with pretend joviality, standing up to kiss her friends. She saw Terry heading in their direction and a red mist flashed across her eyes. She had to fight the urge not to go over and pummel him and shout, 'You gave our children huge burdens to carry. How can you live with yourself and pretend nothing happened, and that everything's all right now? You ruined their childhood and I hate your fucking guts for it. You and that stuck-up—

Stop it! she shrieked silently. *Don't spoil your children's day.*

'Are you OK, Maggie?' Devlin noticed her flushed demeanour.

'Just feeling the heat,' she managed, swallowing down the rage and resentment that surged within her and threatened to erupt into a volcano of vitriol.

Luke, blithely unaware, patted her on the arm and said, sotto voce, 'My wife often feels the heat too, these days.' He laughed when Devlin flashed him a glare.

'Luke, Devlin: great to see you.' Terry patted Luke on the back and nodded at Devlin. 'Looking fantastic as always, Dev,' he complimented.

'Thanks,' Devlin said politely, wishing she could say, *'Cheesy as always, Terry.'*

'Terrific day for a party. Hard to believe our kids are this age, isn't it? Maggie and I love it when Michael's home and they all get together,' he added expansively.

'I'm just going to get some drinks for our guests.' Maggie's fingers curled into her palms as she strove not to rake her nails down his jowly, smug face.

'Beer, Luke, or who's driving?'

'I'll drive home,' Devlin offered.

'Ah, no, have a drink with the girls,' Luke said.

'I have to bring Mam home. I won't be drinking,' Maggie said.

'That settles it then,' Dev decided. 'You have a beer, Luke. I'll have a Coke if you have one, Maggie.'

'We got a taxi, so no worries there, buddy.' Terry raised his beer bottle.

'Good thinking,' Luke said. 'We brought Caroline, seeing as she can't drive.'

'Right! So how's business? I signed a new client the other day, a developer. He has great plans for—'

'I'll just go get the drinks, back in a mo.' Maggie could take it no longer. *'Maggie and I'?! How dare you!* she seethed as she hurried into the kitchen.

'Hey, Mom, it's fun isn't it? Hope you're hungry.' Mimi was making cocktails. 'Will I make you one?'

'I'm fine, pet, just getting a beer for Luke and a Coke for Dev. Will you see what Caro and Dervla would like?'

'Sure I will. Mom, it's so funny, Chloé is totally smitten by Finn and he's so kind to her. She's having an absolute ball. I'm very happy for her because she was having to deal with horrible bullies at school.'

'Ah, Finn's the best. It's great he and Michael managed to get time off together.' Maggie smiled at her youngest daughter, whose pragmatic approach to life and all its challenges had always impressed her. 'You should be very proud of yourself for engineering the rapprochement between her and Shona. You've brought this family together. Your dad owes you, big time.'

'I know! He always hoped Shona would forgive him. I was just thinking: remember when Marion Delahunty did the dirty on me and took John McKenna to my Debs when she knew I was going to invite him?'

'I do.' Maggie gave her a hug. 'What's that got to do with your dad and Shona?'

'That lovely lady you used to go to for acupuncture: Dr Tallon? She gave you a book: *The Game of Life* by Florence Scovel-Shinn.'

'Oh yes, Annette,' Maggie exclaimed. 'Sadly she passed away. She was a great counsellor. I haven't read that book in a long, long time.'

'I have it in my bedroom. I dip in and out of it and one part I always come back to: *"No one is my friend, no one is my enemy, everyone is my teacher."* And I think that Dad's lesson for Shona out of all of this was the lesson of forgiveness. Even though it took her a *long* time to get there, she did in the end. And may I say it took *me* a long time to forgive Marion Delahunty!' Mimi laughed gaily as she clunked ice into a glass and poured Devlin's Coke over it.

Maggie couldn't believe the irony. Here was she, filled with something akin to hate, *longing* to kick her ex-husband in the goolies and hurl all the abuse she could think of at him, and her youngest daughter was casually giving her a lesson in metaphysics and forgiveness. A lesson that Maggie had taught *her* years ago. *The Universe has a weird sense of humour,* she thought grimly.

She'd thought she'd forgiven Terry and let go of the past and that they were on an even keel, until today! Today had brought it all back. Today had made her feel an utter failure as a mother. Today had brought guilt, heartbreak, wrath and despair in equal measure. And now Mimi and her talk of forgiveness.

In utter turmoil, Maggie took Luke and Devlin's drinks and walked out into the sunlight with a fake smile pasted on her face, wishing the day could be over so she could get home, scream into her pillow and *never* have to see Terry again.

CHAPTER FORTY-TWO

THE BARBECUE

'Hi Finn. You're doing a terrific job: the aromas wafting around the garden are making my mouth water.' Caroline reached up to give her godson a kiss.

'Thanks, my poor afflicted godmammy.' He grinned.

'I'm doing all the dirty work, and *he* gets the praise.' Michael made a face.

'You're the silent hero,' Caroline lauded, smiling at Chloé who was standing with a spritzer in her hand, posing, as she watched Michael and Finn's friends chatting across the garden from them. 'Good to see you again, Chloé.' Caroline had met Chloé over the years at some of Maggie's family bashes. 'I'm Caroline, Maggie's friend,' she reminded her, 'and this is my friend, Dervla. She's lived in Abu Dhabi all her life and has just moved home to Ireland.'

'Hi Dervla,' Chloé said politely, trying not to stare at Dervla's bump.

There was an awkward silence and then Chloé ventured,

'We went to Dubai once. It was cool. All those designer shops everywhere.'

'We have them too, in Abu Dhabi,' Dervla remarked nonchalantly, studying the other girl's flawless make-up and boho chic. *She'd fit in really well with the crowd in the Dhabi*, Dervla decided, wishing she didn't feel and look like a beached whale.

'I like your sunnies. Are they Dolce & Gabbana?' Chloé leaned closer to have a look.

'Yes, I got them this summer.'

'Dad bought me these in BT in Dundrum.' Chloé took a pair of sunglasses off the top of her head. 'They're called Chloé, so that's why he got them. This,' she pointed to a small shoulder bag, 'is a Chloé mini. I'd love the Chloé tote but it's over a thou and that's *way* too expensive.'

'Oh, that's so pretty.' Dervla forgot her standoffishness as she studied the bag. 'I like the way they have the logo and that it's your name too.'

'Have you been to Dundrum?' Chloé asked.

'Sure, I go in the summer when I'm here. I just haven't been this summer, yet.' Dervla sighed. 'My friends from Abu Dhabi, who come home here too, went to Ibiza first this year. They won't be here till August and I'm not sure when my mom will be home.'

'Oh! That's a bit of a bummer.'

'Totes.'

'What would you ladies like to drink?' Michael asked, as Finn flipped the array of burgers on the grill.

'Um a glass of white, please,' Dervla said without thinking and saw Caroline looking at her, surprised. 'Oh ... eh, better not.' She glanced down at her stomach and blushed. 'A Coke, please.'

'Same for me, thanks, Michael,' Caroline said.

'Coming up. You OK, Chloé?'

'I'm fine,' she said, waving her half-full glass at him. She couldn't afford to get tipsy in front of her parents or she'd be grounded and not allowed to drink spritzers in public again.

Finn ambled off down the garden and came back a moment later carrying a white garden chair.

'Here you go, Dervla, grab this while it's going. I'm going to tell people to start getting their grub so it will be a free for all. Besides, it's easier to eat sitting down than standing up.'

'Oh, em . . . that's very kind of you.' Dervla turned a bright pink under her make-up.

'No worries. You ladies leave your bags there and go grab a plate, get your salads and stuff and I'll serve you first before the hoards arrive.' Finn turned his chicken wings and sparks flew up from the coals. 'Caroline, I'll cut up your meat for you.'

'You're the best godson, ever!' Caroline exclaimed.

'What happened to your arm?' Chloé asked politely as they made their way into the kitchen.

'I fell and tore my rotator cuff; I might have to have surgery on it. It's a real nuisance but Dervla's helping me to manage. She's currently my PA, isn't that right?' She cocked an eyebrow at the teen.

'Yeah, I'm staying with Caroline for a little while. My dad got Covid,' Dervla explained, as they began spooning salads onto their plates.

'Oh that's awful. My mom got it early this year and she was *so* sick.' Chloé forked a helping of Caesar salad onto her plate. 'Would you like some of this?' she asked Caroline helpfully.

'That would be great, Chloé, thanks,' Caroline said gratefully. Dervla hadn't even thought to ask if she needed help.

'Let me get you some croutons and the bacon bits. I love them.' Chloé put her own plate down and circled the serving spoons around the bowl until she had a satisfactory amount of crunchy bits.

'You'd better leave some for everyone else,' Caroline protested, laughing at her eagerness.

'Would you like some hummus?' Dervla followed Chloé's lead.

'Just a small portion will be fine,' Caroline said and Dervla gave her a knowing look.

'Of course,' she murmured. 'Anything else?'

'A few peppers and some coleslaw and I'm done, thanks.' Caroline hid her amusement. She was touched that Dervla was mindful of her food issues and that having seen Chloé being helpful she'd followed suit.

'Hi Dervla, glad you came.' Shona appeared beside them. She had met Dervla twice before when she'd dropped in on Caroline to see if she needed shopping done or lifts anywhere.

'Hi Shona.' Dervla finished putting peppers onto Caroline's plate. 'I'll carry this for you,' she offered.

'Don't forget to fill up your own plate,' Chloé reminded her.

'Here, I'll bring Caroline's plate out, you two tuck in,' Shona said. 'Chloé, the cheesy potatoes are to die for. Mimi makes them. They're sublime! Help yourself too, Dervla.'

'Thanks, I will.' Dervla's stomach growled. 'Sorry: I'm hungry,' she murmured to Chloé when Caroline and Shona headed out to the garden.

'Well, you are eating for two,' Chloé pointed out, and then

put her hand to her mouth. 'Oh! No offence. Maybe I shouldn't have said that,' she added, mortified.

'Unfortunately it's true. I'm preggers and there's nothing I can do about it.' Dervla made a face.

'Poor you. Is it awful?' Chloé asked sympathetically, spooning herself a large helping of cheesy potatoes.

'Yeah, it's the pits, mostly. But the baby started to kick and that's a bit weird but exciting in a way,' Dervla confided.

'Here have some of these.' Chloé dolloped the potatoes onto the other teen's plate. 'At least you have an excuse for putting on weight. I have none. I just like food.'

'Me too, I'll be like a baby elephant if I'm not careful. The consultant warned me to keep an eye on my weight. But she was nice to me.' Dervla helped herself to coleslaw.

'There were some mean girls in my class that sent me a horrible message and called me a fat See-You-Next-Tuesday. Shona saw it and OMG she busted them so badly and threatened the guards and the school principal on them and they haven't come near me since. She's *so* cool. I've been trying to watch what I'm eating but I'm not thinking about it today. Finn – he's my brother's best friend – he's a real chef and I can't wait to have some burgers and chicken wings, they smell delish. He's a great cook. Come on, let's go and get some,' Chloé suggested, as other guests began to serve themselves from the buffet.

Dervla followed the other girl, relieved there was someone of her own age at the barbecue. She rather liked that Chloé had been sympathetic but not OTT about her pregnancy. She'd been sincere and matter-of-fact. She was actually quite a nice girl, Dervla decided. Not at all stuck up or snooty, as Dervla had initially suspected when they were introduced. This barbecue was turning out to be much better than she'd anticipated. She hoped Chloé might like to keep in touch. Perhaps she'd suggest a trip to Dundrum? She must ask Chloé what eyeshadow she was wearing. It was lovely and sparkly: Dervla wouldn't mind buying the same shade. Her kind sister had Revoluted her some money and Dervla was itching to spend it.

Her spirits lifted and she was glad she'd come to the barbecue. It had stopped her brooding about being pregnant. She was having fun. Meeting Chloé had been unexpected. Dervla felt she'd made a friend.

CHAPTER FORTY-THREE

The Barbecue

'Are you OK, Maggie?' Caroline eyed her friend quizzically. It was evening time and the intense heat of the day had cooled. The barbecue was in full swing with music thrumming out of the speakers, over the laughter and chat. The garden had filled up with some of the twins' and Shona's friends. Terry and Denise had gone and Maggie was preparing to collect her bits and pieces to bring her mother home. Devlin had come inside to use the loo before she went home and the three of them were gathered in the hall.

'Headache,' Maggie replied casually. 'I need to take some paracetamol and get out of here.'

'And...'

Maggie lowered her gaze, unable to hold Caroline's probing stare.

'It doesn't matter, Caro. I'll tell you another time,' she said, her lip beginning to tremble.

'Upstairs now. Come on, Dev,' Caroline ordered.

'Little dictator,' Maggie griped but she turned and walked upstairs, followed by her two friends. She led them into her former bedroom, now Mimi's, and sat down on the side of the king-size bed.

'What's going on?' Caroline sat beside her and Devlin sat on the ottoman.

'It's . . . it's something Michael said to me,' she faltered as tears came to her eyes and her voice broke. 'It just floored me. Oh, girls, he told me he was so glad Shona and Terry made up because he felt it was his fault for being sick that day we came home and she found Terry and Denise having it off in the sitting room. He's felt guilty all his life. My poor son carried that burden from childhood and I never knew. What sort of a mother am I, not to know her son was tormented with guilt?' She sobbed uncontrollably as the heartbreak she'd suppressed all afternoon poured out of her.

'Ah no!' Devlin exclaimed, coming to sit on the other side of Maggie and putting her arm around her.

'You're a great mother, Maggie, don't *ever* think otherwise.' Caroline reached across with her free hand and squeezed Maggie's.

'I want to kill Terry. I want to batter him black and blue. I thought I had dealt with all the shit that led to our divorce but this brings it to a whole new level. I hate his fucking guts. Poor Michael. He was such a good child and he kept this from me and I never knew and that kills me, girls. I'm sick with guilt that I failed him.'

'Stop, Maggie. Don't torment yourself like that. You did more than your best,' Caroline said gently.

'When I *think* of myself lecturing Shona to make her peace with Terry. The absolute cheek of me because I'll *never* forgive him because of this,' she said bitterly, taking the tissue Devlin offered. 'I want him to feel the guilt I feel. I want him to suffer like I'm suffering. Like my children suffered. I thought today was going to be the day when we reunited as a family. Little did I know. Only that I wouldn't put the kids through it and embarrass them in front of their friends, I'd have called out that bastard and that Denise cow and let them see the consequences of their actions.'

'Look, go home, have a soothing bath and an early night and don't do anything hasty. The foundations have been laid for a relaxed family wedding in a couple of months' time – what you wanted for Shona – don't forget that. If you can hang on until then before you let him have it, you'll be doing yourself a favour,' Devlin advised pragmatically.

'On the other hand, you don't want to swallow it down and give yourself a gall bladder attack or worse,' Caroline counselled. 'Write out your emotions: your grief, fury, everything you feel. Tear it up, burn it, don't keep it inside you—'

'Write a novel about it, don't waste it,' interjected Devlin. 'There'll be lots of women who'll identify with what you're going through.'

'You can say that for sure,' sniffled Maggie, blowing her nose. 'I was happy coming here earlier. You never know what's going to hit you next, sure you don't. Look at you with your arm, Caro. One minute you're flying around, the next, there's a halt put to your gallop.' She shook her head. 'I give up,' she sighed.

'Deep breaths.' Devlin smiled at her.

'Hmm.' Maggie studied her. 'I thought there was a bit of an edge between you and Luke. What's going on with you pair?'

'Oh! Was it that obvious?' Devlin frowned.

'Only to us who know you so well. Everything OK?'

'Ah, he's pissed off because I'm going after Colin. He doesn't get it. Can't understand why I'd want to put myself through the stress of a court case after all this time. Although I understand where he's coming from, I'm annoyed that he's not seeing it from *my* point of view.'

'It's only because he loves you, Devlin,' Caroline pointed out.

'I know that, Caro, but it's *still* irritating.'

'Try and sort it before you have surgery next week,' her friend advised.

'We'll see,' Devlin said noncommittally.

'I'd better go and get Mam.' Maggie stood up.

'Hold on, you can't go downstairs like that. You look like a panda!' Devlin went over to the dressing table and found some make-up remover wipes and waved them at Maggie. 'Let's do a repair job.'

Five minutes later the trio descended the stairs with Maggie composed enough say her goodbyes.

'Girls, I'll be in touch. Thanks,' she said gratefully.

'Mind yourself. I'd better go and get Dervla: at least she's had a great time,' Caroline said, as Nelsie emerged from the kitchen to make her farewells.

There was a flurry of goodbyes before Maggie started the car's engine and she and Nelsie set off.

'T'was a great party,' her mother said cheerfully. Michael had made her a couple of Tom Collins and she was pleasantly giddy.

'It was,' Maggie said evenly.

'Such a joy to have Michael home again. He's going to come down and paint the shed for me. He's a great boy.'

'He sure is,' Maggie agreed, swinging out of Mornington Avenue and hoping her mother wouldn't natter the whole way home. She had a throbbing headache. She just wanted to deposit Nelsie home and go to bed.

'T'is a pity you didn't see fit to invite Tony and Ginny,' Nelsie remarked. 'It would have been nice to have all the family together.'

'Mother,' – she only called Nelsie 'Mother' when she was very annoyed – '*I* didn't do the invites. It wasn't *my* barbecue and, even if it was, I wouldn't have been inviting that pair,' she snapped.

'That's not very kind, Maggie,' remonstrated Nelsie crossly. 'I hope you'll be inviting them to the wedding!'

'And now that you bring them up, perhaps we should schedule a family meeting with *you* about *your* wishes and desires for the future and what will be expected of Tony, as your power of attorney, should anything untoward arise. Let's see how *that* goes, and see if they'll want to come to the wedding after it.' Maggie had had enough of keeping her emotions suppressed.

Nelsie was about to argue the toss with her but one look at her daughter's grim expression stifled her protest.

They drove home in frosty silence.

CHAPTER FORTY-FOUR

Devlin

'Can you not sleep?' Luke lay wide-eyed in the semi-darkness, staring at the waning moon shining its pale lemon glow on the balcony outside their bedroom, aware of Devlin twisting and turning beside him.

'No.'

'Are you frightened?' He turned over and raised himself on one elbow to look at her.

Devlin sighed. 'I am and I'm not. In twenty-four hours my life's going to change. Hopefully I'll feel a lot better but I'm not looking forward to being plunged into the menopause and what it will do to my body. I've been able to hide from middle age up until now. I have to face it full on from tomorrow.'

'I'm not even going to offer trite reassurances and trivialise it, Dev, because I haven't the right to. I'm just a man. I'll never experience what you're going through. All I can say is I'll support you as best I can.'

'The way you're supporting me with the CCK thing?' It was out of her mouth before she could stop it.

'That's a low blow, Dev.' Luke was taken aback.

'Maybe.' She sighed. 'But it's how I feel.'

'Look, I just don't want you to have to endure what you certainly *will* endure if you go through with this. The strain of a trial. His barristers will take you apart on the stand, be in no doubt of that. The press intrusion. The social media stuff. It's not that I don't support you, Dev,' he said heavily. 'It's that I'm afraid for you.'

'Luke, if women who've been raped, sexually assaulted and coerced don't step up, we will never be safe,' she argued. 'We live with this every day and I'm *sick* of it. Why *should* he get away scot-free and live his life thinking it was OK for him to do what he did? The more of us who take a stand will make a difference to the young women coming up behind us. What if something like that happened to Lynn if she'd lived? Or Shona and Mimi or Nenita's daughter?'

'I know, Devlin—'

'No Luke, you *don't* know,' Devlin said quietly.

He lay back down and stared up at the ceiling.

'Don't be mad at me, Luke,' she whispered.

'I'm not mad at you,' he said, with a break in his voice, and she turned and saw a tear trickle down his cheek.

'Ah, Luke.' She turned to him.

He turned and put his arms around her, burying his face in her hair. 'I love you, Dev, more now than I've ever loved you. I want to mind you and protect you and stop horrible things from happening to you. You've endured so much but I'll be at your side every step of the way,' he said huskily. 'Please don't take on too much and give yourself time to get over this major surgery you're facing into.'

'I will, Luke, I promise. With you beside me, I can face anything. You're my rock. You always have been. You'll never know how much I love you. Ever.'

She snuggled into him and felt his arms tighten around her. The sensation of being in her lovely, safe bubble – that always happened when they were in each other's arms – returned and eventually she relaxed and drifted off to sleep.

'So depending on what I see when I go in, if I need to take everything out you're OK with that, Devlin?' Anthony Lane stood beside her in his scrubs as she lay on the trolley in the room adjacent to the theatre.

'Yes, Anthony, do what you have to do.' Devlin nodded.

'Hopefully I can do it with keyhole, and it would be good to save the ovaries too, but I might have to cut you.'

'I've been opened up before. Fortunately my modelling days are over.' Devlin smiled up at him.

He patted her arm. 'I'll leave you in the expert care of my colleague here and I'll see you later when it's all over.'

The anaesthetist had already inserted the cannula so she said comfortingly, 'I'm going to put you out now, Devlin. Enjoy the sleep. You're in good hands.'

'I know,' Devlin agreed, wondering whether would she get past the count of three. In all the anaesthetics she'd had over the years, she'd always wanted to get to four. She didn't even make it to two as the anaesthetic took hold instantly without her even realising it.

*

Luke stared at his phone, willing it to ring. It was after 2pm and it seemed a lifetime since he'd left Devlin at the door of the hospital. She hadn't wanted him to come in with her, even though he was desperate to.

'You'd only be hanging around waiting, while they do all the check-in paperwork. You won't be allowed come to the ward. There's no point and I'd rather kiss you goodbye in the car,' she'd said leaning across to kiss him passionately. 'That was *good*,' she added seductively and he'd had to laugh, as he always did when she was teasing him.

If anything had gone wrong, the hospital would have phoned him, he knew that, but it didn't assuage the deep knot of anxiety in his stomach that would only dissipate when he heard her voice again. Luke felt so helpless, so out of control. He would cut the grass, he decided. It would give him something to do and he wouldn't have to do it when she was home recuperating. Thank God Maggie is coming, he thought with relief. She'd be such a reassuring presence and her nursing experience would be just what Devlin needed.

He'd just pulled the lawnmower out of the shed when his phone rang. Praying it was his wife, Luke saw the video call was from her.

He seemed to be all fingers and thumbs as he pressed the green icon.

'Hi, I'm done. I'm back in my room,' Devlin said groggily, her eyes showing how drugged she was.

'Did it go OK? Are you in pain? Will I come in?'

'No, beloved, stay put. I'm not in pain and I'm going to sleep. Just wanted you to know I was done. Let Finn and the girls know,' she slurred. 'I love you.'

'I love you too. Sleep well.' He saw her smile woozily and then she hung up and he felt a wave of relief wash over him. At least that ordeal was over for her. Luke was thankful for small mercies as he scrolled for Finn's number to tell his worried son the good news

'I had to take everything out, the endo was everywhere, and I wasn't able to do keyhole surgery, Devlin. Sorry about that.' Anthony Lane stood at her bedside later that evening.

'It's OK. I'm just glad it's done,' Devlin said. 'Thanks.'

'The nurses will be in and out to you tonight, doing your vitals. You know the score but sleep as best you can.'

'I will,' she murmured, her eyelids beginning to droop already.

The rest of the evening and the night passed in the netherworld of drugged sleep interrupted by noisy bleeps and nurses taking her blood pressure and temperature. Luke had come in around six-thirty and was there when she'd got the much longed for tea and toast. The tea was the nectar of the gods. It always was after a surgery and she knew he was relieved to see her eating the buttery toast.

He was a big softy at heart and, just as Luke never wanted her to worry about him, she never wanted him to be worried about her. *I'm so lucky*, she thought gratefully as he bent to give her a tender kiss when he was leaving. A wonderful son and husband, with her at their centre: Devlin acknowledged that she was a very blessed woman.

Freshened up after a bed bath, Devlin lay back against her pillows the following day, feeling a vague discomfort around her pelvis. The nurses had got her out of bed for a little walk around the room and, when it was over, she was glad to get back in bed, exhausted after the disturbed night and the after-effects of surgery. She couldn't believe that a gynaecologist had asked Maggie's friend if she felt OK to go home twelve hours after her total hysterectomy.

She'd video-called Luke and Finn earlier, so now she picked up her phone and found Maggie's number.

'Hiya, how are you doing?' Maggie asked eagerly.

'A bit sore and tired but I'm glad it's finally done and dusted,' Devlin said. 'And it's a gift to have the catheter.'

'A life saver,' laughed Maggie. 'No running to the loo to pee. You look good.'

They were making plans for Maggie's stay when Devlin felt a weird prickling all over her body. A surge of intense heat flooded her and her jaw dropped.

'Oh Lordy!' Maggie exclaimed, watching her friend's chest and face turn crimson as a wave of warmth washed over her.

'Cripes, Maggie: it's happening! I thought I was having hot flushes before but they were *nothing* like this!'

'Stay calm, Dev, it'll pass. Welcome to my world, dearie. Don't worry. Anthony will sort you out and I'll bring you some black cohosh, evening primrose oil and a little fan. At least we're heading into winter. A small consolation but it's better than plummeting into menopause in the height of summer.'

'It's *horrendous*!' Devlin wailed, flapping her hand up and down to try and create a cooling breeze.

Maggie tried not to laugh but failed. 'Sorry, I know,' she said sympathetically. 'Until you've endured it you never *quite* understand.'

'Do women ever get a break?' Devlin demanded as another rush of heat enveloped her, dampening her nightdress.

'Tragically no, but on the positive side you'll get to the stage where you take no bullshit anymore and you won't care what people think. You'll become "unseen",' she air quoted, 'invisible, to all intents and purposes, and that in its own way brings liberation. Oh and your offspring will patronise you unintentionally and you'll want to slap them *hard* sometimes,' Maggie said cheerfully.

'Stop, Maggie,' laughed Devlin. 'I'm in the horrors enough.'

'You'll be fine. I'll see you on Monday. It's really kind of you to have a hysterectomy so I can come and stay with you, guilt-free.'

'You're welcome.' Devlin blew her a kiss. 'See ya.'

Maggie blew her a kiss back and hung up. Devlin lay against her pillows, her hair limp and damp against her head, and thought apprehensively, *What fresh hell is this?*

CHAPTER FORTY-FIVE

Maggie

Maggie packed her toiletries bag into her case beside her make-up. Her laptop was in its shoulder bag. She was ready to leave. 'Glasses, keys, phone.' She did her final handbag check, as always, before closing the bedroom door and heading downstairs.

Nelsie was in a snit with her. She had an appointment with an ear, nose and throat consultant later in the week and Maggie had told Tony he'd have to bring her.

'I can't. I'll be at work,' he protested.

'I'll be at work too. I'm up to my eyes and I'm also staying with Devlin to mind her after her hysterectomy, so I'm not available,' Maggie said. 'I've given you plenty of notice, so you can take time off or reschedule your working day. I do it all the time, bringing Mam to her appointments. Toodle-oo.'

Nelsie had not been pleased when she'd heard Tony was taking her. Maggie had seen the flare of nostrils, the tightening of the mouth, and heard the tut of disapproval, but her mother hadn't said anything except a cool, 'I see.'

The atmosphere had been chilly but polite when Maggie popped in to see her mother the previous evening before she went to bed, but she'd ignored it. Nelsie could get over herself. She'd given Tony power of attorney and made him her next of kin: *there are consequences to choices made and she can deal with it,* Maggie thought unsympathetically. After the initial shock and hurt of hearing what had transpired with her mother's legal affairs, during Covid, Maggie had begun to see it as a small blessing. Tony, whether he liked it or not, was having to do more for their mother's care than ever before because Maggie was putting her foot down.

She locked up her house, threw her case into the boot and drove over to Nelsie's.

Her mother was tidying up after her breakfast. 'I'm heading up to Dublin now,' Maggie said.

'You're going very early.' Nelsie sniffed, unimpressed.

'Devlin will be fecked out before 10am. The good old days of keeping a patient until after lunch are gone. She was lucky she got four nights in.'

'Give her my best,' Nelsie said. 'How long will you be staying?'

'As I've told you before, probably the week,' Maggie said evenly. 'Your big shop is done and Tony can bring you to get anything extra if you need it.'

'I hate putting him out,' Nelsie moaned. 'He's very busy at work, you know.'

'Aren't we all?' Maggie felt her blood pressure rise. 'See you, Mam. I'll call you.' She gave Nelsie a perfunctory kiss on the cheek.

'You should have never moved back to Wicklow,' Maggie

muttered to herself, getting into the car and slamming the door shut. Nelsie never acknowledged how hard she worked, *ever*! Did she think Maggie just blinked and had finished scripts and books on her desk?

'Get over it,' she told herself crossly, starting the engine, annoyed that even as a middle-aged woman she still felt the need to be recognised by her mother as Tony or any man's equal.

Once she got onto the M11, the Sugar Loaf to the left of her, the sun-speckled sea and curving coastline to the right, Maggie began to relax. She was looking forward to staying at Devlin and Luke's. It was a gorgeous house with incredible views and it had a pool.

Nursing Devlin wouldn't be difficult. Maggie planned to get a good run at her writing and do some relaxing by the pool, if the weather kept good. And, of course, she'd keep in touch with Nelsie, she acknowledged, whizzing past Coynes Cross at a hundred and twenty, listening to Leonard Cohen sing 'Halleluiah'.

Halleluiah indeed: I'm free for a week, Maggie thought merrily, her mood improving by the minute.

'Why don't you change into a sundress? It wouldn't be as warm as the tracksuit,' Maggie suggested to Devlin. Luke had helped her into the lounge, sat her on the sofa and then went into the kitchen to make a pot of tea for the three of them.

'That's a good idea, I'm baked,' Devlin agreed. 'I wore the tracksuit because they told me to wear something loose around the waist going home but it's warm, warm, warm.'

'You sit here,' Maggie said, packing some cushions behind

Devlin's back and helping her lift her legs onto the sofa. 'I'll run up and have a look in your wardrobe for a dress.'

'You're so good to me, Maggie,' Devlin said gratefully.

'Nonsense. I intend to have a lovely holiday as well as getting a few chapters written. Working from home is fraught with distractions. Working from here will be a joy,' Maggie assured her.

Devlin laughed and yawned. She'd been awake since 6am when the night nurse had arrived to take her vitals and say goodbye. She'd had her first unassisted shower before breakfast and felt a bit wobbly after it, so had lain on the bed wrapped in her towel for a while, before managing to dress.

A doctor had written up her prescriptions and officially discharged her and Devlin was shocked at the 'here's your hat, what's your hurry?' vibe, when housekeeping staff came into the room to begin the turnaround for the next patient, about five minutes after she'd finished her breakfast.

Ten minutes later she was sitting in the foyer with a bag of dressings and her case, carried down by the nurse who had escorted her off the ward. The shock of real life, as staff and patients hurried to and fro, made her feel tired and a bit weepy. Devlin had had a little haven up in room 287, where real life had been left at the door and she had been cocooned and minded. She'd never been so glad to see Luke when he came striding through the entrance looking fraught as he searched for her.

'Sorry I'm late. I didn't think you'd be chucked out so early.' He kissed her and grabbed her case. 'I have the car on flashers at the set down so you won't have to walk too far,' he said, taking her arm.

Devlin walked slowly, relieved to be able to lean on her

husband. They stepped out into the fresh air. 'Oh that's lovely,' she breathed, inhaling as he opened the door for her. Sitting down was painful and she gave a little gasp as she gingerly eased herself onto the seat and lifted her legs in.

'Are you OK?' She saw the alarm on his face and was mightily glad Maggie was coming to stay with her for a few days. Poor Luke would be fussing around me like a mother hen, she thought ruefully.

'I'm fine, Luke, just a bit slow. No need to panic,' she assured him.

'Right! Let's get you home.' Luke hoisted her case into the back seat. He turned to her and clasped her hand when he got into the car. 'Thank God that's all over. Now you've to lift nothing heavier than a book or a glass for six weeks, that's what Anthony Lane said, and that's what will be happening,' he said firmly.

'Yes, beloved,' Devlin replied meekly, not telling him that she felt so wrecked she'd be doing *exactly* what she was told.

Three days later, Maggie was changing Devlin's dressing when her phone rang. She ignored it. Whoever it was would have to wait. 'He's so neat. Those stitches are terrific. Your wound looks very healthy, Dev. He did a great job,' Maggie approved, swabbing the site with antiseptic before tearing open the new dressing. Devlin laughed at Maggie peering intently at the scar below her belly. She had her mask and surgical gloves on and her dressing pack laid out neatly.

'How lucky am I to have my own personal nurse?' Devlin said gratefully, as Maggie's phone rang again.

'Oh for God's sake.' Maggie threw her eyes up to heaven,

bagging up the old dressing and her surgical gloves and mask. 'It's Mam. What's up with her now?' she said, seeing Nelsie's number flash up and answering the call. 'Yes, Mam, I'm just doing Devlin's dressing.'

'Tony just phoned me; he can't bring me to my appointment. Some Zoom thing's come up for their division and he has to be at it. He told me to cancel and make another appointment but I was waiting months for this one. You'll just have to come and bring me. I'm sure Devlin won't mind.' Nelsie sounded hassled.

I bloody mind, Maggie wanted to yell but she swallowed it down and said, 'I'll be there. Be ready to leave in an hour. Bye.' She hung up. 'Argh!' she snarled resentfully.

'What's up?' Devlin eyed her.

'Bloody Tony *has* to attend a Zoom conference that's come up and he wants her to cancel but her sinuses are really bad this year, so I don't want her to have to rearrange. This appointment took *months* to get.' Maggie groaned again.

'Aw, Maggie. Look, go home,' Devlin urged. 'You've been so good to me and I'm feeling stronger every day, honestly.'

'You don't seem to understand. I *want* to be here. I'm having a lovely time. Your op is incidental and, besides, it's not a full week yet since you've had it. I'm coming back as fast as I can. Trust me,' Maggie said firmly. 'It's not *all* about you. And we've planned to binge watch the documentary about Juan Carlos and his shenanigans tonight.' They'd devoured *The Billionaire, the Butler, and the Boyfriend*, covering the scandal of the L'Oreal heiress, Liliane Bettencourt, the night before. Caroline was calling over to spend a couple of hours with them as well.

'We can watch that anytime. Do what you have to do with your mam. Luke will feed and water me.'

'I will, don't worry. I'll head off when you've had your shower and we've put your sexy stockings back on.'

'I hate those feckin things.' Devlin looked at her compression stockings with distain.

'Do a few walks around the garden with Luke today. We'll take them off for good on Friday,' Maggie advised, rolling them down off Devlin's shapely legs.

'Yes, nurse!'

'Get into that shower.' Maggie pointed. 'And don't give me any of your attitude.' They smiled at each other as she slid an arm around Devlin and helped her off the bed. 'You're doing great, Dev. Well done,' she encouraged as they walked into the ensuite and Maggie turned on the shower.

Devlin knew Luke would have helped her in all the ways Maggie was but spending time with her friend was such a treat for her. It was like old times when they'd been young women immersed in each other's lives, she thought, as she stood under the jets of hot water and soaped herself. It would have been nice with Caroline too tonight, the three amigas back together; pity Tony had snookered their plans.

That brother of Maggie's was some dose, Devlin reflected. Caroline's brothers had taken *her* for granted a lot when they were younger too, although they'd stepped up when her father had needed looking after. Luke was very caring of his parents but they were still able to care for themselves. Her husband was a good man, Devlin thought gratefully, looking forward to when her wound was healed and they could snuggle together in bed. Luke was insisting on sleeping in Finn's bedroom until she was more recovered. She was lonely for him.

'You OK in there?' Maggie opened the shower door a smidge.

'I'm fine, just fine, Maggie,' Devlin assured her and to her surprise she truly was feeling well. No more bloat or nausea or abdominal pain, apart from the discomfort of the surgery after-effects.

At last, she thought optimistically, lifting her face to the streaming water. At last I'm going to be normal, after all these years of feeling gank.

'She was a very nice lady, wasn't she?' Nelsie chirruped, as she and Maggie walked back to the car park. 'And at least I know I can have surgery as a last resort, if the new medication and the nasal washes don't work. I'm a bit peckish now. Will you bring me something to eat, Maggie, before we go home?'

'I will,' Maggie agreed. 'I'm hungry myself. Would you fancy some corned beef and cabbage?'

'That would be lovely. Where would we get that? Is Blackrock not a bit posh for it?'

'That's not where we're going,' Maggie said, opening the car door for her mother. 'We're going to the Grange, in Deansgrange.'

'Perfect. Sure that's on the way home. Now tell me how Devlin's getting on?' Nelsie settled herself into the front seat, all ready for a natter, relieved that her appointment was over and it had been Maggie who'd brought her. It would be nice to have her daughter home again. It was always a comfort knowing that she was just across the way.

Twenty minutes later they were tucking into a hearty lunch. Maggie was ravenous after driving down to Wicklow and back to Dublin. Nelsie, who always had a hearty appetite, was enjoying her corned beef.

After apple pie and ice cream, and a coffee, Nelsie patted her tummy and said, 'I won't need to eat until tomorrow. I'm as full as an egg.'

'Great. I'm glad you enjoyed it.' Maggie took her credit card out of her wallet. 'Why don't you go to the loo while I pay and then I'll follow you in,' she suggested.

'Good thinking,' agreed her mother, yawning.

They'd just passed Cornelscourt when Maggie saw with satisfaction that Nelsie had nodded off. The nap would do her mother good and revive her after the stresses of the morning.

She hummed to herself driving along the N11. The early afternoon traffic was light enough and twelve minutes later she turned into an estate of smart town houses and parked at a corner house with a navy BMW parked outside.

'Mam. Mam, wake up: we're here.' She shook her mother's arm gently.

'Wha . . . Wha?' Nelsie stirred and opened her eyes. 'Are we home, already? I must have slept the whole way.' She blinked, and blinked again, when she looked out the window. 'What are we doing at Tony's?'

'I'm dropping you off so he can drive you home when he's finished work,' Maggie said jauntily.

'You're not coming home?' Nelsie was confused.

'I'm not. I'm going back over to Devlin's. I'll get out and ring the doorbell while you gather yourself.'

Moments after the bell chimed Tony opened the door. His jaw dropped when he saw her. 'What are you doing here?' He saw their mother getting out of Maggie's car. 'What's going on?'

'Nothing,' Maggie said airily, standing back to let Nelsie step in front of her. 'I've brought Mam to her appointment for you and she did well. So you can drop her home whenever you're finished with your Zoom meetings. I won't come in. Well done, Mam, glad it all went well and that you enjoyed your lunch. I'll talk to you tomorrow.' She blew her a kiss, walked back to her car and drove off, leaving her mother and sibling standing slack-jawed in dismay.

'Deal with that, bro!' she said giddily, chuckling at the look of astonishment on both their faces.

'Well done you.' Caroline raised her glass to Maggie. They were sitting at Devlin's kitchen table devouring Luke's chowder and homemade brown bread. He was in the lounge, eating a bowl of it too, watching a football match. The girls were having a good girly chat.

'It was kinda liberating all right,' Maggie admitted. 'I was so mad the whole way down to Wicklow this morning. Helplessly furious and resentful that yet again he got to duck out of something and Mam expected me to pick up the slack. And then, just when I was turning right at Lil Doyle's, it came to me. I thought, yep, I'll take Mam to her appointment and I'll bring her to lunch and then I'll drop her at Master Tony's. I'm not driving back to Wicklow again when I've a date with my gals to look forward to. So here I am.'

It was great for her friends to see the twinkle back in Maggie eye. She'd been very flat and down in the dumps after Michael's revelation at the barbecue, Caroline thought.

The musical tinkle of a phone interrupted them and Maggie frowned. 'Now what?' she grumbled, getting up to go to the island where she'd left it.

She frowned when she saw her ex-husband's missed call.

'It's Terry! This is his third time to ring me. Why can't the fecker leave me a message? I better call back in case there's anything wrong. Excuse me,' she said stepping out into the garden.

'What's up, Terry?' she asked when he answered on the first ring.

'I've been trying to get you all day, Maggie,' he reproved.

'I was in the Blackrock Clinic with Mam and I'm having dinner with friends right now. Is anything wrong?'

'Is Nelsie OK?'

'She's fine. What is it you want, Terry?'

'I want to meet up with you to discuss the wedding. Shona told me she'd booked that place in Wicklow,' he announced self-importantly.

Typical Terry. He obviously thought that just because he'd made his peace with Shona, he could just muscle in and take over. Perhaps she should meet up and get it over and done with, Maggie thought irately.

'When were you thinking?'

'Sooner rather than later. The summer's flying by. Are you free this week? We could have lunch. My treat.'

'Friday,' said Maggie. She'd still be in Dublin so she wouldn't have to drive up from Wicklow to see him. She could nip into town on the Dart. 'Meet me at Ristorante di Napoli on Westland Row at 12.30. Now I have to go—'

'Westland Row! I've never been to any restaurant there. I was going to bring you to Shanahans or Guilbauds.'

So very Terry, Maggie thought, wanting to eat somewhere posh. They were too awkward for her to get to, the Italian beside the Dart station suited her just fine. 'Terry, my dinner's getting cold. It's a lovely restaurant; I go there every time I go to the National Gallery. It's handy to get to. Does the day and time suit?'

'Eh . . . yeah.' He was taken aback by her attitude.

'Fine, see you then. Bye.' She clicked, off not waiting for his farewell salutation.

'Sorry, girls,' she apologised. 'Terry wants to meet up to discuss the wedding.' She grimaced. 'I suppose I'd better get it over and done with. I told him I'd meet him on Friday.'

'Are you going to tell him anything about what Michael said?' Devlin asked.

'It will be hard not to.' Maggie dipped some brown bread into her creamy chowder. 'Why should I have to suffer the guilt on my own? What do you think, Caroline?'

'You have to do what's right for you, Maggie. Get it off your chest if it makes you feel better. Could you wait until *after* the wedding? The family sea is flat calm right now; do you need to make the waters stormy? Would it make things awkward and uncomfortable? Sometimes it's important to pick your time,' her friend counselled.

'You're so wise, Caroline. Knowing me I'd have said it to him and walked out. We'd all be back at square one,' Maggie acknowledged drily. 'I'll take your advice but he better not push me too far because his day of reckoning on that one is coming.'

CHAPTER FORTY-SIX

MAGGIE/TERRY

It was drizzling as the Dart trundled across the Clontarf Railway Bridge and the grand panorama of murky sea, Dublin Port and the ESB chimneys, cheerful against the glum skies, came into view. The melancholy weather matched Maggie's mood. It was the nearing the end of her thoroughly enjoyable sojourn with Devlin and Luke, before she went back to the realities of everyday life. The last thing she wanted today was to meet up with Terry and pretend that everything was normal and that she was pleased to see him and excited to share plans for Shona's wedding.

Maggie hadn't phoned her eldest daughter to let her know she was meeting up with Terry. She wanted to see what he had in mind for the wedding. He'd better not want to big it up, she thought crossly when the train stopped at the station and a smattering of people got on dressed in rain gear, so different from the summery outfits everyone had sported for the past couple of weeks during the mini heatwave.

Luke had dropped her over to Howth station so she wouldn't have to bother looking for parking. He'd told her to text him when she was at Sutton on the way home so he could be waiting for her. He'd insisted when she'd demurred. He was so appreciative of her coming to stay for the hardest week of Devlin's recuperation.

'Luke, I was really glad to do it and to tell you the truth it gave me a great break too,' she said when he thanked her profusely, driving down from the summit. '*And* I got to have some of your divine chowder.'

'I'm cooking a potful for you before you go home. You can freeze it,' he told her, swinging into the station. 'I'll get fresh crab meat for you when I'm getting the prawns and mussels.'

'You should set up your own brand of chowder, you'd make a fortune.'

'My mother made me swear not to tell the secret ingredients in her sopa de pescado stock. It's from an old Andalusian recipe.' Luke laughed. 'See you later.'

Luke was a sound man, as the Dubs would say, Maggie reflected, wishing with all her heart that she'd been lucky enough to marry a sound man. Instead she was about to meet her ex whom, this very moment, was the last person on earth she wanted to spend time with.

She emerged into the rain on Westland Row, pulled up the hood of her rain jacket and hurried towards the Italian restaurant. She'd taken the precaution of booking a table and was relieved she'd arrived before Terry. It would give her time to compose herself. Maggie took off her coat, ordered a white wine spritzer and scrolled through her emails and messages while she was waiting.

'Howya?' Maggie heard Terry before she saw him as he leaned down and kissed her cheek.

He shrugged out of his russet rain jacket. Barbour, she noted. Denise always has him smartly dressed, she thought sourly.

'Lunch is on me,' he said expansively, taking the menu from the waiter who glided over to their table. 'What are you drinking?'

'I'm fine with this.' She indicated her spritzer. 'And I don't need the menu. I'll have the Caesar salad, thanks.'

'Grand. And what will you have for your main?'

'That is a main,' she pointed out. 'I don't need a starter. The salad's more than enough.'

'You women, I suppose you're on a diet for the wedding. Denise is doing some sort of intermittent fasting carry-on.' Terry threw his eyes up to heaven.

'I'll have the steak please, rare. And the Caesar salad for my ... eh ... for the lady,' he amended. 'And a glass of the house red, please.'

He'd been about to say 'my wife', Maggie realised, and it gave her a little jolt. It was hard to believe she'd once been married to the faintly florid, middle-aged man sitting across the table from her.

'Now, let's get down to the wedding.' Terry was all business, eager to make plans.

Maggie held up her hand. 'Terry, Shona and Aleksy are the ones we should be meeting to hear what they want. As far as I know it's to be a very simple ceremony with just family and close friends. They haven't changed that from day one.'

His face fell. 'Surely *we* can invite a few guests? I presume Caroline and Devlin are coming? I'd like to invite some of my friends too.'

'Terry, Caroline and Devlin are like aunties to Shona. They were very good to her, and the twins, when we broke up,' she reminded him with an edge to her voice. 'Finn is one of Shona's best friends.'

'Oh, I suppose so,' he conceded as the waiter arrived with his wine. 'I just feel bad that I've been to a few friends' weddings and I'd like to reciprocate.'

'You and Denise,' she dropped in his second wife's name deliberately, seeing as it was Denise who had accompanied him to the weddings, 'will be able to reciprocate and invite whomsoever you wish when Chloé gets married.'

'That will be ages away.'

'Perhaps Mimi or Michael will want a big wedding when their day comes.'

'I just thought now that things are OK with Shona there'd be a bit of leeway on the guest list,' Terry said peevishly. 'I'll ask her and see what she says.'

'Terry, if you want my advice, don't. Leave them be and don't start any arguments, now that you're talking again. I'm stepping back and letting them do what they want. I'll show up on the day and do whatever Shona wants me to do.'

'That's a bit casual for the mother of the bride, if you don't mind my saying.'

'It's a casual kind of wedding,' she said calmly, 'and it suits me fine.'

'Is she having bridesmaids? Do you think she'd consider letting Chloé be one?'

'Terry, I've never been to a handfasting ceremony. I don't know what she's doing yet, all I know is that she's booked the Latin Quarter for forty guests.'

'*Forty!* That's all that's coming to the wedding?' He was aghast. 'I've had a bigger lunch party!'

'They're saving for a house,' she pointed out, smiling at the waiter who placed her meal in front of her.

'I'll pay for the wedding. And I'm sure you'll chip something in too, if it's money that's holding them back. We won't let that be the problem, surely.' He cut his steak and stabbed a piece with his fork.

'Terry, are you *listening* to me and Shona?' she asked exasperatedly. 'She doesn't *want* a big wedding. Leave her be.'

'OK, OK.' He held up his hands in surrender. 'But it's disappointing. I'm her father: I wanted to give her a day to remember. What's the story about walking her up the aisle? If there *is* an aisle.' He wiped his mouth where red meat juice had dribbled.

'I don't know. I'm sure we'll find out what they want soon enough.'

'If you could put in a good word for Chloé to be a bridesmaid, she'd be thrilled. You know,' he took a slug of wine, 'I was so worried about her for a while. She was going through stuff with some little bitches at school and she was thoroughly miserable,' he confided. 'I was at my wits' end. And then Shona met up with her, and now she's got this new friend she's hooked up with – that young pregnant lassie Caroline introduced her to – and she's back to her happy self again. I can't tell you how relieved I am.'

Maggie felt her throat constrict. She swallowed and took a sip of wine to help the food down her neck. How *dare* he sit in front of her and tell her how worried he'd been about his miserable daughter when his only son had gone through his childhood feeling guilty about something that was not his fault, because Terry was an utter arsehole? Her fingers tightened around her knife and fork. She wanted to stab him viciously and tell him how he'd ruined *their* children's childhoods. She remembered Caroline's words about calm family seas and bit her lip, struggling to keep the harsh words inside her.

'Excuse me, Terry. I've got to go to the loo.' She pushed away her chair, grabbed her bag and stood up. Maggie made her way to the Ladies and managed to get into a cubicle before throwing up as quietly as she could. *Deep breaths*, she told herself, *deep breaths*. She couldn't stay at that table with him for a second more, calm family seas or not.

She made some running repairs to her make-up, wondering how Caroline could ever voluntarily make herself sick. She hated puking.

'Terry, I'm sorry, I have to go. I've just been sick. I think I have a bug.'

'Christ.' He recoiled. 'Don't give it to me. I thought you weren't your usual chatty self all right.'

She'd forgotten how much of a hypochondriac he was. 'Thanks for the lunch.' Maggie pulled her coat on. 'If I hear anything new about the wedding plans, I'll let you know.' She walked out of the restaurant into a deluge. She was glad it was raining, she thought, as she faced into the wind and made her way to Pearse to catch the Dart, with tears rolling down her cheeks.

'Just let me get through this wedding without saying anything to him,' Maggie prayed fervently to whomever was listening out there in the Universe, as the train pulled out of the station ten minutes later.

The sooner Shona and Aleksy's wedding was over the better for her own sanity. She took a notebook out of her bag and began writing furiously. 'Waste nothing' was the advice often given to writers. *One of these days Terry Ryan is going to end up in a book, for sure,* Maggie thought savagely as her pen flew over the pages and she wrote her anger, grief, guilt and resentment out of her.

CHAPTER FORTY-SEVEN

Caroline/Mick/Dervla/Sally

'I've five viewers coming to see the house tomorrow,' Mick said, stirring a spoonful of sugar into his coffee. He and Caroline were sitting in Bistro 49 having a coffee and toasted sandwich. July's balmy weather had changed and August had blown in with gales and torrential rain. Dervla and Chloé had met up in town and Mick was collecting his daughter off the Dart, in Clontarf, after meeting up with Caroline for a catch-up.

'That's great news, Mick. Thank God you got those tenants out.' Caroline cut the crusts off her sandwich before taking a bite.

'Selling up was the only way to do it. It was a pain in the ass,' he grumbled. 'The RTB were *hopeless*. No wonder small landlords are leaving the market in their droves. But in a way it's going to be a fresh start. Even though I got the house in the divorce, it still feels like Sally's.'

His ex-wife had got the gîte they'd bought in France, as an investment. She never had any intention of returning to live in Ireland.

'She's coming home for two weeks, next week. She's in France with Ciara at the moment.' Mick took a bite out of his toasted sandwich.

'How does Dervla feel about that?' Caroline asked.

'She's not as hostile towards her as she was and I know I have you to thank for getting her to make contact with Sally after her prenatal appointment. I think she's looking forward to her mother's visit. I'm going to book into a B&B. That apartment is too small, even if I give her my room and sleep on the couch.'

'Don't do that. I've two guest rooms, Mick. You're welcome to stay at my place,' Caroline said, pausing mid-sip to look at him.

'I'm not going to impose on your kindness again, Caro, but thanks for asking,' Mick said firmly.

'Don't be daft, we're friends. I've got empty rooms. I'll be working. You'll probably want to be spending time with Sal—'

'Not if I can help it,' Mick declared. 'We're divorced at her insistence. She can entertain herself. I'm still pissed at her wanting to take Dervla to Spain for an abortion without telling me. That really was the end of it for me.'

'Perhaps you could sort things between you when she's home?'

'No, counsellor friend, but thanks for the suggestion.' Mick smiled at her. 'To be totally honest about it, it's not a terrible hardship being divorced now. We're very different personalities. It was rearing a family that kept us together, when I look back on our marriage. The oldest two have left home and are doing well. Sally wanted to spread her wings and live the Emirati lifestyle. I'm done with that. Have been for a long time. We were doing fine as a divorced couple, co-parenting, until Dervla got pregnant. There's no going back or sorting things between us, Caroline. I'm done.'

'Fair enough,' Caroline responded. 'It doesn't change the fact that there are two free bedrooms in my house. Look, I have a favour to ask: so if you take the room I'll ask the favour,' she bargained.

'I don't need to take a room to do you a favour,' Mick said, exasperated.

'You do! It's a big favour.'

'All right then, but that's blackmail. Shoot!' He eyed her guardedly over the top of his coffee mug, speculating on what she was going to ask of him.

'I was wondering if you'd give the car a run for me. I'm afraid the battery will go flat. I'm giving it another week before I start driving again,' Caroline said serenely.

'And that's it?'

'Yep and you've already said you'd take the room so you can't back out.' She grinned.

Mick stared at her and burst out laughing. 'You're something else, you know, behind that demure little façade.'

'Demure, *moi*? Never.' Caroline grinned. 'You'd better get going; you've five minutes to get to the Dart station. Give Dervla my love and tell her not to forget our date to have a massage at City Girl next week.'

'As if she could forget it: she's really looking forward to it. Can I come?'

'Gals only,' she said.

'That's sexist.'

'Tragically yes!'

'I'll see you, Caroline. Thanks for everything. How about we take a spin out to the Hill of Tara on Sunday?'

'Oh yeah! I'd love that. Perfect.'

'We can bring a picnic if the weather improves.'
'Even better.'

She watched him pull up his hood and as he walked out into the stormy weather Caroline wondered would Sally ever come to regret letting him go?

> Hi Caroline Mom wants to know if she could come and see u. She wants to thank u for your kindness to me. Anytime that suits you would suit her. D

Caroline read Dervla's WhatsApp message and paused before replying. Would Dervla be accompanying Sally? Caroline was back at work so it would have to be a weekend visit or an evening one. She didn't want Mick feeling irritated by a visit to her house from his ex-wife while he was staying, either.

She scrolled through her work diary and saw that she had a free slot of an hour and a half on Thursday morning. That would be more than enough time to entertain Dervla's mother. Meeting up for a coffee somewhere handy would be best all round.

> That would be lovely, Dervla. I look forward to seeing Sally again. I've a free slot to meet on Thursday morning. Clontarf Castle is a nice place for morning coffee. See her there around 10.30. Caroline X

'Clontarf Castle! I thought she'd invite me to her home. I was dying to have a look around.' Sally made a face.

'She's probably coming from her clinic. She's back at work

fulltime after her accident and she's very busy,' Dervla said knowledgeably.

'So you keep telling me,' Sally replied tartly.

'Well she *is*,' Dervla declared. 'She's got her own business and she employs quite a few people as well. I'd like to be independent like her.'

'Huh! Getting pregnant isn't exactly the way to go about being independent, Dervla,' Sally countered.

'Caroline's friend Devlin was a single mother and she opened a gym called City Girl that was very, *very* successful. They're having a big party to celebrate its thirty-fifth birthday next year. Having a baby didn't stop her and it won't stop me,' Dervla said huffily.

'Are you coming back to Abu Dhabi when you've put the baby up for adoption?' Sally queried, pouring herself another coffee. They were sitting at the kitchen counter in the apartment. It was the start of the second week of Sally's holiday visit.

'I don't think so.' Dervla shrugged. 'Cesca's going to university in Lisbon, Shazza wants to live with her sister in Jordan: everyone will be moving on.'

'You won't be going to university. You'll be missing too much school in the autumn to get your grades.' Sally studied her nails that she'd had done the previous day.

'I might go to France, to see Ciara. She said I could if I wanted. I'll decide after I've had the baby.'

'But you won't be staying in Ireland with your dad?' Sally probed.

'I don't think so. I haven't decided yet.'

'I see.' Sally glanced out the window at the rain-soaked

maple trees. 'This weather is enough to send anyone into a depression. I miss my pool and the heat,' she groaned. 'How's the house sale going? Your father never tells me anything.'

'There's a few people interested,' Dervla said diffidently. She hated when her mother was prying about her dad's business.

'What about those tenants that were living there?'

'They had to leave when Dad put the house up for sale. It was the only way to get rid of them without having to wait years going down the legal path. I felt very sorry for Dad but I think it will work out well in the end.'

'And where's he going to buy a house when the sale goes through?' Sally quizzed.

'Don't know, Mom. Ask him?' Dervla uncurled hers legs from the high stool she was sitting on and said, 'I'm gonna have a shower. Will I WhatsApp Caroline and say you'll meet her in Clontarf Castle?'

'Sure. Why not? Do you think she's interested in your dad?'

'What?' Dervla stared at her.

'Does she fancy him? Does he fancy her?'

'They're *friends*, Mom. She knew him before *you* did.'

'OK, don't bite my nose off ye wee crabbit. I was just *wondering*,' Sally drawled.

'You know something, Mom, having a true friend after all the fake so-called friends out there means a lot. And I'm glad Dad has a true friend. Cesca's mine.'

'Aye, no one wants the friend with forty faces, as my mother used to say. I met Cesca's mom in Spinneys before I left. Cesca hasn't told her about your ... eh ... condition, it seems. She never mentioned anything to me about it.' Sally changed the subject.

'No,' Dervla muttered. 'Her parents are very strict. They might stop her from being friends with me, so we decided to say nothing. Cesca would have come over to stay for a week if we had a bigger place. Living in a two-bedroom apartment is a bummer.'

'Tell me about it. Ciara could have come over too and we could have been together for a nice little holiday if those damn tenants had moved out when they were supposed to.'

'I'd love to see Ciara. She's going to come when I'm having the baby.'

'Oh! Good. Do you want me to come too?'

Dervla studied her mother. She was sure Sally had only asked because she felt duty-bound and not because she desperately wanted to be by Dervla's side for the birth. This baby was simply a source of irritation to her and all Sally wanted was for the child to be adopted ASAP and then be forgotten about and for life to get back to 'normal' for all of them.

'You're fine, Mom. If Dad hasn't bought a new house by then we'll be a bit stuck for space,' she said offhandedly, letting Sally off the hook because, to tell the truth, she didn't want her at the birth. Her mother had always, subtly, made Dervla feel she was a nuisance. Dervla only wanted people around her for this momentous event in her life that wanted to be there. Her dad and Ciara would get her through. A thought struck her. Caroline would support her. Staying that extra week with Caroline, when her dad had Covid, had been really enjoyable. They'd truly bonded after the prenatal visit. Dervla liked and appreciated Caroline's honesty and matter-of-fact attitude to things. She liked that Caroline had told her about her bulimia and her counselling sessions with her own therapist, and Dervla liked feeling needed. It had felt good to help her dad's friend while she was in the sling. She'd really enjoyed doing her make-up for the barbecue. Caroline was someone she knew she could go to with a problem.

When Dervla had told her she was giving the baby up for adoption she hadn't tried to change her mind or make her feel bad. She'd just said Dervla must do what was best for both of them. That had been *such* a relief.

Her phone tinkled and she saw a snapchat from Chloé. That was another good thing that had happened to her since she'd come back to Ireland. She and Chloé were becoming good friends.

> Me and Sarah are going to hang out in Powerscourt Centre around 2 if u want to meet up for a coffee.
>
> Would love to thanks. See u there. X

Dervla wouldn't say anything to her mother about where she was going. Sally would jump at the idea of going shopping in Powerscourt. It was her favourite place in town. Dervla wanted to hang with her friends, unencumbered, the way Sally did with her crowd when she was in Abu Dhabi.

Five minutes later she was standing under the steaming shower, the scent of her Inis shower gel wafting around her, feeling the happiest she'd felt since leaving her old home.

Caroline watched the glamorous blonde stride through the elegant foyer of Clontarf Castle and gave her a wave. Sally was wearing white Ralph Lauren straight-leg jeans, a red crepe

V-neck Tommy Hilfiger blouse with a DKNY tote slung over her shoulder. She oozed sophistication and confidence. 'Bout ye?' she greeted, her northern accent as pronounced as ever. She leaned across the table Caroline had stood up from and air kissed both her cheeks.

'Hi Sally, good to see you again.' Caroline smiled. 'I was sorry when I heard about you and Mick.'

'Ach, we grew out of each other.' She sat down opposite Caroline and crossed her legs. 'I wanted to live my life again once the kids grew up but Mick's an ould stick-in-the-mud. He wanted to come home. I couldn't bear the thought of mouldering away in this wet, dreary little island. I couldn't wait to get out of the wee North all those years ago. I'll not be going back there, either.'

'To each their own,' Caroline replied, thinking how disloyal this woman was to her ex-husband. 'You look great.'

'You can't beat the ould Botox and fillers.' Sally laughed showing perfectly veneered white teeth. 'You look very well yourself. Dervla tells me you're very busy.'

'Plenty of people out there with problems, unfortunately,' Caroline said, catching a waiter's eye. 'What will you have? Sally?'

'Coffee's fine for me, thanks.'

'A cake, a Danish, or croissant?'

'No, definitely not! I need to watch what I eat if I want to keep fitting into my skinnies. I miss swimming in the pool every day. It's great exercise. Pity it's so hot in Abu Dhabi this time of the year,' Sally moaned.

'Coffee and a green tea for me, please.' Caroline smiled at the waiter.

Sally opened her tote and took out a gift-wrapped box. 'I just wanted to thank you for your kindness to Dervla when Mick's dad had the fall and when he had Covid.' She handed her the box.

'There was no need for this, Sally. I was glad to be able to help. Mick was very kind to me when I went out to Abu Dhabi,' Caroline told her.

'Still you went above and beyond, having Dervla to stay,' Sally declared. 'Not many would take a stranger, and a pregnant stranger at that, into their home.'

'I was glad to help out.' Caroline opened the box and took out a soft Dries Van Noten printed silk scarf in pale greens and russets. 'That's lovely, Sally, thanks very much,' she said appreciatively.

'I got it in BTs. There's a gift receipt if you want to change it. I wanted to get something that wouldn't swamp you. You're such a delicate little thing,' Sally said. Caroline wasn't *quite* sure if it was a compliment or not. 'And thank you also for putting Mick up while I'm here. Our family is imposing on you big time.'

'It's not an imposition in the slightest. I have the room.' The waiter arrived with their refreshments and Caroline thanked him and held out her card to pay. Sally ignored him and carried on talking. He might as well have been invisible.

'Dervla says you have a fabulous house and garden.'

Caroline laughed. 'It's fine. It suits me. It's handy for shops and my office and I like being near the seafront.'

'A woman of means. I envy you in ways.'

'Why's that?' Caroline was intrigued.

'A wealthy widow. No husband or kids to worry or annoy

you. Beholden to no one. Life to live as you please. What's not to like?'

'I'm sure you're the envy of many too, living in Abu Dhabi in a villa with a pool. And shopping malls, gold souks and parties galore,' Caroline responded, trying to keep her tone neutral. *How dare you be so smug telling me what I haven't got, as if I didn't know? What do you know about my life?* she wanted to say.

'True,' Sally agreed, sipping her coffee. 'I like my life but I'd like it even more if the house and pool were *mine*. You don't have to depend on the whims of a man for your affluence. Faisal's very generous, of course. We have a great life. He loves partying and so do I and he's good in bed, and long may it last, but until the ring's on your finger out there, nothing is yours. To be honest, I'm glad Ciara's in France. And if Dervla goes to live with her after she puts the baby up for adoption all the better. The Emirates will always be a better place for men than women, no matter how enlightened they think they're becoming,' she said pragmatically.

'I enjoyed my time there,' Caroline replied, astonished at the other women's frank appraisal of her relationship with her new partner. 'But I wouldn't want to have lived there permanently.'

'You might have married Mick if you had. You were on the scene long before I was.' Sally eyed her quizzically.

'I wasn't looking for marriage when I went there. I'd just come out of a bad one.' Caroline glanced at her watch. 'I need to be going, Sally. I've a session booked in for 11.45am. It was great seeing you again. Thanks for the scarf. And good luck with Faisal.' She stood up. She'd fibbed about the session. It was for noon but she'd had enough of Mick's ex.

'Oh! Of course. You're a career woman. You know what, Caroline?' Sally arched a perfectly shaped eyebrow at her. 'You'd suit Mick down to the ground and he'd suit you. If you want him you have my permission.' She gave a sweet smile.

'You know what, Sally? I don't *need* your permission for anything, thankfully. And I don't *like* being patronised. And Mick is *not* a commodity to be given away. Have some respect for him, yourself and the marriage you had. Cheers.' Caroline turned and walked towards the entrance, leaving Sally astounded and the boxed scarf on the table.

'Up yours, lady,' Caroline muttered, running down the steps to her car, thankful she was driving once more. She hoped she'd never have to see that shallow, cynical woman again. And, she thought angrily, Mick is well rid of her.

Sally watched Caroline walk towards the exit, her chic floral summer dress floating gracefully behind her. *Understated, classy elegance*, she thought. Caroline wore her wealth lightly.

She'd misjudged her. Thought she was still the shy, quiet person she'd encountered when they'd lived in Abu Dhabi. There was nothing shy or quiet about the calm, reserved woman who'd put Sally in her place so sharply. Sally had wanted to have the upper hand, should Mick and Caroline get together. She'd wanted Caroline to know that *she'd* been the one to end the marriage. She'd been the dominant woman in her ex's life. Caroline would be second best.

It hadn't worked out like that, she thought irritably, stuffing the unaccepted gift back into her bag. Caroline had left her feeling not only miffed but also strangely disconcerted. Sally's flashy lifestyle seemed somewhat tacky in comparison to the other woman's and she was sorry she'd opened her big gob about Faisal and his unsettling reluctance to commit.

Annoyed with herself, Sally finished her coffee and decided against going to have a nosey around the area where Caroline lived, in case Mick saw her.

CHAPTER FORTY-EIGHT

Devlin/Nenita

'Let me tell you how a historic sexual abuse case is dealt with, first of all. Oh and of course I'll be engaging the services of a barrister and a senior counsel if you go ahead.' Devlin's solicitor Janet Redmond poured tea into the three Orla Kiely mugs in front of her and offered Devlin and Nenita milk and sugar.

She was a statuesque, attractive woman with a calm demeanour that was very reassuring. She'd been Devlin's solicitor and legal advisor for City Girl since its inception. It was like they had grown up together, Devlin reflected, remembering her first meeting, more than three decades ago, with a young and ambitious solicitor who was already making a name for herself.

They were seated in a small meeting room off Janet's suite of offices in a large redbrick house on Northumberland Road.

Luke had driven Devlin and they had met Nenita and her husband in the Schoolhouse for coffee beforehand. Although they had offered to attend with them – and Devlin knew Luke would like to be there – Devlin and Nenita had said they'd prefer to have the initial meeting with their solicitor alone.

'It's much easier this way, just ourselves, isn't it?' Devlin asked as she and Nenita walked along the affluent tree-lined street.

'Absolutely. We both know the men don't really want us to press ahead, even though they're being supportive.'

'*Exactly*,' agreed Devlin, turning into the coble-lock driveway of the elegant redbrick house. 'I know they'll be with us all the way but let's just do this bit on our own.'

Sipping her tea as Janet read over the detailed notes Devlin and Nenita had prepared for her, Devlin wanted to know what was involved in the process now that they had taken this first step.

'You'll go to a garda station to make a statement. There's no statute of limitations on sexual abuse. You can bring a family member and a support worker from any of the victim-support groups, like the Rape Crisis Centre. I've had my secretary type up what I'm telling you here, because it's natural that you won't remember it all.'

'Thanks, Janet. It's great to know there's support out there,' Devlin said gratefully.

'There is. A lot,' Janet assured her. 'You just need to know where to look. Once you've made your statement to a uniformed garda, who will explain the process to you, you'll no longer work with someone in uniform. An officer from the DPSU – that's the Divisional Protective Services Unit – will come to visit you, or meet in neutral territory. They're specially trained garda officers. They'll take a statement again, from each of you, although as they are pushed to their limit there might only be one officer dealing with both of you.'

'That's good. I don't want my children to know there's anything going on, so I'd prefer not to meet the officers in my home.' Nenita looked troubled.

'That's completely understandable, so you have the option to choose where to meet up. On the second visit you will be asked questions about what you've said previously and on the third meeting you'll revisit the entire narrative and see if any new information has come to mind. There can be anywhere from three to ten visits depending on what the officer or officers feel is required.' Janet looked at them steadily. 'Once the garda investigation is completed and if a file is sent to the DPP, should you decide to proceed with the case, be aware that victims are very often made to feel like a perpetrator.

'You both need to be prepared for this,' Janet warned. 'You may be accused of attempted blackmail. You will certainly be accused of lying. The onus will be on us, your legal team, to disprove that. You'll be asked did you flirt with him? Did you in any way encourage him? You were, after all, young and pretty and in awe of him.

'You'll be asked, Devlin, why have you left it so long to bring this case. Is it for vengeance? Because the truth is you were rebuffed by Mr Cantrell-King. Did you think that by getting pregnant he'd divorce his wife and marry you?

'You'll be asked how many sexual partners you had before Mr Cantrell-King and if any of *them* could have been the father of your child.'

The questions – relentless, probing, accusatory – came at her like bullets. Devlin was shocked.

'And *you*, Mrs Santos?' Janet turned to Nenita. 'Why *did* you keep the soiled garment? That was very clear thinking for someone who was allegedly distraught. Did you have an ulterior motive? Did you intend to blackmail Mr Cantrell-King at a later stage? You say he previously offered you money to drop the case? Are you holding out to see if you'll get more by bringing this case to the wire?'

'No, I'm *not!*' Nenita jumped to her feet, outraged. 'This is *not* acceptable.'

Janet held up a hand and motioned for her to sit back down. 'It's all right, Mrs Santos,' she said gently. 'I want to demonstrate the tack the other side will be taking. I want you both to be prepared. They will be defending their client *vigorously*, just as we will be prosecuting your cases equally forcefully.'

'Oh!' Nenita sat down, deflated, and glanced over at Devlin, whose heart was thudding in her chest. Janet had warned them that they would face intense hostile questioning. She hadn't been exaggerating.

'The opposition will try their best to demolish your case and make the encounters seem consensual and welcome. This is *not* about justice. It's about the letter of the law.

On the plus side, because of the DNA evidence you have Cantrell-King will have to explain how it got there. It won't be easy but I think you have a good chance of securing a conviction, if you proceed.' Janet paused and turned to Devlin. 'I should advise you, Devlin, because of your public profile there will be a lot of media interest in this case. Ask yourself if you're prepared for this.'

'Let me talk it through with Nenita and I'll let you know, Janet. Thanks for all the info. We'll get back to you,' Devlin couldn't hide her dismay.

'This is the time for you to make the decision to go forward or not. Have a good think about it. I'll be here if you both decide to go ahead.' Janet stood up to escort them out.

'Sounds really grim and scary, doesn't it?' Devlin exhaled as they walked down the steps.

'Very.' Nenita made a face. Much worse than I thought. I don't think it's fair to put you through this. You're only in the early days of recovery after your surgery.'

'This is my third week, I'm flying it,' Devlin fibbed, tucking her arm into Nenita's.

'Our men won't be happy.'

'Luke *did* warn me it would be rough. That's why he's reluctant for me to go ahead. How horrible that we might be made to look like blackmailing bitches. You'd wonder how barristers and the like are able to defend rapists and abusers when they probably know, deep down, that they're guilty as hell.'

'And that's how CCK and others like him get away with it,' Nenita said sadly, as they reached the hotel and went into the lounge to reunite with their anxious husbands.

'How did it go?' Luke stood up and hugged Devlin.

'It was tough, very tough, just like you said it would be. Nenita and I have a lot to think about.'

His arms tightened around her. His wife looked pale and tired. He truly did not want her to go through with this horrendous ordeal. But Luke said nothing. The choice was not his to make.

CHAPTER FORTY-NINE

Devlin/Nenita

A week later, sick with apprehension, Devlin waited for Nenita to join her for their first meeting with their legal team. She'd never been in the Four Courts before. Devlin felt she was in the middle of some TV drama as groups of bewigged and gowned barristers huddled in groups speaking animatedly and sometimes loudly, while others swept past across the Round Hall of Gandon's grand edifice. Prisms of late autumn sunlight streamed through the magnificent dome above them. How young so many of them were, how supremely confident they seemed, Devlin thought, watching a young legal eagle in a black mini and white blouse stride past, carrying a load of documents, her gown flying behind her. She looked to be in her absolute element and Devlin hoped the young woman was and not just having to put on a façade.

'Hiya, Devlin, sorry I'm late.' Nenita arrived, breathless. 'The bus was delayed at the Luas crossing for ages.'

'No worries. Janet's not here yet.' Devlin gave her a reassuring hug.

'This is scary, isn't it? It makes it very real. I'm tempted to run away,' Nenita confessed.

'Me too,' Devlin agreed, a part of her secretly wishing she'd never agreed to back Nenita up.

'There you are,' their solicitor greeted them, tapping Devlin on the shoulder. 'Our consultation room is booked for eleven. Denis and Frank, our barrister and senior council, will meet us there. We can order tea or coffee if you'd like some. Follow me. I got a text from Frank to say they'll be with us in ten minutes.' Janet led the way, across the Round Hall, leaving behind the noisy buzz. 'Here we are, nice and private.' She opened the door to a bright airy room with high ceilings and sash windows, overlooking a green space. Devlin felt the knots in her stomach loosen a little. Nenita, looking stressed and pale, sat down at the rectangular table.

'Are you OK?' Devlin asked, concerned.

'I'm very nervous but we're here, Devlin.' Nenita took a deep breath. 'Let's see how today goes.'

'Why don't we order some refreshments?' Janet suggested, tucking an escaped strand of grey hair behind her ear.

She was ordering tea and coffee when the door burst open and a tall, windswept, grey-haired man barrelled in, looking harassed, followed by his younger, smiling colleague.

'Sorry I'm late. I had to walk from the Criminal Court,' the older man apologised.

'No worries, Frank. Would you like a tea or coffee?' Janet offered.

'I'd kill for a cup of tea,' he said, holding his hand out to Devlin. 'I'm Frank Kinsella, your SC,' he said.

'Devlin Delaney.' She returned his firm handshake. 'And this is Nenita Santos.'

'I'm Denis Hannan, your barrister.' The younger man shook hands too.

'Let's sit down and review our notes,' Janet invited, motioning to the chairs opposite her for Devlin and Nenita. Denis sat beside the solicitor and Frank sat at the head of the table.

Devlin swallowed hard as the gowned legal eagles took their seats. Now, here in the intimidating atmosphere of the Four Courts, it truly hit home that the path she and Nenita were taking was going to be a soul-destroying ordeal if they wanted justice. She felt Nenita's hand slide into hers under the table and squeezed it. They were in this together for better or worse. She told herself that they could back out if it all got too much.

CHAPTER FIFTY

Devlin/Luke

'There's some personal post here for you, Dev, and the gang sent this to keep you going.' Madalina handed her a gift basket of champagne and strawberry-dipped chocolates.

'Ah! They're good.' Devlin was warmed by her staff's kindness. They had sent her a massive hamper of pampering goodies the week after her surgery.

Madalina had driven over to have a meeting in person, as Devlin was itching to get back to work properly now that her six weeks' recovery period was almost over. She wanted to keep herself busy to stop thinking about the court case. They worked for an hour, mostly on the anniversary event. Even though it wasn't until March the following year, Devlin was determined to keep on top of things and have her ducks in a row for the big celebration gala. The PR firm she'd hired had created a terrific buzz about it and the requests for corporate tickets had trebled.

'We're not going to have enough room for everyone who wants to come from the membership, so I think we should encourage them to have their tickets bought by Christmas. Lily also suggested we do a draw between now and Christmas to give invites to three winners. Leave a box at reception. The members can fill in their names and addresses. We could do the draw the day we close for Christmas.'

'Perfect! That will give women who can't afford a ticket a chance to come. Fabulous idea. Well done, Lily,' Devlin enthused. Lily was one of the receptionists and Devlin loved that there was such team spirit among her staff. Everybody was invited to contribute suggestions at the three-monthly staff meetings held in City Girl.

Devlin felt invigorated when her PA left. She was feeling so much better now that the effects of her surgery were wearing off and she was on a mild dose of HRT, which had lessened her menopausal symptoms considerably.

The meetings with the garda from the DPSU were reassuring and nearing their conclusion. The file was being prepared for the DPP and she and Nenita kept themselves going by telling each other that if the worst came to the absolute worst they could withdraw their charges at the last minute. In their heart of hearts they knew they were committed to going ahead with the case. The work and effort being put into the case by the garda and their own legal team was incredible. But it was a nerve-wracking process from the moment they had gone to the police station to make their statements, even though the garda on duty couldn't have been kinder or more helpful.

The die had been cast. Closure will come one way or another, Devlin mused as she began opening a stack of get-well cards from City Girl members.

*

'Just go easy on abdominal exercises and lifting weights, if you're going back to the gym. Swimming is the best exercise you can do right now. We'll have a chat when you're ready. Anthony Lane had a quick look at Devlin's wound and left the examination room, followed by his chaperone nurse.

'So!' he said when she was sitting in front of him, at his desk. 'You had endo attached to both ovaries and the bowel and adenomyosis inside your womb. That's very, very painful, as you well know—'

'*Not* all in my head,' she interjected dryly.

'It's still so frustrating to meet patients who are being told this by their GPs and consultants,' Anthony said exasperatedly. 'Far from being in your head, Devlin. Hysterectomy was certainly the best course to take in your case.' Devlin thought of the superiority of the previous consultant she'd seen and wanted to smack him *hard*.

'My advice to you is to go live your life as normal and I'm here if you've any problems.' Anthony smiled at her. 'Questions?'

'Um . . . When can I have sex with my husband again?'

Anthony looked at his watch. 'Depends how long it takes you to get home.'

Devlin laughed. 'Thanks, Anthony. I'm forever in your debt.' She shook hands with him, paid her bill at the reception desk and walked out into the waiting room where Luke was sitting.

'How did it go?' he asked as they walked out onto the street.

'I've to live my life as normal and he's there if I need him.' Devlin tucked her arm into his.

'Brilliant news.' He smiled down at her. 'I'm taking you to lunch to celebrate. Where would you like to go?'

'Let's go somewhere nearer home,' she suggested. The traffic on the drive into the city had been heavy. 'We don't want to get stuck in the school run.'

'Good thinking, Wonder Woman.' Luke clicked on his car fob.

'We could have tapas in Octopussy's.' Devlin got into the car, as he held the door open for her.

'You're on,' Luke approved.

They had a delicious lunch in the small seafood restaurant on the West Pier, watching the trawlers sailing in and out accompanied by flocks of squawking seagulls.

Devlin had had two glasses of chilled Chardonnay to celebrate and she was relaxed and a little giddy when they arrived home.

Luke dropped his car keys into the dish on the hallstand and was about to walk into the kitchen when she caught hold of his hand. 'Where are you going?'

'Into the kitchen to put the fish we bought into the freezer,' he said surprised.

'Oh yeah, forgot about that.' She followed him in and when he'd put away the fish, she said, 'Wash your hands: they'll be stinky.'

'Yes, boss,' he saluted and did as instructed. When he'd finished she drew him into an embrace.

'I asked Anthony when I could have sex,' she murmured.

'You didn't, Dev!' Luke exclaimed.

'I did! He said whenever we got home.'

'He'll think I'm a demanding husband or a sex maniac.' Luke was a tad horrified.

'Well, you're neither. But *I'm* a demanding woman and

possibly a sex maniac so get up those stairs, mister, and service your wife!' Devlin slid her hand down to his crotch.

'*Devlin!* You're unbelievable! I hope I never meet that man,' Luke said ruefully.

Devlin grinned and put her hands on either side of his face. 'I've a brand-new tube of KY and I'm horny and I adore you and it's been a long six weeks.'

'I *always* do what I'm told,' Luke said, meeting her gaze, and the spark that was always there between them ignited. Laughing, they walked upstairs to their bedroom.

CHAPTER FIFTY-ONE

Caroline/Dervla/Mick

When Dervla said 'I'm nervous,' it seemed like the most natural thing in the world for Caroline to take her hand in hers, as they hurried along Parnell Street to the Rotunda. The teenager's fingers clasped tightly around hers and Caroline said reassuringly, 'I'm sure everything will be fine.'

'Thanks for coming,' Dervla said. 'It's my first ever baby scan.'

'I'm *delighted* you asked me.' Caroline squeezed her hand. 'Mine too!'

Dervla giggled. Mick had dropped them off and was parking the car in the Ilac. Caroline wondered why Sally hadn't timed her holiday to be here for the scan. Probably because if she didn't see the baby herself it was possible to be more unemotional about it, Caroline reasoned in counsellor mode. Dervla had made her bed and could lie in it in her mother's eyes. Sally was as uninvolved as she could be to protect herself.

'I hope everything is OK with the baby,' Mick said agitatedly fifteen minutes later, while they waited outside as Dervla was being prepared for the scan.

'We'll deal with whatever occurs,' Caroline said steadily. 'The important thing is to be calm for Dervla's sake.'

'I know, I know. I was with Sally for our three's scans. It was nerve-wracking but exciting. Dervla's just so young, Caroline. I feel I let her down by not being more protective of her after the divorce.'

'Mick! Stop! You're a great father. Always there for her. It wasn't down to you alone,' Caroline exclaimed. She wanted to add, *If Sally hadn't been swanning around Abu Dhabi and shown more of an interest in what her youngest daughter was doing things might have been different.* But it wasn't her place to judge or assign blame, she reminded herself, and kept her mouth shut.

'You can come in now.' The sonographer popped her head out the door and they followed her into the small darkened room, where Dervla was lying on the bed. Her round belly was uncovered as she waited for them, looking so nervous Caroline wanted to sweep her into her arms and hug her. She stood at one side at the top of the bed. Mick stood at the other, holding Dervla's hand.

'Ready?' The sonographer rubbed some gel onto the baby bump and moved the probe around. They all gave an 'Oooh' of excitement as the image of the baby appeared on the screen. 'That's the head. You can hear the heartbeat, strong and healthy. The arms, the legs, the umbilical cord,' the sonographer spoke as she moved the probe around.

'Em, where would you see if it's a boy or a girl? I'm trying to see if there's a ... a ...' Dervla stuttered, trying to find the polite word. She'd almost said 'dick'.

'You want to know the gender?' The sonographer asked, smiling at them.

'Yes please?' Dervla said hesitantly.

'It's hard for you to see but it's a girl.'

'Oh! I'm glad.' Tears filled Dervla's eyes. Mick's eyes were glittering too and Caroline had a lump in her throat. She wanted to *beg* the teenager lying on the bed not to put that little baby up for adoption. But the counsellor in her knew she could do no such thing. The decision was Dervla's and Dervla's alone. Whatever course she took, she'd have to live with the consequences for the rest of her life. Either way it would not be an easy path.

'That was very exciting.' Mick patted his daughter's hand as they sat in Chapters Bookshop afterwards. Dervla had chosen hot chocolate for her treat. She was so relieved that the scan was over and everything was OK with the baby.

Her mind was in a whirl. Now that she knew the baby was a girl, it made everything seem more real. She was going to have a *daughter*. She would be giving her daughter away for adoption. Some other woman would be raising her. She looked at her Dad's kind smiling face and burst into tears.

Mick put his arm around her as she sobbed into his chest. 'It's all right,' he said comfortingly. 'That was a big moment for you, of course you're emotional.'

'It's just . . . it's just now that I know the baby's a girl and I'll be giving her up for adoption . . . and she's my daughter and I don't know what to do. I don't want to be responsible for a baby.'

Mick looked at Caroline in dismay and sent a silent plea for help.

'Dervla, it's a while yet before you have to make the ultimate decision. Why don't we get in touch with social services and the adoption agencies? You can arrange to have your baby to be placed in a foster home if you're not ready to make the decision about adoption. Fostering gives you leeway that adoption doesn't, because after the revocation period passes in the adoption process, you can't get your baby back if you change your mind,' Caroline explained gently.

'Thanks,' Dervla hiccupped, wiping her eyes with the serviette she handed over to her. 'You're very wise.'

'I deal with clients who've been in your position. It's a difficult one, so don't rush into anything. Your dad and I will help you as best we can. Let's just celebrate that the baby's healthy and strong today. We can discuss all the options in the next few weeks,' Caroline suggested.

'Great idea,' Mick said, mightily relieved that Caroline had taken charge. *How kind of her to say 'we'*, he thought. He'd be in an utter heap if he was handling this on his own. 'Let me get you another hot chocolate and a treat,' he offered, noticing that Dervla had finished her drink. He got up to go back to the counter.

'Poor Dad, I'm such a worry to him. You're very good to us, Caroline.' Dervla took a deep, steadying breath.

'That's what friends are for, Derv. He was a great friend to me when I first went to Abu Dhabi after my marriage broke up, and besides, I'm being nice to you because I don't want to lose the best office tidier and organiser I've ever had,' she joked, warmed by the teenager's heartfelt words.

'I did a good job, didn't I?' Dervla grinned. 'Your office was a disaster.'

'I know,' laughed Caroline. 'My office at work is ship-shape and tidy but when I come home, and all that post is waiting and I'm tired, I just shove it all into the office and say I'll deal with that later. You're the only person that's ever seen my shame.'

'Really?'

'Indeed.' Caroline grinned. 'There was six months' filing to be done there and lots of shredding.'

'*Lots!*' agreed Dervla, laughing, as Mick arrived back with a steaming hot chocolate and a plate of cakes. His phone tinkled and he looked at the number.

'Sorry, I have to take this,' he apologised. 'Hello, Laura. How's it going? Any news?' He listened intently. 'Fantastic, thanks so much. Bye.' He beamed at them. 'This *is* a day of celebration. That was the solicitor. The sale's gone through. The house is sold. Well done, Mason Estates. Time to go house hunting!'

'Are you going to stay in Drumcondra?' Caroline nibbled on a piece of the carrot cake he'd thoughtfully got for her, knowing she'd not want anything too calorie laden.

'I like Clontarf, Dad. It's nice being near the sea. On hot, sunny days in the summer when I was staying with Caroline, I pretended I was still in Abu Dhabi,' Dervla commented, licking buttercream off her fingers.

'Oh!' Mick looked at her, surprised. 'Do you miss it much?'

'Yeah!' She sighed. 'I miss Cesca and Shazza and . . .' She was about to say Faisal's swimming pool but she stopped herself in time, not wanting to upset her father. 'It's so cold here now.'

'It took me a while to adjust to the climate when I came home,' Caroline remarked. 'I wore layers that first summer.'

'I hadn't really given much thought to where I'd buy. I did

think of staying around Drumcondra because we're used to it,' Mick said. 'I might be able to afford Clontarf if I go for a three-bed. We don't really need a four-bed like we had in Drumcondra.' He looked at Dervla. 'But did I not hear that you're thinking of moving over to France with Ciara at some stage in the future? So it won't really matter to you where I buy.'

'I won't be going for a while, Dad. Maybe even a year, who knows?' Dervla answered.

'I'm teasing. What do you think, Caroline? You worked for an estate agent, way back.' He smiled at her.

'I suppose it depends what you're willing to spend. Clontarf's pricy but so's Drumcondra. If you *are* going to buy in Clontarf don't buy on the seafront. It's prone to flooding.'

'Good tip. I better get my finger out and start looking. You have a look too, Derv. The sooner we can move out of the apartment the better. If Ciara's coming home for the birth it will be a bit cramped.'

'Don't forget I've two beds free,' Caroline reminded him.

'I'm not going to impose on you any more then I have, Caroline,' Mick said resolutely.

'Give over,' she scoffed, winking at Dervla. 'Derv and I are buddies, aren't we, Derv? Buddies can have buddies and their dad or their sister to stay.'

'That's what buddies do, Dad.' Dervla grinned.

Mick laughed. 'I'm outnumbered. I surrender.'

'Have to go to the loo. Get your phone out and start Googling houses for sale.' Dervla stood up.

'Yes, Your Highness!' He saluted and she laughed at him and gave him a peck on the cheek before she left the table.

Mick turned to Caroline when they were alone. 'Caroline, I can't ever thank you enough for all—'

'Stop, Mick.' She held up her hand. 'You were so kind to me all those years ago, when I was a lost soul. You have no idea how *delighted* I am to repay that kindness. And it's not a hardship in any way. Getting to know Dervla has enriched my life. All my wonderful honorary nieces and nephews are all grown up now and I miss seeing them as much as I did. I've been given a new lease of life.'

'Do you think she should give the baby up for adoption? I'm so torn about it, to be honest. It's a no-win situation no matter what she does. If she keeps it, she's tied. She'll never have the chance to have the life her sister and brother have: travelling, no responsibilities except for themselves, having fun, being carefree. If she puts it . . . no, *her* up for adoption will that haunt her for the rest of her life? It will haunt me.'

'There's no easy answers, Mick. It's a pity she's so young. All you can do is to keep supporting her as you are. And I'll help in any way I can.'

'You're a blessing in my life, Caroline,' Mick said with such heartfelt sincerity that Caroline felt warmed to the very core of her.

'It's a girl. She's a strong, healthy baby. Dervla's fine too.' Mick could hear laughter and chat in the background and guessed that Sally and Faisal were entertaining. 'I won't delay you,' he said.

'No, it's fine. Has she said any more about putting the baby up for adoption?'

'That seems to be the plan currently,' Mick said flatly.

'Good. It's the best thing for both of them.' Sally took a sip of her wine. 'If she wants to come back here when it's all over that's fine too. Your apartment's very cramped really.'

'Speaking of which, the house sale went through today so I'll be looking for a new place ASAP.'

'Great. How much did it sell for?'

'More than I expected,' Mick said cagily. 'I won't need a four-bed, so I'm going to downsize with the next one. Anyway, I'll let you go. You're entertaining. Night, Sally.'

'Night, Mick,' she replied but her ex-husband had already hung up.

A spike of sadness pierced her. The family home was gone, finally. It had been a happy place once, before discontent had overtaken her. Now her final link with Mick was broken. Steadfast, responsible, affable Mick, who at the back of her mind she'd felt she could always go back to if the worst came to the worst.

That might not be so easy now, if anything went wrong between her and Faisal. Since she'd come back to Abu Dhabi after her month away in France and Dublin, Sally had felt there had been an imperceptible change in him. Something she couldn't *quite* put her finger on.

CHAPTER FIFTY-TWO

COLIN CANTRELL-KING

Colin Cantrell-King opened his front door and felt the heat of the house envelope him. It pleased him. The weather had turned cold and it was getting dark much earlier. He switched on the hall lamp and made a mental note to change his timers to come on earlier.

He hung his overcoat on the hall rack and went into the immaculate, tiled kitchen and opened the slow cooker on the counter top. The smell of beef stew filled the kitchen and he inhaled the aroma, his mouth watering.

His housekeeper had left the table set and had left two chunky slices of Vienna roll wrapped up in a pristine white linen napkin. He'd butter it to mop up the gravy. Sometimes a home-cooked meal was just the thing, he thought contentedly. He hadn't felt in the humour for eating out tonight.

'Alexa, play Dean Martin singing "Volare",' he instructed, decanting a bottle of Rioja Gran Reserva he was particularly fond of, humming with Dino as music filled the kitchen. Later he was going to book flights to Portugal for a well-deserved golf week at his villa on the Algarve. The late-autumn heat would be good for him. Some of his golfing friends were making plans to be out there at the same time. Just what he needed after the stressful year he'd had.

All that ghastly business with Devlin Delaney and her nasty little foreign collaborator seemed to have blown over. No doubt they'd been advised they'd get nowhere taking a case against him. He was in the clear, Colin congratulated himself as he ladled the stew into a bowl. He hadn't heard a peep from them since he'd called Madam Delaney at work and given her a piece of his mind.

Colin ate with relish, enjoying his accompanying wine and the music that filled the kitchen. It was nice sometimes just to be by himself, no matter how fond he was of his lady friends.

The jangle of the doorbell woke Colin out of a deep sleep. 'What... what time is it?' he muttered, disorientated. He struggled to see his alarm clock. 7.15am: he'd slept in. He shouldn't have drunk the whole bottle of wine last night. Who could be knocking on his door at this hour of the morning? He staggered out of bed, rubbing his eyes, and opened the heavy drapes on the big bay bedroom window. A man was standing at the gate, a car parked on the road behind him.

'What the hell?' Colin grunted. He wrapped his dressing gown around himself and stomped downstairs, irritated when the bell rang again and resounded around the silent house.

'Hello?' he said gruffly through the intercom.

'Colin Cantrell-King?' A deep voice echoed around the hall. 'Can you open your gate and front door please? It's An Garda Síochána.'

Colin stared at the intercom, shocked. His heart began to pound, his insides turned to ice and his mouth went dry. He pressed the button on the panel and he could hear the gates creak open. Taking a shaky breath, he unlocked the front door as the guard ran up the steps.

'What's all this about, garda? It's very early to be ringing someone's doorbell,' Colin said in his most superior tone when he opened the front door to his unwelcome visitor.

'Good morning, sir. Sorry about that. We like to catch people before they go out. I'm a member of the Garda Síochána.' The garda flashed an identity card. 'May I have a word please? Preferably not on the steps.'

'If you must,' Colin blustered. 'I didn't break a red light on my way to the hospital, did I? I had an emergency patient last week,' he lied. He didn't operate anymore, just recommended private patients who needed surgery to other colleagues, but he wanted the garda to know whom he was dealing with.

The garda stepped inside and closed the heavy front door behind him. 'Colin Cantrell-King, I'm arresting you under section section four of the Criminal Law Act of 1997 on suspicion of the rape of Devlin Delaney in your consulting rooms in . . .'

Colin stared at the guard, dazed. He could see the man's mouth moving but he was in such shock he couldn't take in what was being said.

'. . . sexual assault and digital rape of Nenita Santos . . .'

Those two bitches had shopped him. They had actually gone to the police about him. He was going to be arrested and questioned. Right now, this minute.

'You are not obliged to say anything unless you wish to do

so but anything you say can and will be taken down in writing and may be given in evidence.'

Colin opened his mouth to protest but no sound came out. He knew his arrest would ruin his reputation and his life, no matter whether he was found guilty or not.

'It's all a tissue of lies, of course. They were trying to blackmail me and when that didn't work they went to the guards in an act of pure spite.' Colin sat in front of the barrister and senior counsel he'd hired to defend him. The best money could buy. He felt he was in a nightmare. The humiliation of being questioned like a common *criminal*, in a garda station after his arrest. The terror of being brought to court, charged and released on bail with his passport confiscated almost matched the utter degradation of being filmed and photographed walking down the steps of the court with his solicitor and the resulting announcement in the media of his arrest.

And now, trying to concentrate on the questions his two legal eagles were asking him when all he wanted was to hide away somewhere where no one knew him. He was going to move to Portugal when all this farce was over, Colin decided wildly.

'You're *absolutely* certain there's no truth in either of these accusations?' Colin heard the question being repeated. The senior counsel stared hard at him. Colin stared back defiantly.

'Absolutely none,' Colin retorted. 'Gentlemen, may I say, just between us, women *were* attracted to me when I was younger. It went with the territory. I had many offers *but* I was a happily married man. I didn't need to force myself on any woman, you understand.'

'What about the uniform with the DNA evidence on it?' The barrister – a lanky, balding chap – took his glasses off and polished them before putting them back on and eyeballing Colin.

'It was *all* consensual. She threw herself at me. It was pitiful really: she fell head over heels for me and she was beautiful. I'm afraid I forgot my marriage vows briefly, to my shame.'

'And the Delaney woman who had your child, did she fall head over heels in love with you too?' The senior counsel interjected suavely, never lowering his scrutiny.

Colin was mortified. His gaze dropped briefly. 'Unfortunately, yes. She was naive. A great reader of romance novels. Excuse me for a moment: I need to use the rest room.' He stood up and walked out of the consultation room, utterly disconcerted.

'Guilty as fuck,' the senior counsel said, yawning.

'We'll get him off,' the barrister declared, whipping out his phone to Google Devlin Delaney.

'*Oh my God!* Did you see him on the news, Nenita? He looked absolutely *shattered*.' Devlin tucked the phone under her ear and poured herself a cup of tea.

She'd been alerted earlier, as had Nenita, by their DPSU garda that Colin had been arrested early that morning, questioned and brought to court.

'Not so superior now, Devlin, is he? Even to see this is enough for me to feel vindicated,' Nenita said triumphantly. 'Now everyone knows what he's like.'

'I'm glad they took his passport. He can't sneak off to Portugal to hide out. And he's been directed to sign on once a week too. What an indignity for him. I wonder will anyone else press charges now that we've set the ball rolling?'

'It will be interesting to see, for sure,' Nenita replied. 'The can of worms has finally been opened.'

PART FOUR

CHAPTER FIFTY-THREE

Devlin/Nurse McGrath

'Devlin, there's a young woman here in reception, insisting on seeing you. She says she's Amanda McGrath and that you knew her grandmother and it's important,' Lily, the receptionist on duty, explained to Devlin. She was in her office sifting through the names of City Girl's original members she wanted to invite to the anniversary party.

Devlin remembered Colin Cantrell-King's nurse, a stern-faced, reserved type of woman who went to Mass daily and seemed very religious. What on earth did her granddaughter want with her?

'Send her up, Lily, thanks,' she said, standing up and walking over to the window. It was a raw, cold day and a dour sky hung over Stephen's Green, threatening rain. A short while later Madalina knocked on her door, walking in with a young woman in tow.

'Amanda McGrath for you, Devlin.'

'Thanks, would you get the bistro to send up . . .' she turned to look at the young woman, 'tea or coffee, Amanda?'

'A latte would be great if that's OK,' the young woman answered nervously.

'A latte and a mug of tea for me, thanks, Madalina.' Devlin pointed to the sofa by the window. 'Take your coat off and let's sit down, Amanda, and you can tell me what I can do for you.' She studied the young woman who was unzipping her coat. In her early twenties, an attractive brunette with a short bob and feathery fringe, she was small and wiry looking. Her dark-lashed green eyes dominated her face. 'How is Nurse McGrath? She must be quite elderly by now.'

'She's well. She's in her early seventies, sprightly and well able to look after herself.' Amanda's nervousness dissipated in the face of Devlin's easy manner.

'I didn't know she was married.'

'She wasn't.' Amanda shook her head. 'My mother was born out of wedlock.'

'Oh,' murmured Devlin, trying to hide her astonishment. 'I had a child out of wedlock too, in the early nineties. It was hard going then. I hope Nurse McGrath didn't have too rough a time when she went through it. It's so different now.'

'Gran *did* have a hard time. Her parents disowned her. If it wasn't for my other grandmother, my mother would probably have had to be adopted.'

'Thank God then for that grandmother.' Devlin smiled. 'I hope your mother and Nurse McGrath are in a good place these days.'

'My mother's dead. She died by suicide,' Amanda said flatly as one of the girls from the bistro arrived with the refreshments.

'I'm terribly sorry to hear that, Amanda,' Devlin exclaimed. 'That must be very, very difficult for you both.'

'It is. And it's one of the reasons I'm here. My grandmother sent me to ask if you would meet up with her. She'd like to talk to you about – as she calls them – "private matters".'

Devlin tried to hide her dismay. Nurse McGrath had not been an easy work colleague and had never tried to hide her disapproval of Devlin and her 'immodest, unsuitable clothing' that she wore to work. Devlin clearly remembered the day the nurse had told her that coming to work in a black sleeveless vest top worn with black trousers was entirely inappropriate for the workplace.

'Don't mind Reverend Mother,' Colin had laughed when she'd told him. 'I think you're dressed *entirely* appropriately.'

Devlin, of course, had been delighted with her boss's response.

'Where would she like us to meet?' Devlin queried.

'Gran was hoping you'd come to her house but if you don't have time for that – she knows you are a very busy woman – she wondered would Bewley's suit?' Amanda replied, taking a sip of her latte.

'Did she say anything about Colin Cantrell-King being arrested?' Devlin asked hesitantly.

'Yes. She asked me to tell you these are the "private matters" she needs to talk to you about.'

'I see. Where does she live?'

She lives in Booterstown, not far from the Dart. It's easy to get to,' Amanda said eagerly. 'Here's her address and phone number, so you can text her if you decide to meet her. I'm on an early lunch break: I'd better get back.' She stood up and held out her hand. 'Thanks for agreeing to see me, Devlin. My grandmother admires you greatly.'

'Really?' Devlin was surprised.

'Oh yes! She used to tell my mother that being a single mother hadn't held you back and you were inspiring.'

'That's nice to hear,' Devlin murmured as Amanda pulled on her coat.

'Gran's inspiring to me too,' Amanda said. 'She fought hard to keep my mother and she's always been there for me. Please don't keep her waiting too long for your decision.'

'I won't. I'll text her now to arrange a meeting,' Devlin said.

'Thank you. Bye.'

'Bye,' Devlin echoed as Amanda McGrath strode purposefully out the door.

Devlin was glad of her chunky scarf pulled over her ears. A biting, easterly wind blew in off the white-capped, churning sea as she crossed the Rock Road and turned right towards the address Amanda had given her. Five minutes later she turned down a small side road and onto a neat row of terraced cottages.

Nurse McGrath's cottage was at the end of the terrace and even in the harsh wintery weather the pots of red, white and purple cyclamens and the fat red berries on the skimmia under the windows were gloriously vibrant against the white pebbledash.

Devlin rang the doorbell. Moments later the door opened and a tall, bright-eyed, grey-haired lady stood there.

'Nurse McGrath?' Devlin said, hardly able to believe that her old colleague was as elderly as she was. Of course it had been more than three decades since she'd last seen her, Devlin reminded herself.

'Devlin,' the woman said, holding out her hand. 'Please, come in. And call me Annie,' the older woman said warmly, and Devlin was astonished at how different she was from the stern-faced hatchet she'd worked with all those years ago. Never in a million years would she have thought then that she'd be calling Nurse McGrath by her first name.

Annie led her into a narrow cream-and teal-painted hall and opened the door to a bright sitting room where a blazing log fire burned. 'Let me take your coat. I've the kettle boiled: will you take tea or coffee?' Annie offered.

'Tea would be lovely, thanks,' Devlin said.

'You sit down there by the fire. It's freezing cold out there. Did you drive or take the Dart?'

'I took the Dart. It's so handy, isn't it?'

'I'd be lost without it,' Annie declared, taking Devlin's coat and scarf. Devlin sat on a comfy sofa and gazed around, studying the photos of Amanda and a young woman Devlin presumed was Amanda's mother on the mantle and sideboard. Amanda's mother carried an aura of sadness about her, even though she was smiling for the camera. She was the image of a younger Annie but she reminded Devlin of someone else. Just as she was about to look more closely, Annie appeared carrying a tray with two mugs of tea, milk, sugar and a plate of homemade tea brack.

Devlin jumped up. 'Let me take that from you.' She took the tray from Annie and placed it on the small coffee table in front of the sofa.

'Thank you, Devlin. My fingers are a bit arthritic and this weather doesn't help. Milk and sugar?' she asked.

'I'm sorry to hear about your hands. My mother suffered arthritis in her later years. It's painful.' Devlin splashed a drop of milk into her tea.

'Do have some tea brack. My secret ingredient is brandy: it's the only way I take alcohol,' Annie confided with a twinkle in her eye. *This is not the repressed, reserved woman that I remember,* Devlin thought as she took a slice of the fruity treat.

'Amanda told me you have private matters to discuss,' Devlin said when both of them were sitting down, Annie in her armchair and Devlin on the sofa, sipping their tea.

'I do, Devlin, and can I first say I was so sorry to hear of the loss of your little girl all those years ago. What a tragedy for you, after overcoming such difficulties.'

'Thanks, Nurse ... em ... Annie. There's always the *uaigneas* for my beautiful little daughter. She's in my heart but life goes on and I live with it. I hear from Amanda that you too lost a daughter,' she said gently. 'I'm very sorry for your grief.'

'It's a very hard loss; I grieve for Antonia every day. She found life too hard in the end. Seeking but never finding what she was looking for.'

'And what was that?' Devlin asked.

'A father's love. A man to replace the father she never knew.'

'Oh, how sad.' Devlin didn't know what to say. 'Was it recent?'

'Ten years ago. Amanda was eleven. Antonia – I called her that because Saint Anthony has always been so good to me,' Annie confided, 'well, she'd been in a depression for months. She'd go through bouts of it. Her ex had left her for someone younger, prettier and less emotionally needy, and Antonia never got over yet another rejection. It seemed to be a pattern with her. The men she had relationships with were always older, wealthy and ultimately unobtainable, just like her father. It has not been an easy path with my daughter. At least now she's at peace,' Annie said sadly. 'But,' she straightened up, 'her father is still very much alive and trouble has knocked on his door, I'm led to believe. I can't bring myself to have much sympathy for him.'

'Understandable,' murmured Devlin who, while she felt very sympathetic towards Annie, having heard her sorry saga, was keen to find out what 'private matters' the elderly woman wished to discuss with her.

'I hear our ex-boss has been arrested on charges of historical sexual assault.' Annie changed the subject.

'Yes, indeed,' Devlin said firmly. She hoped that Annie wasn't going to ask her to drop her charges against Colin. Was that why she was here? *Oh no*, Devlin thought. Why had she not foreseen this? Out of some misguided sense of loyalty towards Colin, was Annie going to put her in an awkward position?

You idiot, Devlin! she cursed herself, waiting uneasily for Annie to say her piece.

CHAPTER FIFTY-FOUR

Devlin/Annie/Colin

Annie picked up a folder from her little side table.

'I've something that might interest you,' she said matter-of-factly.

'What would that be?' Devlin was wary.

'It's a record of payments my child's father made towards Antonia's upbringing.'

'And how would this help me?' Devin couldn't fathom what Annie was going on about.

'Devlin: our children shared the same father. They would have been half-sisters.' Annie's blue eyes stared steadily into hers. 'Colin raped me too.'

'Oh my God, Annie!' Devlin couldn't believe what she was hearing. Dazed, she lowered her mug as her hand began to shake. 'Was this after me, after I'd left?'

Annie gave a dry laugh. 'Devlin, he never looked at me like that again after I gave birth to Antonia. She was about seven when you came to work for Colin. That was why I was so stern with you,' she sighed. 'I could see what was happening. He was making you fall for him the same way he'd made me. You might not credit it but I was once pretty and carefree. A good nurse too, believe it or not,' Annie said spiritedly. 'I was working in the maternity hospital where Colin worked and he took a shine to me. He'd opened up his private rooms the year before and his nurse was taking maternity leave and wasn't going to come back. He asked me if I'd come and work for him.

'I thought I was on the pig's back with the offer. Nine to five, no night duties, freedom to come and go as I pleased. I decided to rent a bedsit and get out of the nurses' home. It was so strict there and I *loved* dancing.'

Devlin sat, dumbfounded, trying to fit the perception she had of Annie together with this carefree young woman she was hearing about.

'Anyway, Colin started flirting and being charming and I was shocked. He was married. His wife was beautiful and elegant and I couldn't make out what he saw in me, a little country bumpkin from Meath.' She shook her head, reliving the past as though it were yesterday.

'One afternoon, after he'd seen the last of his patients, I was tidying up the examination couch and he launched himself on me, told me he was madly in love with me and he had to have me. I said no, of course, and I struggled. That made him worse. He ... well, it was all over very quickly. He took my virginity and my self-respect and gave me a cross to bear – not my daughter,' Annie added hastily. 'For years after that day and becoming pregnant outside of marriage, I felt I had to beg forgiveness from God. I used to go to Mass every day to atone for my sins.' Tears came into Annie's eyes.

Devlin had a lump in her throat and she reached over and took the other woman's hand. 'I'm so sorry for what you went through, Annie. So sorry,' she managed, as memories of the loss of her own virginity surged back with an intensity that shook her. 'Why did you stay working for him?'

'Oh I left that day, I can assure you. I found a job as a nanny and I worked there for three months before I finally worked out that I was pregnant. I kept the job until I was six months' gone, when my employer copped. I was showing, even though up until then I'd disguised it under loose sweaters. So I was pregnant and jobless and I went home to my parents and told them. My father called me a slut and told me to never darken their door again. My mother gave me fifty pounds, her life savings, and brought me to Dublin to a Mother and Child home. I stayed there until I gave birth.

'The nuns told me they were putting my baby girl up for adoption. It was the best choice for her to have a good life, because I wouldn't be able to give her one.' Annie shook her head. 'I was stubborn, Devlin. I'd fallen in love with my baby and no one else was going to raise her. So one day I said I was going for a walk with her. I packed my bag and put it into the buggy. I had a great friend, another nurse, and she met me and I stayed in her flat until I got one of my own. I was able to pay a month's rent out of the fifty pounds my mother had given me. I knew where Colin lived so I took the bus over to the Merrion Road and when his car was gone I walked up the steps and knocked on the door. A maid answered. I told her I used to work for Colin and I'd come to show Mrs Cantrell-King my new baby. She let me in, never suspecting anything. I felt real mean doing it but I had to provide for my child.

'Jessica Cantrell-King came into the room that the maid had shown me into. I always remember she was wearing a beautiful lilac twinset and pearls. Anyway, when she came into the room I stood up and handed her the baby. "Meet your husband's daughter," I said.' Annie drew a deep breath. 'The poor woman nearly died. "He will lie when you confront him," I told her, "but he raped me. I was his nurse. It lasted less than a minute and I was a virgin and I got pregnant. I have no money to feed my child. I need your help because my family have disowned me. If you don't believe me, a blood test will confirm the paternity."'

'God, that was brave of you.' Devlin was still holding Annie's hand and Annie put her other hand on top. 'I was *desperate*. Like you were when you went to London after getting pregnant – I read about you in your interviews. We both did what we had to do.

'Anyway, Jessica gave me two hundred pounds and asked me for my address. I gave it to her and you can imagine my surprise when she turned up two weeks later with a form for a Post Office account, into which she told me she would be lodging seventy-five pounds a week. When my baby was one she would fix me up with a job and childcare, she told me. All she wanted was to be able to see Antonia on a regular basis. I couldn't believe it. I didn't want to pry and ask her if she had said anything to Colin.'

'Wow, that was supportive,' Devlin said. 'I always found her very standoffish on the phone.'

'She gave that impression but she wasn't really. Jessica was very nice, actually, and over the years she would let slip things to me about the life she endured with that bastard. I wasn't the first "dalliance", as she called it. She loved him but she'd eventually realised that he'd only married her because her family was wealthy and he needed money and contacts to set up a successful practice. Jessica's family was able to give him both.'

'Why did you go back to work for him?'

Annie took a sip of her tea. 'I went back because she asked me to. She knew he'd never look at me as an object of desire again. He liked them young and fresh, she said once. She was drunk, when she said it. Jessica started to drink heavily as the years went by. She organised for me to work part-time with him and paid for a child minder.'

'Didn't you feel weird going back to work there?' Devlin asked. She knew she couldn't have done it.

'It was hard, *very* hard. I'll never forget that first day. I was sick to my stomach.' Annie grimaced at the memory.

'He was very professional. Called me Nurse McGrath as though nothing had happened between us. He said, "Two things. I never want to hear anything about your child. And there's to be no mention of what happened between us, *ever*." That was all he said and, after that, it was as if the past had never happened. After the first week, I began to feel more OK with it because it meant I could raise my child without having to go on social welfare and worry too much about money.

'Once, he had told a couple they were infertile and couldn't have children. They were crying in the waiting room and he was in his office, irritated with them. I couldn't help it and I said to him. "You have a daughter. They would give anything to have a child. Have you no compassion? How can you not want to know about your own child?"

'"Shut up, Annie," he said — the first time he'd called me

by my name since I went back to work for him – "as far as I'm concerned I have no child."

'I left soon after you left, Devlin. I heard on the grapevine that you were pregnant and were living in London. I saw the way he behaved with you. What I know now to be grooming. That had been me once. And then one day you were working there and the next you were gone with no notice given or anything. So when I heard you were pregnant I figured he was the father. I couldn't bring myself to work there anymore. I told Jessica I'd had enough. I didn't say anything about you. I didn't know if she knew. She understood. She made Colin give me a glowing reference.

'She still came to visit Antonia. Jessica loved her. When her father died she inherited quite an amount of money. She gave me the deposit and more for this cottage.'

'That was very decent of her. What a sad life she led.'

'She'd a very busy social life,' Annie observed. 'She loved opera and the ballet and she did a lot of entertaining for Colin. I think she had a relationship with someone—'

'Oh I *hope* she did,' Devlin said fervently.

'Me too. Cantrell-King treated her appallingly. She deserved some happiness.' Annie nodded. 'Anyway, it's all in the past. But I want you to know that I have a record of all the payments I received from Jessica for Antonia's upbringing. I have the details of the deposit she gave me. I went to an accountant years ago to see what tax was due on it but Revenue said it wasn't all a gift; it was child maintenance, which was decent of them.

'I also have a signed statement here, from a solicitor, which will be very advantageous to our case when we take it.'

'*Our* case! When *we* take it?' Devlin repeated, confused.

'I'd like to join you and the other woman taking the case against Colin Cantrell–King, Devlin. I want my voice to be heard after all these years. I want to do it for Antonia and Amanda. Our children are dead, but his grandchild isn't. He *will* acknowledge them all whether he likes it or not. And I also want to do it for me and for Jessica. We didn't matter to him. Our feelings were of no importance. Well, they'll matter now. He'll acknowledge all of us one way or another. What do they call it now … gaslighting? Well, the gaslighting is over. We have a voice, as do you and that other woman. He *will* hear them.'

Annie stood up and held out her arms and both of them wept as they hugged each other tightly.

'The other side has sent us these documents. It seems another litigant has joined them. An Annie McGrath. Your former nurse. We've been advised she'll be making a statement to the guards and pressing charges.' The senior counsel handed over a sheaf of pages to Colin, whose sharp intake of breath sounded loud in the small consultation room he and his legal team were gathered in.

Colin read the first document, on headed notepaper, and his face sagged in shock.

> I, Jessica Frances Cantrell-King, wish to make it known that my husband, Colin Cantrell-King, is the father of Antonia McGrath, now deceased, daughter of Nurse Annie McGrath.
> Colin Cantrell-King is the grandfather of

Amanda McGrath, daughter of Antonia McGrath (deceased).

Antonia McGrath was born as a result of the rape perpetrated on Annie McGrath in July of the year 1983 by my husband, Colin Cantrell-King.

I also wish it to be known that my husband provided me with revenue to pay monthly maintenance for his child, Antonia, with Annie McGrath.

Amanda McGrath, his grandchild, is entitled to make a claim against my husband's estate, in the event of his death.

'This is *preposterous*. Jessica was probably as pissed as a newt when she made this statement. Or else she was being blackmailed,' Colin exploded as he read the damning indictment.

'It's been witnessed and signed in a solicitor's office. If your wife gave any appearance of being drunk that would not have happened. You might like to read a copy of the statement provided by Annie McGrath to the garda. You will note that the description of the alleged rape is very similar to the ones provided by Ms Delaney and Mrs Santos,' the senior counsel said gravely.

'But . . . but . . . I won't stand for this – this *abomination*. This assault on my good character,' Colin raged.

'Unfortunately a jury might not see it like that,' the barrister interrupted his tirade. 'We're in a spot of bother here, Colin.'

'Whose side are you on?' Colin barked, rounding on him.

'It's not a matter of sides.' The senior counsel tapped his pen against the table. 'It's about evidence and the law and we have to put it to you that this new accuser and the added material supplied are extremely detrimental to your case. The best defence we can put up is conspiracy to commit blackmail against you, by all the litigants. However, that will be hard to prove and you will remember there *is* the DNA evidence Mrs Santos provided. And I presume paternity for both deceased children can be proved if needed.'

Colin glared at him but there was nothing he could say.

'You can of course go to trial and see what a jury makes of the evidence,' the senior counsel continued. 'Or you can plead guilty and forgo the trial. The choice is yours. We will follow your instructions. Take some time to deliberate upon it and advise us of your decision. Good afternoon, Colin.' He stood up, nodded to Colin and his solicitor. *Like a beaky black crow,* Colin thought, glowering at him. The barrister followed him, robes swishing as they went.

'Right then, Colin. I think the senior counsel has put the options available to us quite clearly. Let me know when you've thought about it and are ready to make a decision on how to proceed. I've another consultation so I'll take my leave,' his solicitor said briskly and then he was gone. Colin was alone in the room with the sheaf of photocopies his senior counsel had presented him with.

So, Jessica had got her own back on him from beyond the grave. How devious of her. I didn't think she had it in her, he thought contemptuously. 'Drunken sot,' he muttered furiously.

Colin shoved the pages into the file, grabbed his coat and walked out of the room. He was passing through the Round Hall when he saw one of his golf buddies. 'Hello, Jeremy,' he said chummily, thinking how dignified and imposing the other man looked in his wig and gown.

The barrister looked at him briefly, recognised him and, not breaking his stride, walked past Colin without a backward glance. Colin stopped dead, shaken at the snub. He'd already seen little groups stop their conversations when he'd walked into the clubhouse bar. He'd noticed his golf partners were making excuses not to do a round with him since news of his arrest had got out, but he'd never been deliberately snubbed.

I'm done for! I'm a gonner, Colin realised, fear seizing his guts in a vice grip. *I'm ruined, a pariah, and I'm going to end up in jail for the rest of my life.*

CHAPTER FIFTY-FIVE

The Wedding

'Oh Mam, isn't it such a *gorgeous* morning?' Shona stepped out onto the patio and raised her face to the much-wished-for September sun. The country was experiencing an unexpected late Indian summer. The previous week there'd been torrential showers and thunderstorms. 'What a stroke of good luck. The gods and goddesses are with us.' She danced exuberantly, barefoot on the paving slabs, raising her arms to the sky and Maggie felt an overwhelming love for her eldest daughter wash over her.

'We didn't need to put the Child of Prague out,' Maggie remarked, patting the statue's head. Nelsie had given it to them the night before.

'Put it out, just in case. Better to be safe than sorry, Shona,' her grandmother had advised sagely.

'Yes, Gran,' Shona kissed her grandmother and Nelsie's eyes welled up.

'Mam! Are you OK?' Maggie was taken aback by Nelsie's tears.

'Ah, I was just thinking of your father. She was his favourite, you know, although he never let on. He always treated them the same but Shona was his little pet. He'd have been so proud to see her walking down the aisle.'

'Ah Gran.' Shona's eyes shone with tears. 'I loved Granddad very much. I knew I was his pet. But then I was his first grandchild,' she pointed out. 'It's not exactly an aisle I'll be walking down, Gran, don't forget,' she reminded her.

'It will be grand whatever it is,' Nelsie assured her. Maggie had warned her months ago when Shona had broached the matter of having a handfasting that Nelsie was to zip it about getting married in a church.

'I'll be saying nothing,' Nelsie retorted back then. 'It's all different to our day and that's as it should be. Young people have their own way of seeing things. And I like the handfasting idea, if you must know. It's older than the Church. We had it in Ireland long before we had that lot with their pointed hats and long frocks.'

'We did,' Maggie had agreed, relieved. Her mother surprised her sometimes with her enlightened attitudes.

'Not that I'm giving out about all the priests. Father Brendan and Father Harry are great men and kind with it. I haven't given up on *all* of it.'

'That's good to hear, Mam.' Maggie knew some of her elderly relatives had been shocked by her divorce but Nelsie had let them know in no uncertain terms that Maggie had done the right thing and if they knew about Terry's carry-on they'd agree. Maggie had never given her mother the full details about the straw that had broken the camel's back; she'd just said Terry was with another woman and they'd been together in their home when Maggie wasn't there. If Nelsie knew what Shona had seen she certainly wouldn't be on such good terms with her former son-in-law, Maggie was in no doubt.

She and Shona had come back to the house with the statue and following the old custom had placed it in the garden, even though the night was clear and starry and good weather was forecast for the wedding day.

And what a cracker of a day it was, Maggie thought gratefully. 'I better put the fry-up on. Mimi and Michael will be back soon.' She threw a few crumbs into the garden for her robin who always came for breakfast. The twins had gone down to Latin Quarter to put the finishing touches to the flowers and decorations. After breakfast the four women were going to Classic Cuts, in Ashford, to get their hair styled before coming back to Maggie's to get their make-up done.

Maggie and her children had had a poignant but happy family night that past evening: reminiscing, joking and laughing. Knowing how much it would mean to her kids, Maggie had, with some difficulty, put aside her own anger and had sent Terry a text the day before asking him if he'd like to have supper with them. She hadn't told Shona and the twins of the invite. When the knock came to the door, Shona had answered it and seen her father on the step. She'd burst into tears of happiness. It was the first time in years they'd been together as a family, just the five of them. Listening to the hoots of laughter downstairs while she stood in the bathroom, she'd looked at herself in the mirror and said aloud, 'You're a good person, Maggie Ryan, even if having him here is giving you frigging heartburn.'

She still had heartburn the next day. Better not have a fry, she decided, flinging sausages into the air fryer and placing strips of bacon on the grill.

'That smells good.' Michael came in the back door and put his arms around his mother. Maggie was a tall woman but her son was three inches taller than her and she snuggled in against him. She couldn't believe that her easy-going boy, who was always getting up to mischief when he was a child, was now a tall, strapping young man.

'You can't beat a mammy fry,' he approved as she put brown bread onto a pan sizzling with butter.

'You'll have to clean up after the mammy fry: we've to go to get our hair done.'

'So have I,' he joked. 'Sure I will. Cinders will do everything, as usual.'

'What would I do without you?' She looked up at him, laughing.

'You'd be rightly stuck,' Michael said, nicking a sausage out of the air fryer.

'Get away and call your sisters. I'm just going to fry the eggs,' Maggie said happily. What a joy to have such precious time with her children.

Two and a half hours later Maggie, her daughters and Nelsie left Classic Cuts, looking a million dollars thanks to the ministrations of the hairdressers who had made such a fuss of them when they arrived.

'This is *very* exciting' Nelsie said perkily as they drove home to get their make-up done. Shona had persuaded her grandmother to have light make-up for the photos and Nelsie, who had needed little persuasion, was eager to embrace the new experience.

Two make-up artists that Shona often used when filming were waiting for them, chatting to Michael, and for the next hour the kitchen resembled a beauty parlour. Halfway through the proceedings, a car crunched across the gravel drive and Shona saw her dad and Chloé get out. Denise thankfully remained in the front seat.

'Hello, sis. Good timing,' she greeted warmly, when her half-sister followed Terry in, carrying her dress in a garment bag.

Chloé beamed. 'Hiya,' she said happily.

'Your hair's lovely,' Mimi complimented.

'All my work,' said Terry, and they laughed. 'I'll drop Denise down to the village for a coffee and you can text me when you're ready for me. You all look so beautiful,' he said and, for a moment, when his eyes met Maggie's she saw sadness and regret flash across them.

'We won't be too long,' she said. Maggie didn't need any more conflicting emotion on top of what she was feeling already. She was praying that she'd get through the giving away part without bawling.

'Right, Dad, off you go. I'm done. Chloé, you sit here.' Mimi took charge, much to her mother's relief, as Terry was ushered out the door. 'Shona: upstairs to put your dress on. Gran: make us all a cuppa before we go.'

Nelsie, who was admiring herself in the mirror and wondering what magic the make-up girl had used to make her eyes so bright and blue and her skin so creamy, said, 'Right oh, ya little tyrant!' She was enjoying herself immensely.

Twenty minutes later Shona descended the stairs, a vision

in an ivory satin V-neck, half-sleeve, tea-length gown with sandals to match. Ivory and pink roses were entwined through her hair: she carried a small bouquet of the same. Chloé gave a little squeal of delight. 'You look out of this world, Shona.'

'Do *not* cry, Mother!' Mimi warned Maggie, who was desperately trying to hold it together. 'Your mascara will streak.'

'You remind me of my youngest sister when she got married.' Nelsie was enchanted. 'Tea dresses were all the fashion after the war. You look radiant, dear!' She would have cried but Mimi's stern gaze gave her pause and she swallowed hard and cleared her throat.

'Ya scrubbed up well, sis,' Michael – looking like a tanned Greek god in a light blue Oxford shirt and cream chinos – approved. He had been putting ribbons on his father's car with Terry, who'd arrived back five minutes previously, when Maggie had texted him. He'd followed his son into the kitchen and came to a sudden halt when he saw his daughter in all her bridal glory.

'Shona!' Terry said, his voice breaking.

'Do *not* cry either, Father! You will set our mother and grandmother off. Photos quick: we need to get going. Shona doesn't want to be late, sure you don't, Shona?' Mimi appealed to her sister who was also struggling not to cry.

'No ... no, I want to be there on time.' Shona composed herself. 'Last photos and we're going.'

Fifteen minutes later, the photographer was happy with the group shots and Michael waved his car keys. 'Come on my little chicks, time to go,' he said to Nelsie, Mimi and Chloé, gallantly taking his grandmother's arm and opening the car door for her. He made sure her hat stayed on while the two bridesmaids edged themselves gingerly into the back, not wanting to crease their fit-and-flare dusky pink midi dresses.

'So here we are, just the three of us.' Shona smiled at her parents. 'We made it, finally. And I'm so glad we're OK and a happy family again,' she said gratefully. 'I'm a very lucky bride. Let's go and have a wedding to remember.' She kissed each of them and then the photographer began fussing around and the moment was lost.

'If you want to see me arriving under the arch down there, you better get your skinny ass in gear and get out of here because I'm leaving now,' Shona told him, jokingly. He was a friend from college who was a bit of a perfectionist.

'Right, I'm done. I'll see you down there.' He grinned. As Maggie placed Shona's bouquet beside her on the back seat, she said, 'I suppose I better get in the front.'

'I suppose you better,' agreed her daughter, and Maggie wondered what Denise would be thinking when she saw the three of them arriving. Today was hard for the other woman, she imagined, but at least Shona had met her halfway by asking Chloé to be a bridesmaid. *Not my monkeys, not my circus*, she told herself, repeating one of Caroline's mantras, as she got into the front seat and picked up the whiff of whatever overpowering perfume Terry's wife wore.

'Right, girls. All ready? Off we go,' Terry said jovially, getting behind the wheel and starting the engine. 'Your prince awaits.'

A buzz of excitement rippled through the assembled guests as they stood around the lantern-festooned, flower-bedecked patio of the Latin Quarter. A quartet of musicians played soft melodies in the background and tables, with tasty treats in ceramic bowls, dotted the seating areas beyond. A faint smoky scent from the pizza ovens mingled with the scent of roses and clematis and the herbs that grew in various pots around the grounds.

'Here she comes,' Chloé gave a shout. She and her friend Sarah and Dervla – who had been invited with Caroline and Mick – had been standing under the arch keeping an eye out for the wedding car.

Aleksy – watched proudly by his parents and siblings – was standing with Michael and his best man, his brother Filip, under the gazebo where he and Shona were to be married. He straightened his tie nervously. Aleksy loved that Shona was on time. She'd told him that she had no truck with keeping a bridegroom waiting. 'I wouldn't do that to you, my darling,' she'd promised him when they said goodbye to each other the day before the wedding.

He heard the bridesmaids greet Shona and his heart swelled with love and joy when they moved behind her and Aleksy saw his bride. She was standing between her parents under the flower-draped ancient stone arch that led from the street into the magical venue.

The quartet took up their instruments and began to play *'Amigos Para Siempre'*. As the evocative music filled the air, Maggie and Terry walked their daughter under the arch, with her bridesmaids behind them, until they reached the red carpet that led to the gazebo. They kissed her and Shona drew away from them and walked alone to where Aleksy stood with his arms open to embrace her.

'Friends forever,' he murmured against her hair and the choir of birds in the trees above them enhanced the melodious notes of their love song.

'Friends forever,' Shona whispered against his cheek as their celebrant began his words of welcome to all who had gathered with them to witness their wedding.

'It was a beautiful service, Maggie,' Caroline enthused, 'and you look stunning.'

'I told you that dress was perfect for you,' Devlin said smugly. The trio had gone shopping in Gorey a month before the wedding and seen the perfect dress in one of the many boutiques on the main street. It was a pale lemon and blue chiffon midi dress with an off-shoulder neckline, that floated ethereally when she moved. Her hair was in a loose up-do, wisps framing her face. And even Maggie, who didn't spend much time looking at herself in the mirror, had to admit she looked great. She hadn't worn a hat. Neither had Caroline or Devlin, knowing it wasn't a posh affair. Denise's red wide-brimmed creation with a big bow at the side took pride of place in the hat stakes. She was wearing a fitted cream dress with tiny buttons up the back that clung to her curves and a red clutch and red shoes accessorised the ensemble.

'Bit bridey looking, isn't it?' Devlin had murmured to Caroline when she'd seen Denise's dress.

'Not going to be outdone, for sure. Just think it's a bit OTT for the kind of wedding we're at.'

'I'm just so glad it all went well and we can relax now. I wasn't too sure about the walking up the aisle bit with Terry,' Maggie confessed. 'Shona did it perfectly. She didn't want to be "given away" so it was nice to walk her to the gazebo and let her go to Aleksy herself.'

'I know it's hard for you, Maggie, but it was so moving to see you and Terry at her side,' Caroline remarked.

'You know, if Michael hadn't have told me about feeling guilty for being sick that day, I'd have been as happy as Larry today. I'm trying hard not to dwell on it but it's a struggle, I can tell you, when I see Terry being the life and soul of the party here and me knowing what I know.' Maggie sighed.

'But Michael's having a great time.' Devlin pointed to where he, Finn, Luke, Mick and the best man were laughing uproariously over at the pizza oven, scoffing canapés. 'So try to enjoy every second of today.'

'You're right. And I *am* enjoying it, and Caroline,' she turned to her friend, 'Mick is an absolute dote.'

'He is, isn't he?' Caroline smiled. 'He's such a great friend. I'm delighted to see him enjoying himself; it's not been easy for him the last few months. Thanks for asking him and Dervla.'

'We were delighted to. Shona insisted,' Maggie assured her, secretly thrilled that Caroline had brought a plus one. It did her heart good to see her darling friend having fun and being carefree after the rough patch she'd gone through.

'Nelsie is having a ball,' Devlin observed, seeing Maggie's mother chatting away to Maggie's friends, from Flemings Shop in Barndarraig, who'd come for the afters.

'She was disgusted Tony and Ginny haven't come despite being invited. *I* on the other hand am very glad not to have them here. I know that's an awful thing to say about your own brother and his wife but do I look as though I care?' Maggie took a drink of her Prosecco and laughed.

'It's such an informal, carefree wedding. I love the vibe of this place,' Devlin said as a group of Aleksy and Shona's friends began an impromptu session, playing banjos, guitars and mouth organs. One girl was thrumming away on a bodhrán. Devlin's eyes lit up. 'Come on, girls. Let's get on the dance floor and do our best Riverdance impression.' Laughing heartily, the three of them took their shoes off, sashayed onto the floor and began to dance a slip jig, roared on by the other guests who all joined in too.

'Your aunts are great fun,' Dervla said enviously to Chloé, watching Devlin, Caroline and Maggie doing their Irish dance. 'My mom loves a trad session too. They have lots of them in the Irish Club in Abu Dhabi.'

'They're not my real aunts,' Chloé corrected her, 'but they're just brill. Caroline's very kind, isn't she?'

'Yeah, I've really got to like her.' Dervla shoved a cushion behind her back. It was aching and the baby was lying on a nerve that sent shooting pains down her left leg.

Sarah had gone to get more drinks for them and they were on their own, sitting on a sofa, in a snug little seating area that opened out onto the grounds. Dusk was settling and the lights threaded around the Latin Quarter were beginning to twinkle brightly. The heaters had been turned on to take away the faint evening chill and there were plenty of soft throws for guests to wrap up in if they were cold.

'You OK?' Chloé asked solicitously.

Dervla's lower lip trembled. 'I'm scared,' she whispered. 'And I feel so fat and ugly. And I wonder will any boy ever want to marry me? And I hate my life.'

'Oh, Derv.' Chloé scooted over beside her friend and put her arm around her. 'Will I get Caroline or your dad?' she asked anxiously.

Dervla shook her head. 'No,' she gulped. 'It's so nice to see my dad having fun because I know he's so worried about me.'

'You're not fat and ugly. You have beautiful eyes and I'd kill for your nose. It's so dainty, not like my schnozzle.'

Dervla laughed in spite of herself. 'You haven't a schnozzle, Chloé.'

'I take after my dad with the nose,' Chloé sighed. 'But look, when the baby's born we can Zoom and do exercise sessions three times a week. They have great ones online. You'll have your figure back in no time,' she said confidently.

'I don't know. I'm longing to get into my real jeans and not have to wear tents. It would have been fantastic to have been able to wear my Kate Spade halter tonight and dance with all those hot boys.'

'They're a bit old. They're in their late twenties and thirties,' Chloé demurred.

'Who cares, they're hot.' Dervla sighed, wiping her eyes when she spotted Chloe's friend heading back their way. 'Thanks for being a good friend, Chloé,' she said gratefully. 'After I've had the baby next month maybe we could go and have a spa day somewhere.'

'Ooh yeah! I'd love that. That's a plan,' Chloé enthused, giving her a hug. Dervla cuddled into her, knowing she was lucky to have two real, good friends in her life. Things were never as bad when you could tell them your fears. Somehow she knew Chloé and Cesca would be her friends forever. They'd be like Devlin, Caroline and Maggie. Three besties.

'Maggie, our taxi has arrived. We're staying in Powerscourt tonight. We're not going to go to the Arklow Bay for the dancing.' Terry came and stood beside her. It was dark, nearly 9pm and the bus Aleksy and Shona had hired to take them, Aleksy's family, and their guests to the Arklow Bay hotel, where they were all staying, had pulled up outside Latin Quarter.

'I'm not going either,' she said giddily. She'd been drinking Prosecco all afternoon and was a tad tipsy.

'I just want to thank you for everything you've done for our children. You're a great mother and you were a great wife and I'm sorry about the way things turned out, because I was a dickhead.' Terry was a bit maudlin. He'd had quite a lot to drink and his eyes were slightly glazed.

'We did well,' she said lightly, unable to bring herself to say that he was a great father, no matter how tipsy she was. 'One down, two more to go. And there's Chloé too, of course. Enjoy your night in Powerscourt. I better go and say goodbye to Caroline and Mick.'

'Oh! Yeah, right.' He threw his arms around her and hugged her tightly. 'Thanks, Maggie.' He said it with heartfelt sincerity that, in spite of herself, Maggie returned his hug because she knew he truly had little real understanding of the havoc he'd caused in her life. It was just the way he was.

'Terry, we shouldn't keep the taxi waiting. Go and find Chloé and Sarah.' Denise tripped over to them in her Jimmy Choos, not impressed at the way her husband was embracing his ex-wife.

'Thanks for coming, Denise. Chloé was a delightful bridesmaid,' Maggie said politely.

'Er . . . yes. It was kind of Shona to ask her.' Denise wrapped her pashmina around her and gave an exaggerated shiver.

'It was, *very*,' Maggie said pointedly and had the satisfaction of seeing a faint blush rise to the other woman's cheeks. 'Now, I think they're getting ready to give Shona and Aleksy a send-off. I must say goodnight to the guests,' she excused herself and walked towards a cheering group who were beginning to gather for the send-off for the bride and groom.

'Mam!' Shona threw her arms around her. 'Thanks for everything. We had the best wedding *ever*. I love you so much.'

'I love you too, Maggie, and thank you.' Her new son-in-law enveloped both of them in a bear hug.

'Won't you come over to the hotel for breakfast in the morning?'

'Of course I will, my darlings. Now go, have fun with your friends and dance the night away.'

'I'm gonna throw my bouquet,' Shona declared, standing up on a chair. There was a rush to gather in front of her as she turned her back to the crowd and, laughing happily, threw the flowers over her shoulder.

'Lucky you,' shouted Chloé as the bouquet hit the top of Dervla's bump and she caught it. Everyone cheered, much to her mortification.

'I wish I'd caught it,' Sarah said enviously as Dervla looked at the wilting flowers in astonishment.

'Now, see,' murmured Chloé to her friend. 'A boy *will* ask you to marry him. It's a sign.'

'You think?'

'I do.'

'Congratulations, Dervla.' Shona stepped off her chair, gallantly assisted by her husband. 'I hope you enjoyed the wedding.'

'I did, thanks,' she said shyly as Mick put his arm around her.

'We'll see you when we're back from the honeymoon. Bye everyone, see you at the hotel whoever's coming and thanks a million to all of you,' she called out to the assembled guests. Cheers and good wishes followed the happy couple.

Maggie stood watching her daughter embrace Terry before she stepped onto the bus, tears sliding down her cheeks. She was very happy for Shona. Aleksy was a good man. She prayed to the Universe that her child would have more luck with her marriage than she'd had.

'Well done, Maggie.' Devlin slid an arm around her waist.

'You played a blinder.' Caroline squeezed her hand.

With her two best friends standing by her side, Maggie waved her daughter and son-in-law off as the next chapter in their book of life began.

CHAPTER FIFTY-SIX

Caroline/Mick/Dervla

'Ow!' Caroline yelped as her consultant put her arm through a range of motions that caused her considerable pain.

'Sorry,' he said, prepping a cortisone injection.

It was painful. Right into the bone and she cursed that dangerous manhole cover she'd tripped over. The consultant put a plaster on the injection site and helped her on with her jacket before they walked out to his desk where an image of her X-ray was on a screen.

'I was hoping you wouldn't need surgery, Caroline, but I'm afraid you do: the tear hasn't healed. I'll get Grainne to book you in but because I've given you a shot of cortisone I can't operate for three months. You can go home the same day of surgery if you're OK after the anaesthetic. You'll be in a sling for six weeks and no driving.'

'OK, thanks, Hannan,' she sighed, not relishing the prospect ahead of her.

'I'll see you on the day,' he said, standing up. 'You'll be fine.'

'I'm in good hands,' Caroline replied as they walked out to reception to confirm a date for the operation. Her shoulder pain had got considerably worse in the past few months and Maggie had insisted she go back to the shoulder consultant. Hannan Mullett was the 'best in the country' her friend had said firmly.

'So I'll be out of work again for at least a month this time and I'll be needing to cut back. In fact, I'm thinking of going part-time permanently after my surgery in January,' Caroline informed her colleagues, at the meeting she'd convened to tell them her news.

'You're dead right, Caroline. We have three months until your op in mid-Jan. That will allow us to scale down your appointments. I've already changed your list to afternoons only, starting from next week, as you asked. Do you think Dervla will deliver on time? Wasn't her due date sometime the first week in October? That's this week.'

'You know the way it is, Tara. Babies come in their own sweet time. Everything's normal with the pregnancy, thank goodness. So Friday's supposed to be D-Day.' Caroline smiled at the office administrator.

'Great. I think that's everything. I'll get the minutes typed up,' Tara said briskly, tapping on her iPad.

Caroline was glad to get home that evening. Her arm and shoulder ached after the examination and injection that morning. She ate a dish of chicken casserole that she'd cooked in the slow cooker and popped an anti-inflammatory capsule and two painkillers. Night had crept in as she ate dinner and she realised that the clocks would be going back the following week. *Where has the year gone?* Caroline wondered, flicking on the logeffect fire in the fireplace in the kitchen and turning on the lamps.

She sat on the small sofa in front of the fireplace, scrolling through her messages. She'd texted a few friends and colleagues who referred patients to say she was having surgery and she'd be cutting back.

Some of the responses were kind and helpful but a few left her open-mouthed. Margaret Flannery, a colleague, had written,

Hiya, I'll refer anyone I need to to Niall. Cheers. 👍

Katherine Reidy had written, KK, no worries. 😊

When both of *them* had had surgeries, Caroline had sent flowers and a pamper pack. They were always on her invite list for parties and social gatherings and they invariably got in touch with her when they needed advice. And not even a word of support or commiseration from either of them. Why am I surprised? Caroline, thought, disgruntled. Will I ever learn? She'd known them long enough to know any sympathy or assistance would never be forthcoming when *she* was in trouble. She hadn't heard a peep out of them when she was in the sling after the fall. She needed to cop on to herself and stop giving away her good energy to 'Me! Me! Me!'s who didn't deserve it. That's what I'd be telling my patients, she thought wryly, making herself a green tea.

The meds made her feel sick and sleepy so Caroline switched off the fire and went upstairs to have a bath and an early night.

She had her earbuds in and had fallen asleep listening to a

meditation video when the sound of her mobile ringing roused her. Disorientated, she scrabbled around the bedclothes for it and said a groggy, 'Hello.'

'Caroline, we're in the Rotunda. Derv's gone into labour and you told me to ring you when it happened. Sorry for waking you.' Mick couldn't disguise the stress he was feeling and she sat up and was instantly awake.

'Will I come in?'

'Ah no, I don't want to drag you out in the middle of the night,' he said but Caroline knew he was only being thoughtful.

'I'll be in,' she said.

'I'd love it if you would but she's only started and it could be another twelve hours or more. They'll only let one of us in at a time, anyway. I was just wondering if Ciara could come to you in the morning if I'm not home? She's managed to get a 6am flight but she doesn't have keys for the apartment.'

'Well, how about if I come to the hospital at around six-thirty and you go to the airport and bring Ciara back to mine? Then perhaps both of you have a sleep and come back in around lunchtime. The beds are ready for guests,' she offered.

'Are you sure?'

'Certain,' Caroline said firmly. 'Give Dervla my love and tell her I'll see her early in the morning. And if anything changes ring me *immediately*.' She would set her phone alarm for 5.30am.

'You're a lifesaver, Caro!' Mick said gratefully.

'Don't worry, I'll be getting my own back. I've to have surgery on my shoulder in the New Year and I'll be in a sling for six weeks. I'll be needing your help then.'

'We'll be there,' he assured her. 'Don't you worry. See ya.'

Now that is how true friendship works, Caroline thought, smiling in the dark as she settled back down to get as much sleep as she could manage before her early start.

'It hurts, Dad,' Dervla whimpered, her face flushed and contorted in pain as another spasm hit her.

'We're going to set you up for the epidural very shortly, Dervla. Breathe like you've been taught at your prenatal classes.' The student midwife was reassuring. 'Inhale, hold, exhale. We'll be moving you into a delivery suite as soon as one's free. It's busy here tonight.'

Dervla did her best to breathe like she'd been taught, squeezing Mick's hand tightly.

'Caroline's coming in at 6.30am. I rang her and told her.' Mick wiped her forehead with a paper tissue.

'Oh good,' Dervla grunted, face twisted in agony.

'And something else to cheer you up: Ciara managed to get a 6am flight, so when Caroline comes in I'm going to go and pick her up at the airport. I asked if it was OK for Caroline to be here when I'm not, because you can only have one birth partner attending. And they kindly said yes. The good thing is, the epidural will be working by then and you won't have any pain.'

'Phew!' Dervla said as one loudly groaning woman was pushed in to the pre-labour ward alongside her.

I'm gowned up and ready to go in Caroline texted Mick, just outside the delivery suite.

Out in a sec he texted back and moments later he came through the door.

'How's she doing?' Caroline asked.

'She's a trooper. She's in there listening to her music and doing exactly what she's told. The epidural's helped enormously and the staff are fantastic.'

'Oh good. Here.' She handed him a bag with a flask and a bacon and fried egg butty wrapped in tinfoil. 'Get that down you before you go to the airport. You have Dervla's keys to my place if Ciara wants to have a snooze. There's clean towels in the ensuite and the heating and water's on.'

'Ah, you're the best. I *love* bacon butties,' Mick said. 'I better change out of this gear and get a move on. You can go on in and thanks a million—'

'Stop thanking me and get going.' Caroline knocked on the door and went into Dervla's suite.

The lights in the large airy room were dimmed and she had her earbuds in, listening to her music. When she saw Caroline she gave a broad smile.

'How's it going? This is a great room.' Caroline pulled up the chair beside the bed.

'They're new suites. Cool, aren't they? Once I got the epidural it got much easier. It's just going on *so* long. I'm eight centimetres dilated. The second stage will start when I'm ten. That's when things really get going and all the hard work starts.'

'Well, I'll be with you until your dad gets back and anything I can do to help just tell me.'

'I'm so glad you're here, Caroline. Thanks so much.'

'No need for thanks, darling. I'm honoured to be a birthing partner to you. It's the first time I've ever been one.'

'It's a bit scary.' Dervla's lip wobbled.

'You have a brilliant team who know what they're doing.

It will be fine,' Caroline comforted, giving Dervla's hand a squeeze as her midwife came in to check up on her.

By the time Mick came back at lunchtime, Dervla was beginning her second stage of labour and was very tired. 'Your dad's here, sweetheart. So I have to go. Just think, this time tomorrow you'll be in your ward and it will be all over. I'll be in as soon as I'm allowed to, to see you. And your sister's here as well.' Caroline dropped a kiss on her damp hair and was rewarded with a hug and a teary smile.

'Thanks, Caroline. Tell Ciara I'm dying to see her.'

'I will, pet,' Caroline replied as the midwife said briskly, 'Now, Dervla I need you to push.'

Caroline slipped out to be greeted by a shaven and showered Mick. 'It's heating up in there: hopefully it won't be for too much longer. Keep in touch and let me know how it's going.'

'I will and—'

'Don't say it,' Caroline grinned. 'Get in there!'

'OK,' he laughed. 'Ciara's flaked out in your guest room.'

'Excellent. I'll feed her when she wakes up. If Dervla's allowed visitors after the birth, I'll bring her in. See you.' She gave him a peck on the cheek before he knocked on the door and went in.

It was good to feel the fresh air when Caroline stepped out of the hospital and she inhaled deeply, walking to where she'd parked in the early hours. She hoped Dervla's labour wouldn't go on for much longer. She felt very protective of the young teen and couldn't imagine how Sally wouldn't want to be by her daughter's side for the birth. At least Dervla's sister was home to support her. Caroline had met Ciara and her brother once at a reunion bash, years ago, when they were quite young. She'd thought then Mick and Sally and their children were the perfect family.

Was there such a thing? Caroline had seen so much family strife in her years of practice that she doubted it. She yawned and joined the stream of traffic heading out of town, wondering what sort of a family would Dervla's baby end up with. It pained her to think of it but that was because she had always wanted a baby, Caroline conceded, and she couldn't think of anything more heartbreaking than handing one up for adoption – but it seemed to be what Dervla wanted, understandably. She was only sixteen. There were difficult decisions to be made: all Caroline could do was support Mick and Dervla as best she could.

'One last big push, Dervla,' the midwife urged. Gathering every ounce of energy she had, Dervla pushed her baby into the world and fell back exhausted against her pillows.

'You did it, Derv, well done.' Mick had tears in his eyes as he clasped his daughter's hand. She'd made him promise not to look at what was happening, being mortified in case he'd see her lady bits, so he'd kept his eyes on her face and encouraged her every step of the way.

A little cry made her heart lift. 'Say hello to your daughter, Dervla.' The midwife laid a squirming little bundle in her arms and, as Dervla looked down at her, the baby's eyelids fluttered open and a pair of beautiful brown eyes stared up at her. Dervla felt like they looked right into her soul.

'Oh, Dad, look. She's *beautiful*.' Tiny little fingers curled around Dervla's and her heart melted with love. Mick looked at his youngest daughter holding his first grandchild and his heart was fit to burst. He swallowed hard. 'A beautiful baby and her beautiful mother. I'm so proud of you, Derv. So very, very proud.'

CHAPTER FIFTY-SEVEN

Caroline/Mick/Dervla/Ciara/Sally

Caroline had kicked off her shoes and lain down on her bed, intending to have a short nap. When she'd got home from the hospital, she'd seen the guest room door closed and guessed Ciara was asleep after her early start. She made herself a cup of tea and a ham sandwich and checked her emails while she was eating. She tidied the kitchen after her, before going up to her bedroom.

Caroline had sent texts to Devlin and Maggie to tell them Dervla was in labour. Dervla had video-called Chloé while Caroline was with her and Chloé promised to come and visit as soon as Dervla gave the go ahead. Everybody who needed to know knew what was happening.

Caroline pulled the soft throw over her and yawned. Minutes later she was fast asleep.

'I brought you a cup of tea. I figured you shouldn't sleep too long or you won't sleep tonight.' A soft voice roused her from her sleep and, disorientated, Caroline sat up and brushed her hair out of her eyes to find an attractive young woman standing beside her bed, holding a mug of green tea and a biscuit.

'Oh ... thanks. Ciara, hello. I only meant to have forty winks,' Caroline explained, taking the mug. 'Did you get something to eat, yourself? Some hostess I am.'

'I did. I took the liberty of having some of that chicken casserole. I hope you don't mind.'

'Not at all, I'm glad you made yourself at home. What time is it?' Caroline noticed it was almost dark outside.

'Just gone five.'

'Cripes, I slept for the whole afternoon. Any word of Dervla?' she asked anxiously.

'She had a baby girl. Seven pounds. All fine. Dad's downstairs. He told me you liked green tea.'

'Oh that's *wonderful* news. Let me get up and go down.' Caroline shook the throw off her and swung her legs over the side of the bed. 'I'll be down in two minutes.'

Ciara laughed. 'No rush. I'll see you downstairs.' She looked like Mick, Caroline saw. She had the same open, friendly eyes and straight nose. Her thick brown hair had auburn glints in it and fell around her shoulders in a wavy curtain, framing her oval face.

Caroline took a sip of tea and went into her ensuite. Switching on the mirror light, she did a double take. Her face and chest were as red as Rudolph's nose.

'Bloody cortisone.' She groaned at the side effect of the injection, washing her face and slapping on some moisturiser and serum before applying foundation. It didn't completely hide her red glow but it dimmed it. She sprayed some perfume on her neck and wrist, brushed her hair and headed downstairs.

'Congratulations, Mick! I'm so sorry I wasn't here when you arrived,' she greeted the new grandfather, who was eating a Big Mac.

'Don't be daft.' He stood up, wiping the crumbs off his mouth, and gave her a hug. 'She had the baby about two hours after you left. I wouldn't let Ciara wake you. She's an absolute dote, Caroline. Big brown eyes and a surprisingly strong grip,' he said proudly. 'Poor Dervla's wrecked so she's settled in her room now and going for a sleep. They said she could have short visits. Two visitors max, around seven. Visiting hours are until eight, so if you want to go in with Ciara that's fine. I'll go in tomorrow. But if you're tired I'll bring Ciara in.'

'Oh, I'd *love* to see them,' Caroline said eagerly. 'If that's OK with you? I can drop Ciara over to you afterwards.'

'Perfect.' Mick sat down again and devoured some chips. 'I'm ready to fall into bed myself.'

'There's another room down the hall beside Ciara's,' Caroline offered.

'Thanks but I better get home and start preparing for baby's arrival. I'm giving Dervla my room because it's the biggest and has an ensuite.'

'Well, I'm just saying again and I won't say it anymore. There's two bedrooms here if either of you need them at any stage.'

'You should put up a B&B sign. Anyway, I'm viewing a house on Saturday. It's over in Killester. A three-bed bungalow.'

'Great,' Caroline enthused.

'If you're free and doing nothing want to come with us?' he asked diffidently. 'No worries if you can't.'

'Sure. I'd love to. I can use my old skills to see if there's any damp or woodworm.'

'Caroline used to work as an estate agent, many years ago,' Mick explained to his daughter.

'Cool. I work in property sales in France. I love it.' His daughter looked surprised that Caroline had worked in the same business.

'Of course. Your dad told me. Between the two of us we'll give it a good going over.'

Mick left half an hour later and Caroline and Ciara chatted about the difference in selling properties in France and Ireland. She was easy to talk to and Caroline liked her vibrant personality.

'I'll just pop in to visit for five minutes, to give the two of you time together,' Caroline said when they got into the car to drive to the hospital. 'Dervla was so looking forward to you coming to stay.'

'My poor little sis,' Ciara said sadly. 'What a predicament to be in at her age. I really feel for her.'

'Me too,' Caroline agreed. 'She's got a difficult choice to make. To offer the baby up for adoption or to keep her. All we can do is support her as best we can.'

'Do you think she should keep it?' Ciara asked.

'It doesn't matter what I think. It's Dervla who has to make the decision. I always wanted children but I wasn't blessed with them, so I'd be a bit biased towards keeping. But raising children in today's world isn't for the faint hearted and Dervla's very young.'

'I know. She wants to come and live with me. She can't face going back to Abu Dhabi and, besides, her best friend will be going to uni in Lisbon next year,' Ciara said.

'That's understandable.' Caroline drove onto Ballybough Road. 'Anyway, she doesn't have to make a decision immediately. Let her hormones settle, because she'll be in a heap, and we can see how it goes,' Caroline advised and Ciara began to understand how her dad and sister were so fond of the woman sitting beside her. She was so calm and easy to talk to and very honest. Ciara wondered why Caroline hadn't had children even though she wanted them, but didn't like to ask.

Twenty minutes later they were hurrying down the hospital corridor that led to Dervla's room. Tears slid down Ciara's cheeks when she saw her little sister in her pink polka dot nightie lying against the pristine white hospital pillows and the small cot beside her bed where the baby slept peacefully.

'OMG!' Dervla exclaimed. 'I've been dying for you to get here, Ciara,' she said, hugging her sister tightly. Thank God she has a great sister, Caroline thought, moved by their obvious love for each other.

'Caroline, look at the baby, isn't she a tiny little thing? I breastfed her and she was fine *and* hungry. They told me it was good to do it soon after giving birth, when she was wide awake, but they said she'll sleep a lot.' Dervla was bubbling, on a high now that the pregnancy and birth were finally over.

'She's *adorable*,' Caroline exclaimed as she and Ciara bent over the cot to look at the sleeping baby with her tiny little hat on.

'My very own little niece. Dervla she's *amazing*. What are you going to call her?' Ciara asked.

'I'm going to call her Katie Michaela – after Dad,' Dervla said firmly.

'He'll be so chuffed. It's a gorgeous name,' Ciara approved. 'I thought you were going to call her Taylor after Taylor Swift?'

'Nah! I had a rethink. Taylor's a bit American. As soon as

I saw her the name Katie popped into my head. I don't know why. But I like it.'

'It's perfect for her,' Caroline said. 'And now I'm going to leave you two sisters to have a natter. And I'll see you and Katie Michaela again, soon. Sleep well, pet. You did great.' She kissed Dervla. 'I'll see you when visiting hours are over, Ciara. I'll be down in the café in the foyer.' She took one last look at the baby, waved to the girls and left them alone.

'Caroline's really lovely, isn't she?' Ciara took her sister's hand in hers. 'You and Dad are lucky to have a friend like her.'

'You can say that again. I don't know what we would have done without her,' Dervla said fervently.

'Em . . . have you called Mom yet?' Ciara ventured hesitantly.

'No, Dad told her.' Dervla made a face.

'Maybe we should do it together—'

'She wanted me to have an abortion behind Dad's back. If it was up to her, Katie Michaela wouldn't be here,' Dervla said resentfully.

'I know,' Ciara soothed. 'I think she was just trying to do what she thought was best for you.'

'OK,' conceded her sister grudgingly.

'We could call her granny just to annoy her,' Ciara suggested mischievously. Dervla tittered.

'Hi Mom, it's all over. You're a granny,' Dervla said jauntily when her mother's face appeared on the screen.

Sally was taken aback as she stared at her two daughters on her iPad screen. 'Oh . . . oh, I suppose I am.'

'Here's your new granddaughter, Mom.' Ciara took the phone from Dervla and held it over the cot, where the baby still slept soundly.

Sally studied the sleeping baby. 'She looks so tiny. I forgot how small babies are,' she said slowly.

Ciara handed the phone back to her sister.

'Your dad said everything went fine, Dervla.'

'It did, Mom. He was with me most of the time and when he went to collect Ciara Caroline was allowed stay so I wouldn't be on my own.'

'That was kind,' Sally replied.

'Caroline's *very* kind,' Dervla said pointedly. 'Hope you're having a good time in Abu Dhabi.'

'It's busy again. Thankfully the weather's cooled a lot. I've ordered some baby clothes from BT for the baby.'

'Her name's Katie Michaela. Michaela, after Dad – because he's a *great* father. Thanks for the clothes,' Dervla responded with barely disguised animosity.

Ciara took the phone back. 'I think it's time Dervla had a nap. Visiting hours are almost over. Talk soon, Mom, take care.'

'I suppose you're going to say I was being a mean girl.' Dervla was defensive as she snuggled under her bedclothes.

'Nope! I'm saying nothing. Now tell me all about the labour, from start to finish. '

'Even the gory stuff?'

'Even the gory stuff.' Ciara nodded, as Katie Michaela slept on soundly, blissfully unperturbed by what her future might hold.

Sally poured herself a G&T and wandered out to the pool. She stared up at the Arabian sky where a crescent yellow moon hung suspended in mid-air. That same moon would be shining over the hospital in Dublin where Dervla had had her baby. *I haven't been much of a mother*, Sally admitted dejectedly. Guilt had been nagging her all week as she waited for news of the birth.

Should she book a flight home? Where would she stay? She wouldn't be able to stay in the apartment. It only had two bedrooms. Sally had a couple of friends in the city; she could stay with them, she supposed. Hotels were enormously expensive now. The Skylon and the other hotels near the apartment were booked out; she'd already had a quick check. She'd left it way too long to book any place decent with her dithering.

Sally took a long drink of gin and sat into the swing chair. Crickets chirruped incessantly but she'd got so used to the sound of them she didn't notice it. It was a damn nuisance Mick had decided to sell the house because of the carry-on with those bloody tenants. Whenever he bought his new one, she wouldn't feel entitled to stay. It would be *his* house, not the family home that the one in Drumcondra had been.

This worried Sally. Something was going on with Faisal, she was sure of it. He was in Dubai now. When she'd offered to accompany him, he'd told her he had back-to-back meetings and he'd need to focus on his work. *Front-to-front meetings don't you mean?* she'd wanted to say. Since she'd come back to Abu Dhabi her feminine instincts were on full alert for infidelity. His welcome though warm was distracted. He wasn't as interested as he used to be in sex and he was going to Dubai a lot.

Sally needed to save her money. She'd gone a bit wild after the divorce and spent a fortune on the good life. If she ended up on her own there would be precious little to spend. The cost of living was high and she would only be able to stay in the Emirates as long as she could support herself. She could always go to France and live in her gîte if the worst came to the worst, she supposed.

'Granny!' Sally muttered. The girls had said that deliberately to rile her. Tonight she felt like her own old granny: ageing, tired and disillusioned. Life wasn't turning out as Sally had planned and now she had a grandchild to complicate matters. She desperately hoped Dervla would have the baby adopted.

Dervla shouldn't have named her. She shouldn't become too attached to the baby, so it would be easier to hand her over for adoption. Katie Michaela: the dig about Mick being a great father had stung, as intended, but Sally couldn't argue with the fact that her ex-husband was a far better parent than she was right now.

'Oh my goodness, it's so long since I held a baby.' Caroline held out her arms for the precious bundle and gazed into a pair of bright, brown eyes staring back at her.

'Hello, missy,' she cooed. 'Aren't you *so* beautiful?'

'She *is* beautiful, isn't she?' Dervla said proudly, as Mick fussed around putting cushions at her back and putting a soft pouffe stool under her legs.

Caroline couldn't describe the feeling of bliss as the baby's little downy head, with her shock of black hair, nestled against her.

Ciara was making tea for everyone in the apartment, which was gleaming and immaculate for Dervla and Katie Michaela's homecoming.

Dervla still hadn't come down to earth on her third day after giving birth. When all the fuss died down and Ciara was back in France and Mick was working, it would hit her then, Caroline knew.

'It suits you.' Mick smiled at her, as he gently caressed his grandchild's face with his finger.

'I loved minding my friend's kids when they were babies. When they were older they used to come on stay-overs. Hard to believe they're adults now,' she told him as Ciara placed a mug of green tea on the coffee table and took out her phone to take a photo of Caroline holding the baby.

'I'll send it on to you,' the young woman promised, clicking away.

Later that night, studying the photos, Caroline remembered the pleasure she'd had holding the baby. She knew there was no upper age limit to adopting a child, although she would be strictly vetted. A single woman in her mid-fifties. A recovered alcoholic and recovering bulimic: not a great candidate for an adoption agency assessment. It would be selfish of her to even consider it, Caroline acknowledged, going upstairs to have an early night.

Fostering might be an option, she mused, brushing her teeth. She could certainly provide love, care, security and a nurturing environment for a child but that would require a rigorous assessment too. The best she could do for the time being was to be as supportive of Dervla and her baby as possible, she decided, but it was a shame her past was now blocking something she had dreamed of all her life.

'No point in crying over spilt milk, or feeling sorry for yourself,' Caroline said crossly to her glum reflection in the bathroom mirror. A fleeting temptation to go down to the fridge and comfort eat its contents came and, thankfully, went.

CHAPTER FIFTY-EIGHT

Colin Cantrell-King/Amanda

Amanda McGrath put her bike on its stand and pulled her woollen hat down as far as it would go. It was freezing. The weather forecast was for snow. People were talking of a white Christmas. Her breath curled in front of her in wispy silvery whirls and frost sparkled on the gravel beneath her feet.

She studied the car in front of her. A silver Merc. He must be home if the car was here. It was lucky the gates weren't locked. She could see lights on in the basement. Movement in the kitchen.

She took a deep breath and crunched her way across the gravel to the door in the basement. If he was downstairs there was no point in going up the wide steps to the main front door. She rooted in her backpack, took out a white A4 envelope and pressed her finger on the bell.

'Yes?' A grouchy voice crackled on the intercom.

'I have some post for you?'

'Stick it in the letterbox, please.'

'I just want to make sure it's the right address. Mr C Cantrell-King?'

'Hold on a minute.' Moments later the door opened and a tall, well dressed elderly man stood in front of her, peering out into the dark. He held out his hand for the post, hardly looking at her.

'Hello, Grandfather,' Amanda said coldly, handing him the envelope. 'Happy Christmas.'

Shock followed by anger crossed his features. 'Who are you? What are you doing here? How *dare* you invade my privacy?' he growled, incensed.

'Oh, I dare all right. I just wanted to say to you that I look forward to your trial in the New Year. I'll be there every day for my dead mother, my grandmother whom you raped and for me. And I'll be telling the newspaper and TV reporters just what a shit you are. You might have ignored my mother from the day she was born but you won't ignore *me*, Grandfather.'

Before he could respond, Amanda turned on her heel, marched over to her bike and cycled out onto the road without a backward glance.

Shaken and unnerved by the encounter, Colin banged the door shut and walked back into the kitchen. Typical: on the one day he'd forgotten to close the damn gates. He'd kept them shut since he'd been arrested and filmed but things had quietened down coming up to Christmas and he'd grown careless.

He had not had a good day. His lady friend Gayle had ended their relationship, by text. She hadn't even had the good manners to phone him or meet him face to face. He'd been damn generous to her over the last few years. He'd brought her to the Algarve, regularly, to play golf and stay in his villa. They'd gone on cruises around the Greek islands, eaten in Michelin restaurants: the works. And this was the thanks he got. He could remember every word of the cold, insensitive text.

> Colin, I feel in view of your on-going situation we should end our relationship. Friends in our set are asking me about it, which is embarrassing, and I don't want to be involved. I wish you all the best in the future and thank you for your kindness in the past. Affectionately, Gayle.

'*Affectionately*, Gayle,' he muttered sarcastically, tearing open the envelope that cheeky young woman had thrust at him.

Photos fell onto the kitchen counter. A young woman – Annie – holding a baby. A toddler with a gap-toothed smile.

He drew in a sharp breath when he saw the photo of his wife, looking uncharacteristically happy as she gazed at the baby she was holding. And another one of her, looking much older and with the ravages of alcoholism showing in her face, with a young woman who, to his surprise, looked like him. They were standing with a little child in her communion dress, the picture of innocence and happiness. The daughter and grandchild, he supposed.

He scraped his half-eaten dinner into the bin. He wasn't hungry. He poured himself a brandy, took a small notepad and pen from a drawer and trudged upstairs to the TV room. He switched on the lamp beside his armchair before walking over to the window to pull the heavy curtains.

It was snowing, the swirling white flakes drifting lazily down to blanket the ground below. In the houses across the road he could see the lights of Christmas trees spilling their festive illuminations onto the frosted gardens. A wave of loneliness and self-pity engulfed him. He drew the drapes, remembering how, in his heyday, the house would be tastefully decorated for the many Christmas parties and dinners he and his wife hosted.

Not one Christmas party invitation had dropped into his post box this year. He'd been abandoned. His so-called friends and colleagues had made themselves judge and jury and determined that he was guilty.

It's neither here nor there whether I am or not, Colin thought angrily. They could at least give me the benefit of the doubt. He'd sent many patients to Johnny McGregor, whom he'd considered to be a friend as well as a golfing buddy. Gayle had told him the McGregors' daughter had got married, two weeks ago, and neither she nor Colin had been invited but half the club membership had.

Colin couldn't hide from it anymore. He was a social outcast and there'd be no coming back from it no matter how the trial turned out.

He had all that to face in January. It *would* be a circus. It had been bad enough when he'd been arrested. He still had nightmares of that ghastly day with cameras flashing in his face and RTE filming him as he made his way down the steps of the court.

Colin had stopped watching the news so as to not have to see defendants in court cases hiding behind scarves and masks climbing up those same steps. Colin shuddered. He couldn't even bring himself to imagine what it would be like if he was jailed. He'd hoped against hope his legal team would win his case, but the development with Annie had added a whole new layer to deal with. He could still avoid the trauma of a trial by admitting his guilt, he had been advised, but he wasn't bloody guilty of the things they were accusing him of, Colin raged. He wasn't some common rapist!

He went over to his well-stocked drinks cabinet and slid a wooden panel aside to reveal his safe. He keyed in the password and took out an envelope. Colin topped up his brandy glass, poured a separate glass of tonic and sat comfortably into his armchair. He scribbled a note on the pad and placed it on the side table. 'Alexa, play Chopin's Nocturnes opus nine, number two,' he said. He shucked the tablets in the envelope into his hand and swallowed them, washing them down with the tonic. He raised the brandy goblet to his lips. The golden liquid was soothing him and Colin let the music flow over him as he drank the brandy, took more tablets and refilled the glass when it was empty.

After a while he felt a delicious lethargy envelope him. All the enormous stress he'd carried since he'd received that dreadful life-changing letter from Devlin Delaney all those month ago, floated away. His muscles relaxed and his eyelids began to droop. 'One more drink and then you can sleep,' Colin told himself, taking one last long draught of his brandy. He placed the glass on the side table with a shaky hand before wooziness swept over him. Colin's head drooped down to his chest and he began to snore loudly: his breathing harsh and raspy as the city outside slept, eerily silent under a soft mantle of snow.

CHAPTER FIFTY-NINE

Devlin/Nenita/Annie/Amanda

'Dead! *Dead!*' Devlin repeated, stunned. 'I don't know what to say. You're *absolutely* sure?' Devlin asked her garda support officer, walking away from the kitchen radio so she could hear better.

'Yes, absolutely, Devlin,' the officer replied. 'He was found this morning by his housekeeper. It's fairly certain it's suicide but we won't know until the results of the toxicology tests are back from the lab. There was a note concerning his burial arrangements and some tablets were found and he'd been drinking. I just wanted to let you know before it gets into the papers. It's already on Twitter. I'm going to phone Nenita now. Take care, Devlin. Ring me at any stage if you feel the need to.'

'I will. Bye.' Devlin put her phone down on the kitchen counter, her thoughts a jumbled mess as she tried to absorb what she'd just heard. Colin was dead. It seemed so unreal and hard to fathom. The sounds of Bing Crosby singing 'White

Christmas' drifted from the speakers, adding to the surrealism of the moment.

Numb, she poured herself a coffee from the bubbling percolator and sat down at the island. Devlin stared out unseeingly at the whirling snowy blizzard that was blocking the view across the bay.

Colin Cantrell-King was dead. It was over. There'd be no court case.

The coward, Devlin thought scornfully. He took the easy way out.

What pushed him over the edge, she wondered? Stress. Anxiety. Apprehension. Fear. She and Nenita had experienced all of those life-sapping emotions in the years that followed their assaults at Colin's hands, and the months that had followed making their statement to the guards. Emotions that hopefully were twice as intense for him because he faced the prospect of going to jail. Her phone rang and she knew it was Nenita before she even looked at it.

'Can you believe it?' the other woman asked.

'No,' Devlin replied. 'Or maybe I can. It's all very, very bizarre.'

'We won't get our day in court. We won't get to see him jailed. *That* is my regret,' Nenita said sorrowfully. 'But we won't have to put ourselves and our families through the ordeal of a trial either, so there's that to be thankful for.'

'That's one positive,' Devlin agreed. 'And at least we can console ourselves that we made our stand and he had to face the consequences of his actions. And the public, no doubt his peers included, knew about it too. He was ruined, and he knew it, and for that I'm very glad, Nenita,' Devlin added.

'Me too.'

'Have you told your husband?'

'Not yet. I wanted to ring you first. Have you told Luke?'

'Not yet. I was waiting for you to ring. I better go and put him out of his misery because it's been a burden on him too. I'll ring Annie and Amanda too, as soon as I've told my son, and let them know before it's announced on the news or in the papers. Mind yourself, Nenita. Let's meet up soon.'

'Sure, Devlin. And thank you for standing by me.'

'We held each other up,' Devlin said. 'Take care.'

She sipped her coffee, hearing Luke coming down the stairs. He walked into the kitchen carrying a small box.

'I knew it was somewhere where we put the decorations,' he said, taking out a beautiful handcrafted Belén his mother had given them for their first Christmas. Luke saw the expression on her face. 'What's up? Who were you talking to?' He was instantly concerned.

'CCK's dead.'

'*What?*'

'The guards think it was suicide. There was a note about his funeral arrangements and they found tablets and evidence of drinking. They won't know for sure until they get the tests back.'

'Good God!' Luke sat down at the counter beside her, as stunned as she was.

'He took the cowardly option,' she said, shaking her head. 'He would have been able to get morphine tablets or other opiates easily.'

Thank God the bastard's gone. Pity it was so easy for him, Luke thought silently as relief poured a silent balm on the fears he'd carried for Devlin since the whole ordeal began.

'How do you feel about it?' Luke asked cautiously, not wanting to appear too jubilant after she had put so much energy into bringing him to trial.

'Numb, angry, relieved. But, as I said to Nenita, at least he had to face up to what he'd done. And I've not an ounce of regret that his last months were miserable for him,' Devlin said vehemently, finding it hard to believe that it all was over.

'He had to live with that, for sure, and the social contempt.' Luke stood up and put his arms around his wife. 'It will probably be on the evening news. Perhaps you should ring the girls, too,' he suggested.

'That's a good idea. I'll call them,' Devlin agreed, picking up her phone to call her son.

'*Great* news, Mom,' said Finn bluntly when she told him what had happened. 'I hope the scummy bastard rots in hell. I'm so glad you won't have to endure a trial. That's the best thing about it. I can't wait to get home next week. I'm gonna give you such a hug,' he said affectionately and Devlin felt her heart lift. She knew they *would* have a good Christmas, now. She'd been dreading it. Going through the motions of decorating City Girl. Treating her staff to their Christmas celebrations, all the while thinking about what was ahead of her in January. Now there was nothing to worry about. The burden had been lifted. Life could go on without anxiety hanging over her like a heavy black cloud. *Can it really be that easy?* she asked herself, perplexed.

'I'm gonna hug you right back, mister,' Devlin replied gaily before hanging up.

'We're so lucky,' she said to her husband. 'Let's put your mother's ornament on the mantelpiece and really start the festivities.' She picked up the Belén with its colourful, intricately handcrafted nativity scene and hand in hand they walked into the lounge.

'I need to let Annie and Amanda know what's happened,' Devlin said after they placed the ornament carefully on its traditional spot.

'OK. I'll bring in the tree and get it started.' Luke couldn't wait to decorate. He was such a child at heart sometimes. Devlin reflected on how strange it was to be decorating for Christmas when a man who had shaped her life so radically was lying dead on a slab in the city morgue.

'Well, he won't be resting in peace,' Annie said when Devlin told her the news. 'But at least his last days were miserable. To tell you the truth, I'm glad I don't have to face the ordeal of a trial. I was fully prepared to go through with it but the Almighty has seen fit not to torture us with it. And, Devlin,' she continued, 'I can go to the next world, when it's my time, safe in the knowledge that Amanda will have a roof over her head and whatever she's entitled to inherit from his estate. I can't ask for anything more.'

'You're right, Annie. That's one big positive from the whole affair. Perhaps the four of us could meet up after Christmas, to celebrate our new beginnings, in January. It would be good to have some closure on the whole rotten business.'

'I'd like that very much, Devlin,' Annie said eagerly. 'I'll be looking forward to it.'

'Not surprised, really,' Caroline said thoughtfully. 'It was his way of being in control, as he always was. A trait common in abusers.'

'Good! No loss to the world. And it means you can put it all behind you as best you can and focus on the anniversary gig next year. That's going to be one hell of a party and now you'll be able to enjoy it,' Maggie, ever the pragmatist, declared bluntly.

'Oh yeah! I'd kind of put that to the back of my mind because I was getting consumed by the trial and all it was bringing with it,' Devlin confessed.

'Well, get your party vibe going again. We City Girls have a lot to celebrate.'

'We sure do,' Caroline agreed, smiling down at the baby asleep in her arms. 'Dervla has decided I should be called Nantie by Katie when she's able to talk. "Na" for Nana and "antie" for auntie. Good, isn't it? Nantie.'

'Oh, that's so sweet,' Devlin enthused.

'Love it!' Maggie clapped.

'Right gals, I better be off. Luke's doing the tree in the lounge so I should muck in. See you soon.' Devlin blew her best friends a kiss and clicked off their call.

'I would have been by your side if the trial had happened. You *know* that, don't you?' Luke said sombrely later that evening when they sat together on the sofa. They were watching the headlines at the start of the news flash up on the screen.

'I know that, beloved,' she said, cuddling into him, wondering would Colin's death be covered by the Six One News.

It was in the second half of the show that the segment about Colin came up. They watched in silence as his impressive redbrick house appeared on the screen, with a policeman standing outside, and a hearse driving out the gates.

'An elderly man was found dead in his house on the Merrion Road earlier today,' the newsreader said. 'He has been named as retired gynaecologist Colin Cantrell-King. Mr Cantrell-King was due to face trial over accusations of historical sexual abuse and rape in the New Year. A garda investigation is underway on the circumstances leading to the death. Foul play is not suspected.' And then it was over and the next item, a story about a Christmas walk for charity, appeared.

Devlin shook her head, still perplexed by what had happened. Watching the news had made it real for her.

'It's over now, Devlin. *Try* not to dwell on it. There's a new year coming: let it be a fresh start for all of us,' Luke said firmly.

'Yes, Caroline.' She looked up at him from the shelter of the crook of his arm, her eyes crinkling in a mischievous smile.

'Smarty,' he laughed and bent his head to kiss her.

'Goodbye and good riddance, ya poxy dose.' Amanda threw another log on the fire and watched the flames lick around the edges. If he was getting cremated, the flames would be engulfing her detested grandfather before long. Amanda was not one bit sorry that she had called on him with the family photos. Annie had pointed out his house to her and Antonia many years ago, when they had taken the Dart to the Merrion Centre to do some Christmas shopping.

Amanda didn't care if her visit had tipped Colin over the edge. Meeting him that once, seeing his arrogance and distain towards her, ensured that she felt not one iota of guilt. No guilt but some shock, she had to admit. Amanda had been stunned when her grandmother told her the news of Cantrell-King's death earlier. She wondered whether her visit had been caught on CCTV and if she would be questioned.

She didn't care. All she had done was given him copies of family photos. There was no harm in that. But *she* knew her words and the photos might have encouraged her grandfather's decision to end his life. Amanda vowed that she would take that knowledge with her to the grave. Annie, Devlin and Nenita would never know her part in the reckoning Colin Cantrell-King had faced in the hours prior to his death.

CHAPTER SIXTY

DEVLIN/CAROLINE/MAGGIE

'This is so handy, Maggie. Good thinking. What Dart did you get?' Devlin settled into her seat in Il Caffè di Napoli. It had just gone midday.

'Sandymount. It's the easiest to get parking.' Maggie put her phone on silent and shoved it into her bag.

Christmas had crept up on them almost before they knew it. Devlin and Luke were flying to Barcelona that evening. Maggie had driven up from Wicklow, dropped Nelsie to the house in Ranelagh then got the Dart to meet the girls. She was spending Christmas in Dublin with her children.

Caroline had hopped on the same Dart Devlin had taken in Howth and they'd all arrived at the restaurant on Westland Row in fifteen minutes.

'How are you doing, Dev?' Maggie asked after the waiter had handed them their menus. 'You look much better than you've looked in ages. You've got your vibrancy back,' she noted, delighted to see Devlin's blue eyes bright and shining with good health. She'd had her ash blonde hair styled in a sophisticated, layered cut that suited her.

'I feel much so better,' Devlin confided. 'And of course I don't have to face a trial in January. That's such a load off my mind.' She shook her head. 'It's still kinda hard to believe CCK topped himself and there's not going to be a trial. I'm mightily relieved. I would have gone through with it, for Nenita and Annie, but it was taken out of our hands and I can tell you I won't be sorry to see the end of this year,' she said fervently.

'We all had our rough patches for sure. It's been a tough year,' Maggie observed. 'I dealt with Tony as best as I could. I sent him a text yesterday saying he could entertain Mam for New Year and if he dares take one cent off her I'll report him to the Elderly Abuse unit in the DPSU. The one that you told me about, Dev. *And* I got through the wedding despite Terry and his arseholery. And Shona's happy out. And *you*, darling, Caro,' she turned to her friend sitting beside her, 'fought your demons head on, ended up in a heap with a torn rotator cuff and *still* managed to take a pregnant teenager and her baby under your wing,' Maggie declared in admiration.

'But look at us, though,' Caroline said. 'Here we are to celebrate *us*. We always have each other's backs. Maggie, you should write a book about us,' she joked, delighted they'd made time to get together.

'I will! And I'll call it *Three Mighty Women*.'

They laughed heartily before getting down to the business of deciding what to have for their annual Christmas lunch.

Christmas

'What's going on?' Caroline asked Dervla when the young woman opened the door to the apartment looking stressed and flushed. She could hear the baby crying in the bedroom. She'd got home from the girls' Christmas lunch just before three and decided to nip over to Drumcondra with a carton of Dervla's favourite beef stroganoff. Caroline was longing to see the baby too. She hadn't seen Katie for four days.

'I think she's got colic and the boiler's not working and the place is freezing and Dad's gone to get another electric fire, because the landlord says he won't be able to get it sorted until after Christmas because he's tried three plumbers already and they're all booked up because everyone's heating goes dodgy in the coldest spell of the year. And I can't even have a shower until the immersion heats up.' Dervla looked as though she was ready to burst into tears.

Caroline followed her into the bedroom and watched her pick up her wailing child.

'Please stop crying, baby,' Dervla begged, rocking her back and forth.

'Is she hungry?' Caroline sat on the rumpled, unmade bed.

'No, she guzzled her feed. I think she's having a growth spurt and she drank so fast it gave her wind.'

'OK! This is what's going to happen,' Caroline said firmly. *'I'm* going to wind the baby. *You're* going to pack enough clothes and her bits and pieces for you and Katie to stay at mine for at least a week. And,' she arched an eyebrow at Dervla, 'did I see the car seat in the hall?'

'Yep. Dad had to take it out in case the new electric fire wouldn't fit in the back seat around it.'

'How fortuitous.' Caroline, smiled, taking the howling baby from the fraught young mother and holding her over her 'good' arm. She began to rub Katie's back in gentle, circular motions. 'I'm going home to a lovely warm house and you're coming with me. You're going to have a long lingering bath with loads of pampery stuff and if Mick's not home before we leave he can follow us.'

'*Really?*'

'The sooner you get packed, the sooner we can get going,' Caroline laughed, as Katie gave a huge burp and let loose a machinegun rattle of farts. 'Ah, you poor little dote. Did you have bad wind?' she clucked, tucking the baby onto her left shoulder and loving the feel of her against her cheek.

'A week?' Dervla was unsure. 'But it's Christmas in two days.'

'I know! I'm afraid you'll have to endure Christmas in my house with its warm radiators and glowing stoves and hot water all day. Do you think you could cope?'

'Oh Caroline, I just *love* you,' Dervla exclaimed in delight. 'You're so good to us.'

'I just love you too, and this little one.' Caroline laughed at Dervla's relief and excitement.

'Oh my days, a week in that gorgeous room.' Dervla's eyes sparkled as she began to pack babygrows and romper suits into a holdall. The intercom rang and she went out into the hall and pressed the buzzer. It opened the hall door and she saw Mick on the screen, struggling into the foyer with a large box. 'It's Dad. I'm just going down to help him, Caroline,' Dervla called, putting the door on the latch.

'OK,' she whispered as Katie softened into her shoulder and a tiny contented snore escaped her lips.

'Dad, Caroline's come to our rescue. She wants us to stay with her until the boiler's fixed. Even over Christmas,' Dervla announced merrily, grabbing onto the box that that her father was hauling up the stairs.

'We *can't* impose like that, Dervla,' Mick exclaimed. 'This fire will heat the place up fine and we can put the small fire in your room.'

'Aw, Dad!' she cried, crestfallen.

'No. It's not fair. Anyway, Caroline's going to her brother for Christmas.'

'Oh!'

They manoeuvred the box into the hall and Mick saw Caroline standing at the bedroom door with the baby. 'We'll be fine, Caroline. Thanks for your really kind offer but—'

'Ah, Mick don't say no. Dervla and I have plans to have a girl's pampering night. And you're babysitting for us. Isn't that right, Dervla?'

'Yeah! Yeah, it is,' Dervla agreed, even though it was news to her. She hoped against hope that her father would relent.

'I can still babysit here.' Mick took his scarf off and hung it up on the hallstand. There were snowflakes still on it.

'Mick, the place is very cold. Look at Katie's little nose. It's red. Electric heating's not great: it dries out the air. You can't stay here for Christmas. It's going to snow heavily later, according to the forecast. Come on, pack up and come over to my place.'

'Please,' Dervla begged.

'But you're going to your brother's, Caroline,' he protested.

'They won't mind. I'll visit them in the morning while you're cooking the dinner,' Caroline countered. 'Please, Mick.

Imagine having Katie with me for a week. She can sleep in my room and Dervla can have some good rest.'

'You're mad!' he sighed. 'Are you *sure*?'

'We'll have fun, won't we, Derv? And if the heating's not sorted when Ciara comes for New Year, we can bring your blow up bed for her. Now come on, before we get snowed in.'

'I never knew you were this bossy. And I think it's a slight exaggeration to say we're going to get snowed in.' Mick could see he was getting nowhere fast. Dervla's evident excitement at going to stay with Caroline – and his friend's observation about electric heating – won out.

'OK. I surrender. But I *am* cooking the dinner,' Mick decreed firmly.

'You *are*!' Caroline assured him, her brown eyes glinting in amusement. 'Why do you think I asked you?'

Even though it was mild by Irish standards, Devlin wanted to make sure her Spanish mother-in-law Josefa was well wrapped up as she sat on the fold-up chair Luke had carried from Finn's apartment to the Sagrada Família. They were on Carrer de la Marina, in front of the magnificent cathedral's Nativity façade. Children's choirs and musicians from neighbourhood choirs were preparing to offer a repertoire of traditional Christmas carols from Catalonia and around the world. Devlin tucked a soft cashmere throw around Josefa.

'*Gracias querida.*' The elderly woman patted Devlin's hand with her thin bony one. '*Esta es una noche especial.*'

'*Sí.* It *is* special, *Madre.*' Devlin smiled down at her. 'It'll be so lovely to be all together for Christmas.' In her mid-eighties, Josefa was still agile. As was Luke's father Liam who was standing beside his son, nearly as tall and erect as Luke was. Finn was alongside his grandfather. They were having a discussion about different ways of cooking shellfish.

Josefa and Liam spent the winter months in Seville, where Josefa was from, and the rest of the year in Ireland in their home in Malahide. Finn sometimes took the high-speed Renfe to visit his grandparents when they were in Spain. He was close to them. Luke had persuaded them to fly up from Seville to spend Christmas Eve and Christmas Day in Barcelona. He'd booked a room for them in his and Devlin's favourite hotel, for their Christmas present, and bought their plane tickets. He and Devlin would fly back with them to Seville, and spend a few days with them there, before coming back to Dublin for New Year.

A wave of anticipation rippled through the crowd when the conductor raised his baton and the sweet, poignant, pure young voices of the children's choir filled the star-studded sky with the evocative traditional Catalan carol 'El Noi de la Mare'.

Luke's arm slipped around her shoulder. 'You OK?'

'I'm *fine*, beloved.' Devlin smiled up at him, covering his hand with hers. He held her close as his deep baritone joined the multitude of voices around them singing the chorus.

And then, for one magical moment, Devlin felt the faintest breeze caress her cheek like a feathery kiss and somehow she *knew* her daughter and aunt – who had been like a mother to both of them – were with her.

Maggie really didn't want to go, but Terry had begged her. 'It will be the first Christmas in years that we've been together *happily*, as a family.'

She wanted to say it didn't matter to her; she'd always had her children close, why couldn't he just take them out for a meal? But Mimi, Michael, Shona and Aleksy were looking forward to it, plus Nelsie loved eating out, so Maggie found herself dressing to go to lunch on Christmas Eve, something she'd never done before. Usually she was slaving in the kitchen but this year Shona and Aleksy were cooking Christmas dinner and Maggie was finding it a bit strange to be a lady of leisure at Christmas.

Terry had booked Roly's in Ballsbridge and had thoughtfully arranged a taxi for Maggie, Nelsie, Mimi and Michael. Shona and Aleksy were coming from town. She'd have a couple of stiff drinks if Terry put her sitting beside Denise, Maggie had decided earlier, but her spirits lifted enormously when Terry greeted them at their table and confided that his wife wouldn't be able to join them because of a migraine.

Yay, there is a God, Maggie thought, lying through her teeth and saying insincerely, 'Oh that's a shame.'

Chloé, looking festive in a glittery red dress, said, 'Hi Maggie, Happy Christmas!' and kissed her.

'You look beautiful, Chloé.' Maggie complimented her warmly. She liked the teenager and Caroline had told her that she'd been a very supportive friend to Dervla.

It was a jolly lunch, with much ribbing and joshing between the siblings, with Nelsie interjecting her tuppence worth and Maggie relaxed and began to enjoy herself. She caught Terry's eye at the end of the table. He raised his glass to her and smiled and she raised hers and smiled back. *I'll take this*, she thought, listening to Chloé laughing at something Shona was saying. No point in hanging onto the old miseries anymore and giving them free lodgings in her head or stressing her long-suffering gall bladder. A new tradition, born today, for the blended Ryan clan was better than a warring family any day.

PART FIVE

CHAPTER SIXTY-ONE

CITY GIRL'S 35TH ANNIVERSARY PARTY, MARCH 2025

'This is it, team. Thirty-five years of this fabulous iconic gym and spa and it would never have been as successful as it is without you.' Devlin smiled at her staff. 'Some of you have been here with me from the beginning.' She nodded at Liz, the MD, who had been her first PA. 'And others have come later and become part of our City Girl family. I cannot thank you enough for your hard work and your loyalty to me. It's you all who create a peaceful, friendly, nurturing environment.

'To say thanks and to celebrate us there'll be an extra thousand euro in your paycheques this month and Madalina has envelopes with your names on, with a thank you note from us, and a little gift.' Cheers and claps greeted this announcement and Devlin laughed.

'Right, let's go party, City gals and boys. Doors opening in ten minutes. Let's give our guests a night to remember. Happy anniversary, everyone!'

'Thanks, Devlin.'

'Woohoo!'

'You're the best boss, EVER!'

The cheers were long and loud and then Liz held up her hand. 'Devlin, before we go, we have a little presentation of our own to make. You know how we feel about you and you're right: we *are* a family. So on behalf of all of us, I'd like to ask Aoibhinn to present this gift with our love, admiration and great good wishes.'

Aoibhinn, the spa manager, stepped forward with a large, elegantly wrapped parcel and handed it to Devlin.

'Be careful, it's sort of delicate,' Aoibhinn warned. Devlin didn't know whether to laugh or cry, she was so overwhelmed with emotion.

'Let me help.' Madalina, ever practical, removed the paper to reveal a bubble-wrapped painting.

'Oooh!' Devlin gasped when she saw the beautifully rendered image of the City Girl building on a summer's day. Dappled foliage from the trees brought even more vibrancy and perspective to the redbrick Georgian building and she could almost feel the buzz of the street emanating from the brush strokes.

'It's an M. H. Hensley.' Liz pointed to the signature of the up-and-coming artist whose murals were gaining recognition. She had painted a stunning mural with soothing Persian overtones on the new private party tearoom in the renovated attic space of the building.

'I *love* it. Thank you all *so* much. How thoughtful,' Devlin managed to say before tears slid down her cheeks.

'No! *Don't* cry,' squawked Maria. 'You'll ruin your make-up.'

'Sorry,' sniffled Devlin, half-laughing, half-crying at her beauty therapist's rebuke.

'Come up to the room with me. I'll sort you,' Maria instructed.

'Yes, Maria,' Devlin said docilely. 'I better do as I'm told. Thanks again, you gorgeous people. You're the best I could ever have wished for.'

'Devlin, that dress is fabulous!' Caroline raved at the black sequinned form-fitting long-sleeved gown. It had a dramatic V at the back.

'It's a Don O'Neill. I treated myself,' Devlin confessed. 'I love his designs, they're so flattering.'

'He gets women, doesn't he?' Caroline remarked.

'You're looking gorgeous,' Devlin returned the compliment. Caroline was wearing a ruby silk halter neck with a ruched skirt and slit at the side. The colour was perfect for her brown-eyed, slender beauty. 'Here's Maggie.' She waved excitedly. Devlin had told the girls to come early so she'd have a chance to talk to them before the guests started arriving. Dervla and Chloé had come with Caroline and were sipping Prosecco at Reception.

'Wowza!' Maggie exclaimed when she saw her two friends. She was wearing a delphine cape gown in midnight blue and she looked like a goddess.

'Wowza yourself, Maggie,' Devlin exclaimed. 'I could never wear a dress like that. You're *so* lucky to be tall.'

'Beneath these sparkles, under this frothy cape, are the arms of a middle-aged woman,' Maggie said dryly. 'Caroline, I'd die to have sculptured arms like yours and still be able to wear a halter neck.'

'A gym addiction has its benefits,' Caroline smirked and they laughed heartily.

'Girls, I better get going. I see the photographers gathering and my PR manager is looking for me. Coming, Helen!' she called to the elegant blonde woman who was looking her way. 'Do you want to be in the photos?'

'Nope!' Maggie grinned. 'Sorry for your troubles.'

'Go strut your stuff,' Caroline said. 'We'll enjoy looking on.'

'Meanies. See ya later.' Devlin put on her public face and sashayed into the foyer to join her team. Soon they would open the doors and welcome all the City Girls who were beginning to arrive.

CHAPTER SIXTY-TWO

Maggie/Terry

'Excuse me, Devlin, someone's collapsed in the foyer. We've called an ambulance,' Madalina interrupted Devlin and one of the guests who was thanking her for a wonderful party. It had been a very successful, fun evening and people were leaving.

'Oh no! I'll come right away.' Devlin excused herself and hurried to the ground floor, where she saw a group standing around a prone man. Maggie was attending to him. *Once a nurse always a nurse*, Devlin thought gratefully.

'Excuse me. Let me through, please,' she said and was horrified to see that the man on the floor was Terry. Her eyes met Maggie's briefly and Devlin heard her friend say reassuringly, 'There's an ambulance on the way, Terry. You'll be fine,' as she knelt by his side, holding his wrist to take his pulse.

'What's wrong with him?' Denise knelt on the other side of her husband and took his free hand, her face white with shock.

'Pain's bad, Mags,' Terry groaned.

'Take deep breaths. Don't talk,' she said calmly, loosening

his tie and belt as Shona and Aleksy pushed their way through the people gathered in the foyer.

'Daddy,' Shona gasped, falling to her knees beside Maggie. 'Are you OK?'

'I'm fine, sweetie, don't you worry.' He tried to smile but it was more of a grimace.

A woman in a purple gown pushed through saying, 'I'm a doctor, let me through, please, and get me a glass of water.'

'He's having a cardiac event. I'm a nurse.' Maggie stood up to let the doctor take her place. 'The staff are bringing the defib from the gym, in case we need it,' she murmured before the woman hunkered down beside Terry.

'Hi, I'm just going to get you to take an aspirin for me. You're not allergic to them, are you?' the doctor asked as someone handed her a glass of water.

He shook his head. Beads of sweat ran down his face.

'Chew it slowly,' the doctor ordered, taking a tablet from a blister pack in her evening bag.

'OK.' Terry did as he was bidden, taking a small sip of water from the glass she held to his lips.

'Any previous cardiac episodes?' she queried.

'No.' Terry squeezed his wife's hand. 'Sorry for ruining your night.'

'Don't be silly,' Denise said, trying not to cry as the wail of a siren and flashing blue lights lasered through the windows and alerted them that the ambulance had arrived.

'I'm glad Chloé's gone to stay with Dervla. I wouldn't like her to see me like this.' Chloé and Dervla had taken a taxi back to Caroline's earlier on, where Mick was babysitting Katie.

'You'll be all right. I'll bring her into the hospital to see you tomorrow.' Denise burst into sobs when the paramedics gently moved her out of the way and took over. Within minutes Terry was placed on a gurney and wheeled out to the waiting ambulance.

'Maggie, Shona.' He raised his head and called them weakly and they hurried to his side, earning a glower from Denise, who was accompanying him to the hospital.

'Don't worry, Terry, you're in good hands now,' Maggie said reassuringly, taking his hand in hers once more.

'We did good, Maggie. We're OK, aren't we?' Terry clasped her hand tightly. She could see the fear in his eyes and felt for him.

'We did *very* good, Terry. And yes, we're fine now. One big happy family again,' she comforted him.

'Shona, you know I love you very much.' He took his daughter's hand in his just before he was lifted into the ambulance.

'I love you too, Daddy. Hurry on and get well so you can visit us in our new house.' She leaned over and kissed him on the cheek.

'I will.' He nodded and then he was whooshed up and into the ambulance where Denise was already seated. The doors closed and it drove off, wailing like a demented banshee, into the night.

'Mam, is he going to be all right?' Shona asked and then dissolved into tears as Aleksy, Devlin and Luke came to comfort them.

'I'd hope so,' Maggie said shakily, the effort of appearing calm and professional leaving her spent. 'At least he didn't go into cardiac arrest.' She turned to the doctor who was standing to one side. 'Thank you for all your help and for the aspirin.'

'I always carry them for just such an event. Hard to call it. I hope it all goes well,' she said quietly.

'Thanks,' replied Maggie miserably, watching Aleksy try and console his weeping wife. Terry played golf so he had some level of fitness but his lifestyle wasn't healthy. He was overweight and too fond of the good life. That was not going to stand him in good stead, she thought, realistically. He was going to have to go on a life-changing health regime once he was out of hospital.

'I'm so sorry for ruining your party, Dev, especially as it had all gone so well,' she said dejectedly when they turned to go back inside.

'Don't be daft, these things happen. I just hope Terry will get better: that's the important thing.' Devlin put an arm around her and gave her a hug.

'I don't know whether to go to the hospital now with Shona. I don't know if Denise would want us there. She's very definite about me knowing my place as the ex. It's really awkward being in this sort of situation. I need to ring Mimi too, and Michael. Thank God Terry and Denise got to go and cruise the Arctic with him after Christmas. Terry was *so* proud of him. He had photos all over Twitter and Facebook.'

'If you feel you want to go to the hospital, go, Maggie,' Caroline said firmly. 'I'll drive you.'

'I think I will, thanks, Caro. I don't have a good feeling, to be honest. I don't know why. But I don't want to say that to Shona.'

'Come on then. Let's go. Shona,' Caroline called over to her godchild. 'I'm bringing your mum to the hospital. Do you want to come?'

'Thanks, Caroline. I *do*. I want to make sure Dad's going to be all right. Can Aleksy come?' she asked, wiping her eyes.

'Of course he can. I'll go and get the car and meet you outside.'

They drove across town to St James's in silence, each lost in their own thoughts. Maggie couldn't shake the unease that shrouded her. Shona sat in the back with her husband's comforting arm around her, giving silent thanks that she had made her peace with her father. Whether Denise approved or not, she'd be able to visit him often in hospital and at home to encourage him on his journey to wellness.

The traffic was light due to the lateness of the evening and Caroline dropped them at the entrance so they could go straight to A&E, while she looked for parking.

Maggie, Shona and Aleksy hurried across the concourse to where a cluster of ambulances was gathered. In front of one, they could see Denise standing in her silver lamé dress, hands up to her mouth, a paramedic standing by her side. She saw them coming towards her.

'He's dead!' she screamed hysterically. 'Terry's *dead*!'

CHAPTER SIXTY-THREE

THE FUNERAL

> Shona considering your history with your father, which caused him much grief and stress if you prefer not to be involved in his funeral Mass that's fine. Mimi and Michael are doing a reading. If you do wish to be included you can bring something to the altar at the Offertory. Please let me know ASAP.
> Denise

Shona read the text from her stepmother and felt as though she'd been kicked in the stomach. Denise had never been friendly towards her, understandably, but in the immediate aftermath of Terry's death she had been downright hostile towards her step-daughter.

'What a bitch,' she muttered, rereading the text again just to make sure she wasn't making a mistake. Denise had made it very clear to Maggie that she would be organising the funeral, when Maggie ventured to suggest that a non-religious service would be more in line with what Terry might have preferred: he never set foot in a church unless he had to and had no religious beliefs whatsoever. Typical of her ex-husband, Maggie thought. Head in the sand whenever the subject of last wishes had been brought up in their own marriage. He'd never discussed his funeral requirements with Denise either, nor left instructions, so it was up to her as his *wife* to do as *she* wished, Denise had said coldly – emphasising the wife bit.

'She's a wagon, Mam,' Shona had exploded when she heard this.

'It's understandable.' Maggie tried to calm her down. 'She's in shock, she's in denial and she's angry, so she's projecting it onto us.'

Well it *wasn't* OK in Shona's book. How *dare* Denise treat her mother like dirt! Maggie had always been pleasant to Denise whenever they were at a family event. And she had done her best to make her stepmother feel welcome at the family barbecue and the wedding. Maggie, Shona and her siblings had known Terry for far longer than Denise had. We have as much right to make decisions about Dad's funeral as she does, Shona thought furiously as she began tapping her response on the phone.

> Denise, I don't appreciate your attitude. And may I say; if you'd had some decency and not had sex with my father in our own home, when I was a child, there would have been **no** issues with my dad, so accept your part in it. I'm glad Chloé never had to see what I saw.

She wasn't even going to sign it, she thought bitterly. Mentioning Chloé brought her half-sister to mind. The teenager was beside herself with grief, unable to accept that the father she adored was gone and she would never see him again. Shona pitied her from the bottom of her heart. After all, she knew exactly what Chloé was going through. Shona stared down at her phone. If she pressed send that would be the end of her dealings with Denise. There'd be no going back. But it would impact on her relationship with Chloé too and that growing bond was precious to her.

Be the bigger person. Don't react, she told herself as her index finger hovered over the harsh words she'd written. Sighing deeply, she deleted what she'd written and wrote instead, Bringing the offering up is fine. S

'You did a good thing for Chloé,' Aleksy approved when she showed him the text and told him how she'd wanted to respond. 'And a good thing for you. You kept away from the drama.'

'Very unlike me.' Shona gave her husband a watery smile, grateful beyond measure for the comfort of his loving arms.

It was the sight of her son – eyes glittering with tears as his father's coffin was placed on his broad shoulders to carry him out of the church – that undid Maggie. She had sat stoically throughout the Mass, hardly able to believe that Terry was lying in that coffin at the top of the altar. She had made to go into the row behind her children, Denise and Chloé but Michael had put his hand on her elbow and said, 'Your place is with us', giving Denise a stern, wordless stare when she'd looked put out.

On either side of her, each holding her hand, Mimi and

Shona wept. Maggie's heart ached for her children. Later she kept her head down, following Chloé and Denise – in her Louboutins, click-clacking her way down the aisle – to the soaring refrain of 'You Raise Me Up', Denise's choice of music to end the Mass with.

Shona, Mimi and Michael had had no input into the funeral or the service. They might as well be distant relatives. Maggie was disgusted with Denise's lack of magnanimity. She could understand that the other woman was in shock and was grieving. They all were, but this was a time to join together: not be divided. Whether Denise liked it or not, Terry had three children from his first marriage. They deserved to be treated with respect.

They stood underneath the leaden sky watching as the coffin was placed into the hearse. As Shona and Mimi were surrounded by condoling friends, Maggie went to find Devlin and Caroline. Michael walked over to her, took her arm and said, 'Come with us, Mam. People want to offer their condolences to you too.'

She touched his face gently. 'You're a great son, Michael. Your father would be very proud of you.'

'And of you, Mam. You're so dignified and—'

Whatever he was going to say was interrupted by his grandmother.

'Michael: you and Mimi were excellent. Every word of your readings could be heard. There's nothing worse than mumbling,' Nelsie praised.

'*Mam!* What are you doing here?' Maggie stared at her mother, looking elegant in a black trouser suit with a pink floral scarf draped elegantly around her neck. 'I thought you were looking at the funeral online. That's what we agreed.'

'Of *course* I was coming. I'm here to support my daughter and grandchildren.'

'Who gave you a lift?' Maggie asked, touched at her mother's declaration of support.

'No one. I drove up myself.' Nelsie hugged her grandson, dwarfed by his size.

Holy Divinity, Maggie thought in dismay. Nelsie wasn't driving half as much as she used to and certainly not driving up to the city.

'I put my sat nav on. Sure it was grand. Handy that it was on the Southside and I didn't have to come too far on the M50. I might not go to the crematorium though,' she said, as Shona arrived to give her a hug.

'Aleksy will bring you to the crem, Gran. I've to go in the funeral car. And after the meal we can bring you back here to collect your car.'

'That's very kind, dear,' Nelsie approved, secretly delighted that she was going to go for the meal. She had a few things to say to Madame Denise, funeral or no. Better to have her say on a full stomach after the meal. She was feeling a bit peckish.

'Chloé, I'm very sorry that your dad has died. I don't know what I'd do if the same happened to me,' Dervla said earnestly as she reached the top of the queue of friends who were sympathising with the teen.

'Thanks *so* much for coming, Dervla, that was *really* kind of you,' Chloé said. 'My friends are so good to me.' She hiccupped and burst into tears, as she drew down the blanket that was lightly wrapped around Dervla's baby and stroked her little face.

Katie gave a wide gummy smile. Chloé smiled back despite her distress. 'She's so cute.'

'She loves her Auntie Chloé,' Dervla said kindly, taking a clean baby wipe out of her bag. 'Let me fix your mascara. It's run a bit.'

'Thanks, I know I look a sight.' Chloé sniffed.

'You don't. And anyway it doesn't matter how you look on the worst day of your life. You just ring me whenever you want and if you want to come for a sleepover anytime just let me know.' Dervla was aware that more people were queuing behind her to talk to Chloé.

Mimi, who was standing next to her half-sister in the receiving line, reached out and squeezed the younger woman's hand. 'If you ever need a lift over to Dervla's I can take you,' she offered. 'Honorary aunties are important and you're Katie's.'

'Sisters are important too.' Chloé squeezed back. Even though her mum didn't make much of an effort with her dad's first family, Chloé couldn't even begin to explain how much the kindness of her siblings was helping her get through this horrible nightmare that her life had become.

'Terry would have hated every minute of the church service,' Maggie said to Caroline and Devlin as they took a few moments together in the crowded church grounds. 'A Mass just to show off that she's the grieving widow. Has she ever been in a church in her life? Oh God, I sound bitter and twisted,' she groaned.

'You're not bitter and twisted,' Caroline remonstrated. 'He would have hated the religious part of it, yes, but he'd have liked the big crowd that's shown up. Denise has made it about her. It's a declaration of her status as wife and chief mourner.

She and Chloé are *"the"'*, she raised her fingers in air quotes, 'family. It's a classic power statement from a second spouse. Don't take it personally.'

'I feel for my children. They were excluded from any decision-making about the day. Couldn't even choose their readings. She could have sent Terry off in a horse and cart to a bog for all I care but they're his children. If it weren't for them I'd go home right now. The thought of going to this damn meal after the cremation.' She glowered. 'Honestly, it's sickening having to be civil to the former friends who dropped me like a hot potato when we divorced and now they're all being unctuous and nice. Bloody hypocrites. I've had such a job being polite to some of them.'

'Look, after today all you have to do is keep in touch with Chloé, if you still want to.' Devlin linked her arm in Maggie's. 'There's only a few hours left to go, hang in there. As soon as you've eaten, you can slip away home and get into an Epsom salts bath and relax. You'll have your children around you. Look at old photos, laugh, cry and remember the good times,' she advised.

'And there *were* good times.' A tear slid down Maggie's cheek. 'When our babies were born we were very happy, until he took up with that Ria Kirby one and it all went downhill after that. He was a selfish, womanising charmer and I'm damned if I'm going to confer sainthood on him now that he's dead.'

'You don't have to. You can say what you like to us, anytime, but you've been so good at handling the divorce. You made sure Shona, Mimi and Michael kept up their relationship with him.'

'Well, the twins anyway. It took Shona years but, girls, I'm so thankful she made her peace with him. What a nightmare it would have been for Shona if she hadn't. We were so fortunate to have the wedding and that fun, family Christmas Eve lunch.'

'*You're* the one who should have sainthood conferred upon her. Deep breaths, Saint Margaret of Wickla. I think your mother's looking for you.' Devlin saw Nelsie heading in their direction.

'She drove herself to the church, to support me. That touched me a lot, in spite of everything that's gone on between us. No sign of Tony and Ginny, needless to say. I'll talk to you during the week. Wish me luck.' Squaring her shoulders and taking a deep breath, Maggie walked towards Nelsie but was waylaid by yet another sympathiser.

Michael walked back into the function room and looked around for Chloé. She was sitting by the window holding Dervla's baby. He walked over.

'Hiya, girls,' he said. 'Your baby's beautiful, Dervla.'

'Thanks,' she said shyly.

'Chloé, we're heading off soon, come over to our table with me to say goodbye.'

'Sure.' Chloé handed Katie back to Dervla. 'Bye bye, princess, see you soon.' She kissed Katie tenderly.

'I just want you to know something,' Michael said, putting his arm around his half-sister as they walked between the tables to where Maggie was saying goodbye to Caroline. 'Shona, Mimi and I will always be there for you. If you ever need us, pick up the phone, won't you?'

Chloé nodded and began to sob. Her half-brother's arm tightened around her. 'I'm so, so sad, Michael. I just don't know how I can live without Daddy. This is the worst thing that's ever happened to me.'

'Me too,' Michael said miserably as they arrived at the table. Shona and Mimi jumped up and embraced their siblings and Maggie wept to see their grief, knowing that all they could do was put one foot in front of the other, every day, and support each other as much as they could.

'On behalf of Maggie and myself I'd like to extend our thanks for the meal, Denise.' Nelsie was damned if she was going to call that woman 'Mrs Ryan'. 'It was a grand send off for my son-in-law, better than he deserved if truth be told. But he was a good father to my grandchildren, even if he was a lousy husband to my daughter, who treated him far better than he deserved after their divorce. But then Maggie is a *lady*.' *And you'll never be one*, she added silently, thinking there was no point in rubbing too much salt in the wound. 'Good afternoon.' Nelsie bestowed a cool smile on the people at the table – Denise's parents and siblings – and revelled in the look of shock on the widow's face before she turned and walked back to where her daughter and grandchildren were saying goodbye to Chloé and getting ready to leave.

'I said thanks to that one from both of us: you don't have to go near her, Maggie. Let's leave them to it. We've done what we have to do,' she whispered to Maggie, careful not to let Chloé, who was talking to Shona, hear. 'Aleksy, thanks for driving my car to the hotel. I'll be home in no time. You're a great young man.' She kissed each of her grandchildren and Chloé. 'I'm on the other end of the phone if you need to talk.'

'Thanks, Gran.' Michael stood up. 'I'll walk you out.'

'Maggie, I have an apple tart and a tin of scones in the car, in case people drop by when you get home and you haven't anything to go with a pot of tea. I'll give them to Michael. Drop in when you get back down from Dublin. I suppose you'll stay a few days with the children?'

'I will. Thanks, Mam, I really appreciate your support. Are you sure you'll be OK getting home?' Maggie stood up to hug her mother.

'I'll be fine. I'll be home in twenty minutes. It will take you longer to get home to Ranelagh than it will take me to get to Wicklow,' Nelsie said briskly, nestling into her daughter's embrace. It had been so long since they'd hugged like that. 'When everything settles down, I'd like to have a chat with you about something. We have a few things to sort out.'

'Have we?' Maggie looked her mother straight in the eye.

'Well, I have,' amended Nelsie, sheepishly.

'I'll be in touch. Text me and let me know you're home safe and sound.'

'I will,' Nelsie promised, taking her grandson's arm. 'Lead on, McDuff.'

Michael laughed. 'You always said that to me when I was small and we were going somewhere.'

'I did.' Nelsie smiled back at him. She'd always loved having her grandchildren come to stay when they were small. Terry's funeral had been an opportunity for her to be able to support them.

Nelsie drove home delighted with herself. She'd *finally* put the second wife firmly in her place, not that she'd ever tell Maggie. Her daughter might be upset by what she'd said. Loyalty to family was important, Nelsie felt, and Terry's sudden death had given her a lot to think about.

CHAPTER SIXTY-FOUR

Maggie/Nelsie

Nelsie felt unaccountably nervous as she set the kitchen table for two and placed a plate of cherry-and-walnut scones on the tablecloth. They were Maggie's favourite. She'd baked them first thing this morning for her daughter.

The late spring sunshine speckled the jug of daffodils and bluebells that sat in the centre of the table. The sight of them calmed her. They were such cheerful flowers. She had masses of them in the glade between the two roan trees at the end of her garden. Nelsie loved her spring garden. The scent of the daphne blooms always lifted her heart after the cold, dark days of winter. When they burst into glorious blooms it signalled that the days were getting longer and the weather getting milder.

There was heat in the sun these days. Nelsie knew she should be thankful that she was alive to experience the joy of another spring. There was Terry, now gone from earthly life. How things could change in the blink of an eye.

Nelsie had been stunned when Maggie had phoned to tell

her the news. The last time she'd seen her former son-in-law was at the Christmas lunch he'd treated the family to. It had been most enjoyable, especially as that briar of a second wife of his wasn't there. For his many faults, he'd always been kind to Nelsie during his marriage to Maggie and they'd shared some banter at that happy Christmas Eve do.

Shona and Aleksy's wedding – a day that Nelsie once thought Terry would never have been invited to – was another wonderful family occasion. Shona's reconciliation with her father had made that wedding a day of true family happiness. Nelsie had felt a lump in her throat when Maggie and Terry had walked Shona under the stone arch entrance. And now he was gone. Her grandchildren had lost their father and life had changed to 'before' and 'after' his heartbreaking death.

Nelsie could be gone as quick herself, if the Almighty decided. She wanted to make her peace with Maggie. She wanted to explain things to her. Wanted to explain why she'd made the decisions she'd made. Nelsie knew she'd hurt her daughter. Maggie had been truly shocked when Nelsie had informed her that Tony was her executor and held power of attorney. Maggie hadn't made a big issue about it but she'd stepped back and insisted that her brother play his part in Nelsie's care.

Nelsie sighed a gale-force sigh. Getting old was vexatious to the spirit for sure. Her independence was slowly being whittled away by little things. There was a time when she could climb a ladder to change a light bulb or reach up to her kitchen press to take out her weighing scales and mixing bowl. They'd had to be put in the lower press in her dresser because she could no longer raise her arms much higher than the top of her head. She couldn't prune her shrubs beyond shoulder level, nor hold her hairdryer for long. All these minor irritations were wearing and it was worse they were getting. Maggie had been right about one thing: she should have kept tighter control of her finances in case she had to get more home help. Tony and Ginny had made a dent in her savings and she only had herself to blame for that.

Nelsie stared out the window at the planters of purple and yellow pansies that ornamented the patio. She'd managed to plant those herself. A small triumph. Her son had needed to be nagged to power hose the patio so she wouldn't slip on the flags during the icy winter days. She'd reared a lazy son, Nelsie admitted gloomily. She'd spoilt him as a child, and Rick, and that spoiling had carried on right into adulthood for Tony. The girls had been rightly irate at how much their brothers could get away with.

Nelsie smiled at the memory of Niamh throwing Tony's shirts at him saying, 'I'm not ironing your bloody shirts anymore. Iron them yourself, ya lazy lump,' and then glaring at her mother, saying, '*You* should be making those pair iron their own shirts. Women aren't men's slaves anymore.' It was partly Nelsie's fault that Niamh had never come back to Ireland to live, she thought sadly. She'd been a demanding mother of her two daughters. A distant memory drifted in of her own mother calling Nelsie's grandmother a termagant. They had never got on. Had she been as much of a termagant as her grandmother? Maggie's arrival saved her from having to delve too deeply into that and she was glad of it, Nelsie admitted to herself as she greeted her eldest daughter.

'How are the children doing?' she asked as she poured tea for the two of them.

'The girls are gone back to work. Michael's going back to his ship on Friday. They're stunned. Numb. A sudden death is so difficult to deal with. No warning. No time to prepare. I'm glad they're close. They're helping each other and Chloé.' Maggie sank down on a kitchen chair. She was weary.

'Yes, that's a blessing, I suppose,' Nelsie said, buttering two scones with a generous helping of creamy, yellow 'real' butter, as she called it. Nelsie had no truck with spreads. 'Eat them up. I made them especially for you.'

'Thanks, Mam.' Maggie managed a smile.

'You should be proud of yourself: the way you raised your children. You did a better job than me,' Nelsie ventured.

'Am I a disappointment to you?' Maggie paused mid-bite. She was surprised at the turn the conversation was taking.

'Of course not,' Nelsie exclaimed. 'What I meant was I didn't raise my children to be close to one another and that is *my* failure.'

'Oh!' Maggie murmured, taken aback at this admission.

Nelsie put her cup down. 'Maggie, I know I favoured the boys and particularly Tony when they were children. I never told you or your sister or them that our first child, a little boy, died a cot death when he was nine months old. We didn't know about cot deaths then. I thought it was something I'd done wrong. I blamed myself. We were delighted when our beautiful daughters arrived. Never doubt that, Maggie, but when Tony was born I felt I'd been forgiven for the death of David, your baby brother. And that was why I spoilt him the most.'

'Why didn't you ever tell us, Mam?' Maggie asked, dumbfounded.

'I . . . I couldn't bring myself to,' Nelsie said shakily. 'I buried it deep inside. I couldn't face questions. And even now I still carry the guilt and ask myself was there *anything* I could have done to save our baby?'

'Ah, Mam.' Maggie got up and went to put her arms around Nelsie. 'You couldn't have done *anything*. No parent should feel guilty about a sudden infant death.'

'That's easy to say when you haven't experienced it, Maggie.'

'Mam, you know I don't believe in the churchy type of God sitting in heaven judging people and all of that stuff we were taught, but I *do* believe there is a divine plan to our lives. The cot death was part of . . . of David's divine plan, just as Terry's sudden death was part of his. There's *nothing* to feel guilty about,' she reiterated.

'If it had been Shona, Mimi or Michael at your baby brother's age?' Nelsie stared at her. 'How would you feel?'

'I don't know,' Maggie admitted. 'Devastated I'm sure.'

'No, you don't know, dear, thankfully.' Nelsie patted her hand. 'Now before I say what I have to say, I don't want you telling your sister and brothers about what I've told you. This is between you and me.'

'If that's what you want, Mam,' Maggie replied reluctantly. She felt her siblings should know they'd had a baby brother called David.

'It is. I don't want to ever talk about my little baby again. It still pains me. It might be selfish of me. But that's what I'd prefer.' Nelsie slumped in her chair, drained.

'That's OK, Mam. I won't say a word. Could I just ask you: where's his grave?'

'In the graveyard, of course. He's buried in your father's family plot. Beside his daddy. It's a grave for six. Your nana, granddad, David, your daddy and, when my time comes, me. There's room in there for you if you want, seeing as you won't be buried with the other fella.'

'I always thought David was an uncle. Well, that's what I assumed. It never dawned on me to ask. And you kept all the grief to yourself. How sad.'

'My girlfriends were so good to me. You know the way you depend on Caroline and Maggie? Well, my friends carried me.'

'I'm so glad you had them to support you, Mam. Real friends are a great blessing.'

'Now!' Nelsie said briskly and sat up straight. 'I know you were hurt when I told you Tony has power of attorney for me and that I had my will made. The thing is, Maggie, when Covid happened and they came to stay with me it was such a strange time. I mean, it was awful when Martha Daly down the road died and the poor family could only look in the window at her when she took her last breaths. It was horrendous, they told me. But it made me terrible nervous. And then Tony was asking me about my will and the power thing and he kept at me to get it sorted and said he'd take me to a solicitor. I had to go to the doctor too, to make sure I wasn't doolally. And that's how it happened. He kept saying to me that he'd take care of things and there was no need to be annoying you. You had enough to be dealing with having children to worry about and so on. And that's kind of him, Maggie. You *do* have a lot on your plate and even more so now,' Nelsie declared spiritedly. 'But anyway I was wondering, if you were agreeable, if you'd like me to add your name as an attorney holder. I wanted to ask you before I said anything to Tony.'

'Of course you can. That would be a good idea, Mam,'

Maggie agreed, much to Nelsie's relief. Maggie would make sure that, if anything went wrong with her, she wouldn't be fecked into a nursing home and left there.

'I think I'd like to go back to Garrett Fitzpatrick and have him take care of it. He's a very kind young man and *very* patient. He reminds me of your father. He has that handsome look about him and a fine head of hair, like Ted had. I didn't really take to that bloke of Tony's,' she sniffed, nostrils flaring.

'I think that would be a good idea too, Mam. Garrett is very dependable.' Maggie was delighted Nelsie was going back to the family solicitor.

'Well, let's get it sorted. The sooner the better. I'll speak to your brother today and we'll make a date with Garrett, if that's all right with you.'

'That's fine with me. Now why don't I make us a fresh pot of tea and we can tuck into those delicious scones?' Maggie suggested, kissing the top of her mother's head. Nelsie exhaled. A long, deep breath. She felt as though a heavy burden had been lifted from her shoulders . . . and her heart.

'Tony, I had a long chat with your sister and I've decided to add her to the power of attorney document. It's only fair, really. She's minded me very well for years. I know you didn't want her to be burdened or anything, when you encouraged me to sort my affairs during Covid, but it was a strange old time and I wasn't thinking straight. I want to go back to Garrett Fitzpatrick. He's dealt with the family for a long time and I like him,' Nelsie said firmly. Now that she knew Maggie was agreeable to her proposition, she wasn't going to be browbeaten by her son.

'There's no need to go changing things. You're sorted.' Tony struggled not to lose his temper. 'You're wasting money, Mam.'

'It's my money to waste,' Nelsie said sharply. 'And another thing, don't be asking me for any more money, now. I need to put enough aside to take care of me and have extra home care if I need it in the future. You need to cut your cloth to suit your measure and stop living beyond your means.'

'What's brought all this on?' Tony demanded angrily.

'A sudden death gives pause for thought, Tony. I saw how well Maggie had brought up her children to support each other. They are very caring of each other in this time of hardship. And, to tell you the truth, it made me look at how I spoilt you and Rick in comparison to how I treated your sisters. I shouldn't be handing out large sums of money to you, son, and not giving the same to the others. And anyway, as I say, I need to think of what I might need for the future.' Nelsie felt empowered. Wasn't that what young women were today? *Empowered*, she thought, relieved that she was finally having the conversation with her son that she'd been practising for since the funeral.

'And another thing.' Nelsie had something else to get off her chest. 'It wouldn't have killed you to go to Terry's funeral and be there for your sister and your nieces and nephew. I was disappointed in you.'

'I can't just take time off just like that, and besides they've been divorced for years—'

'That's as may be,' Nelsie retorted. 'But you should have been there. As the young people say these days: do better. Now, I have to go and book a Mass for your father's anniversary. Make sure you're down here for *that*! Bye bye.' Nelsie hung up before her son had time to answer. She knew he was furious with her but she didn't have the energy for his sulks anymore. Her days of spoiling him were over. He'd done very well out of her. From now on it was herself she'd be spoiling, and Maggie too, Nelsie decided. It was high time for it.

Maggie sat in a sheltered nook in her garden, closed her eyes and raised her face to the sun. She'd made an appointment with Garrett Fitzpatrick for the following week. The sooner the legal matters were settled the better. Terry's death had rattled her. There was no telling who might go next. That was always the way after a death, she reflected tiredly. Unease and apprehension for a while until life settled back to something akin to normal.

She was trying to absorb all her mother had told her earlier. It was unbelievable to think that Nelsie had kept the secret of their baby brother's death to herself for all these years. No wonder she'd filled her life with the ICA and charity work and the like. Trying to fill the cavernous hole that her baby's death had left in her life. She could understand now why Tony and, to a lesser extent, Rick had been favoured. Not that Nelsie her done her eldest son any favours. He'd grown into a mean-spirited man with a sense of entitlement because he'd always been given anything he wanted.

Not that that excused her brother's behaviour during Covid. He'd exerted pressure on their mother when she was at her most vulnerable and was still touching her up for money. It *was* elder abuse and he wasn't going to get away with it any longer. Maggie was glad now though that she hadn't gone at him full tilt, as she'd been tempted to, and had a massive row. Playing it cool had been the best strategy.

The whole business had caused a rift between them certainly but so be it. If Tony didn't have enough of a moral compass to see how contemptible his behaviour was, nothing she said was going to change him. And that was a sad thing for him, she thought forlornly, reflecting on the difference in her relationship with her siblings in comparison to the loving bond shared by her children, including Chloé. Not under any circumstances could she imagine any of her children treating her the way Tony treated Nelsie, in her old age. Nor could she imagine them being distant and uninvolved like Niamh was with their mother.

Her relationship with her children was loving and supportive and what she gave them she got back a thousand fold. Motherhood hadn't been easy, especially when she and Terry had separated and divorced. That had been a nightmare time but they'd got through it. And now she was reaping the rewards. Her children were well-balanced, standing on their own two feet, making good lives for themselves and supporting each other, and her, through this trauma and loss. She, Niamh, Tony and Rick had never been that and that was their great loss. If their baby brother had lived would things have been different? Who knew?

Maggie stood up and went to her garden shed and got her secateurs. Michael was coming to stay the night before he went back to sea and she wanted to cook his favourite dinner: corned beef, mashed potato, cabbage and parsley sauce. But first she needed to do something to mark the day that was in it. She snipped daffodils and tulips, growing in clumps around the apple trees, and cut a couple of sprays of forsythia. She locked the back door and set off down to the graveyard on the edge of the village.

She walked briskly, listening to the birds chirruping in the hedgerows and the rumble of a tractor in one of the fields in the distance. There was no one in the stonewalled graveyard and Maggie filled a watering can from the tap at the gate and made her way along the centre pathway. She came to the row where her father and his family were buried and stopped at the well-tended grave that her mother took pride in caring for. Pots of multi-coloured violas and red and white cyclamen rested on the white and black stones.

The granite headstone stood strong and sturdy bearing the names of her grandparents, father and brother. She filled the grave vase with water and inserted her fresh flowers into the round holes on top, arranging them until she was happy with the display. 'Dad, David,' she said, running her forefinger gently over their names, 'help me to have patience with Mam, help Niamh to overcome her resentment, help Rick to become more involved with the family and help Tony to become a better person. And say hello to Terry if you see him.'

A white butterfly fluttered past her to land on the violas and she smiled. A sign, Maggie thought gratefully, that her loved ones, including the brother she never knew, were always with her.

CHAPTER SIXTY-FIVE

Devlin/Caroline

'Hiya! Any chance you might be free for an elbows-on-the table din-dins at mine, tomorrow or Thursday?' Devlin's cheery voice made Caroline smile. 'I know it's short notice but I want to run something by you.'

'Are you cooking?' Caroline asked, amused.

'Well, you know it's not exactly my forte, but seeing as Luke's in London I'll do my best. Oh, and if you happen to be talking to Maggie don't say you're coming to me for dinner. It's just you and me.'

'Oh! OK.' Caroline was taken aback.

'I'll tell you all when you're here, so what evening suits you best?'

'Tomorrow's fine. I don't have any plans and I won't be babysitting.'

'Can you stay the night?'

'I could.'

'Brilliant, pack an overnighter and I'll see you around six?'

'Looking forward to it. I'll bring dessert. See ya!' Caroline replied, wondering why Maggie wasn't invited or even to be told about Devlin's spur of the moment invite. Had they had a tiff? It would be most unusual if they did, and she didn't want to be stuck in the middle of it. In all their years of friendship, they'd never had a real falling out. A bit of narkiness here and there but they were a tight trio who knew each other very well. Devlin had sounded cheerful so there must be some other reason to keep their friend in the dark, Caroline reasoned, wondering what it was.

'Something smells nice,' Caroline observed as a garlicky aroma wafted out of the kitchen.

'My signature garlic bread, and creamy salmon pasta. Even I can't go wrong with that and I cheated and bought a goat's cheese and red onion tartlet starter from the Butler's Pantry.'

'I made a crunchy apple crumble, with apples from my tree, for afters.' Caroline placed her creation and a carton of Bird's custard onto the kitchen counter and popped a tub of ice cream into the freezer.

'Luke will think he's died and gone to heaven when he comes home to that tomorrow. He loves your crunchy crumble.' Devlin approved.

'I know. That's why I made it. Mick and Dervla love it too.'

'I lit the stove. Even though the days are getting much longer, it's still a bit cool at night.' Devlin gave her simmering pasta dish a stir and turned down the heat before turning off the air fryer where the garlic bread was crisping. She poured two glasses of chilled Nosecco, handed one to Caroline and said, 'Cheers. Sit down and tuck in.'

'So what's the deal with Maggie? Why wasn't I allowed to say you invited me to dinner?' Caroline shook out her napkin, took a drink of her sparkling fizz and cut into her tartlet.

'The thing is, Michael and Finn have come up with a plan. Michael and the girls are worried about her with all that's gone on: what with Terry dying and Denise being a bitch about the funeral and that carry on with bloody Tony and Nelsie earlier in the year. They feel she needs a good break, so they want to treat her to a cruise. Finn, God love him, is worried about *me*, having had the surgery and all the shite with CCK and the stress of organising the City Girls' celebration. So between them all they came up with a plan. They want to surprise Maggie with a cruise, on Michael's ship, with us there too and have us stay in Barcelona for a few days before we embark. Michael will be joining the ship in Barcelona after his shore leave, in May.'

Devlin put her knife and fork down and looked Caroline straight in the eye. 'Caro, I'd love if you could come. But I know you've struggled with bulimia again in the past year and the reason you've never gone cruising is because of the food thing. I know it could be a problem for you. All those restaurants that Maggie would love but you'd probably run a mile from. I'd hate you to feel we'd left you out but I'd also hate if you felt pressurised to come and were miserable.'

'Oh!' Caroline murmured, taken aback. Devlin and Luke had cruised several times and Maggie and her girls had taken a cruise on Michael's ship when he'd been a junior officer a few years ago but cruising had never appealed to her.

'You know me so well, Dev.'

'There *is* a huge emphasis on wining and dining on a cruise ship but, you know, you *can* tailor it to suit your needs,' Devlin said. 'Michael's ship is one of the smaller luxury cruise ships. It takes six hundred passengers. The only time you really spend time with lots of the other people is in the restaurants. There's a state of the art gym, two pools, a fabulous spa and great reading nooks. So there's a lot more than food to keep you entertained, as well as visits to the ports. And the veranda suites are *so* comfortable. Michael said the housekeeping staff can turn back the veranda dividers, so we'd be able to have a really long balcony, the length of our three cabins, if you come. It would be so *lovely* for the three of us to get away together after all the hard times we've had,' she said longingly.

'It does sound fabulous,' Caroline admitted. 'And since I've gone back to counselling part-time and being so involved with Dervla and her baby, the bulimia's not so dominant. I guess the baby's filled the ache the food used to. I'm not lonely anymore, Dev. I don't feel empty. My life is so different now. Maybe I *could* come and not be stressed out of my tree.'

'Think about it. Only we need to book soon. The cruises fill up very quickly on the smaller liners and it would be great to go when Michael's on the ship. When we've eaten let's go and sit by the fire and I'll show you some of the videos of the ship.'

'And how are you planning on getting Maggie to go on the cruise if she knows nothing about it?' Caroline asked, spearing a piece of goat's cheese.

'We're going to tell her we're taking a trip to Barcelona for a few days with the boys, before Michael joins the ship. And then we'll go and see him off, or so she thinks, and before she knows it we'll be heading up that gangway! Can you just imagine her face?' Devlin said giddily, getting up to ladle her creamy salmon pasta into a serving dish.

'It's a terrific idea. She so badly needs a do-nothing holiday. The kids are great, aren't they? I love them.'

'They are,' agreed Devlin. 'She raised them well.'

'You did a great job with Finn, too.' Caroline stacked their starter plates in the dishwasher.

'And you, Dervla and Mick are doing a great job with the baby. Has Dervla said anything about the fostering or adoption plans?'

'She's vacillating. And if she's going to go ahead with either of those options, she needs to do it sooner rather than later because it will just be so hard on both of them. Mick's offer on a house was accepted but you know how long the legal stuff takes. Once they're in, there'll be more space for them all. But it's not my place to say anything, so I don't.'

'She's a little dote,' Devlin said. 'The first time I held her I got broody! At my age.'

'I've always been broody. Having Katie in my life has been such a gift. Saying goodbye to her would break my heart,' Caroline confessed.

Devlin's heart sank. To think that after all these years Caroline had found something that gave her life meaning and made her happy and it could be taken away from her. How cruel of fate if it happened.

'Take it day by day, Caroline.' Devlin knew it was trite advice but it was the best she could come up with right then.

'All the times I've told my clients that,' Caroline laughed. 'Practising what I preach is a lot harder.'

'You know, if you decided the cruise wasn't for you, you could always come just for the few days in Barcelona. It would do you good,' Devlin suggested.

'You know what, I just might.' Caroline raised her glass to Devlin. 'It would be something to look forward to.'

Later, lying in bed in Devlin's guest room, listening to the shush-shush of the sea, Caroline thought about the cruise proposal.

Devlin was right. She *could* do with a holiday. The rotator cuff surgery in January had been much more painful than she'd anticipated and the recovery was slow. She could drive but her range of motion was taking a long time to come back. Lovely warm weather and daily swimming would certainly make a difference.

Since Mick, Dervla and Katie had moved in with her on her return from hospital, the three of them had cemented their bond in such a relaxed, easy fashion that it seemed like the most natural thing in the world for them to stay on after her surgery. Mick was truly grateful to be able to do something in return for Caroline's kindness and Dervla became much more confident with Katie because Caroline was there to praise and encourage. When needed, Caroline took the fretful baby for a couple of hours, giving Dervla time to chat to her friends on social media or meet up with Chloé.

They had become so much a part of her life that she couldn't imagine them not in it. Dervla wanted to study accountancy. She had a head for figures and an attention to detail that fascinated Caroline, who'd hated maths at school. Dervla wanted to do the one-year Leaving Cert course in Plunket College in September to get her points for college. But first she had to make a decision about her baby. They knew each other so well now, perhaps it would be OK to broach the subject of making a decision one way or another, casually, Caroline mused. She wasn't an outsider anymore: she was very much a part of their lives and they of hers. She'd do it soon, she promised herself as she drifted off to sleep soothed by the sea's rhythmic lullaby.

'So what do you think?' Caroline put down Katie's bottle and leaned her forward to burp her. She had outlined Devlin's proposed surprise cruise to Mick and was keen for his opinion on what she should do.

'What *you* think is more important than what I think.' Mick made faces at Katie and made her laugh. 'If you were your client, what would you say?'

Caroline laughed. 'I've heard that before. In fact, Devlin said the same thing.'

'And?'

'Well I wouldn't *advise*, that's not my job,' she hedged.

'But you'd point them in the right direction?' He eyed her quizzically.

'I'd say if it was too stressful and they didn't think they could control the bulimia then they should seriously consider the consequences of going. But if they felt they could deal with the food issue, it would be a shame to miss such an opportunity.'

'I'm not a counsellor, so I *can* advise, and I say go for it, Caroline. You'll be with Devlin and Maggie, who know you as well as you know yourself. Stick to your eating routines. Don't make a big deal of it. There's much more to enjoy and the ship looks amazing from the videos you've shown me. Go and have fun with the girls. You deserve it, Caroline. You *need* it,' Mick encouraged.

Katie gave a loud burp. 'Good girl,' Caroline praised, settling her back into the crook of her arm and watching happily as she sucked contentedly on her bottle once again. 'I'll miss her, if I go.'

'She'll be waiting for you when you get back. We all will.' Mick put an arm around Caroline's shoulder and gave her an affectionate squeeze.

Caroline heard the key in the door and her eyes lit up as Dervla and Chloé came into the sitting room. They had been on location in Clew Bay for the day with Maggie and Shona. Shone was filming a segment on Grace O'Malley the pirate queen for the series on powerful medieval women that had been commissioned after Maggie's trip to Carcassonne.

'Did you have a good day? There's chicken and broccoli bake and an apple crumble in the kitchen.'

'It was great,' enthused Chloé, taking off her coat. 'Thanks so much for inviting me to stay. Hello, baba!' She knelt down to smile at the baby. 'It's Auntie Chloé.'

Katie gave a big smile.

'Look Dervla, she *knows* me. She smiled when I said I was her auntie.' Chloé was ecstatic.

Dervla laughed. 'She smiles at everybody, Chloé. Don't you, my darling?' she took Katie from Caroline and cuddled her. 'Hello, my little girl. Were you good for Nantie Caroline and Gramps? Did you miss Mama?' She kissed her and smiled tenderly when the baby hooked her hand around her little finger.

'She was a very good girl. Do you want to finish feeding her?' Caroline asked. 'I've just winded her and she's ready for the rest of the bottle.'

'I'm starving, Caroline: do you mind if we have our dinner first?' Dervla said, planting gentle kisses on her baby's head.

'Of course not. The table's set: enjoy it.'

'We will, we're famished,' Chloé said eagerly, leading the way to the kitchen. She loved Caroline's home cooking.

'Isn't it wonderful that they've become fast friends?' Caroline watched Katie's incredibly long lashes fan over her cheeks as she drank. 'They came into each other's lives when they both needed a friend most. Chloé's so devastated by Terry's death; Dervla and the baby are a godsend to her.'

'Friends do come into each other's lives just when they need them and old friends often reunite when *they're* needed most, don't they? Just like we did,' Mick observed, turning to look at Caroline.

Their eyes met in a moment of profound recognition. And then, like it was the most natural thing in the world, both of them raised their lips to the other and their first kiss was one of utter tenderness, contentment and joy.

CHAPTER SIXTY-SIX

Caroline/Mick

'Do you think we should get married?' Mick propped himself against the pillows and looked at Caroline, who was snuggled in against him. Dervla and Chloé had taken Katie out to the Howth Market on the Dart and Mick and Caroline had scarpered upstairs like two teenagers making the most of a free house.

'If that's a proposal it's not very romantic.' Caroline's lips turned up in a smile.

'I'm asking you what you think first, to see if I *should* propose,' Mick said, straight-faced.

Caroline reached up and caressed his cheek. 'We're together and it's wonderful and I'm so happy, Mick. Do we really *need* to? It's going to be a pain in the ass making wills and sorting properties. You need to leave your house to your children. I've the clinic to deal with as well as this house and shares and so on. I've been married and so have you so we've been there, done that and the rest of it.'

'Are you playing hard to get? That's the best proposal rejection ever,' Mick laughed.

'I'm serious.'

'I know you are: that's what's even funnier. And the thing is, you're absolutely right.'

'I know!' Her eyes lit up. 'Let's have a ceremony like Shona and Aleksy had but without the legal stuff.'

'You're on,' Mick agreed.

'But you'll have to propose properly. I'm not that easy,' Caroline teased.

'I'll go down on one knee but you might have to help me get back up. The old rugby injury is playing up. Seriously, Caroline, I love you. I want to be with you and grow old with you and, if marriage is what your heart desires, I'd marry you in a heartbeat.'

'My heart desires you, Mick. It's so wonderful being a part of your and Dervla's lives, and Katie is a miracle in mine. Do you think Dervla will have her adopted?'

'I have a feeling if you and I are together that might not happen, somehow or another,' he said thoughtfully. 'We have to tell her about us, and tell Ciara, Conor and, of course, Sally at some stage. I want to tell the kids first.'

'I wonder what will they say?' Caroline asked.

'They'll say I'm the luckiest man alive.' Mick bent down and kissed her and Caroline drew him close and kissed him back, delighting in the feel of his body entwined with hers and with the gift of intimacy with a man she loved, having been so long without it.

'Thanks for fitting us in for a Zoom, guys,' Mick said to Conor in Melbourne and Ciara in France.

'Cool, Dad. No worries,' Conor replied and Caroline was

struck by how alike he and his father were.

'Everything OK?' Ciara asked. 'You all right, Derv?'

'Yep.' Dervla waved Katie's little hand.

'So,' Mick cleared his throat, 'the thing is Caroline and I . . . Well, Caroline and I are a couple now—'

'*Yes!*' Dervla couldn't contain her delight. 'Chloé, Ciara and I just knew it was going to happen. We just didn't know what was taking you so long. Isn't that right, Ciara?'

Her older sister laughed at her father's gobsmacked expression. Caroline was blushing. 'That's right, Derv. Dad, Caroline: I'm really happy for you. That's great news.'

'Way to go, guys. Hope you can come to Australia for a visit soon.' Conor gave a thumbs up.

'When's the wedding?' Dervla – ever the romantic – asked.

'We've decided that getting legally married would perhaps cause complications in the future. I want to leave all my estate to you guys without any legal difficulties. And Caroline has her estate to deal with, so it's easier to stay as we are but we're going to have a ceremony for sure.'

'That makes a lot of sense,' Ciara said.

'It was Caroline who pointed it out.' Mick hugged her tightly.

'It's good that you all have a home to come to when you're in Ireland. Mick's waiting for the sale to go through. I'll be helping him decorate but I'll be keeping my house too, in case Dervla and I need a girls' night every so often,' Caroline said lightly.

'We sure do! And when you come home, you can have one with us too, Ciara,' Dervla said happily. 'Dad can babysit.'

'Are you keeping the baby, Derv?' Conor asked.

Dervla was silent for a moment as all eyes turned to her.

'Are we? I *really* want to.' She turned to Mick and Caroline.

'We'd certainly love to, if we did but as always the decision is yours to make.' Mick lifted his grandchild into his arms and gooed at her, making her laugh.

'You know I'm here for you and Katie, Derv. Nothing would make me happier than for the three of us to raise her. I'll mind her when you go to college. We can work everything out. If it's what you really want.' Caroline linked her arm in hers.

'I'm so glad.' Dervla burst into noisy sobs. 'I really couldn't bear to give her up for adoption. I love her so much. I was just afraid you might not always be in our lives and it wouldn't be fair on Dad.'

'I'm in your life permanently now, Derv, and you're in mine. And I *love* your Dad very much. So between the three of us, Katie Michaela is going to have a life *full* of love.' Caroline held her step-daughter-to-be tightly and marvelled that at last, after all these years, she had everything that she had ever wanted. A loving family unit of her own.

CHAPTER SIXTY-SEVEN

MAGGIE

'It's going to be a wonderful break for you, Mam. I *adore* Barcelona. And you'll have a few days with Michael and Finn, as well as being on holliers with Devlin and Caroline. Something to really look forward to. Just what you need,' declared Shona. 'And make sure to take another week off, to get the full benefit from it. I won't pencil in any filming or postproduction work for you.'

They were in the office, having a quick cup of coffee and a sandwich before Maggie did her voice-overs and Shona wrote some scripts for documentaries she was working on.

'It's been ages since I was away with the girls. We've all had such a ghastly time of it over the last year. It will be just what we need and being able to spend time with the lads will be fun.' Maggie opened a bag of crisps and put a few in her ham sandwich.

'I'll book your tickets for you, if you like. Go and find some good locations for filming while you're there: you can claim tax back on the fare as a work expense. If you're going to Barcelona we might as well get the most out of you.' Shona grinned.

'Oh I don't know about claiming tax on it. It's a holiday,' Maggie hesitated.

'Are you *mad*, Mam? Look at the tax you pay, and we all pay, that's being absolutely wasted. Look at the cost of that bloody children's hospital. It was supposed to cost five hundred million and now it's costing *billions*! Look at how much of our money was wasted. Thirty-nine million on a site that was totally unsuitable, and where it is now is no better. Look at one hundred and thirty new electric buses lying idle in depots because there's no infrastructure for the chargers! Don't *annoy* me, Mam,' Shona retorted crossly.

'When you put it like that.' Maggie grinned at her daughter's belligerence.

'I do! I don't mind paying taxes but, bloody hell, taxpayers in this country are being abused big time, and I'm sick of it. I've a good mind to emigrate myself.'

'Ah don't do that, I'd miss you.'

'I'd miss you too,' Shona said fondly. 'Check with the girls about the dates and who you want to fly with. The sooner you book the cheaper it will be.'

'Yes, Shona. Whatever you say, Shona. You're in charge.' Now that there was talk of booking flights, Maggie was beginning to get excited. A jaunt abroad with Dev and Caroline would be such a treat. Good weather, the sun in their faces, heat in their bones. It was an inviting prospect for sure.

'I'm booking her flights and I'll book the cruise from my email. I have her passport number. Michael said you'd be able to download the boarding pass for the flight home from Rome while on the ship, if it's too soon to do it now.'

'Excellent, Shona. You're playing a blinder,' Devlin approved. 'I hope to God I don't let it slip.'

'Me too. I'm petrified. It almost popped out once. I stopped myself just in time!'

'Can you imagine her face when the taxi brings us to the ship instead of the airport? I can't wait! Roll on our holliers.'

CHAPTER SIXTY-EIGHT

Caroline/Mick/Sally/Maggie/Devlin

'Hi Dev, count me in: I'm going on a cruise with my ladies,' Caroline announced gleefully.

The weather had turned cold and mizzly. A Mediterranean cruise was getting more inviting by the minute.

'Yay!' squealed Devlin. 'I'm *thrilled*. Caro, we're going to have such *fun*. Shona's booking everything – flights, cruise, the whole palaver – so Maggie will have no idea. We *deserve* this. I'll get in touch with Michael to firm up the dates. If you like I can book for the two of us and you can fix me up whenever.'

'Are you afraid I might chicken out?' Caroline teased.

'No! It's just I've done it before. There's quite a bit involved and you get inundated with emails. No point in the two of us having the hassle of it. Send me your passport details and I'll do it at the weekend.'

'OK. And Dev . . . I just want to thank you for being so kind and understanding about the bulimia.'

'Ah, give over. Sure haven't Maggie and I had our own issues over the years? You know Shona and Aleksy's wedding song? *'Amigos Para Siempre'*: that's us. I think we should sing it on the bow of the *Seabourn Ovation* – that's the name of Michael's ship – as we sail out of Barcelona. I'll do my best Sarah Brightman quiver.'

'Imagine Michael's face if the three of us warbled that at the top of our voices,' Caroline laughed.

'Knowing him, he'd join in. I'd better go,' Dev said. 'Health and Safety are here making an unannounced inspection and, even though I know the place is spotless, it's always a bit nerve-wracking. I'll talk to you at the weekend. You've made my day. See ya.'

How lucky I am to have such a friend, Caroline thought, sending up a prayer of gratitude. Wait until she told Dev and Maggie about Mick and herself. She would never forget that soul recognition: when *anam caras* – soul friends – reunite. That deep bonding gaze with Mick that was a homecoming for both of them and the exquisite kiss that had sealed it. Both of them were finally in a safe harbour after all the trials and tribulations they'd endured. Their friendship was deep and had strengthened so much in the past year. Now that his children knew about them she felt free to tell Devlin and Maggie the news of her changed relationship with Mick.

So much to look forward to, Caroline daydreamed, before Rebecca phoned to say her next client was on his way up to see her.

'Hi! Everything all right? You're up early.' Sally was surprised to get a call from her ex-husband on a Monday morning. She figured it was 8am in Ireland. She was getting dressed to go to a charity lunch.

'Everything's fine. I Zoomed all the kids last night. They're fine. Dervla and Katie are fine, so nothing to worry about. I just wanted to tell you that Caroline and I are in a relationship and the kids are very happy about it. They like her a lot. I'm waiting on the sale to close on the new house, so that will be there for the kids when I'm gone. And that's it really,' Mick said casually.

'Oh! Oh!' Sally stuttered. 'That's nice for you, Mick. I hope it works out well,' she managed to say, doing her best to hide her dismay.

If Mick and Caroline were a couple now, she couldn't use her ex-husband as a safety net if Faisal ended the relationship with her. Maybe she should go out to Conor in Australia and try her luck out there?

'Thanks for letting me know. I appreciate it, Mick. I'll be home sometime in July so I'll see you then.'

'Sure, see you then, Sally. Mind yourself,' Mick said cheerfully and hung up.

'See you,' Sally said dejectedly, feeling like a balloon that all the air had escaped from. She'd wanted the divorce, insisted on it, and now she had to deal with the consequences. Mick was moving on whether she liked it or not.

'Shona's colleague is working on a programme about successful Irish women and she wants the three of us to do a short interview. Are you on for it?' Maggie asked her two best pals, calling from her kitchen.

'Sure,' Devlin agreed.

'Depends on the date,' Caroline said solemnly. 'It might clash with my wedding ceremony.'

'Your wedding ceremony?' Maggie repeated, perplexed. 'Are you going to a wedding?'

'I am.'

'Whose?' Devlin asked. 'Anyone we know?'

'Mine,' Caroline said straight-faced.

Devlin copped first. 'OH MY GOD!' she shrieked. 'Did Mick propose?'

'*What?*' Maggie wasn't sure what she was hearing. 'Mick proposed? To you?'

'No, to Cinderella!' Caroline laughed.

'Caroline, that's fantastic news. When's the wedding?'

'Calm down, we're not getting legally married because it would cause too much hassle with wills and taxes. We're having a ceremony, something like Shona's—'

'We'll be your matrons of honour!' Devlin interrupted.

'Speak for yourself. I ain't no matron.' Maggie grinned.

'Will it be before or after the cr— eh, Barcelona?' Devlin stuttered, nearly letting the cat out of the bag.

'After,' Caroline said. 'We want to have Mick's new house sorted. So we might combine the ceremony and a house warming. We're not in any rush.'

'Good idea,' Maggie approved.

'Barcelona can be our hen party then,' Devlin said.

'Roll on Barcelona.' Caroline beamed, happier than she'd ever been in her life.

CHAPTER SIXTY-NINE

Barcelona

'Oh this is *fabulous*!' Maggie dove into the rippling waves of the azure Mediterranean and began to swim.

'How does she do that?' Devlin asked as she and Caroline waded gingerly into the sea behind her.

'Watch out, tsunami warning,' joked Michael, and the trio burst out laughing.

'You brat!' Maggie shouted, surfacing and shaking the sea out of her hair. She swam to where he was floating and splashed him, chuckling at his smart-Alec comment. 'Get down straight away!' she advised her friends. 'Don't be wussies.'

'She says that every time,' grumbled Devlin, who was not a water baby like her friend.

'It's much warmer than Brittas. It *is* lovely.' Caroline took the plunge and struck out.

'If you can't beat them, join them,' muttered Devlin, submerging herself with a little gasp. The sea was delightfully tepid and the June sun warmed her as she began a leisurely crawl.

Finn and Michael had driven them a few miles north of Barcelona City to a little cove close to Bogatell beach, which was popular with locals rather than tourists. It was the third morning of their holiday and they were totally relaxed. More relaxed and carefree than any of them had been in a long time.

When they'd first arrived in Barcelona, Michael had collected them at the airport and brought them to their delightful Airbnb on Calle de Valencia. It was a wide, tree-lined boulevard with plenty of restaurants and shops, just a ten-minute taxi ride to the port.

They'd decided to stay in the Airbnb rather than the hotel Devlin and Luke usually frequented, to make it more like a girls' holiday of old. 'If the three of us are in a hotel we'll be in separate rooms and the craic won't be as good. Plus, we won't be able to cook an Irish breakfast for the lads,' Maggie had remarked when they'd discussed where to stay. 'I think we should do an Airbnb. We'd have much more freedom and we'd be together. Easier than in a hotel lounge or one of our rooms to be with the boys.'

'Great idea.'

'Sounds good to me.'

Her friends had agreed wholeheartedly and Finn had pointed them in the direction of a nice area in the city, which wasn't too far from the airport, and was quite close to the port, for when they would be embarking on their cruise. Finn and Michael were keen to make sure everything went to plan.

Caroline had suggested Maggie stay with her the night before they flew to Barcelona, and Shona had brought them to the airport the following morning. 'Here, Caroline, you take the boarding cards: I know you're always so organised when you travel, not like my beloved mother who invariably ends up frantically rooting in her handbag.' She grinned at Maggie, who couldn't argue with her daughter. She was always scrabbling for glasses, car keys and her phone in her voluminous totes. Shona had done the handover so smoothly Caroline had whisked the documents into her travel wallet. Maggie had no idea she wasn't travelling home when she thought she was.

They checked into their building and the boys lugged their luggage out of the lift to their sitting room. Maggie began unloading her goodies onto the coffee table in the stylish cream and blue lounge while Devlin and Caroline explored. She had arrived with Tayto crisps, O'Neill's rashers, Superquinn sausages and Dunne's pudding from Wicklow, which she knew her godson was very partial to.

'I have something for you too, for your voyage,' she said to Michael, brandishing a freezer bag filled with Barry's teabags.

'Ah thanks, Mary Poppins. That bag of yours is a bottomless pit.' He bent down and planted a kiss on her cheek.

'English Breakfast just doesn't cut it for a real tea drinker. You can treat yourself to a proper cuppa when you come off watch. I brought a few for us too, Dev.' She took out yet more teabags. 'Caro, you're on your own with those mint abominations.'

Caroline laughed and said, 'I'm putting on the kettle if you want to join me.'

The apartment was perfect for them. Three bedrooms with Juliet balconies. A small but well-supplied kitchen and a spacious lounge with long French doors that led out onto a balcony overlooking the elegant avenue.

They'd packed a lot into their stay so far: Caroline even

jogging to the Sagrada Família one morning at 6am while Maggie and Devlin were still fast asleep. They had designated their last day in Barcelona as a day of R&R on the beach. Michael was joining his ship at 7am, when she docked in port, the following morning. As far as Maggie knew they would be heading to the airport to get a lunchtime flight home after saying goodbye to her son.

That night they all went to a restaurant across from their apartment. Finn said it served delicious Catalonian food. 'Their la bomba is legendary. You'll love it,' he promised. He'd taken a day off and was enjoying being a tourist in the city he called home.

'I love that stuffed fried potato croquette.' Michael studied the menu. 'I *might* have to order two!'

'I don't know what to pick: I want *everything*,' Devlin announced to much laughter. The waiter poured their wine and lit their table candles while dusk settled softly around them.

'It was a great holiday. The time flew,' Maggie said much later when the two lads waved down a taxi to go back to Finn's apartment.

'We'll just have to do it again,' Devlin said matter-of-factly.

'Absolutely,' agreed Maggie. 'Absolutely.'

'Goodbye, love. Have a safe trip. Keep in touch, see you in the autumn.' Maggie tried to keep the wobble out of her voice when she saw her son dressed in his uniform, standing up to say goodbye to her. She straightened his epaulettes. 'Your dad was so proud of you, Michael. He was always boasting about you.'

'I know, Mam, I know that. You mind yourself too. I'll call you tomorrow when we get to Mahón but send me a text anyway to let me know you got home safe,' he assured her, grinning at Finn and the girls over the top of her head.

'Perfect,' she said, giving him a tight squeeze before stepping back so he could go and hug Devlin and Caroline, who were sipping tea and a tad bleary eyed. It was 6.15am. Michael and Finn wanted to get to the port to see the *Seabourn Ovation*'s arrival. Finn and his girlfriend were saving hard to take a cruise on it in the autumn, when Michael had finished his next shore leave and was back on board.

'Let's go before things get too maudlin. I can't hack it.' Finn stood up. 'Mom, I'll be back for you around lunchtime to collect you for the airport.'

'Text me when you're leaving. We have to be out of here by eleven, so we're going to have coffee in the little crêperie beside us. They'll hold onto our luggage in reception,' Devlin said, ushering them out the door to the lift. 'Drive carefully.' She could see Maggie was upset at the farewells. She stood beside Devlin until the lift doors closed and then she burst into tears.

'Come on, have a croissant and a cuppa,' Devlin urged sympathetically.

'Sorry,' Maggie sighed, wiping her eyes. 'He and Terry were close and I know he's had fun with us here but I know he's grieving too. It's harder for him because he's away from home and away from the girls and me.'

'Of course it's hard but thankfully there are so many ways now to keep in touch,' Caroline comforted, putting some croissants into the microwave and making fresh tea. 'Most parents try and spare their children anything that causes them pain and sadness. It's natural. And a sudden death is harder to get over. There's no preparation.'

'I love that Finn and Michael are such good friends. Finn's been a tower of strength to him.' Maggie sat at the table and slathered butter and blackcurrant jam on the croissant Caroline gave her.

'Me too. They always have been. I'm glad Michael's the brother we were never able to give Finn.' Devlin added milk to her tea and sat beside Maggie.

'And I'm so glad that my soon to be step-daughter's baby is going to have two terrific uncles, as well as her doting aunts.' Caroline lightened the atmosphere.

'Caroline, you have so much to look forward to. We're *delighted* for you,' Maggie said. 'Do you know what we should do?'

'We're all ears.' Devlin grinned.

'After the summer, around mid-October – which is always a lovely time in the south of Spain – we should rent out the penthouse in Mi Capricho. It will give us a chance to have another little reunion. I've a mad busy summer with work ahead of me. Lots of filming and a deadline to deliver a book.'

'Mi Capricho is such a haven. Right on the edge of the sea, looking across to Africa, and sitting in El Capricho eating their divine boquerones al limón ... and sipping cocktails on the balcony at sunset. *Fabulous!*' Devlin clapped. 'Perfect for another of our little minibreaks. Great idea, Maggie. Let's put it in the diary.'

'It's been a lovely break here too,' Caroline said. 'Short but very sweet. We needed it.'

'Right, seatbelts on. Let's go.' Finn smiled at his mother sitting in the front seat of his red Peugeot. Their luggage had been crammed into the boot of the hatchback and they were ready to go.

'Caroline, don't forget to give me my boarding card when we get to the airport.' Maggie rooted in her bag for her reading glasses to have them handy.

'Stay calm. I have everything under control,' Caroline said as Finn indicated and slid out into the traffic. The city was calmer, less frenetic on a Sunday morning, and before long Finn was in the lane to take them to the port.

'Why are we going to the port?' Maggie looked around her in surprise when she saw the sea ahead of them.

'Well, we're OK for time so we have a little surprise for you,' Finn said. 'I've to text Michael when we get to the ship and he's going to go to the starboard side station on the bridge and wave at you.'

'Ah Finn, that's so kind. I haven't seen his new ship. He was on the *Sojourn* when the girls and me went, a few years ago.'

'Yeah, Michael was saying that, so we decided on this little detour so you could see it and give him a wave before we head to the airport.'

They drove over a steep ramp and turned right towards the cruise terminal. The three women exclaimed when they saw the impressive gleaming white cruise liner come into view.

'She's a beauty, isn't she?' Maggie gazed at the ship where her son was a first officer. 'Such a pity you're not into cruising, Caro. Could you imagine the three of *us* on a cruise?' She laughed heartily at the notion.

'Not really. It wouldn't be my scene I don't think. I'd be afraid I'd be seasick ... and all that food. *No.*' She gave an exaggerated shudder. 'Mi Capricho will do me fine for our next reunion holliers.'

Finn came to a stop. 'I'm not sure if I can go any further. This is where passengers check in.' He pointed to a building ahead of them. 'Why don't you walk down around there to the wharf and you'll see the bridge easier,' he suggested. 'I'll text Michael now.'

Maggie opened the door, eager to see her son. Caroline got out her side and they began to walk towards the quay.

'Finn, you put the labels that Caroline gave you last night on the cases and wheel them over to the embarkation station over there. Did you hear Caroline about cruising?' Devlin chuckled. 'She should get an Oscar.' She followed her friends around the embarkation building towards the quay's edge. They were looking up at the massive ship's bridge with its overhang.

'Look! Look, there he is.' Caroline waved excitedly.

Maggie saw the figure of her tall son in his smart uniform waving too. She couldn't make out his face, because of the tinted windows, but she blew him kisses and he blew some back. She took her camera out and snapped some photos to send to her daughters. She thought, with a pang, that she would have sent some to Terry too had he been alive.

'Here, let me take a picture of you and Caroline, with the ship behind you.' Devlin posed her friends and, up on the bridge, Michael gave a thumbs up. 'I suppose we better get a move on,' she suggested when she finished clicking.

They turned and gave a last wave and walked along the dock, the sea breeze delightfully refreshing as the temperature rose in the early afternoon heat.

'Thanks, Finn, that was a treat.' Maggie hugged him when they got back to the car.

'You're welcome, godmother. Goodbye other godmother and Mom. See ya in August,' Finn said cheerily.

'Did you get called into work?' Maggie was surprised at this turn of events. 'Can we get a taxi from here?'

'I'm sure you could get a taxi from here if you needed it, but why would you do that when there's three suites awaiting you on the *Seabourn Ovation*?' Finn's face broke into a massive grin.

'I don't understand . . .'

'The City Gals are going on a cruise. This one, in fact.' Devlin was smiling from ear to ear.

'How? When? Even *Caroline*?'

'Your wonderful children wanted to treat you. My darling son encouraged Caroline and me to go with you – we needed a lot of persuasion,' Devlin said drolly. 'Michael did all the booking and sent the emails to Shona. And here we are.'

'But . . . but . . . what about . . . I don't even have enough clothes packed.' Maggie was flabbergasted.

'Yes, you do,' Caroline informed her smugly. 'Mimi sorted some of your fancy dresses and shoes for eveningwear, some extra ninnies and a couple of pairs of cutoffs. They're in our luggage. You can get the clothes you wore in Barcelona laundered on the ship. So have your passport ready and,' she extracted a small folder from her bag and took out some pages, 'your *Seabourn* boarding pass.'

'I don't know what to say.' Maggie stared at them and the ship.

'Say nothing and get a move on. I'm dying to see my suite and we don't want to be standing here all day.' Caroline pointed to the small queue beginning to form.

'Bon voyage,' Finn said. 'Send me a postcard!'

'And not one of you let it slip,' Maggie said in wonderment as they joined the queue.

'I nearly did,' Devlin confessed, 'but Caroline saved my bacon.'

'And *you*,' Maggie turned to Caroline. 'I thought you didn't like the idea of cruising?'

'I got over myself,' Caroline deadpanned.

Maggie was overwhelmed. 'Unbelievable,' she said. '*Unbelievable.*'

After their bags had been checked in and their photos taken for security, the three of them sat on an outside patio, sipping welcome drinks offered by smiling staff as they waited to board.

'This is very civilised,' Caroline remarked. Now that she was actually checked in, she was eager to get on board. 'I thought it would be much more crowded.'

'Don't forget there's only six hundred passengers, not thousands like the huge liners, and they stagger the boarding times to avoid queues,' Maggie explained, having regained her equilibrium somewhat. An announcement came over the loudspeakers.

'That's us.' Devlin took a last sip of her drink and stood up. 'Come along, ladies.' They were through the last embarkation requirements in moments before heading to the gangway.

'Welcome aboard, Mam.' Maggie saw her son standing at the entrance and felt a lump in her throat.

All of the planning and subterfuge that had gone into this by her children and two best friends. Was there ever a luckier woman in the world?

CHAPTER SEVENTY

THE CRUISE

'What do you think?' Devlin and Maggie followed Caroline into her suite. 'I put you into the middle. We're on either side,' Devlin said, laughing as Caroline oohed and aahed over the luxurious bathroom with its Molton Brown goodies. The walk-in closet had lashings of hanging space and drawers, a safe and a pair of towelling robes and slippers.

'Look at the bed!' A queen-sized bed with plump pillows and cushions looked ready to dive into. 'I love the lounge. Oh look: a bottle of complimentary Champagne. I'll give that to you, Maggie. I'll keep the basket of fruit.' She grinned, as excited as a child. Maggie and Devlin were thrilled for her. The first cruise was always special and on board a ship as luxurious as the *Ovation* it was even more exciting.

'Look at the veranda.' Caroline stepped outside, raising her face to the sun. 'I might never leave this place.'

'And they've opened the dividers for us, like Michael said they would.' Devlin clapped. 'Look Maggie: here's mine and there's yours.' They walked along to peer into their similar suites. 'If we want to have room service breakfast together, or a lunch or dinner, it will be perfect.'

'I never thought it would be like this,' Caroline said in awe.

'Girls, did you ever think when we had hardly a penny between, us all those years ago, that one day we'd be on a luxury cruise ship?' Maggie asked.

'Well, I don't know about you but this woman's hungry. It's a long time since breakfast. Let's hit the Colonnade. It's great for lunch. It's self-service and you can eat inside or outside,' Devlin suggested.

'Good thinking,' Maggie approved. 'Let me dump this tote next door and we're on our way.'

Twenty minutes later, after their luggage had arrived and been put out of sight into the closets, the trio walked up the spiral staircase to the restaurant on Deck 9, the level above theirs. They gave their room numbers to a smiling staff member on reception and walked into the bright, airy restaurant. There were tables of delicious starters, cheese boards and desserts on display. Caroline's eyes widened, gazing at the array of food. The aroma coming from the hot buffet made her empty stomach rumble.

'Let's sit outside,' Devlin suggested, catching Maggie's eye and leading the way through the big doors to the deck at the stern of the ship. They were lucky to get a table by the rail and when they were seated a waiter came to take their drinks order. When he'd gone, Maggie turned to look at Caroline.

'Here's my advice to you, for what it's worth, because I saw a flicker of panic in your eyes when you saw all that grub,' she said frankly. 'Eat the way you normally eat – and you should, if you can, eat more than usual – because the food *is* scrumptious and this is a one-off experience. Don't take any seasick tablets if it gets a bit choppy so if you puke after indulging, you won't feel guilty about it.'

Devlin gasped. Maggie was always so damned *blunt*!

Caroline looked at Devlin's stricken face and back to Maggie who was shaking out her linen napkin. She started to laugh. She couldn't stop. 'Oh Maggie ...' she managed, 'never change. If any of my clients with an eating disorder are ever going on a cruise that's the advice I'll be sure to give them.' Maggie started to laugh and so did Devlin and the three of them hooted until tears rolled down their cheeks.

'Cripes, I have to clench: I'll be lucky if I don't pee myself,' Maggie wheezed.

That set them off again and the tone was set for the cruise of a lifetime.

'It's so good to see Maggie relaxed, isn't it?' Devlin put down her book and watched their friend swimming lazily up and down the pool.

'It's great. She needed this badly. Terry's death took a lot more out of her than I could have imagined,' Caroline remarked. 'I guess she's felt it acutely for her children. But you can see the difference in her already. It's so relaxing here, isn't it?'

'Blissful,' sighed Devlin, stretching on her lounger. They'd got up early to watch the ship docking in Mahón, Menorca, gone exploring, had lunch on the patio beside their loungers and now she was ready for a little late-afternoon snooze.

'A drink, ladies?' An attendant appeared at their loungers.

'I don't think it's too early for a cocktail,' Devlin perked.

'Could I have a Cosmopolitan and one for my friend in the pool, please, and Caroline?'

'A non-alcoholic gin and tonic for me please,' Caroline replied. She'd spent an hour in the gym and a nice cool drink would be just the thing.

'Coming up,' the attendant said as Maggie emerged from the water and wrapped herself in a soft, luxurious white towel.

'I ordered you a Cosmo.' Devlin lifted her shades.

'You look like a fifties Hollywood film star with those glasses.' Maggie grinned.

'Cool, aren't they? Got them in Tunny's in Finglas. But I can't *believe* I've had to get prescription sunglasses these days. How elderly is *that*?

'*Very!* Welcome to my world.'

'At least I can read comfortably. This is an exquisite book.' She picked up *Time and the Tree*, the novel she was reading.

Maggie's phone vibrated on her lounger. 'Mam video-calling: she's probably wondering why I'm not home yet.' She made a face. 'Hello,' she murmured guardedly.

'Are you having a good time on your cruise?' Nelsie's face appeared on screen.

'So far it's fabulous but we're not even a full day cruising yet. How did you know?'

'Shona told me ages ago. I thought it was a great idea,' Nelsie said crisply. 'I have a bit of a surprise for you, myself. Look who the wind blew in.' She angled the phone.

'Hi sis.' Niamh smiled, waving. 'Shona told me what was happening and suggested I come and visit Mam and keep an eye on her while you're gone, so here I am. I'll be here when you get back too. Have a ball and can't wait to see you.'

'Now for ya!' Nelsie chuckled. 'You're not the only one who can do surprises. I'll see you next week and tell the other pair to enjoy themselves.'

'I will, Mam. Thanks.' Maggie hung up. 'Fancy that! Mam and Niamh together for a week.' She unwrapped her towel and fluffed up her pillow.

'That's just peachy, Maggie. You don't have to worry about Nelsie while you're away. I love the way Niamh said Shona "suggested",' Devlin chuckled.

'Exactly.' Maggie grinned. 'Knowing my eldest daughter she probably said, "Get your ass over to Ireland pronto. It's your turn." Cute little madam, she never said anything to me last night when I rang her to thank her. She said Mam was fine and not to worry, that she was keeping an eye on her.'

'No messing with Shona,' Caroline said, smiling at the attendant who had returned with their drinks.

'Girls, this is the life.' Maggie sat on her lounger looking like a sun-kissed goddess. She always tanned well. She raised her glass.

'Absolutely, here's to life on the ocean waves.' Caroline toasted.

'You can say that again, my ladies. You can say that again,' Devlin toasted back. 'Our first cruise together but definitely not our last.'

It was their last night on board. The ship had set sail for Civitavecchia in Rome. They would be out of their cabins by 7am. Disembarking by eight-thirty.

They'd decided to have a room service dinner, in their robes. They'd had massages and facials earlier. The rich oils were soaking into their skin and so they didn't want to have showers and wash their hair.

The room service waiter had set the table for them on Devlin's veranda, with linen tablecloth and napkins. They were eating caviar and the delicious nibbles and dips that accompanied the luxurious treat.

The sun was sinking, streaking the western sky with vibrant orange and pink slashes that coloured the rippling Tyrrhenian Sea golden.

'What was your highlight, Caroline, now that you've survived your first cruise?' Maggie popped a crudité dipped in sour cream and chives into her mouth.

'Definitely exploring my suite and I can honestly say I have *never* slept in a more comfortable bed.'

'I know, they're *heavenly*,' Maggie concurred.

'I loved being invited for the bridge tour and hearing the captain telling you that Michael is a very fine first officer who will go far.'

'I know. I was so proud to hear that and that captain's not a bit smarmy. He's very genuine. His crew love him.'

'He's got very kind eyes and he's interested in people.' Caroline put a small spoonful of caviar onto an unsalted cracker and took a nibble. 'The bridge was very impressive.'

'I liked Sète very much. I love France.' Devlin ate a sliver of avocado.

'Me too. When I saw a Sephora there I knew my prezzie worries for the girls were over,' Maggie said.

'I loved that we got a great table in the fabulous sushi restaurant, at the end of our corridor, without queuing,' Devlin reminisced. She adored sushi and had advised Caroline and

Maggie they should be there early as there was no reservation required but there was always a queue.

'Delicious meal. I was a bit "sea sick",' Caroline air quoted, 'that night. But that was the only time and it was because I pushed myself too far. Recovery is not a straight line, so I'm not beating myself up about that one time.'

'My gall bladder was screeching at me for a few hours afterwards.' Maggie threw her eyes up to heaven.

'What I like about this ship is the relaxed vibe,' Devlin remarked. 'It reminds me of the motto in Le Parker Mèridien that Luke and I stayed in, in New York. Uptown, but not uptight.'

'That describes it perfectly,' Caroline agreed. 'I was surprised how unstuffy it is. Oh and I really enjoyed the train trip to Pisa. I loved Elba and Napoleon's villa in Portoferraio. I guess I just loved *all* of it. And I love the sailing part, like now.' She stared out at the sea beneath them as the ship picked up speed, slicing through the water towards Rome.

'A honeymoon cruise might be the very thing for you and Mick. You could do the one that goes from Rome back to Barcelona. There's different ports to visit,' Maggie suggested.

'Oh! That would be fantastic! I never thought of it. Mick would love this.' Caroline's eyes widened. 'We couldn't really leave Dervla, though.'

'Yes, you could! Auntie Devlin's here. She could come and stay with us. I'd love to have them and Dervla would be able to swim in our pool while I'm having goes of the baby.'

'You're not having Katie all to yourself, madam. I want a few goes too,' Maggie interjected. 'Dervla could have a reiki and massage in Latin Quarter, and stay with me for a day or two, as well.'

'You're as good to me, the two of you,' Caroline said, touched.

'Oh, it's nothing to do with you, Caro,' Devlin assured her. 'It's the *baby*! It's *all* about the baby for us two grandchildren-deprived women.'

Their hearty laughter floated out over the waves as the dusk deepened and the first stars began to twinkle in an indigo sky.

'I was just thinking about something you said, Dev, about remembering when the three of us had not a penny to our names all those years ago,' Caroline said as they sat on the train to Rome Airport.

'And?' Devlin asked.

'I never thought I'd be so wealthy. *Ever!* But when I inherited my mother-in-law's estate, as well as Richard's, it was unbelievable, actually. And I was thinking about when you suggested the honeymoon cruise, Maggie. I said that we couldn't leave Dervla and you were both so kind. But not everyone has a Devlin and a Maggie, and Dervla's actually got great support behind her, and I was thinking about all those young girls with babies who *don't* have great support and are very tied.'

'I felt that often when Lynn was a newborn.' Devlin nodded.

'I got a book, *Poor*, for the library in the clinic. It's by a woman called Katriona O' Sullivan, one of five children who grew up in dire poverty, got pregnant and was a mother when she was fifteen and ended up homeless—'

'I read that,' Maggie exclaimed. 'It won two big book awards the year it was published. It was *very* inspiring.'

'I must read it,' Devlin said.

'You should because look what you made of your life and,

well, she's Dr O'Sullivan now. She went from rock bottom, like you, to gaining a PhD in psychology from Trinity, and speaking at the UN. She's involved in improving working-class girls' access to education, among other initiatives.'

'That's some achievement,' Devlin commended. 'So why is she on your mind?'

'Dervla wants to study accountancy. She's very smart, and of course Mick and I will support her in every way we can, but there are hundreds of young girls with babies who aren't so fortunate and will never get the chance to pursue their further education. I was thinking that I have the other house in Clontarf. The elderly lady who rented it died. I don't want to let it again but maybe I could turn it into a centre for young women who want to go to school or college, where we could advise them on what courses to do, offer baby-minding services, help them when their exams are coming up, mentor them. Support them—'

'That's *a terrific* idea, Caroline,' Devlin enthused. 'If I'd had a place like that to go to it would have been a godsend.'

'Shona could do a documentary on it! I'll narrate it. We could get architects, builders, electricians, plumbers and landscapers to chip in. You know that hugely entertaining programme *DIY SOS* that Baz Ashmawy presented, perhaps something like that!' Maggie's eyes lit up.

'Yeah! We could do some charity events in City Girl for funding. This is getting exciting, girls.' Devlin sat up and took a small notebook out of her bag and began writing. 'We could do a City Girl bursary.'

'I could get some of my writing pals to fund one with me, too!' Maggie offered.

'So much for semi-retirement and taking things easy.' Caroline laughed, delighted with their reaction.

'We're only hitting our prime, gals,' Maggie declared, as the train sped onwards, and they threw ideas back and forth, relishing the prospect of developing the new project Caroline had come up with.

'This will keep us going until we get to Mi Capricho in the autumn,' Devlin commented, hauling her luggage off the conveyor belt.

'Don't you lift that, Caroline,' warned Maggie, elbowing her friend out of the way when she went to slide her case off the belt. It was the last case to collect and they were surprised the luggage had arrived so promptly. 'Girls, thank you so much for the amazing surprise. You've no idea what it did for me. I feel ready for anything after it,' Maggie said gratefully as they pushed their loaded trolleys along the concourse at Dublin airport towards customs.

'It was our pleasure, Mags,' Devlin assured her.

'And now I might even have a cruise addiction. I want to go on another one *soon*!' Caroline joked. 'We've nothing to declare here, sure we don't?'

'Do you think if that fine thing there asked me if I'd anything to declare, and I said, "Yes, I'd love you to give me a ride," would I get anywhere?' Maggie quipped as they walked past a handsome young customs officer.

They were snorting laughing as they emerged into the arrivals hall.

Caroline's face lit up radiantly when she saw Mick, Dervla and Katie waving at her.

Maggie was enveloped in bear hugs from Shona and Mimi. And Devlin, abandoning her trolley, ran into Luke's outstretched arms and knew she was home.

EPILOGUE

'We did it! Can you believe it?'

Caroline gazed around the large, airy, open-plan ground floor of the new centre for single mothers and their babies. It was opening day and a frisson of excitement swept through the guests when Shona and her film crew pointed their camera at the podium to capture the opening ceremony.

Dervla, while keeping an eye on Katie, who was happily toddling around meeting other little pals, was talking to two of the young women who were starting college in the autumn. She'd finished her second year of accountancy in Plunkets and was telling them what to expect when they started back to college.

Luke, Mick, Michael and Finn were chatting to the builders who had done a superb job transforming Caroline's old cottage into a beautiful building, full of light and warmth.

Mimi and Chloé were overseeing the lavish buffet donated by local hotels, delis and supermarkets.

Mary, Yvonne and Breda, the house mothers, were standing, laughing, on the flower-filled patio, having just finished their interview with Maggie. The large, private, landscaped garden with play areas for the children and sheltered little nooks for relaxing or studying in was full of tradespeople who had so generously given of their time and expertise to assist with the revamp. A gaggle of Maggie's writer friends who'd contributed a bursary were gathered in the gazebo having a catch-up, punctuated by gales of laughter.

'You did the most of it. You should be so proud—'

'No, Dev, we did it *together*. The three of us,' Caroline insisted. 'We all contributed in our own way. We all left our mark here and I'm glad the builders made us write our names on one of the wooden beams in the kitchen.'

'When we're in our dotage, we'll be able to look at it and remind ourselves of who we are.' Maggie grinned. She'd just spent five minutes rummaging in her bag for her glasses only for Devlin to point out they were on her head.

'*Some* of us are in our dotage *already*,' Devlin wisecracked.

'Smarty boots,' laughed Maggie.

'Shona wants us up on the stage, I think.' Caroline could see her godchild waving at them.

'Pity, I like standing at the back watching,' Maggie said.

'You get up there and you after getting Botoxed. Don't waste it.' Devlin gave her a nudge.

'It's not *too* McDonalds Arches, sure it's not?' Maggie ran her finger over her eyebrows and smooth forehead. 'The TV cameras are so unforgiving. Honest to God the crevices on Everest had nothing on the ones around my eyes. Does it look *too* obvious that I've been *"done"*?'

'No, it's great. You don't look "done" or plastic. You look *refreshed*,' Caroline complimented. 'I might get some myself.

But then I might develop an addiction to getting "done",' she joked.

'Don't ever let them near your lips. That's a dead giveaway and I've never seen a good lip job,' Devlin warned as they made their way towards the podium, where Caroline would be getting mic'd up ahead of her speech

'Ready to go, women?' Caroline asked them, smiling.

'As ready as we'll ever be,' Devlin assured her.

'We're right behind you, missus.' Maggie smiled back.

'Raring to go,' said Caroline. 'It's time to finally get Stepping Stones up and running.'

As Caroline began her speech, welcoming Dr O'Sullivan, the keynote speaker, and all the guests, Devlin and Maggie linked arms, standing behind her, as the next exciting chapter in their precious and enduring friendship began.

ACKNOWLEDGEMENTS

As always, my first acknowledgement is to my Spiritual Team: Jesus, Mary, St Joseph, the Divine Feminine Energy of Mary Magdalene, Saints Michael and Anthony (the stalwarts) and all my Angels, Saints and Guides. For all the wonderful joys and gifts, I've been given in my life, I give thanks. And for my precious mother and dad who are now with them. My books would never be written without the Divine Inspiration that you have sent me in every book that I've written.

Thanks to:

My Beloved, my anam cara. A very patient man.

My sister, Mary, my greatest supporter, and to Yvonne – a sister more than a sister-in-law. I'm so blessed to have you both.

My brothers, nieces, nephews and in-laws. I'm so lucky to have a wonderful, caring tribe.

Breda Purdue, Helen McKean whom I met through my writing career and who are now my dearest friends.

Debbie Sheehy, Pam Young, Aidan Storey and Mary Helen Hensley: my soul tribe.

Ciara Geraghty and Caroline Grace-Cassidy, two mighty women, whose podcast *Book Birds* inspired me to write *City Girls Forever*. They made me see *City Girl* in a whole new light, after thirty years, and I will forever be in their debt.

And Heidi Murphy, bookseller, who also read an early draft and has supported me and my books enormously throughout my writing career. And a huge thanks, too, to all my great writing pals. Always supportive and fun to be with.

My much-loved and always reassuring agent, Sarah Lutyens, and all the team at Lutyens & Rubinstein who work tirelessly on my behalf and always have my back.

A big thanks to my lovely, patient accountant Mary Burke.

Simon Hess, Helen McKean, Declan Heeney and the Gill Hess team Jacq, Gillian, and Patricia, who have done stellar work for years to get me to No 1. My gratitude knows no bounds.

My new editor, Louise Davies, huge thanks for the kindness and patience you showed in our first collaboration. And to SJV, Rich, Clare and also Caroline Hogg, my copyeditor, and Charley Chapman, my proofreader, my cover designer, the sales and marketing teams and all my dear Schusters – another book hits the shelves because of our great teamwork.

My Schusters in Australia, South Africa and India, far away but much appreciated for the great work you do on my behalf.

All my translators, foreign publishers and sub agents, it is such a thrill to see my books in other languages.

Mr Hannan Mullet, Grainne Roche, Finn and Orla, Dee, and Mr Denis Collins and Sheena Murtagh, SSC. I am in your debt and am so grateful for all you've done for me. And to the staff in Blackrock Clinic for all your kindness.

A heartfelt thanks to the wonderful staff in the Breast Check Clinic, Eccles St, who were so kind to me. Grace Carey, Kamfunti (K) Kanyama, Marissa Hearty, Dr Jennifer Kerr, Dr Niamh O' Mahony, Nicola Delaney and Dr Anna Heeney, and Jacinta O'Reilly and the staff in the Mater Hospital.

Garrett Fitzpatrick, legal eagle. Wild at heart!

Dee and Ray O'Callaghan, Eileen, Bernie and Anne in Flemmings shop, and Sandra, Noreen, and the girls in Classic Cuts, my Wickla tribe are a blessing in my life.

A MASSIVE thanks to Booksellers everywhere, who sell my books, and to the bloggers and reviewers, too. We authors are always so grateful for all that you do for us. Our gratitude knows no bounds.

As always, a HUGE thanks to my readers, worldwide. This book is dedicated to you with all my love.